The Particolored Unicorn

An Entertainment

Jon DeCles

ACE BOOKS, NEW YORK

D0003815

Portions of this book were
copyrighted © 1982, 1983, 1984, 1985
& 1986 by Jon DeCles.

This book is an Ace original edition.
Portions of it have previously appeared
in substantially altered form,
but the completed book has never
been previously published.

THE PARTICOLORED UNICORN

An Ace Book/published by arrangement with
the author

PRINTING HISTORY
Ace edition/December 1987

All rights reserved.
Copyright © 1987 by Jon DeCles.
Cover art by Darrell Sweet.
This book may not be reproduced in whole or in part,
by mimeograph or any other means, without permission.
For information address: The Berkley Publishing Group,
200 Madison Avenue, New York, New York 10016.

ISBN: 0-441-65192-5

Ace Books are published by The Berkley Publishing Group,
200 Madison Avenue, New York, New York 10016.
The name "ACE" and the "A" logo
are trademarks belonging to Charter Communications, Inc.

PRINTED IN THE UNITED STATES OF AMERICA

10   9   8   7   6   5   4   3   2   1

A roar and sudden heat caused Piswyck to jump back from a cage that held a small dragon. It was too young to do him much harm, and he pitied the poor beast its future in some dank dungeon, breathing out its life to send warmth through the pipes of somebody's castle.

Then the wind changed and he knew he was close to the corral of unicorns.

He put his head close to the heavy wooden bars and peered around.

This was a mistake.

The unicorns were quick of eye and nose, and even quicker to notice the presence of a possible deliverer from their purgatory.

"Hey, here sir, *me* sir!" cried the first to spot him, and it came galloping toward him at full tilt.

"No sir! Not that one, *this* one! This most humble and . . ."

"I, sir, am brave!" came a third voice, and . . .

"Most kind one, I can speak Sanskrit! But listen: *Asatoo Maa Sadgamaya . . ."*

They thundered toward the fence, and Piswyck had to jump back in order to avoid being skewered.

"Is there one among you who is not white?" he asked. . . .

"The Particolored Unicorn most certainly does run through a full spectrum of adventure."
—Esther Friesner
author of *Harlot's Ruse*

To my wife, Diana Paxson, do I dedicate this book, the very first of my works I think might be worthy of her.

—But this book was a lot of work, and not only on my part. I would therefore like also to dedicate it to the other people who helped. To the Chandelle School of Hang Gliding, who got me off the ground: thanks, George, Janine, especially Wolly, and the others. To my agent, Tracy Elizabeth Blackstone, who liked it from the start. To Joel Hagen, who has often given me hours of his knowledge and advice, and visions of faraway peoples. To Robert O. Becker, M.D., and Gary Selden, who wrote a great book and whom I've never met. To Richard Lawrence, who came in at the last possible moment and kept me airborne.

—To Elton Wildermuth, who spent years proofreading it and arguing genteelly about things he didn't like. Thanks, Mr. and Mrs. Nitnorth!

But—how can I thank the Piswyck Club?

How can I thank Rowen Sherwood for walking up and offering money to keep it going? Jim Oliver for expressing faith beyond the call of miracles? The people who gave me room to read the chapters at conventions when the story had received the *nastiest* rejections I'd ever seen? The people who put me up in their homes so I could read? Richard Corwin for drawing me pictures?

How can I thank Kevin Moore? —I'll find a way!

I can thank Gian Carlo Menotti by telling you to listen to his music. And I hope that I can thank my publishers by making them rich!

—Jon DeCles, March 20, 1986

Contents

1

The Particolored Unicorn

There were only three things in the world that Piswyck wanted.

The first was his inheritance: the castle on the hill; the stables filled with fine horses; the vineyards that produced the best blue wine in all Carsonne; the tapestries; the jewels... But that would have to wait. His father was still very much alive and lively, and he loved his father much. The inheritance would come in due time.

The second was Miranda, but she was far away, held by her wicked uncle in a dutiful bondage against the day when he could marry her off in trade for some suitable prize of power. She would require rescuing, but that would require a trip to Far Bermuda, and an assault on her uncle's fortress. And Piswyck well knew the limitations that he must overcome in order to be able to face so fell a wizard as Miranda's uncle.

The third was the particolored unicorn that he had just espied, and that, at least, was within his grasp; so long as he was willing to endure the censureship of the town, suffer the displeasure of the Countess, and defy all-powerful fashion, which since time immemorial had dealt in *white* unicorns, with golden or silvered horns; or at the greatest variance, perhaps a black one with a horn of ivory.

Piswyck fingered the embroidered salamander on the Montana Bib that Miranda had secretly sent to him at Midsummer. The twelve pearl buttons fastened the bib securely enough to his doublet, he was sure, and yet... It was the end of the rainy season, and the long, muck-filled aisles between the pens of animals were singularly uninviting to a young man dressed in some of his favorite things.

But, if he wanted the unicorn . . .

Piswyck stepped down from the wooden platform into the aisle, and sank up to mid-calf in the muck. He looked down with despair at his white hose, and realized that he had seen the last of his favorite silver boots. The stinking stuff oozed down inside and he could just imagine the kind of jokes that would be made when he got home. But it would not be the first time he'd endured jests. There had been the time when he'd got into his father's smoking equipment, and had tried one of the tiny fire spells . . .

But that was of no consequence at the moment. The ordeal at hand was to make his way through the mixture of mud and offal that is omnipresent where animals are penned, and find the particolored unicorn.

He sloshed down the long aisle, looking into each pen through its rough wooden fence. He had seen the unicorn for only a moment, a flash of bright color amidst the prancing of a small herd of the usual white beasts. It had leaped, and he had frozen it with his inner eye, a vision glimpsed afar from his position at the ramps to the transport station. He had been on his way home when he saw it, and now . . . But again, no matter; it would not be the first time he'd been late.

Most of the pens were full of ordinary animals: horses, kine, tigers for house wardens, dogs for field service. The smell was not pleasant, for the pens were never cleaned. The owner of the stockyard, Krakmalnic the Seller, had often voiced the opinion that animals stayed there only so long as a man might ride a dromedary, and therefore there was no need to see that the comfort of the animals was more than that of a human.

A roar and sudden heat caused Piswyck to jump back from a cage that held a small dragon. It was too young to do him much harm, and he pitied the poor beast its future in some dank dungeon, breathing out its life to send warmth through the pipes of somebody's manor or castle. He reached into his pocket and extracted part of a pork bun he'd been munching since lunchtime, and tossed it through the bars to the obviously unhappy animal.

Then the wind changed and he knew that he was close to the corral of unicorns.

There is one kind of stink to an herbivore, such as a cow or a horse, and there is another kind to a carnivore, such as a tiger or a dragon. Piswyck knew the smells, for he had done his share of hunting for his father's table, and had the usual hunter's knowledge of fewmets and traces. That the unicorns were omnivores, if picky ones, he also knew; so when their smell assaulted him on the breeze it was a quick matter to follow his nose directly to the big corral wherein a dozen of them were incarcerated.

He put his face close to the heavy wooden bars and peered around.

This was a mistake.

The unicorns were quick of eye and nose, and even quicker to notice the presence of a possible deliverer from their purgatory.

"Hey, here sir, *me* sir!" cried the first to spot him, and it came galloping toward him at full tilt from the other side of the corral.

"No sir! Not that one, *this* one! This most humble and . . ."

"*I, sir, am brave!*" came a third voice, and . . .

"Most kind one, I can speak Sanskrit! But listen: *Asatoo Maa Sadgamaya . . .*"

They thundered toward the fence, and Piswyck had to jump back in order to avoid being skewered as they rushed toward him in their eagerness, poking their heads between the bars, all talking at once in that beautiful piping voice so like unto a contralto who has swallowed a clarinet; and all falling suddenly silent as, in his haste to retreat, Piswyck's boot slipped from under him and he went down, flat on his back in the mud and ordure.

There was a moment of quiet horror. Piswyck could see in the several animals' beautiful, heavily-lashed round eyes the abject fear that his predicament inspired. They stood aghast, wondering if he would take this as an ill omen and leave without rescuing any of them.

Piswyck let out his breath. He certainly did not want to draw one in, considering his circumstances. He cleared his throat.

"Is there one among you who is not white?" he asked.

The unicorns continued to stand stock-still, none speaking. Then there came a laugh, from behind the fence.

"I think that not a one of them is white," the voice of the laughter said. "Though once they all were whiter than the snow. Now all of them must dance in shit and mud, forgetting noble parentage and blood!"

There was an angry murmur from the herd.

"I had more in mind colors than stains," Piswyck said, slowly getting up from his submergence in the mire, and noting the ruination of Miranda's needlework.

"Some dyes for noble colors come from roots," the voice said. It was deeper, Piswyck noted, than the voices of the white unicorns, though no less musical. "And roots are nourished in the slime and mud. Are not then things the same, both dye and stain?"

"Not all colors are dyes," Piswyck said, trying to wipe some of the filth off himself, and only making the mess more complete. "Some colors are added by artifice, it is true. But the tail of the peacock is born to the bird, and these white fellows of yours were all given their snowiness by their parents, not by a paint pot. Just so do I suspect the case with you."

Piswyck walked to the side of the rails where the herd had thrust its collective head through and peered between the palings to where he thought the owner of the voice should be.

He laughed.

From far away the poor beast's condition had not shown, but from here it was obvious that it had been in the pen for some time without benefit of a bath. Its hooves were caked with filth, as were its fetlocks, and the mud was somehow more offensive against its bright colors than on the snowy surfaces of the other creatures' pelts. A bright yellow left-front leg was smeared to brown, and a dusky-rose right-front leg was mired worse. The olive-green back-left leg, the color of which came all the way up on the hindquarter, now looked more like a goose turd than an olive. The right-back leg should have been as scarlet as blood, but now it was dark as blood that has dried; and thinking this, Piswyck noted that there were sores on the legs and feet. The unicorn's tail was black, with streaks of grassy green, and its back had a huge mottle of orange that started above the scarlet right-back leg and ran all the way forward to the neck, where the rose-pink mane fell across it. Partway up, the neck itself acquired a patch of dark garnet red that went up and encompassed one ear; but most of the neck and the head were of a most wonderful blue, dark and rich and the perfect contrast to the chrome-yellow circle that went round one bright eye. In that circle, and in the cerulean darkness that surrounded the other orb, were eyes of honeyed amber.

And the horn was not gold, nor standard silver, nor even the exotic ivory that had been bred into black unicorns. No, the spiraled spike that sprang from its forehead was clear carnelian, like a liquor made of late summer sunsets.

Piswyck laughed again. Now he had a full view of the creature he was pleased. His mind's eye had not painted the picture wrong.

The unicorn met his eyes for only a moment. Then the beast turned away, twitching its tail at him.

"Be not unkind," the unicorn snapped at him over its ocher shoulder. "It adds not to your grace!"

"Your pardon," Piswyck said. "It is just your cynicism at the mess these others have had to endure, when you are in just as bad shape. Why, if anything, you're a bigger mess than they are!"

"He's been here longer," said one of the white unicorns, in a voice low with fear.

"There's no demand for his kind," said a second unicorn, almost whispering. "And you know what happens to those who are not sold by the time they have eaten their price in provisions."

"Why, no," said Piswyck. "I do not."

"They are *eaten!*" said the colored unicorn, turning back to face Piswyck.

The amber eyes were full of defiance, but the veil was thin over terror and loathing.

"And some of them are wont to go with grace," the colored unicorn continued. "But some of them will fight until they die. Yet even those with hearts of hardest steel are wont to end as nothing but a meal!"

The beautiful dark voice held incredible bitterness.

Piswyck let his eyes drop. This time it was he who was embarrassed to meet the other's gaze.

He saw again the sores around the creature's feet. He would be a fool to buy a lame unicorn, he thought. But he did not feel like asking the beast to walk for him. And he had an uneasy conviction that even if there was a limp, he would buy the unicorn anyway.

"Have you a name?" Piswyck asked, looking up.

The unicorn returned his gaze curiously. There was a spark

in its eye, as if his question kindled hope where philosophy had been wise enough to kill it.

"I might have had a name, but long ago," the unicorn said. "If so, my memory has washed it out."

"Then I shall have to think of one for you," said Piswyck.

The unicorn's head jerked, just a little. It knew what he was saying, but it was afraid to believe.

"Do you know your price?" Piswyck asked.

The other unicorns laughed.

"Krakmalnic will ask seventy," said the one who spoke Sanskrit. "Offer him twenty and our companion is yours!"

They all laughed again.

"But hurry!" cautioned the one who said he was brave. "Time runs short in the glass for our companion. This day is set to be his last!"

Piswyck felt his skin crawl. So close!

"I shall hurry!" he said, and turned and headed for the small wooden building where Krakmalnic did business.

Krakmalnic the Seller of Beasts was a fat and a powerful man. Piswyck had seen him from afar many times, heard stories about him from childhood, and even been in his presence a few times when, as a child, he had tagged along with the household steward to buy new kine.

There are those who let their flesh own them, and there are those who own their flesh: Krakmalnic was the latter of these. He was fat because he liked to eat, but under his fat was still the power of the wrestler who, in his youth, had wrestled at the Royal Games and won many a lady's favor.

It was true that his long and drooping mustaches had lost their flamelike color, and that the bright red hair had dwindled to a little halo that rested on his ears; no ladies now danced anxiously outside his dwelling, hoping to catch sight of his powerful shoulders. But his eyes were still sharp, and what he'd lost in attraction for the women he made up for in attraction for their gold.

It was said that Krakmalnic was on very good terms with the Countess. He always had something new for her, some exotic pet on which she might dote for a while. And if the Countess doted, all the ladies in Carsonne doted with her. If the Countess had a new creature, why, nothing would do but that all the ladies should have for themselves one just like it. Thus was the power of almighty fashion. And thus was the simple magic that brought to Krakmalnic's pockets a tithe of all the money that was spent for luxury between the high mountains of the Pyreen and the impassable waters of Hercule.

And if, as was rumored, Krakmalnic's service to the Countess extended beyond the supply of exotic pets, who was there to complain? Such sinister tales were better left untold. Better that it should be remembered how grateful Krakmalnic was to the Goddess for his good fortune, and that he never killed a bitch dog for any reason.

As Piswyck burst in upon him, Krakmalnic was at his leisure. He had his filthy booted feet up on the table that served him for a desk, and near at hand he was roasting some bits of meat on skewers over a brazier. The smell of the roasting meat was intoxicating, redolent as it was with spices and herbs, and it reminded Piswyck that he had not really eaten enough since noon.

"Sir!" Piswyck gasped, having run all the way. "You have a unicorn I wish to buy!"

Krakmalnic raised his bushy eyebrows, looking his young visitor up and down and clearly displeased that his repast had been interrupted before it had begun, and by so distasteful a visitor at that.

"So?" queried Krakmalnic. "Indeed?" He lifted his booted feet from the table and let his chair come down with a crash. "You seem already to have taken half his produce without payment. Are you sure it is the unicorn you want?"

Piswyck felt himself flush, was embarrassed by his own blushing; then he realized that it didn't matter. His face was too dirty for it to show.

"I am sorry to appear before you in this condition," Piswyck said, "but I fell while I was looking through the pens." He squared his shoulders and tried to regain a smidgen of his dignity.

"I didn't think you bought that coat on purpose," said Krakmalnic, his rusty voice rumbling and maybe about to laugh. "Which one is it you want? Oh, they're all the same to me, but I know a young man like you will have picked a favorite already. The one who speaks Sanskrit? He's a nice choice. Or the one who plays chess? I wouldn't recommend the one who boasts about his bravery all the time—"

"The particolored one!" said Piswyck, interrupting.

Krakmalnic cocked a bushy eyebrow at him. Piswyck

could see the coins begin to glitter behind the Seller's eyes. Now the bargaining would begin.

"You wouldn't want *that* one!" Krakmalnic said decisively. "He's completely out of fashion, and besides, he has bad habits."

"Oh, but that *is* the one I want," said Piswyck. "I am bored to death with fashion! Everyone who has a unicorn has a white one, or at best a black one. The colors, the pretty horn——"

"But he's gone lame," said Krakmalnic, rising from his chair and reaching over to turn the skewers.

Piswyck laughed. "I know he's lame. But that should be to my advantage, now shouldn't it? I don't want him as a steed, only as a pet for my garden. He'll look stunning amidst the white camellias! And if he's lame, perhaps the price is not so high . . ."

Krakmalnic stood up straight at the suggestion of a lower price. "The price of such a beast would be high in any case," he said. "Perhaps beyond you, boy! Why, the difficulty of introducing the color genes from a Hyacinth Macaw to get that blue color to his head, and that yellow around his eye . . . Why, that alone would be worth a fortune! And the other colors— But you are right, to some degree; the price must be less because of his lameness. Except for one thing: I have set my heart, after having him about for so long, on a coat made of his hide! Can you not imagine what a rich treasure that would be? The only particolored unicorn coat, I dare say, in all of Westron Landea. Perhaps in all of Latter Earth!"

Piswyck's eyes opened wide. "Sir! You would not!"

"Oh," said Krakmalnic with a smile, "but I would! Now, find yourself some other creature for your garden, boy. Perhaps a golden Harpie would look good with your white camellias? . . . And let me have my coat."

He picked up one of the skewers and looked at it critically, then smiled politely and proffered it.

"Would you care for a bit of meat? I think it's done!"

Piswyck recoiled, remembering what the unicorns had said about creatures who outlived their keep.

"Sir," he said, "you could have a much finer coat with the money I would pay for the unicorn. There are many fine coats available, from many lands, and all of them unique. Besides which, if no one has bought the unicorn, then surely a coat made of his hide would be as unfashionable as the beast himself."

Krakmalnic chuckled. "That may be true. But there is also the meat to think of. You know, do you not, that I eat the beasts I slay? How much food could I buy when I had bought the coat? And then, there is all the food the unicorn has eaten. That must be paid for as well."

Piswyck noted that the man was willing to dicker. That meant his heart was subject to his purse strings.

"These things are considerations," Piswyck said, trying to get a little of the initiative. "You may be correct in assuming that the price is too much for me. But sir, how shall we ever determine whether I can make it worth your while to forgo the coat and dine on another victual unless you name a price?"

Krakmalnic grunted, then took one of the chunks of meat between his teeth, delicately pulling it off the spit and thereby giving himself an excuse for not answering immediately. He chewed the hot meat gingerly, and looked about for something to drink. Piswyck noted a certain disgruntlement in his manner as he did this. Was it that the point had been reached too soon? So many merchants viewed this bargaining in the light of a seduction. Krakmalnic found a bottle of wine, pulled the cork with his teeth, swallowed some, and the meat with it, then spoke: "One hundred and five golden rodrics."

Piswyck gasped, then gagged as the smell of his clothes was drawn in with his breath.

"But *sir!*"

"I am doing you a favor, young man. The creature is ill-tempered. He farts, and worse: he speaks in iambic pentameter! Now be happy that my desire for a many-colored coat has saved you your sanity. For surely to keep a particolored unicorn would drive a young man such as you mad in no time at all."

Krakmalnic laughed, presumably at some private joke concerning what he'd said. It made no sense to Piswyck, so he assumed it to be some literary allusion.

"I will give you sixty," Piswyck said.

Krakmalnic laughed again, but this time at the offer. He popped another chunk of meat into his mouth.

"Best forget it!" he mumbled around his meal. "It is most probably too late in any case, for today is the day that I have ordered him slain and his hide sent to the tanner. Even now, my man Bloth may be swinging him up by his hind legs and bringing his sledgehammer down on his skull."

"Seventy then!" blurted out Piswyck, sure that this was a bargaining, but not really sure.

"I could not dream of it!" said Krakmalnic. "There is more to be considered than what I have told you. I have invited several of my friends to a feast, with unicorn as the main course. Why, if I sell you the colored one, I shall have to slay one of the others to take its place at dinner."

"Eighty!"

"Are you sure you would not care for some of this most excellent meat? I have marinated it for two days and two nights in herbs and wine, and—"

"Sir!" said Piswyck, *"I want the particolored unicorn!"*

From Krakmalnic's beatific smile, Piswyck knew that he had capitulated completely.

"And I have told you for what price I would part with this rarest of treasures. Surely you understand a matter of commerce?"

Piswyck took a deep breath. "One hundred," he said. "And my father will make a coat of *my* hide when he hears it!"

Krakmalnic looked at him intently upon mention of his father. Piswyck had made no secret of his identity, but with so much mud and offal all over him it was certainly possible that he had not been recognized. The slightly sinister relationship between Krakmalnic and the Countess crossed his mind. That the Countess was his father's enemy was well known, but . . .

"Let me see the money!" said Krakmalnic suddenly.

Piswyck reached into his burse and drew out some coins. He laid them on the table before Krakmalnic.

"This is all I have with me, but I am sure I can bring you the rest by tomorrow afternoon, when my father—"

Krakmalnic sank into his chair with a thud, and bristled. "What is this? What is this? You come to me pleading with me to give up my coat, my dinner, and now you want me to do it on *credit?*"

Piswyck was about to protest that his father's credit was good anywhere, but something stopped him. Krakmalnic's manner had changed, ever so subtly.

"No, young man," Krakmalnic continued, warming toward anger. "I have not been in business this long to be made a fool by the likes of you! If you want this unicorn, then bring me the cash! And quickly! The softness of my heart cannot be extended forever. I will give you an hour, no more. If this is not a youthful game you are playing, an attempt to cheat me, then you will be back. If not—well, I shall have my supper, and my coat! Now be off!"

For seconds Piswyck was rooted, startled by Krakmalnic's sudden anger, bewildered by the something else that flashed in Krakmalnic's eyes. Then the situation crystallized and he realized that he did not have time to figure out implications or worry about peculiarities of character. He had to get home, get the money, and get back in time to rescue his unicorn.

Without even retrieving the coins he'd laid down on the table, he rushed out. Would he be able to explain his desire to his father? Would he be able to move fast enough?

Behind him he heard Krakmalnic rumbling into laughter. But there was no time to wonder why.

He ran toward the transport station, but realized even as he ran that the Snail Train would be too slow. He veered and headed for a nearby stable, but as he ran in the door he cursed himself for a fool, for he had left all his coins on Krakmalnic's table.

There was nothing for it but to pay with four of the twelve pearl buttons that fastened the ruined bib to his doublet. Miranda would be furious enough that he had ruined the bib, with all the elaborate work of the embroidered salamander. Now she would be doubly furious that he was using the buttons to pay his bills. But there was no other solution. He needed a horse!

He galloped the poor beast till foam flew from its sides, but it got him home more quickly than any other means of transport could, short of magic. As he rode up the last length toward the great gates of the castle, across the Azure Field (planted, it was said, by Boswyck, the second marquis) with its hundreds of different blue-flowering plants, he was barely conscious of the small crowd of servants gathered at the gatehouse, or the horses tied up in the courtyard.

It was such an automatic thing for him to leap down from whatever steed he was riding and toss its reins to a waiting groom, that he did so even now; and he was only returned to the reality of his outer condition when the groom, quite insulted, snarled at him and threw the reins back.

"Dandion, it's *me*, Piswyck!" he said, realizing that he must look like a walking dung heap. "Where's Father? I must speak with him quickly!"

"He's in the library, sir," said Dandion, grabbing the reins back, and looking quite bewildered to see his master under so much filth. "But sir—"

But Piswyck didn't wait to hear whatever it was the groom was saying. He rushed straight across the courtyard, up the broad steps of the main entry, and directly toward the library, not even kicking off his filthy boots as he careered down the hallway. Time was of the essence. He had to get the money and get back before the unicorn was killed.

The vision of the poor beast strung up by its hind legs, the blood gushing from its smashed skull, was so vivid that he could almost see it. What if he were too late? What if he could not persuade his father to let him have the money?

He pushed open the great oak door of the library and rushed in. Then he stopped dead in his tracks.

Row on row of shelves filled with books stretched to either side; reaching a ceiling as high as two normal rooms set one atop the other. Several tables were stationed about the room, piled high with the books that his father had most recently had reason to consult, for his father was a magician in his own right, although specializing in such abstract processes that most people would mistake him for a scientist or a scholar.

At the far end of the room was his father's great desk, with its globe, its traditional human skull with a candle on it, and several of the mathematical devices his father had, from time to time, used for his instruction. Beyond the desk was the fireplace, so large a tall man might walk into it to warm himself when the fire was low.

Above the fireplace, hanging on the stonework of the chimney, was an ancient shield bearing the arms of their line: *Purpur, a candle argent.* It was the very shield that Astwyck the Great had born at the Battle of Baldeborg, and there were all kinds of legends about it. Once, when he was a young boy, Piswyck had climbed up and examined it closely. It had seemed to him no more than an ordinary cuir-bouilli shield.

Seated at the desk was his father, and to either side of him were armed men, one of whom held a rapier to his throat.

His father, the Marquis Oswyck, looked Piswyck straight in the eye.

"Hemford!" his father snarled, calling him by the name of one of the grooms about whom they frequently joked. "What do you mean by entering this room in such condition? No, don't answer that. Only get out of here! Can't you see that I am . . . indisposed?"

Piswyck stood frozen. What was happening? He looked from his father to the man who held the sword at his throat. It was Lomfroth, the villain who acted as tax collector and special spy for the Countess. That could mean only that the Countess had, as they had long suspected she someday might, moved against his father.

Piswyck's eyes shot back to lock with his father's. Did his father really take him for Hemford?

No! His father's eyes burned like ice into his. His father knew who he was, and was telling him to *get out!* To run. Justice might be served later. For now it was more important to get the heir to safety.

"Yes sir!" Piswyck said, making a little bow and tugging at his manure-soaked forelock in a gesture that he hoped fervently would look like that of a servant. He backed out of the room as clumsily as he could, pulled the big oak door shut, turned, and ran down the corridor.

His father a prisoner in his own house!

The Countess herself the adversary; she, who, with her foreknowledge, knew the whereabouts of the Appearing Egg!

Someone stepped out from behind a stuffed bear, and Piswyck felt his well-trained hand go to his dagger.

"Stay your hand, young Master!" hissed a subdued but familiar voice. It was Alberta, his nurse from childhood. "I am not here to harm you, but I think everyone else is!"

She looked around in fear and agitation. "That damnable Lomfroth," she half whispered, "has filled our house with spies. But there's no time for me to tell you what's come to pass in the last three hours. Only know that those among the servants who are loyal to you are preparing to act! . . . But I must give you this!"

She reached into her ample bosom and pulled out a letter, stained and soggy with her sweat.

"It is from Miranda!" she said. "Things are worse with her as well. It seems as if the whole world is flying apart!"

Piswyck nodded dumbly.

"Now go!" said Alberta. "The Countess has seized the castle, but her full force is not yet here. She used the power of the Egg to move some of her men within our defenses, and sent a few more by horse, disguising them as messengers. Those are searching for you everywhere. Did you not see them in the courtyard?"

Piswyck remembered the horses tied up in the courtyard, but no actual soldiers.

"No mind!" Alberta said, fluttering her old hands. "You must escape before the rest of the troops arrive, if you are to escape at all. You must go—far away. To Miranda, if you can! If you can win against her uncle you will have *his* weapons at your disposal. Then you may have a chance against the Countess. Remember, the Egg is not invulnerable! Now *go!*"

Piswyck started to take his old nurse in his arms, then thought better of it. He did not want to cover her with dung and thereby give away the fact that she had seen him.

"Here," he said, pulling off six of the remaining eight pearl buttons, so that the Montana Bib now hung by only the top two. "Things may go hard with you from now on. These will help you survive if you are turned out."

Alberta started to protest, but there was a noise behind them, down the hall. Piswyck pressed the dirty buttons into her hand and she pushed him, and they were parted. He stumbled off, gaining his balance and running again as if he'd never stopped. He glanced over his shoulder briefly, but Alberta had once again melted into the shadows amidst the stuffed animals.

Go, yes, Piswyck thought as he ran.

To Miranda, yes.

But how?

He dare not return to his rooms for money. They would be waiting for him there. He dare not go to the family coffers, for *surely* they would be there.

It occurred to him that it would have been more sensible to keep the pearl buttons, for they could at least be traded for food, if not used outright as money in any land.

But, among the few bits of magic that his father had been willing to teach him was the axiom that helping another in need was a very good way to short-circuit one's own troubles.

With that in mind he resolved to go *first* to Krakmalnic's stockyard and rescue the particolored unicorn. Good sense did not offer any solutions to the moment's miseries.

He rushed out the great front doors of the castle and into the courtyard. He hoped desperately that Dandion had shown the good sense to keep his rented horse at ready.

But it didn't matter. One of the guards Alberta had mentioned was in the courtyard. The way he was hitching at his hosen showed what little errand had kept him from his duty, and the wicked smile that broke out across his face showed that even a simple soldier could add two and two.

"The young marquis, I believe?" the guard queried, stationing himself between Piswyck and the horses and drawing his sword. "Will you surrender, or shall I take the Countess your head?"

Piswyck gauged the distance between them. The guard had a sword, while *he* was armed only with a dagger. Still, there were two body lengths between them. He had a chance.

"What? Me surrender?" he asked.

He made a split-second prayer of thanksgiving to Saint Genesius, then grabbed the upper-left corner of the Montana Bib with his right hand and ripped it off his doublet. The two remaining pearls popped toward the guard, and Piswyck yelled *"Swine!"* as he threw the manure-soaked garment in the guard's face with all the force he could muster. And while the guard was reacting to the spectacle of his opponent ripping his clothes off, and then to being hit in the face with a pile of shit, Piswyck did a forward handspring that brought his filthy silver boots into hard and powerful contact with the guard's jaw.

It took only a moment. No more than a good feint with a sword by a skilled swordsman. But it was a display of gymnastics, not swordsmanship, and was therefore not what the guard had expected by way of self-defense.

Piswyck had a chance!

The guard was knocked backward with almost enough force to break his neck, and he was dazed.

Piswyck fell flat on his back.

The guard shook his head and fought to recover his advantage, throwing off the filthy bib and clutching his sword, which, despite the drop-kick to his jaw, he had not released.

Piswyck, flat on his back, threw his legs up in the air. He reached up and pulled his dagger from his boot. He threw his legs forward again, using their momentum to carry him to his feet. Then he hurled himself on the downed guard, landing with both his knees in the man's belly, and driving his dagger in under the man's jaw and up into his brain.

It was so quick and so complete that the dying man barely had time to bring his sword in line and drive it into Piswyck's shoulder. Not even a decent price for the transaction! Piswyck had learned in early classes that arrows are useless against swords, and swords against daggers, provided the conditions are right.

"Sir!" Dandion cried, and he had a *fresh* horse ready! "They're coming!"

Piswyck pushed himself up from his opponent's body, pulling his dagger free and giving it a blood shake as he did so. He thrust the dagger back into his boot and pried the dead man's sword out of his fingers, then ran toward the gatehouse.

They were coming, all right! As he ran he saw five or six of them emerge from the South Wing, at least ten from the great main doors which he had just exited, and more from the direction of the stables.

The odds were not good.

But there was Dandion, holding a fresh horse, and what had old Alberta said about the retainers preparing to act?

He grabbed the reins from Dandion, put his foot in the stirrup, and leaped up onto the horse. He noted that it was Shadowflight, one of his father's fastest.

The horse reared as one of the Countess's minions tried to grab at its bridle. Piswyck slashed with the borrowed sword and cut off a hand. As the horse came down, its hooves crushed the skull of another enemy, giving the converging militia graphic reason to back off for a moment; and in that moment Piswyck spurred Shadowflight and shot for the gate.

It would be only long enough for them to mount, he thought, and then there would be hot pursuit.

But no! As he cleared the gate three old men appeared, still crouching but ready to spring. Alberta had said the servants were preparing to act, and act they now would. They were wearing the shaggy wildman outfits that were used to lead all the village parades. It was an honor long held by the retainers of the Marquis, a custom that went back too many years to be certain of its origins. They had huge clubs, and rattles, and masks that made them look like devils. There was one shaggy blue wildman, and one bright saffron wildman, and one devil-red wildman; and wildmen always frightened the horses.

Piswyck shot by, thinking how brave they were to risk their lives for him, and chuckling as he imagined them humbly setting forth the story of how they were practicing for the festivals when lo! So many soldiers on horses had a'come a'galloping out of the gatehouse and . . .

As Piswyck sped down the road between the fields of blue

flowers he heard the commotion behind him. Neighing, hoof thunder, shouts. Frightened horses and cursing men.

The family had always been proud of its retainers' abilities at acting.

He laughed out loud, and began plotting his course. Escape was only the beginning. He must rescue the unicorn and get both it and himself out of the Countess's reach as quickly as possible. He must find a way to get to Far Bermuda and rescue Miranda.

It had occurred to him that it might be possible to rescue Miranda without confronting her uncle, but that now seemed inadvisable as well as unlikely. He needed more from the uncle than Miranda. He needed powers, and the ability to wield them.

He would most likely have to make the passage by ship. Travel by air was subject to too much scrutiny. There were only so many balloons aloft, and the spells that guarded them against foul wind and weather made them stand out like beacons. If the Countess wanted him, she could take the time to scan all the balloons aloft each day.

Kites, of course, were out of the question on a journey so long.

No, it would have to be a ship, and not a respectable one. Sea captains of respectable mien did not like to get involved in politics, or magic. They were too vulnerable.

A pirate might be good, but a smuggler would be better. That would mean crossing the mountains to Serrique. No port in the world had better pirates or smugglers than Serrique!

But with what could he pay for their services? For that matter, how was he going to get the unicorn?

And, for that matter, was getting the unicorn even a good idea? It was very noble to consider rescuing the doomed beast, but a man traveling alone is in danger enough when he is trying to hide. How was he to remain inconspicuous in the company of a particolored unicorn? He'd might as well wear a big sign proclaiming him to be a choice object of profit for itinerant bounty hunters!

And the unicorn was lame as well. It would not only attract attention, it would be a liability!

Precisely what, Piswyck wondered, was he doing? Going after a beast for which he could not pay and which would surely provide more of a handicap than any sane man needed.

Perhaps Krakmalnic was right; to keep a particolored unicorn would surely drive a young man to madness.

And here was the evidence: here was the young Marquis Piswyck, in deadly danger, galloping for all he was worth to rescue the creature, despite all his most logical objections made to himself!

It was in such a state of doubt and bemusement that he continued on until at last he came to the back of the stockyards and dismounted.

It was obvious that he must steal the unicorn. There were no other alternatives. One thing that having a magician and metaphysician for a father had done for Piswyck was to acquaint him with the relativity of all things.

Stealing was wrong. But dying was wronger.

He walked quickly along the fence, looking in here and there to see what the different pens housed.

Horses here. Llamas. Overly large serpents, which had known a certain fashion five years before, but which now mainly slept in the sun, too rank of flesh to be eaten. A gryphon. (Gryphons had also once been fashionable, but they were as stupid as they looked and made messy pets at best.)

The unicorns.

"Here!" Piswyck called, as quietly as he could. "By the back fence!"

There was a small, unquiet stampede as all the unicorns converged on him and began to talk at once.

"Sir, too late—"

"Bloth—"

"To the abattoir!"

"Quickly!" said the one who spoke Sanskrit. "Follow along the outer fence. You may not be too late!"

Piswyck ran, terrified. Past camels. Past stacked cages of monkeys and apes. Past exotic birds. Past a shrouded dark pen with an obscure warning on it.

His feet slipped and slid as he ran, and he kept falling into the muck. It didn't matter. The only part of him that was still uncoated with the stuff was the white patch on his chest, where the embroidered salamander had been.

It was like running knee-deep in cranberry sauce, he thought wildly, his heart pumping. It was like slow-motion running in a dream.

Ahead he saw it, the abattoir: a raised wooden structure

with a ramp at one end, and hanging in the shade of its roof, rows of animal corpses, upside down and bloodless.

And at the far end, a big, lumbering man who had to be Bloth was fastening a manacle around the hind leg of the particolored unicorn.

"Wait!" Piswyck called out. "There's been a change! I've come to get that unicorn!"

Piswyck climbed up on the wooden platform and raced down the rows of dead animals to where Bloth stood beside the unicorn. The unicorn was quivering visibly.

"A change?" asked Bloth, his broken teeth showing as his smile opened like a shark's. "Well then, show me the token!"

The blankness Piswyck felt cross his face was fleeting, but Bloth was quick enough to catch it.

"Ah ha! The master thought you might try some such ruse. You would not be the first! He warned me: no token, no unicorn! We are not fools here, young Marquis!"

Hearing himself thus addressed, Piswyck was stunned. He felt like a domino at the end of a long line of dominos. Far away he could feel the first domino tipped over, as a long line of logic crashed toward him.

Bloth knew who he was. That meant Krakmalnic knew who he was. If that were true, then Krakmalnic knew he was good for the money . . . unless Krakmalnic had known something else, something such as the Countess's plan to move against the Marquis Oswyck.

Piswyck pulled the borrowed sword from his belt and shot it to Bloth's throat.

"Unfasten the manacle!" he commanded, already sure that the Countess's troops must be on their way.

"Not a chance!" Bloth laughed, and he hurled himself backward off the platform, a drop of six feet into a pile of manure.

Piswyck stooped to unmanacle the unicorn's leg, but the iron ring was locked. He stood and looked down at Bloth; but Bloth, despite his size, was not slow. He had moved quickly to a lever near the wall, and now he threw it.

Gears began to grind and the chain from which the manacle was suspended began to move. Piswyck followed the chain with his eye and saw that all the chains dangled from a central train, which led upward over an inclined wheel. It was so arranged that the manacle would be slowly and inexorably raised until the poor unicorn, like countless beasts before him, was lifted up by his hind leg. His muscles would all be ripped as he hung there in pain, waiting for the release that only a blow from Bloth's butcher's mattock, or a cut throat, would bring.

Piswyck jumped down into the manure pile and moved on Bloth with lightning speed. But Bloth, grinning like an insane wolverine, was ready for him. He had his huge slaughter hammer in hand and raised.

"You want to fight?" Bloth laughed, taking a position between Piswyck and the lever. "Maybe you want to have your brains bashed out? Your puny sword against my hammer?"

Piswyck really had no time for the niceties of form, and a little bit of muck wasn't going to distract Bloth in any case. Something quick was in order; the unicorn hadn't said a word, but it was making sounds in its throat, sounds of fear as the chain pulled it along.

"You have two choices!" Piswyck said, drawing himself up and hoping it showed under the slowly drying shit. "You can give me the unicorn now, and let us both be on our way. Or you can try to stop me taking revenge on you and your master."

"With the Countess hot on your heels?" Bloth asked contemptuously, playing the one card that Piswyck knew he would play.

"How long," asked Piswyck, "would it take to ruin your master with *this?*"

His father had taught him a little magic. Precious little, he'd always thought, but each time he'd asked, his father had told him that magic was too expensive for a young man. That it was easier to do things the hard way. That a young man should be sowing wild oats instead of following the Wild Hunt.

But his father had taught him, on the grounds that he might need the skill for survival some frosty winter, to make a little bit of fire.

This Piswyck now did, in the straw of the manure pile.

And manure being one of those substances given to spontaneous combustion, it took only a second for a great gout of flame to erupt.

"Now see who, and *what*, you shall fight!" snarled Piswyck. His back was to the fire, but he could see the flames reflected in Bloth's eyes.

"You little bastard!" shouted Bloth, swinging his great bloody hammer.

But Piswyck expected that card, too. He waited for the upswing, when Bloth's arms were raised over his head and his rib cage conveniently exposed. Then he stepped to the side and drove his sword in under Bloth's arm, straight to the heart.

There was a shriek.

Piswyck glanced up. The manacle had lifted the unicorn's leg clear of the floor. Its feet were scraping the wood, trying for traction. It was beginning to panic, and it might injure itself.

Bloth was still standing, the hammer upraised, a look of surprise on his face. Piswyck stepped behind him, and pulled out the sword, deftly dodging the geyser of blood that erupted from the puncture as Bloth died. As the butcher toppled, his own hammer fell from his hands to crush his skull. Piswyck turned and threw the lever controlling the chain to off.

The terrible grinding of the gears stopped.

Piswyck took a deep breath.

Immediately he regretted it. The smell of shit had been bad enough. The smell of burning shit was worse.

He stooped and rolled the remains of Bloth over. There was a chatelaine's ring on Bloth's belt, so Piswyck cut the belt off with his sword, took the keys, and hoisted himself up to the platform. He tried several keys, quickly found the right one, and unlocked the manacle from the unicorn's leg.

"I don't know why I'm doing this," he muttered as he undid the fastening. "The last thing in the world I need is a lame, particolored unicorn with me while I'm trying to escape."

"I'm not lame!" said the unicorn, his voice still shaky and forgetting his pentameter for the moment. "But a few more minutes and I would have been, believe me! Now quickly, tell me what it is you need!"

"To get away from here as fast as I can," said Piswyck. "Why, can you help me with it?"

"As fast as any horse that is alive," said the unicorn. "My ancestors were cross-bred with the wind. But what now can we do about the fire?"

"Let it burn," said Piswyck, noting that the manure pile was now an inferno, and that the blaze was spreading quickly up the old rafters of the abattoir, and that the unicorn's speech had resumed its rhythm.

"And what of all the living creatures here?" the unicorn asked, gesturing around the stockyard with its horn. "To die in fire is a ghastly death!"

It was a genuine moral point, but one that Piswyck would rather not have thought about at that precise moment.

"Have you any suggestions that would take less than a minute?" he asked.

"Begin by setting all the monkeys free," said the unicorn. "They are not bright, but they can open locks. The little men with masks will do as well, if not much better, once they know the cause!"

Piswyck saw the vision instantly. And more: the confusion it would cause in the town. An aid to his getaway.

He followed the unicorn quickly down one of the aisles to where the cages of monkeys, some dyed, some natural, were awaiting sale. He undid the cage fastenings while the unicorn chattered in what for all the world sounded like monkey talk, and then he let them out.

And though some of them immediately sped for safety, a good number of them began working to open the cages of other animals.

The "little men with masks," the raccoons, were steadier in applying the efforts of their tiny, perfect hands to the cage fastenings. There was an ancient battle between raccoons and locks, as was well known to all wizards.

"The ones who'd eat us, you will have to do," the unicorn said, sensibly enough. "The tigers and the lions and the bears."

Piswyck nodded. "You go to the fence, where the other unicorns are," he said. "I'll meet you there. If danger presents itself, run. And oh, I left a horse there. If I am to ride you, then send him home!"

The unicorn nodded once, then trotted off, shaking its mane and catching the glow of the growing fire in its translucent carnelian horn.

Piswyck made his way to the carnivore pens and began opening them. It wasn't a comfortable feeling, letting out a lot of tigers; but they were, after all, meant for house wardens, and were presumably no more dangerous than wolves or dogs.

He was in the aisle that had first led him to the unicorns, uncomfortably close to the front of the lot, when Krakmalnic appeared, flanked by two guards wearing the Countess's yellow livery.

"So!" Krakmalnic roared at him. "It is *you* who are making all this trouble! I might have known! I *did* know better than to trust you! But it's too late for your unicorn, young Marquis! Bloth—"

"Bloth is dead!" said Piswyck, summoning up all the presence of command his father had been able to teach him. "I might have forgiven him, had he not known the details of my lineage. I might even have forgiven *you* your bloodthirsty lusts, had you not known who I was! But you conspired with the Countess to do me harm!"

Krakmalnic laughed.

"Your forgiveness isn't worth the shit you're covered in, boy! It's your *head* that will pay for your wreckage of my stockades!"

Krakmalnic started forward, still flanked by the two guards.

But as Krakmalnic had come upon him, Piswyck had been about to free the last of the carnivores. As the Seller strode toward him down the aisle, Piswyck pulled the bolt and opened the gate for the baby dragon. The gate made a strong barrier across the aisle, with Piswyck on one side and the dragon, Krakmalnic and the guards on the other.

There was a blast of heat beyond the barrier, and cries of dismay.

Piswyck didn't wait to find out what was happening. It was only a baby dragon, after all. He ran to the unicorn pen.

The white unicorns were free and already galloping toward the hills. The particolored unicorn was waiting.

"Now can you ride without a saddle, friend?" the unicorn asked.

"If need be!" answered Piswyck.

"Then do, and let us leave this dreadful place!" the unicorn said.

Piswyck mounted the particolored unicorn, and they were off.

2

Over the Mountains and to the Sea

Three days later they found Bethzda. A big water troll had tied her feet together with one end of a long rope and hung her upside down, stark naked under the bridge. The rope was looped over an outcrop of failing abutment, and fastened to an old log. She was thus stowed like a string of garlic until it was time for the troll's supper. The troll himself now lay asleep on a sandy shelf the river had made by silting out.

Piswyck and the particolored unicorn moved quietly in the water, back downstream, downwind, around the river bend to where they could talk.

"I can't say that I'm over fond of the idea of taking on a troll with only a sword," Piswyck whispered. "Not to mention this sword wound in my shoulder!"

The flight from the flaming stockyards through streets filled with frightened humans and maddened wild animals (some traditional, some genomythological) had left no time for washing the offal out of the wound, so an infection was setting in. Thus the bath in the river, which had led to their discovery of the naked girl held captive by a troll.

"I don't think we can leave the girl to die," said the unicorn.

"No," Piswyck agreed. "But this is not the ideal time for a side venture. As soon as the Countess has restored order she'll have her men after us, and if she wanted my head before she'll want it now still fastened to my body, so that she can sever it herself!"

"One starts to think the world is made of teeth," the unicorn said. "The Seller wanted me to serve his guests, and now this girl is dinner for a troll."

"Over the mountains and to the sea will not be the journey I'd hoped it would be," said Piswyck. "But at least we won't stink like a stockyard as we go."

By now the water had served to wash away most of the accumulated road dust and ordure. The unicorn's colors were gleaming bright and Piswyck was anxious to see what his new steed would look like dry and in the sunlight. Piswyck's clothes were stained beyond hope of restoration, but once they'd hung from a branch for a while to dry (now that he'd washed them) they would be tolerable.

"I think the biggest danger is the girl," said the unicorn. "If she should start to scream, the troll will wake."

"She looked unconscious to me," said Piswyck. "I'd have thought her dead except that I could see her breathing; that and the fact that I know trolls only eat live food."

"That gives the rescue even less appeal," gulped the unicorn.

"Necessity seldom has the virtue of appeal," said Piswyck.

He waded to the shore and drew his sword from beneath the shrub where he'd concealed it. Then he reluctantly put on his still-wet clothes. There was no sense going into a fight naked if he could avoid it.

"From the way the troll is lying, I think our best bet is for me to sneak up on him; then, when I'm close, you make a commotion. If you can distract his attention, I'll have a chance to get in a good thrust."

"That wound that makes your shoulder stiff and red?" queried the unicorn.

"As fortune would have it, my opponent was also right-handed. A few inches more and it would have been my heart. As it was, it was my left shoulder; so although it is painful, my good sword arm will still work. Ready?"

"It sounds as good as any other plan," said the unicorn.

Piswyck waded back into the water and they moved quietly back upstream. As they approached the bridge the smell of carrion assaulted their nostrils and they noted piles of badly cleaned bones on the shelf near the troll. Most were the bones of goats, sacrificed by people who simply had to get across the bridge and who knew the troll was there. But there were human remains as well, testifying to the eternal ignorance of road conditions that would probably always plague the unwary traveler.

Piswyck looked up at the girl hanging upside down. It was not the best position from which to judge a woman's beauty, and certainly not the right circumstance for doing so in a leisurely manner; but even thus, she was not uncomely. She was lithe of limb, pale of skin, with breasts that hung like cantaloupes, and long—very long—black hair. As Piswyck looked at her she opened her eyes, which were green. He put his wet finger to his lips, but the intensity of her gaze quickly made him understand that she was not a woman given to idle screaming.

Piswyck and the unicorn moved slowly out of the water. This took an interminably long time, for it was important that the sound of water sloshing off their bodies should not give away their presence. When the water had drained, Piswyck moved carefully toward the far edge of the sand shelf, where the troll would not be able to see him if it opened its eyes.

The troll was truly ugly, as trolls were bred to be, but worse: it lacked character. If it had been definite in its ugliness, with pronounced fangs and deep-set eyes, it would not have been so bad. Stone trolls were like that. But this was a water troll, which was almost like a human, only larger; and softer, flabby, as if it had a pudding in its lineage. It had clawed hands and feet (there was dirt, or something, under its nails) and a hideous mouth full of teeth. But whereas a stone troll had teeth like an Allosaurical nightmare, this water troll resembled grounds for an orthodontic lawsuit.

It could also have used a good cologne, Piswyck noted as he carefully approached the sleeping brute. Life in close proximity to water had not proved adequate to its hygiene.

Piswyck got very close, still downwind of the troll's flabby nostrils, and moved the point of his sword toward its throat. But the thing lay at such an angle that to reach its throat he would have to place himself directly before it, and therefore within easy reach of its claws. A troll's toenails, Piswyck recalled from his father's lessons on mythozoology, were designed chiefly for disemboweling.

He looked up in frustration and caught the unicorn's amber eye. The unicorn tossed its head and gestured with its horn, but Piswyck was unable to interpret. It occurred to him that it was very difficult to play charades with someone who didn't have hands.

He looked up at the girl, catching her gaze. Her eyes were green, like pools of deep summer algae. Her hands moved, gesturing, interpreting the unicorn's plan.

Piswyck was to be ready. The unicorn would make a commotion, as planned, but from a different position. When the troll awoke and sought to rise, its throat would be within reach, and Piswyck could cut it.

Piswyck looked to the unicorn. It nodded agreement.

He felt his own throat, to see just where the jugular vein was, then positioned himself where he could slice at the troll's fat neck. He would have liked to behead it at a stroke, but its neck was fatter than a bull's!

The unicorn neighed; or, rather, shrieked like a horse in terror. It surprised Piswyck, for it had not occurred to him that the unicorn could do that. Though why a creature who could speak with raccoons and monkeys should not be able to—

The troll's eyes opened and it let out a snarl mixed with a hiss. Its breath was awful! It started to lumber up from its rest.

Piswyck drove his blade into its throat with a hard thrust, then pulled the sword backward, slicing out as he did so, ripping the flesh, jumping back to avoid the gout of blood.

But there was no gout of blood. Though the troll *looked* somewhat like a human, it wasn't built like one. There was no jugular vein conveniently near the surface, as there was in a human. Only a mass of fat, and some nerves. The nerves' existence could be verified by the roar of pain the troll let out.

The troll turned on Piswyck.

"Run!" the woman screamed from where she hung. "Save yourselves!"

The troll snatched at Piswyck, but he did a backspring out of its reach. He owed Saint Genesius another candle. The troll lunged at him.

The thunder of hooves on sand echoed from the stone cave the bridge formed, and the unicorn attacked. Head down, it galloped full tilt and drove its carnelian horn into the troll's rump.

The troll roared twice as loud and whirled to see its new assailant. But the new assailant was now attached to its victim by its only weapon. The spiral horn was stuck in the troll's rear. As the troll turned, the unicorn was yanked off its feet. The sheer force of the turn hurled the unicorn's mass away from the troll and, as the horn was freed, the unicorn was slung up against the stone wall, and dazed.

The troll reached to its punctured posterior and felt the wound, from which something was oozing that was not quite blood. It opened its ugly mouth and issued a long, mournful wail.

Piswyck took advantage of the moment and ran up behind the troll. Crouching low, he sliced at the back of its ankle, inflicting a deep cut. He hoped the thing had something like an Achilles tendon.

Whether it did or not, the pain thus inflicted was excruciating to the creature. It stood bolt upright, lifted its leg to grasp its ankle, and fell over backward toward Piswyck.

In the split second of the troll's fall, Piswyck saw it coming. He raised his sword, grasped the hilt with both hands, and let the monster's own weight drive the blade straight through the middle of its body, right where its heart should be.

The experiment did not determine whether or not the troll had a heart, but it did determine where the heart was not. The falling troll tried to pull away from the pain piercing it, leaving Piswyck crushed under its bulk with only his head and one arm sticking out and all the wind knocked out of him. The troll roared even louder and began to writhe.

"Help!" Piswyck gasped.

"Get me down!" commanded the naked woman from her pendant attitude. "We can use this damned rope to get that damned thing off him!"

"How?" cried the unicorn, dancing back and forth. "I haven't any hands to untie knots!"

"Trolls haven't any brains to tie them with!" she responded. "It just looped the rope around that log. Roll the log and the rope will come free!"

"But if I do you'll fall down on your head!" protested the unicorn.

"I'll fall into the water and I can swim!" she said. "Now hurry."

The unicorn trotted to the log around which the rope was wrapped, pushed it with his horn, and rolled it. The rope unwound, secured only by friction, and the woman fell into the river.

"Help!" Piswyck gasped again. The monster had started rocking back and forth, trying to reach behind itself. Whether it was Piswyck or the sword that it wanted was not apparent.

The young woman surfaced and pulled herself ashore, quickly undoing the clumsy friction knots that bound her feet.

"Have you ever pulled a wagon?" she asked the unicorn, shaking water from her hair.

"I'm pleased to say I certainly have *not!*" snapped the unicorn, visibly offended at the thought.

"Neither have I!" she said. "But we're going to do it in tandem now!"

She stood up, made a quick and amazing knot in the rope, then began whirling it over her head. It spread out in a circle, like a hempen halo, and expanded. Then she twisted her arm just so and the lasso flew deftly over the troll's head. She pulled and the noose tightened. The troll grabbed for it and nearly yanked it out of her hands.

"Here!" she shouted, running sideways and wrapping a loop of the rope across the unicorn's chest. "Let's go!"

They strained. The noose tightened. The troll made a strangled howling. It stopped grappling with the rope and clawed at its neck, by which it was being dragged. Slowly the thing rolled over, off Piswyck.

As the troll rolled, Piswyck pulled his sword free of the creature's back, staggered to his feet gasping for breath, and tottered away from his adversary.

Unfortunately, pulling the troll off Piswyck had put the troll on all fours, and from this position it was able to climb once again to its feet. Its wounds were oozing, but it still had a lot of fight left.

"Move him into the sun!" Piswyck gasped, his breath starting to come back.

The troll started moving toward the woman and the unicorn, following the rope to its tormentors.

"I think the troll's between us and the sun," cried the unicorn, and so it was, for the sun was at Piswyck's back.

Piswyck took a deep breath, feeling his heart pound. Then he ran toward the troll, let out his best war cry (the one that always frightened his nurse, old Alberta), and drove in his sword as high up as he could: where the troll's kidneys should have been, but where the troll's kidneys apparently were not.

He pulled the sword free as the troll whirled around toward him. He hoped he had its attention. He stumbled backward, trying to look as tired as he felt, toward the place where the sandbar gave out and the sunlight fell on a deep pooling of the river.

"Now he's mad!" cried the woman, as if the fact needed confirmation.

Piswyck eyed the water. It didn't seem advisable to try to escape a water troll in its own element, but there wasn't any other alternative. He threw his arms up and dove.

But as he threw his arms up his left shoulder wrenched with an agony like lightning striking. As he hit the water he realized that fighting with one arm was one thing, and swimming quite another!

He broke the surface, coughing, blinked his eyes, and looked around. The troll was wading in after him. Into the sunlight, but also into the water. Did the water cancel the effect of the sunlight? And where was his sword? Had he dropped it when the pain hit? He looked down into the water. The bottom was a mass of twisted roots. He glanced at the shore. A tight growth of willow trees, of course!

"Get up on the bridge!" he shouted, and coughed; then he turned and swam desperately toward the tangle of willows.

The troll roared and Piswyck shuddered, detecting a certain note of satisfaction in the roar. He was in the water, which was where the troll liked to be best. A vision flashed across his mind of a string of live fish, strung through the gills and waiting to die. His shoulder shrieked.

The water got shallow suddenly. Piswyck stretched his body straight as an arrow and glided in over the mass of roots. He hoped the troll would tangle in them. He pulled himself the last meter with a breaststroke, then reached up and lifted himself up into a tree. The pain tore at him and he thought he would faint. But he knew it would hurt more before it got better, and he didn't want the troll to catch the scent of the blood that now spilled from his wound.

He was grateful that the human body pumped adrenaline as a result of fear, and that adrenaline was an anesthetic.

He gauged spaces and distances with a practiced eye, then used his legs to propel himself further upward into the willows just as the troll reached the shallows. Leaping, he caught hold of an overhead branch, brachiated briefly, then clambered from tree to tree, using his legs as much as he could, depending on the right arm and trying to avoid using the left. He heard the troll roar, and then the sound of huge branches breaking as the troll began to tear its way through the trees. He was in too much pain to pray, but he thought briefly of Saint Genesius and was grateful for his tumbling lessons.

The green darkness of the woods lessened, lightened, and then he was swinging out onto the dusty road. The troll roared

behind him, trees snapping. The naked woman and the particolored unicorn waited where the road went up and over the
stone bridge.

"Can you do that rope trick again?" Piswyck asked.

"Won't have to," the woman said. "The troll's so dumb
he's left his necktie on!"

"Hide around the corner," said Piswyck. "I'll get him to
follow me up on the bridge. When he goes by, tie the end of
the rope to the bridge. I think it's long enough. Now quick,
hide!"

The woman and the unicorn dashed back around the abutment just as the troll ripped apart its last willow tree and
roared triumphantly at finding Piswyck.

"Your mother was a septic tank!" shouted Piswyck; then he
turned and ran up the road to the middle of the bridge, where
he stood and waited, hoping the troll understood at least the
tone of the insult.

For a moment the troll stood still, staring at him with its
pus-yellow eyes. If what they said about trolls and sunlight
was true, thought Piswyck, then the creature should have
enough sense of self-preservation to stay out of the stuff.
Since this one was not sticking to the shade . . .

The troll lumbered up the road toward him. The sunlight
didn't seem to be having much effect. Suppose all that stuff
about sunlight was only superstition?

The woman darted out from behind the abutment, grabbed
the end of the rope, and looked around desperately for a place
to tie it. Suppose there wasn't any place to tie it?

She found an old iron rail, probably meant for tying horses
in the days when the road had tolls instead of trolls. She tied
the rope. The troll moved faster and lunged at Piswyck. He
dodged, but its filthy claws raked his right arm.

"You bastard!" Piswyck snarled, aware of the understatement he was making regarding the troll's genes. The troll
made a gargling noise, the closest thing to pleasure it had yet
expressed. Then it lunged at him again.

Piswyck danced back toward the parapet, where old rocks
had crumbled leaving a gap in the ancient wall.

"Let's see how well you can swim this time!"

He stuck his thumbs in his ears and waved his fingers,
sticking his tongue out just in case he was being too subtle.
The troll lunged again, but as it did Piswyck turned and dove

off the bridge, gritting his teeth against the pain and trying to relax as he hit the water.

He didn't relax enough and he hit the water like an egg falling from the nest. He felt splatted. It was all he could do to avoid tangling himself in the willow roots at the bottom, but he did and quickly surfaced, looking for a way to escape in case the plan hadn't worked.

There was no troll in the water.

Good!

He looked up.

Not so good. Still no troll, and the beast should by now be dangling from a noose halfway down to the water.

The troll appeared, still on the bridge, and Piswyck almost thought the thing was *smiling!* It had pried loose one of the big stones of which the bridge was made. It raised the small boulder high over its head, then hurled it down at Piswyck.

Piswyck scrambled in the water and the boulder missed him, but the shock as it hit the water dazed him. By the time his wits cleared the troll had another rock and was taking aim.

Then Piswyck heard the sound of hooves on the stone bridge above, and abruptly the troll jerked, buckled, barely avoided dropping the rock on its own head, and pitched forward. Troll and boulder both fell off the bridge and Piswyck scrambled to get clear.

When his head cleared this time the troll was exactly where he wanted it: hanging by its neck halfway between bridge and river, in full sunlight. It was feebly clawing at the noose. Above, at the gap in the bridge's wall, the particolored unicorn stood looking down at him. The sunlight caught in its carnelian horn, and glinted in its amber eyes. The sunlight showed Piswyck what he had not really seen before, the unicorn's bright clean colors. One eye looked down on him from a proud head of wonderful blue, the other from a circle of chrome yellow. Troll blood dripped from the carnelian horn, and the rose-pink mane hung limp with sweat.

The naked woman appeared. Her green eyes contrasted strangely and beautifully with the amber eyes of the unicorn.

"I thought sunlight was supposed to kill them!" she called down.

"I think it will, sort of," said Piswyck, treading water. "Eventually. As I recall what my father taught me when I was ten, it's like a very bad sunburn. Their bodies respond by sending calcium to the surface, which is why it looks as if they turn to stone. Actually they die of something like acute psoriasis!"

"How horrible!" she gasped.

"I'd put the thing out of its misery if I knew how," Piswyck said. "Can we continue this conversation when I'm dry? My shoulder hurts."

"Oh!" said the woman, shaking her head as if to restore reason. "Yes! Hurry! We've got to get out of here! The Countess has troops patrolling the road for you!"

"Then you know who I am?" asked Piswyck, still treading water.

"Of course!" snapped the young woman. "You're the young Marquis Piswyck. And I'm one of the Countess's troops."

Piswyck blinked.

"And oh, yes—I'm Bethzda, daughter of Amerdeen, who used to be a weaver. Now hurry!"

Piswyck didn't want to hurry. He wanted to lie down on the sand shelf in the sunlight and sleep for a week or two. Instead he took a deep breath and dove, searching the willow roots until he found his sword.

As it happened, Bethzda had no wearable clothes, so Piswyck's tunic became her dress. She wore the soggy top and he wore the soggy bottom, and they both mounted the somewhat disgruntled unicorn and rode away.

"We got the message just as the sun came up," Bethzda told Piswyck and the unicorn as they traveled. "As usual there was some dragon doo about the Marquis Oswyck experimenting with forbidden magicks . . ."

"What? But my father would never—"

"I never believed it! In the old days no one would have believed it. But now, with things so bad, some of the simpler folk are willing to believe anything if it offers a shred of hope. I would like to believe, too, but I know too much about the Countess to trust her with two words in a row. My father was a wealthy man once. He grew spidersilk and leatherleaves. He had a plantation of the newest kinds of new bamboo."

As Piswyck rode with his arms around her waist he was able to feel the tenseness creeping into Bethzda's body as she spoke.

"One day the Countess rode through his plantation with a hunting party. She admired the certain purple of a chlamys my father was wearing, and, it seemed, my father as well. She spent the night with him and in the morning convinced him that nothing in Latter Earth could make her happy but a whole room done in his elegant purple silk."

She laughed bitterly, and to Piswyck it seemed that the lovely softness of her body was now as hard as the calcified troll they'd hanged in the sunlight.

"That was the rarest of purples, and my father had to travel to far Tyre to get the little shellfish from which it was made. He sank all he had into the venture, sure that almighty fashion would smile on him. But when he returned the Countess just laughed at his gesture, and purple stayed out of fashion for years."

"My father told me," said Piswyck, "that in her youth the Countess was the most beautiful woman in the world. He said that everything she did was a picture of charm and grace. But then she discovered that she knew the whereabouts of the Appearing Egg, and the fascination for the thing and its power corrupted her."

"I'm glad its power isn't absolute," said the unicorn, his colors dark with damp now because he was sweating from the load. "She yet may have some virtue we don't know."

Bethzda gave a little snorting laugh.

"Better to throw away a pomegranate that has only one good seed left," she said. "The time wasted finding the one seed will buy a dozen healthy fruits."

"I would be satisfied with just one seed," the unicorn sighed, "for mention of it calls to mind my feed!"

Piswyck noted that his own stomach was remarkably empty.

"You can graze when we get to shelter," said Bethzda.

"Graze?" queried the unicorn indignantly. "What do you think I am, some kind of horse?"

Bethzda glanced over her shoulder and Piswyck saw her green eyes filled with surprise.

"Unicorns are omnivores," he explained. "And finicky!"

"I don't think finicky is quite the word," said the unicorn, continuing to be offended. "Refined in taste is what I'm bred to be!"

"Well," Bethzda laughed, bemused, and her body softening as the topic changed. "I'm afraid we are short on pomegranates and caviar this year. But will that clump of trees ahead interest you? I think it is an abandoned pear orchard, and there should be pears ripening there by now. We might even find some aloes for the marquis's wound."

They made an amiable lunch of not-quite-ripe pears and just-a-little-too-ripe blood oranges, and to accompany the meal they chose a vintage spring water that dribbled from the chin of an old stone lion in the kitchen garden of the ruined farmhouse. There were aloes, and Bethzda lost no time in dressing and binding Piswyck's wound with a poultice of the stinging clear jelly the plant produced. When this was done Piswyck and Bethzda reclined head to head on an old stone wall and the unicorn moved slowly about the kitchen garden, sniffing at herbs.

"You said you were part of a patrol," Piswyck said, stretching.

"I fly a kite in the service of the Countess," said Bethzda. "Keeping watch over the country from the sky. My father's fortune is gone, as I said. Someone has to support us, and I like flying. Let me make clear, Marquis Piswyck, that I did not set out to rescue you this morning. I won't blow any free wind in your direction! I was doing my duty, and if I'd been with my flight mates when I saw you, I would probably have spotted on you. On the other hand, if I had been alone . . . well, I will seldom avoid a chance to throw sand in the Countess's butter! Now, of course, it's all different. I am resolved to help you in any way that I can, so long as it does not compromise my father."

He nodded.

"My father, however," Bethzda continued, "my father will wax ecstatic at the chance of spotting on the Countess this big!"

"How did you end up in the troll's cupboard?" Piswyck asked. "Did the Countess send you to kill it, and you got caught instead?"

"The Countess?" asked Bethzda. "Why no, of course not! Why should she do that? The water trolls and the stone trolls and all the rest are her pets. She's the one who turned them loose, to close the roads and prevent travel."

"What?" Piswyck sat up abruptly.

"You mean you didn't know?" asked Bethzda, astonished. "Why, she started last fall, when she loosed the stone trolls in the mountain passes. Why do you think there have been no visitors in Carsonne this year?"

It hadn't really occurred to Piswyck that there was a dearth of visitors. But now that she mentioned it, he hadn't seen anyone from outside since last midsummer, when Miranda had sent him the ill-fated Montana Bib.

"I was looking for you," Bethzda continued, "and I flew my hang glider down too low to get a look under that bridge. The bridge is a good way from my base, so I didn't know about the troll. The wind changed and I lost the lift and was forced to land. As soon as I touched down the troll picked up my kite and plucked me from under it; just as easy as taking eggs from a hen! Well, not quite as easy. My harness hook wouldn't come loose, so the troll had to tear me out of the harness and my clothes to separate me from my glider. I'm just lucky he didn't break any of my bones in doing it."

"If the mountain passes are closed with trolls," said Piswyck, "then how am I going to get to Serrique?"

"To Serrique?" asked Bethzda.

"And ultimately to Far Bermuda," he said.

"In two months' time you won't be able to. The winds will change and the snows will set in. But for a while yet you can fly."

"I've never done any hang gliding," said Piswyck. "Nor, I suspect, has my unicorn."

"Then I shall have to teach you both," said Bethzda, as if it were no more to learn than shuffle dancing.

Was she serious? Piswyck wondered. "Teach a unicorn to fly?" he asked aloud.

"I do not think a unicorn should fly," said the unicorn decisively.

"And I don't think a unicorn should die," said Bethzda, just as decisively. "If you stay in Carsonne, the Countess will post a reward. Eventually you will be caught. Besides, flying is easy. The only dangerous part is the landing, and I'll teach you that first."

"I don't think they make gliders in my size," the unicorn protested.

"Gliders are made for pilots, not the other way around," said Bethzda. "I admit you're a little bit unusual. Your kite will have to be larger than most. But you have advantages from the outset. Humans have to train for a long while before they can run with a load on their back, bent over facing the ground. You'll be able to do it with ease!"

"But—" started the unicorn, but Piswyck interrupted,

pointing to a flight of yellow triangles that had appeared in the sky near the horizon.

Bethzda watched intently for a moment, then gathered up the orange peels and pear cores and rushed both Piswyck and the unicorn into the ruins of the farmhouse.

"They won't land without a reason," she said, directing the unicorn to lie against a wall, then covering him with pieces of rubble. "It's late enough in the season that the fields we came through won't show our passage. All we can do is hide, and hope. Just remember that they're silent up there. Don't move, don't even breathe too fast."

Piswyck and Bethzda slid in under the narrow shelter of an old table that lay against another wall. The tunic rode up as they squirmed in and Piswyck found himself pressed against her virtually naked body.

"This is not only uncomfortable," said Bethzda, "it's embarrassing!" With a deft squirm she pulled the tunic off and tucked it under her head as a pillow. "You haven't told me the unicorn's name yet."

"He doesn't have one yet," said Piswyck, perceiving that the situation was, indeed, embarrassing (but delightful) and that if they stayed in this position long the intimacy of their relationship must surely expand.

She snuggled against him.

"It takes hours to look over an area this size, even with binoculars. They will give careful scrutiny to this ruin, but I don't think we've left any traces. Still, we'll be here a long time. It will probably be more amusing if you take off your silly pants."

Piswyck had not had any reason to study the customs of the people who flew hang gliders, but he had no wish to offend the proprieties of his hostess and possible benefactress, so he did as he was told.

The next morning Piswyck and Bethzda saw the unicorn for the first time in his full glory. The bath in the stream had washed him, and the rest of a night had refreshed him, and the sun just after dawn had dried him out. His rose-pink mane fluffed in a gentle morning breeze. His colors seemed to absorb the sunlight and return it newly cleaned and tinted. When he twitched his tail the black caught highlights of blue and the green streaking was even greener than the fields of mown stalks that surrounded the orchard.

He is like a pile of living jewels, thought Piswyck.

"He's like candy," said Bethzda. "You know, that kind of colored crystal candy that you can see through? Sometimes it comes in little disks and sometimes there's a hole in the middle, like a doughnut. At the festivals, when I was little, they used to sell it in the shapes of little gods and goddesses. You suck on it, and it's tangy, and it comes in lots of different colors and flavors. When the sunlight falls on it, the colors are just like those of your unicorn. I think I always liked the olive-flavored candies best!"

"Oh why must everyone see me as food?" complained the unicorn, tossing his head.

"The trouble is," laughed Piswyck, "that everyone can *see* you! What are we going to do about that?"

"Why, we shall have to travel in the night," said the unicorn.

"Or else disguise you," said Bethzda.

The idea of a disguise did not appeal to the unicorn, but Bethzda's idea for doing so proved so clever that they decided to do it. It offered not only the luxury of travel by day but the opportunity of confusing the enemy.

There was plenty of clay in the part of Carsonne through which they traveled, so on some days they would find a bank of red clay and paint the unicorn all over, and he would become a roan. On other days it would be white clay and he would be a gray. On one occasion Piswyck was possessed by a veritable artistic frenzy and the unicorn had to submit to being a pinto. There was no way to disguise the fact that he was a unicorn, but from a distance the effect was . . . the best they could manage.

Bethzda continued to wear Piswyck's tunic (now dry) and he continued to wear his hosen, and it was no greatly unusual sight to see a bare-chested young man with his short-shifted young woman riding through the hot autumn fields on their unicorn.

They rode across the fields, away from the roads, like youngsters from the farms who paid no heed to politics. By this method, and circuitous routes, they took five and a half days (and nights) to make a day and a half's journey to the leatherleaf forests of the foothills. The unicorn had gone a little lame from the strain of having two people ride him much of the time, and the conversation had turned to friendly silence by the time they finally came under the purple shade of the trees.

As they walked beside the unicorn in the coolness Piswyck contemplated the fact that he had grown to like Bethzda a great deal. He liked her open sexuality, her hard courage; she was quick of wit and a mother of invention when the going got rough. She saw things in a light so fresh it dazzled him.

It occurred to him that he would very much like to take Bethzda along as a boon companion to Far Bermuda. But it also occurred to him that Miranda, his intended, might find it disconcerting to discover herself rescued by her fiancé and his mistress—assuming that the rescue proved successful!

That day passed and on the next day they came to the first of the silk plantations. They skirted the stands of mulberry trees widely, for although the spiders were mostly docile there had been more than one fatality ascribed to a herd of excited spiders.

Clumps of mutant bamboo appeared, and persimmon orchards for the beer trade. Then they were through the more prosperous part of the forest. Ruined homes appeared, then stretches of dark forest festooned with white and dusty gray cobwebs, abandoned and dangerous dells where the wild spiders dwelt.

Finally they came to the ruins of a large, half-timbered manor. Bethzda signaled Piswyck and the unicorn to wait, then walked into the courtyard. Piswyck could see her walking about idly, whistling absently to herself. He recognized an ancient folk tune called "I Want to Hold Your Hand."

At length an unobtrusive little door to one side was hurled open and an old man came running out, dropping his crossbow and throwing his arms around Bethzda.

"Bethzda, darling!" the old man cried, tears running down his cheeks. "They said you would not come back!"

"I near did not," Bethzda said, hugging the old man to her. "A troll caught me, and would have had me for his dinner save these two friends saved me."

She gestured toward Piswyck and the unicorn where they waited. The old man looked at them and his face beamed with gratitude. It was a round face, with eyes paled by despair, and there were patches of gray discoloration. Piswyck wondered whether the patches were stains or old bug bites. It didn't matter, for now the old tragedies were swept back into the past.

"Now, Father, it will be our turn to save them," Bethzda continued, not giving her father a chance to make a speech. "Do you think we can build a glider to fly a three-hundred-kilogram unicorn?"

The old man looked at the unicorn closely, his gaze sharpening as if he were about to let an arrow fly.

"Not, by any chance, a *parti*colored unicorn, under the clay?"

Without waiting for an answer he burst into laughter, a raucous cackle like a demented turkey.

"Oh, how I *shall* delight to spot upon that coroneted bitch!" old Amerdeen crowed. "Come, my fetlocked friend, we shall start to spin today! A silver kite, I think. The color of the nature of the silk. A kite that will not stand against the dawn sky visible. Such a challenge! A kite not for the colors but the pilot!"

To Piswyck it seemed that they were being needlessly feted for the next two days, but when he spoke of it to Amerdeen he was taken to a great barn of a room in one wing of the manor and shown the loom that two old men were stringing.

"It will have to be a huge kite," said Amerdeen, rubbing his hands together. "The biggest we've ever made, perhaps the biggest ever! And yet it cannot be *too* big. There is a point of diminishing return. I hope the unicorn is strong and swift, for he shall have to go fast to get off the ground. If we make the kite too big, all those delicate ratios won't work out. If we make it too small, then it won't lift him. It has to be just right! We're estimating eleven meters, roughly, for the wing span, which will give us about twenty-three and a half square meters of sail. We could stitch that much sail together, of course, but I think the spidersilk will be stronger and the air flow more smoothly if we make it all of a piece. These looms that we have been piecing together over the past two days are from very old parts. There was once a fashion for great silk tents, many years ago. The looms took up too much space when the fashion passed, but the parts are still with us piecemeal. But you, young Marquis! How is your shoulder?"

"It's better," said Piswyck, flexing the muscles. The aloe had killed the infection and the sword wound was on its way to healing. The raking that the troll had given him was only an angry welt now. Still, he didn't want to have to do any unnecessary handsprings.

"You will have to be much better, much sooner," said Amerdeen seriously. "Once you are in the air things will go easily. But, as with any bird, there is a lot of muscle to getting airborne. You have rested and eaten well. I think now it is time to begin to train you!"

Amerdeen couldn't take them to the usual training hills for obvious reasons, but there were plenty of meadows with steep slopes in unfrequented parts of the forest. Guarded by dells of wild spiders, the old man and his daughter began to educate Piswyck and the unicorn to the air.

The hardest part, Piswyck quickly discovered, was getting up the hill.

The unicorn complained, but he did have four legs, Piswyck noted, so going up a steep hill with a burden on his back was more a matter of inconvenience and indignity than it was anguish. For Piswyck, with a sore shoulder, it was an ordeal.

The glider with which Piswyck practiced was ungainly. Even furled into a long tube it was subject to the whims of the winds, like a backpack that stuck out two meters fore and two meters aft.

The first day they didn't go far up the hill. Amerdeen stopped them and showed them how to unfurl and assemble the glider. The unicorn could not assemble his own (having no hands) or run a check of it, but his mind was quick and his eye sharp, and he made quite sure that Piswyck remembered everything.

There was no glider for the unicorn as yet, but he had to learn the drills, nonetheless. Amerdeen had already made him a harness and for practice it was attached to the largest glider in the neighborhood, one that had formerly belonged to the miller's fat wife. With this much equipment the unicorn could practice his balance.

The first day's lesson consisted of putting on their harnesses, hooking their harness hooks to the kite's center of gravity, and walking through the triangular frame by which the craft was guided. They made sure they were hooked in securely, then hoisted the glider and ran down the hill.

The apex of the triangular steering frame dug into Piswyck's shoulders, and for the first try the pain was all that he could think about. Running down the hill took the strain off the shoulder, but at the bottom he had to pick up the glider and port it back up hill. Then the shoulder really hurt!

After the fifth try the unicorn was veritably dancing with excitement. "I felt it tug at me and try to lift!" he cried.

Piswyck was not so fast a runner as the unicorn, so after carrying the glider up the hill five times he was exhausted. If the wind hit the expanded and stretched sail it flattened him to the ground. Part of him felt like an overgrown child playing with a big toy. Part of him felt that the toy was playing with him. He was sure that the skill to fly must take months to acquire.

Amerdeen seemed pleased in the extreme with his progress.

"You have a talent for it, boy!" the old man said, clapping him on the shoulder and remembering too late the sword wound. "I can see that you've trained for something strong and graceful. A dancer perhaps?"

"A gymnast," confessed Piswyck.

"Ah," said Amerdeen, "one of the finer ways to put a good body on a young boy's bones. You should have no trouble in adapting to flight. Just bend your body more in half when you run down the hill. Pretend you're one of those little feathered dinosaurs, and that you have a big fat tail sticking out behind you!"

The days passed and the wound healed, and Piswyck and the unicorn learned to fly. They learned it with their bodies and they learned it with their minds, perusing the mysteries of ground speed and air speed, learning from Amerdeen and other experienced pilots how to gauge the shape of the air by the way trees and grass on a distant hill fluttered.

"The air is a great ocean," Amerdeen said. "But if you fail in it, you will not float to the top. When you are high up its currents can be more treacherous, and less visible, than those of either rivers or oceans. If we prayed to a god of the air, we would use the words of one of the most ancient pilots. He said: 'The air is terribly unforgiving.' You must learn *never* to make mistakes!"

The mistakes, it seemed to Piswyck, gave their own warnings. If you ran down the hill *just* wrong one wing of the kite would lift you, you would lose your footing, and unless you did just the right thing you took a nosedive. Then if you didn't let go and let the harness protect you, you could have your *other* shoulder cruelly wrenched.

"But remember," Bethzda would say as she massaged his

aching-all-over naked body with heated almond oil, "it is better to hurt a lot and be alive than to hurt not at all and be dead."

The day came when Piswyck could get off the ground and glide from one ridge to another. That was the first plateau. It mattered not at all that he crashed at the other end and knocked himself cold with the impact. He was jubilant when he awoke, despite his headache.

The next plateau came when the unicorn's kite was finished and the unicorn found that he, too, could get off the ground.

It was somewhat frightening for Amerdeen and his old compatriots, for although they had calculated how much ground speed the unicorn would have to attain to become airborne, and how fast the glider would go when it got up, there was a difference between knowing a thing with the mind and seeing it in the air.

"*That's* a critter could spot on you!" said one of the weavers in awe.

They learned maneuvers, and different subtleties in landing, and there was so much to absorb into the mind and the muscles that months seemed to pass. In the moments when Piswyck could stop to think, he realized that he had lost track of time. Was it weeks? Was it months? The seasons in the forest changed more slowly than those that flushed over the plains of Carsonne. It could have been mere days, but for the easing of his aches.

It was such an intense, passionate kind of learning, and so completely absorbing, that even mortal danger seemed to recede, both the danger of the flying and the growing danger of discovery by the Countess. Time, for the nonce, was against him, Piswyck noted.

The most important part of the course was to learn thermaling. They would have to be good at that for they would only have one chance.

To get enough altitude to get over the mountains they would have to make use of the fields that were plowed to send up the patrols the Countess ordered. Freshly plowed land produced columns of warm air and a glider could move into such a column and spiral upward to great heights. Amerdeen said that if it were done just right they would be able to take off, glide down into one of the thermal pillars, spiral up, then catch the late morning winds that rose up toward the top of the mountains. The difficulty would be the timing, for it would have to be done long enough after the Countess's patrols were gone out that no one would swoop down on them from above, yet early enough to catch the uphill wind.

They also learned to sing.

"If you're stuck in a mist or a cloud," Bethzda told them, "you have to make a sound, to be sure that someone else doesn't crash into you. The best thing is singing, for it's easier to sing than it is to talk or whistle, and long, sustained notes travel well through the air."

There were many songs that pilots liked, and there were songs that were good and bad luck. Songs where the voice was at the top of its range were best because treble notes were directional. Songs in the bass register were worst, because bass notes were not directional.

"Singing in various kinds of harmony is ideal," she continued. "Most pilots can do it by the hour; have to! But we can't go into that because it requires a lot of practice and there isn't time. Suffice that your voice must carry a long way, Piswyck, or you'll be in mortal danger should you climb into a cloud."

At. the end they were not nearly ready. They could have used much more practice. But the word came that news of their presence had leaked and there was no real choice anymore between flight and falling prey.

"Whoever . . ." Amerdeen mused tiredly over a hot mug of persimmon beer. "Whoever did it . . . Well, they can't be blamed. The Countess has charms! Oh, how I know it! It is only sad if they got as little for their informing as I got for my sea snails."

Piswyck's body had healed enough by then that making love through the night was not impossible, however imprudent. He and Bethzda slept briefly near dawn, then awoke and saw the pale glimmer of morning light in each other's eyes. With light touches instead of words, they dressed and went to the slope where the lessons had been. The gliders were already assembled for them to save their strength. There were three gliders waiting, as Bethzda was to guide them up the slopes, through the passes that were negotiable by air, and down the other side to a point where they could see Serrique.

"If you should go down in the mountains," said one of the old weavers, "there will be stone trolls waiting, so you have to make it through in one flight!"

"Should we not be armed with more than a sword?" asked Piswyck. "I know the weight is critical, but . . ."

"Even your sword will be useless to you in the air," said Bethzda, fastening herself into the cocoonlike harness and putting on her heavy leatherleaf and carven wood helmet. "The only good weapon in a kite is a spear, and it takes much greater skill than you have to both pilot and fight."

"You fight with spears while high above the earth?" queried the unicorn.

"You don't attack each other," laughed Bethzda without humor. "You slice each other's sails. Once you've done that, trying to kill your opponent is superfluous."

Piswyck got down on his knees, stretched out, and hung from the frame, feeling the straps tighten at his shoulders, his chest, and around his thighs. He drew his knees back up, then stood and walked through the triangle and looked back, checking to see that the harness hook was fastened securely. Then he walked back through the triangle and got down on his knees, to rest until it was time to fly.

"Remember, don't try to fly too close, and watch everything I do," said Bethzda. "You can judge some of what's coming up by the way I move."

She bent over and lifted her kite, letting the broad yellow sail rest on her back. She had deemed it best to take an official kite in the hope that the flight would not be questioned. She grasped the leatherleaf handholds three quarters of the way up the sides of the triangle. She hefted the kite and rested the padded parts of the triangle below the apex on her shoulders; then, still bent, she ran down the hill.

The sail caught. She leaned forward to gain speed, then eased the bar out to lift the nose. As the nose lifted she gently pulled back, dropped her hands to the cross-member control bar, and stretched out her body horizontally. She went smoothly up.

Piswyck was next because once the unicorn was airborne it would fly very fast indeed, and the problem would be keeping ahead of it to guide it.

He followed the same precise routine that Bethzda had, but it was still scary. As he ran down the hill his heart tugged at him, telling him it couldn't possibly work. Then the straps grabbed at his thighs. He kept running, knowing that he'd better have his legs moving if this was a false start. He pulled gently at the frame, saw the ground move faster under him,

grass and flowers and rocks. Then he pushed gently out and
the surge of his weight against gravity, as the sail lifted, told
him that he was going up. He looked ahead, spied Bethzda,
and adjusted himself so that his big, sky-blue kite would follow her. He stretched his body out, letting the pulleys wrap
the warm silk cocoon around him. The sound of the New
Bamboo (well, it wasn't strictly bamboo, but another kind of
grass mutated to gigantic proportions of lightness and
strength) creaking and the silk sail beating and the wind rushing past almost made him forget where he was and what he
was doing. Only when his heartbeat slowed from the thrill did
he check his little rearview mirror and ascertain that the unicorn was also in the air, a particolored pegasus now with
silver wings.

The first part of the flight was beautiful, and not the least part
of its beauty was its uneventfulness. The vast expanse of the
leatherleaf forests stretched out below them, dark green except
where an errant wind ruffled the surface and the rich purple
undersides of the leaves flashed in the bright morning sunlight. Large roundels of lighter green marked the mulberry
trees of an occasional silk plantation with its drifting white
chimera of spider silk.

Piswyck remembered somewhere a reference to the prede-
cessor of the present silk, a stuff made from the cocoon of a
worm; and a reference to the tiny webs spun by carnivorous
spiders. He shuddered at the thought of one of the half-meter
poisonous spiders hunting meat instead of mulberries.

As they approached the plowed fields of the thermaling
columns they saw the last of the Countess's patrols heading
off toward the northwest. Amerdeen's intelligence had so far
proved correct and for that Piswyck gave thanks to the God
and Goddess, and to Saint Genesius as well. Moments later he
watched as Bethzda sailed into the column of warm, rising air,
tilted her glider slightly, and began the huge, lazy spiral upward.

It was a little rougher following her example than Piswyck
had anticipated, for the air was more turbulent than he liked
and knocked him about; but he'd been warned, and he adjusted. As he sailed upward he saw the unicorn come into the
column below him, faster, frighteningly faster, so fast he was
afraid for a moment the unicorn would go right across the
field and exit the column. But then the unicorn was also in the

spiral pattern, joined in the sacred spiral dance that was an ecstasy in its imitation of the Holy Spiral of the DNA molecule. Piswyck felt a rush of awe as he realized that this was the first time he'd ever done the dance in a full three dimensions!

Later, as they spiraled up, the unicorn appeared at the opposite side of the spiral and the sun fell full on its cleanly washed colors. There was no room for mud in the sky! And Piswyck thought that Bethzda was right: they *were* the colors of little crystal candies (though how Bethzda could like the olive-flavored ones he couldn't imagine). He pictured how the unicorn would look, sitting next to the fire in the dark; light and shadow dancing on him, in the Great Hall at Midwinter Festival. Would his children someday see that resemblance to candy?

They got to the top of the column, where the air was freezing cold, and Bethzda took off in the direction from which they'd come: toward the mountains. Piswyck followed her, and only in that moment did he realize the enormity of what they were attempting. He had not really looked at the mountains while they were practicing. He had not wanted to anticipate sharp crags and buffeting winds. Now he had to look up at the gray stone topped by eternal snows and he felt like a mosquito trying to rape an elephant.

A man with relay horses could travel faster on the flat than a man with a glider. But the horses would have to go around obstacles and they would slow as they climbed the mountains. It might be an even race in normal times; but now, with the mountain passes sealed by stone trolls, Piswyck's escape from Carsonne might well be easier than before. He wondered what mad scheme had prompted the Countess to seal off Carsonne from the outside world.

A change in the wind pulled his attention back to flying. The one luxury a pilot could not afford was an easily distracted mind! He checked his mirror and laughed as he observed the unicorn making a turn and going back into the thermal column. Was the creature outstripping him in technique or not? Why, it was *playing* with the air currents, as if it had been born to the sky! It was also delaying its speed, so that it would not overtake and pass Piswyck and Bethzda.

The midmorning wind they had counted on was there, almost waiting for them, and once they were on it they climbed.

They went south of where Amerdeen's ruined silk plantation lay, so they could not see it from the sky, but they could see the great road that led up into the mountains, and which formerly had been the usual route through them. With some trepidation Piswyck realized that there were several guard stations along the road and that if anyone looked up they would be able to see, if nothing else, the flying unicorn.

He hoped no one would look up.

The foliage below them changed and tall conifers appeared. Here and there along the road was a logging town, but even these gave out as the road rose, and the last couple of them seemed to be abandoned. Piswyck put on the mittens that hung by stretch cords inside his cocoon. The air was not just cold now, it was freezing. The sun was high, and a nonphysical chill set into his bones at the thought of flying through the mountains in the dark. Amerdeen had calculated they'd come out of the far crags by sunset if all went well, and that they could stay high above the opposing forests, beyond the mountains, until moonrise. If they made it that far they would be well out of the Countess's grasp.

Piswyck hoped Amerdeen had calculated well, and that things went according to schedule.

They went higher and higher. In his mirror he could see the vast plain of Carsonne, soft and glowing in a rose mist. It was a calm day back there, or so it seemed. It was hard to believe that something so beautiful could exist under a reign of terror. He wondered if they would go high enough to see the distant seas, with their thrashing whirlpools and writhing monsters: Carsonne's Forbidden Coast.

He heard a distant roar and his attention snapped ahead again. The mountains were closer now, and after a moment he discerned the source of the sound as a small avalanche; from this distance it looked like a fairy waterfall misting gracefully down a sheer rock face. He wondered if it were a natural phenomenon, or if some stone troll had stumbled to its doom in the mountain's fanciful ornament.

A broad stone valley stretched ahead, the road below them picking its way through the center like a strand of fallen gray yarn. In some places he saw that boulders had fallen across the pavement. He wondered how long it had been like this.

Up, between the stone walls, and then they seemed to be flying straight at a solid stone cliff a kilometer high. He shiv-

ered for a moment, then saw that the road curved off to the
right, and assumed that the valley must also.

As they approached the wall they saw that the valley did
curve, straight into a bank of thick white clouds.

"Now sing the songs that keep you safe from harm!" came
Bethzda's voice from ahead, singing. Piswyck started to call
back to her, then caught himself. Here in the high wind it was
palpable truth that his words would be shredded if he tried to
modulate his voice in the complex registers and productions of
speech. Song, with its simple pitches and steady breathing,
was much easier; which, as he remembered, was why people
on the stage always sang after they danced.

"What's it like ahead, Bethzda?" he sang in inquiry.

"Broad for most of the way," came back the answer. "With
luck the mists will vanish before we reach the narrows."

Above and behind them came the sensual and powerful
voice of the unicorn, so like a clarinet. "At last I'll get a
chance to sing my fill!"

Piswyck recognized the tune as something from an ancient
opera, and felt a flush of confidence that at least part of their
trio would be on pitch. He hated this awareness instantly, for
every song he knew left his head at that moment, just as they
entered the mists, and he had to fall back on the emergency
trick Amerdeen had taught him. He started to sing the multiplication tables.

The next part of the trip was as much an agony as the first part
had been a pleasure. There was nothing to see, only the
deadly white softness all around. All that he could feel was
the harness chafing against his limbs and the negative feeling
of the cold trying to numb him. It seemed that the cold and the
chafing were warring for possession of his beleaguered
nerves. He could hear just fine. The creaking of the poles that
formed the frame of the glider, the hissing of the air rushing
by, the beating of the sail like the purr of a giant cat. And the
singing: his own voice, croaking out "Ten Times Ten" or "Ten
Thousand Times Ten Thousand"; the unicorn singing something in Old Italian (*Mozart!* That was it, the unicorn was
singing Mozart!); and Bethzda making a sometimes wordless
harmony that blended with them both.

He had to think and feel in four dimensions. There were
the three he moved in, and the dimension of time, *through*
which he moved. The music gave him bearings in the fourth

dimension, for he had to know at all times where he was, and
as well at all times where he was about to be; and where
Bethzda and the unicorn were also about to be. It was not only
the chafing of the harness and the cold throwing dice for his
nerves, he reminded himself. He, too, had a pass at the bones.

Sometimes Bethzda's song gave directions, but mostly she
used it as a beacon, and as a kind of sonar. Piswyck knew that
she was not only sending out sounds but listening intently for
the little echos that came back, divulging by their exact timbre
the presence and position of rocks and snow.

He followed her directions and her voice, literally following blindly. The trio continued interminably. Piswyck began to
wonder just how prolific the ancient Mozart had been.

The mists began to darken, and Piswyck knew that night
must be coming on. Were they nearly out of the mountains?
The cold was not letting up. He reached into the pouch at his
waist and pulled out one of the little cakes made from dried
persimmons, mulberries, and sunflower seeds. He stuffed it
into his mouth and started to chew, then realized as the flavors
flooded his senses that he couldn't eat and sing at the same
time. He gulped it down, nearly choking, then started to sing
again, not even noticing that he had gone back to Elevenses.

By the time the mist around him was black dark softness,
Piswyck was sure his voice would not hold out. The cold
made the singing more difficult. He was creaking now more
than croaking. He legs felt numb no matter how much he
shifted and he was increasingly afraid to shift for fear that it
would affect his flight too much and smash him into a mountain. Even the unicorn had taken to singing slower pieces, and
ahead Bethzda was sounding long tones on a breath, just to
stay audible.

Piswyck felt every moment of eternity passing, not before
his eyes but through his body. Each individual moment was an
eternity in itself. He felt his mind start to slacken from lack of
stimulation. He felt himself slipping into the darkness and the
cold around him. The pain of the chafing was losing out, for
the harness cutting into him was only a finite pain while the
darkness and the cold were infinite.

And then they were out of the mists.

Past dusk blue, the sky heralded their freedom with a banner of stars, and the black slopes below waved to them with a
wonder wind, that peculiar sunset upsloping of air that lifts
and lets you go on when you thought for sure that you had to

go down. They were lifted up as the conifers below rippled. Bethzda ahead, her voice coming now joyfully, Piswyck next, finally giving up on the multiplication and letting go with the alphabet, and the unicorn singing something that began: *"Exultate jubilate!"*

But in his mirror Piswyck saw, bleary eyed, a less welcome sight. There was a kind of natural terrace on the high mountainside, and, even as he watched, five pale gliders stepped into the air seriatim. It was not so dark that he could not see the spears that hung from their hands.

"The Countess's men!" he cried, giving up the song.

"Fly on!" cried Bethzda. "I'll try and slow them down!"

Before he could protest Bethzda slowed and began to drop, gathering speed dangerously. Then she did something Piswyck had heard about but not seen. It was called a chandelle, and Amerdeen had said it was supposed to be impossible with a hang glider. She sailed up, her right wing tipped up; she made a curve that almost took her upside down; and then, at the end of the curve, she straightened out, so that she was now flying straight back toward them all.

"But they have spears!" Piswyck gasped as she came abreast. "You can't fight them all!"

"You'd be surprised!" Bethzda sang at him, and her eyes widened with a wicked smile.

Piswyck struggled desperately with the only turn he knew. He lost altitude, but he finally accomplished it, noting as he straightened out that the unicorn had turned more quickly than he and was already ahead of him.

The trick, Piswyck knew, was to stay well above the enemy. That way they couldn't drop anything on your sail and would have a hell of a time using their spear on it. At the moment the wonder wind was behind him, and all he had to do was ride it to get extra lift. Of course the enemy could use that wind, too, but it would be more difficult for them, since they were lower in altitude.

But what could he do?

He thought about the one piece of magic his father had taught him. To make a little fire. He closed his eyes and concentrated on the sail of one of the kites coming toward him.

Unfortunately, magic has its limitations. The air was cold and the wind was rushing past. Even if he were able to focus enough heat in the sail, he realized, the wind-chill factor would rob it. He could put all of his body heat into it, but it would be hopeless. He'd only end up frozen.

He opened his eyes.

There was Bethzda, right ahead of one of the enemy kites. To his horror, she jammed her bar forward and stalled. She started to fall. Piswyck choked. Was she trying to crash into him? She pulled on the bar and her kite shot forward, and as it did she lowered her legs, as if she were about to land. The toe of her shoe reached down, there was a glint of metal, and where her toe dragged across the top of her opponent's sail a long slash appeared. As she shot off toward the mists they had just escaped the torn kite crumpled and the man under it screamed.

He screamed for a long time as he fell toward the dark pine forest. Piswyck trembled.

Then one of the soldiers was after him, on a long glide toward him, spear lowered.

Piswyck was not yet adept at this sort of activity but he knew a good trick when he saw one. As the enemy kite closed in, he jammed his bar forward and stalled. His stomach churned as gravity disappeared. He pulled the bar back, too far, and almost lost control completely, but the trick had worked. His opponent had passed him by.

Bethzda reappeared from the mists. The enemy kites were turning now, ready for a second assault and no doubt mad about losing their comrade. Where was the unicorn?

"Piswyck, will you get out of here?" demanded Bethzda rhetorically.

"Not without you!" he answered.

"If you run, stupid, they'll follow! I can spot on them from behind!"

"Oh," said Piswyck. He had forgotten in the excitement that he was the fox in this chase, and that there was a prize for his pelt. He started to turn his kite dutifully around, to head for Serrique. But when he had made the turn he realized that the enemy was now between him and his goal; and now the wonder wind was on their side.

And where was the unicorn?

A yell from one of the enemy kites startled Piswyck; then he saw the kite go fluttering downward, not quite out of control but certainly crippled.

"What happened?" he called to Bethzda.

"Aren't you glad dinosaurs don't fly?" she laughed.

Something whizzed by Piswyck and a chill ran over him. He recognized the sound of a crossbow bolt.

"Hey, they're shooting at us!"

"Don't worry!" said Bethzda. "This silk is double bonded with bee propolis. It won't ravel!"

"But suppose we get shot?"

"Get going!" she cried. "If you hang around here talking you *will* get shot!"

There were three enemy gliders now and Piswyck supposed that was something of an even match. But they had all three broken out crossbows and, though it was a dirty trick, it could prove effective. He decided to take Bethzda's advice, if only because it would make the enemy have to turn again— provided he got by them.

He dove, letting his glider pick up as much speed as he dared, hoping he could go under his opponents faster than they could drop to attack him. It was a gamble, but it worked. He shot under them, pulled up, and headed straight into the darkness. If he wasn't skilled enough to fight in a hang glider, maybe he could race! He knew the unicorn could easily outrace anything flying by virtue of its weight. But what about Bethzda?

It was difficult to use his mirror in the gathering darkness. The stars had provided enough light for his mist-bedarked eyes to let him do battle, but long-distance viewing was another matter.

As the moments drew out he began to worry more and more. Where were they? The enemy. Bethzda. The unicorn.

There was only the sound of the night wind rushing past, the creaking of the giant grass members of the glider, the beating of the spider-silk sail, like a fast heart. He strained his senses outward. There was a resin smell from the forests below. The air was growing warmer. The adrenaline had beaten back some of the pain where the straps had cut into him.

Where were they?

Then a sound, like the sound his own kite was making, but a little different. Distant. Then closer. He strained his eyes, reaching into the dark mirror, trying to see.

Nothing.

Then something. Something pale, something not of his friends. One of the gliders of the Countess, coming in from above and behind him, the deadly spear poised like the tail of a wasp, ready to sting.

He tried to pull up. It was no good. He couldn't get altitude quickly enough. The enemy was coming closer, settling down behind him. He could see the man's face in the dark, a smile of anger and vengeance, joy about to burst with the kill. Closer.

Closer.

Then in the nimbus of consciousness which Piswyck had fixed on his enemy a rushing sound appeared, like a kite only faster, like the wind, like the dawn, and he felt rather than saw the unicorn beneath its kite, legs drawn up, head down, its carnelian horn like Parsifal's spear thrown through darkness. The tip of the horn came down and cut the silk of his enemy's sail like scissors, like paper; and, like a stone thrown from a sling, the speeding unicorn pulled up and vanished above them both.

It was a second's vision. The man in Piswyck's mirror seemed surprised, and then he plummeted out of sight and there was only a scream in the night.

Piswyck shivered and flew on.

The air grew warmer and moister, and he could detect traces of ocean air mingled with the resin. The moon rode straight ahead. It was full, and by its white light he made out the unicorn flying dark against it.

With what was left of his voice he called out, and the unicorn heard him. It turned its kite slowly, made its way back, and soon they were flying not far apart.

"Where is Bethzda?" Piswyck asked.

The unicorn was silent for a moment. Perhaps it, too, was tired, Piswyck thought. Then it answered.

"She spotted on the kite that came in first, but then the second one was on her tail. She ducked into the mists again as if that trick was such that it could never fail. I heard a cry, and then another came, and so I think that in the mists they met. His cry was loud and long. I know he died. But her cry never came and so the same may not be true for her; although as yet I hear no voice, nor any trace of song."

Piswyck knew instinctively that the unicorn had waited longer than was reasonable. That he had only come to the rescue when there was no longer any point in waiting for Bethzda.

They flew on, and the moon grew smaller and colder. Piswyck thought about Bethzda in the sunlight, and about the unicorn in the sunlight, and about how the unicorn had twice now saved his life. High in the night sky he thought about the unicorn's bright colors by daylight, and he decided to name the unicorn for a memory of Bethzda.

"My friend!" he called out. "From this moment thy name be Lifesaver!"

Then in the night sky Piswyck cried.

Drinking Crabgrass Wine

In the dawn streets of Serrique, Piswyck and Lifesaver searched for a smuggler, desperate lest delay deliver them unto death at the hands of the Countess. And yet they found themselves dawdling, peering into amber chambers through leaded-glass windows and marveling at ancient architecture. They felt comfortable in Serrique, almost normal for the first time in weeks. While it was true that there were not many particolored unicorns abroad (in fact there were none), there were a great many drunks; and the two of them were now charter to that illustrious company.

It was, of course, the crabgrass wine. Its effects were not only intoxicating, they were mildly psychedelic, heightening all the colors and adding an extra depth to everything. Lifesaver had expressed an opinion, earlier in the evening, that one did not so much have the wine as it had one. It was the only wine that Serrique could produce and, as it traveled not at all, Serrique was the only place in Latter Earth it could be had. It came with the meal (any meal) and there was an abundance of it now in their blood, making concentration difficult, even on the necessary task of staying alive.

As they staggered through an ancient brick arch they heard a scream. Piswyck tried to brush the colorful cobwebs from his mind and focus on the source of the sound. As if obliging his effort at attention there was a second scream.

"*There!* In the shadows!" he said, drawing his sword.

"I'd rather wait till morning for a fight," lamented Lifesaver, but as Piswyck advanced the unicorn followed.

Under the rotting awning that had once been a shop, two big men and a *something* were beating a small man in rags. Piswyck was aware that things were seldom as they seemed, but he disliked the odds.

"Hold!" he cried in his best command voice.

The *thing* turned on him and hissed. He couldn't quite see it in the dark, but it might have been a basilisk. The two men continued the beating. The victim, perceiving possible help, screamed again.

"I said *hold!*" Piswyck all but shouted.

The thing that might have been a basilisk came at him, hissing loudly, its movement a rapid shuffle on many feet. Tendrils shot out of it on all sides, ready to enwrap him.

Piswyck knew that basilisks were poisonous. Whether this was one or not, he wanted to take no chances. He sprang backward as the tendrils reached for him, then leaped left as it spread the writhing mass and came at him again.

It was fast, but Piswyck was a gymnast. As it changed direction he somersaulted past it, then threw his momentum into a circular cut with his sword that severed the creature's head from its body.

There was a small, intense blast of heat and yellow light as the sword passed through the thing, its blood and the steel of the sword making bad chemistry together. Piswyck felt intense pain as drops of the monster's blood spattered on his hand and burned like acid.

There was another scream from the direction of the rotted awning and Piswyck turned to see one of the two attackers spitted on Lifesaver's spiraled carnelian horn. The remaining assailant, seeing that the odds had changed, turned to run. But the little man he'd been beating grabbed his leg and sank his teeth into his tormentor's thigh, just above the knee, then shot his fist up with surprising force into the big man's balls.

Piswyck looked back at his burning hand, then at his sword, which was now glowing with a sickly yellow light and disintegrating even as he held it. As the gnawing corruption of the steel that the monster's blood was causing encroached on the quillons he threw the weapon from him and let out a cry of pain.

"Yeow!"

Almost as quickly as the cry had escaped, the little man in

rags was at his side, fumbling through the tattered remains of a large burse.

"Quick," said the little man in a raspy voice, "I'd better treat that!"

Before Piswyck could do more than hurt, the little man pulled out a bottle of crabgrass wine, unstoppered it, and poured it over his hand. As Piswyck stared in blurry amazement, the man then spit on his hand quite thoroughly and added the gooey contents of a small ceramic jar. The pain began to subside.

"What were they after?" called Lifesaver, doing a little animal dance with his sharp hooves near the head of the remaining malefactor. The malefactor merely clutched his groin and groaned.

"Secrets," said the little man diffidently, tearing a long strip from his ragged garment and binding the salve to Piswyck's swelling hand. "That's what they all want. That's my stock in trade. But these fellows didn't want to pay for them! What's a poor fellow to do when they want to rob him of his secrets!"

"You sell *secrets?*" Piswyck asked.

"Ah, yes!" said the little man proudly. He had bushy hair, Piswyck noted, though the color was indeterminate in the gray dawn shadows. His face was angular, perhaps once handsome, but he walked with an extreme stoop, as if carrying a heavy load. "If you will allow me to introduce myself: I am Skylatch, Seller of the Secrets of Serrique. I make it my business to know everybody else's business and, for a fee, can arrange to transgress a little business for almost anybody!"

Skylatch laughed, a shallow little laugh.

"Well," said Piswyck, sighing through a wave of butterfly-colored emotions. "It may be that we have stumbled across the right party. My friend and I have had little success in discovering anything in this city but the availability of crabgrass wine, even though what we seek is something the city is famed for."

"And what might that be?" asked Skylatch, his eyes lighting with a smile.

"A smuggler," said Piswyck.

"But one whom we can absolutely trust," added Lifesaver, tapping his prisoner's arm gently with a hoof when said prisoner started to rise.

Skylatch laughed again, a little louder this time. "Are your goods very precious then?" he asked.

"Our goods are ourselves," said Piswyck. "As precious a cargo as it is possible to own."

"Ah," said Skylatch, "an intrigue. You must escape from someone or something!"

"As much that as *to* someone," said Piswyck. "I am not only pursued but must, perforce, perform a rescue. For these reasons my friend and I must seek secret passage to Far Bermuda. Because my, uh, fortune, is in dispute we must put the venture on credit."

Skylatch laughed again, then whistled with astonishment.

"It's not much you want, young friend! The journey to Far Bermuda is a perilous one. Sundered Seas, monsters of the deep . . . and know you not that the oceans of Latter Earth are dominated by the Black Elves?"

"All this I know," said Piswyck, "and perhaps that is why I have put off the journey for so long. I have held it my duty to rescue my betrothed; but it has been easy, because of the perils you name, to say to myself that I lack the maturity, or the advancement necessary to marshall forces. Now I am unable to stay at home and tend to business as usual, so I must sally forth and do my duty as best I can; and in so doing perhaps acquire the weapons to wrest my own rightful inheritance from the hands of my usurper!"

"Amen!" said the unicorn.

"As pretty a speech as I have heard," said Skylatch sympathetically. "But alas; not the first time I've heard such. Serrique is full of outcast noblemen seeking a way to win back their homes. They require an army, or a potion, or a spell, or some rough magic. But you, at least, want something a little different. That may be to your credit.

"Listen, young friend. You have saved my life so I will give you some secrets in trade for it. I must admit that they are the kind of secrets so widely known you would probably have found them out by morning, but no matter! What you need is a smuggler whom you can trust. Now, there *are* no smugglers who can be trusted, but it is possible to bind them so that they will do what you wish. The way to do that is to gain the graces of she whom they trust and serve."

"The Goddess?" asked Piswyck, somewhat taken aback.

"No, no!" Skylatch laughed, somewhat bemused at the idea, and at such innocence. "Not one so grand, I fear! No, it is she who rules the Mirror Court whom you must seek. Madame Leudecia Roseboom!"

"The Mirror Court?" asked Piswyck.

"Aye," said Skylatch. "That court of the underworld that so perfectly mirrors the High Court of Prince Paul the Impotent, who in theory rules Serrique."

"Oh," said Piswyck. The tone of Skylatch's delivery made it obvious that this was one of those things that "everyone" knew about—like Dame Harriett's World-Famous Prune Pies.

"She is not beautiful," said Skylatch, "but once she was, perhaps, the most beautiful woman in the world. At least, enough men thought so to amass her fortune and give her power. Now she sits like the Queen of the Toads atop a pile of gold that would slay a dragon by sheer envy. You will need some entry to her court, for not everyone who seeks will find, as the saying goes. But it is possible that you have some talents?"

"I can swim," said Piswyck, "and I am not a bad tumbler. I can do a bit of hang gliding, but we've both had to sell our gliders to the silk merchants to survive the past three days in Serrique. My swordsmanship is adequate, but nothing for exhibition; and it would not suit my needs to sign up with her palace guard."

"And what about your unicorn?" asked Skylatch.

"He can sing, and rather well," said Piswyck. "Does she like music?"

"It depends upon the kind," said Skylatch.

"Lifesaver has a wealth of music at his command," said Piswyck expansively. He was perhaps exaggerating, for he had only in the last few days become aware how all-consuming was the unicorn's passion for melody.

"A wealth may be insufficient if it is not of the correct coinage," said Skylatch. He turned to Lifesaver. "Tell me, do you know anything dirty?"

Lifesaver blinked.

"I mean," clarified Skylatch, "songs that treat of explicit sexual material in a demeaning and derogatory, although humorous, manner."

"I know those old motets that Mozart wrote," said Lifesaver, "but those must all be sung in several parts. Beyond that, there's a lay by Robbie Burns; and after Paris sank beneath the sea, great Pandit Boosh wrote songs to make one blush with Schönberg's system grafted on a beat."

"All rhetoric to me," said Skylatch, "but yet it may be just the thing to get her attention. Come, new friends, I will lead

you to the door and introduce you; but beyond that my acquaintance would prove more a burden than a blessing. A man
in my business is welcome nowhere unless there is a buyer for
his market."

The streets of Serrique were crowded with buildings like semi-
precious stones, tumble polished and piled one atop another in
a mad yet subtle display of dark and lustrous color. Whether
the stone towers were made of jasper Piswyck knew not; the
effects of the crabgrass wine came and went, and sometimes a
darkly glowing jewel of a doorway shifted ever so slightly and
became mere stone. The moon was a pearl above pearly onion
turrets at some moments, at others a bead of ice threatening to
fall and shatter on crenellated parapets. As they walked the
ever-brightening sky slowly picked out new colors as shadows
shifted and dissolved.

But then the balance between the brightening morning and
the closer crowding buildings began to reverse. The upper
stories reached out over the street in the most ancient style of
architecture, and the sunlit sky was no more than a jagged
ribbon high overhead. There were still lamps lit in the windows of the lower floors, and needfully.

The thin sounds of early morning gave way to those of
people waking. The smell of the streets was eclipsed by the
steamy scent of breakfasts cooking behind closed doors. Piswyck was reminded that all their money had been used up the
night before, and there was not much prospect of breakfast in
Serrique without it.

They came at length to a great triumphal arch made of cut
and polished tiger's eye, and decorated with hundreds of
statues of nondescript camels. Piswyck couldn't imagine what
it commemorated and forbore asking Skylatch as he suspected
the reason for the erection had been long forgotten. The street
that once had passed beneath it was now a dead end. A brick
wall blocked the far portal of the arch very effectively.

Skylatch led them under the arch, turned left, and preceded
them down a previously concealed stairway. Torches fastened
in niches in the wall provided flickering light, and their
shadows dancing on the walls produced an eerie yet amusing
ballet as counterpoint to the castanet clicking of Lifesaver's
hooves on the stairs.

At the bottom of the stairway was a huge bronze door,
wrought with bas relief depicting the inhabitants of alien

worlds. Skylatch lifted a knocker cast in the shape of a trib-wing and let it fall. A resounding *bong* summoned the door-keeper, a woman named Gladys who looked out at Skylatch with disdain. Her hair was dyed pink and done up in knots with festive ribbons of many colors.

A brief, stilted conversation provided introduction of Pis-wyck and Lifesaver, then Skylatch bid them good-bye and Gladys admitted them to the Mirror Court.

There was no antechamber, no entryway, no hall. Only the one bronze door separated the outer world from the gigantic chamber that, Piswyck thought, might have been copied from a devil's pleasure palace. Enormous tripods supported brazen pots of fire to light the place with russet hues. Sweet smoke also issued from the flame, incense laced with divers drugs, no doubt. There were dozens of tables piled high with foods of every description, from a simple whole roast bull to a sal-tity of marchpane done up in a shape that Piswyck found both stimulating and disturbing. Tall silver fountains ornamented with baroque cherubim bubbled chilled crabgrass wine, and musicians vied with one another to produce the greatest possi-ble cacophony from stages situated all around the circumfer-ence of the room. Some of the musicians had dancers performing with them, some had singers, some both. There were people on stilts, wearing masks and juggling flaming knives over the heads of the throng that filled the room. A lone prestidigitator stood on a table and pulled yards and yards of yellow silk from a robin's egg held deftly between his thumb and forefinger. Mounds of pillows were piled thick with writhing bodies attempting passion; and all, all of this was multiplied a million times or more, for the great hall of the Mirror Court was paneled all around and over the walls and ceiling with broken chunks of mirror in a multiplicity of sizes and shapes.

A crowd of naked people painted purple careened off the wall and, resuming the steps of some strange dance, drew Piswyck and Lifesaver in among them.

"I think it not amiss that we should eat!" Lifesaver said as the currents of packed humanity began to pull Piswyck away from him. Without waiting for agreement he sank his teeth into a small pudding as they were swept past the table on which it sat. Piswyck wondered what the charge might be, then let his grumbling stomach take over. He wrenched a drumstick from a large dressed fowl and bit into it. When he turned back from the table Lifesaver was farther away in the crowd, chomping on bunches of green and black grapes.

He pulled free of the dancers and addressed himself seriously to the dinner. The fowl was cooked in citrus sauce, and delicious. There was a thick, moist bread, and whipped butter. Melon balls laced with paper-thin slices of preserved meat took his attention for a few bites, then there were cheeses. Without thinking he took a crystal goblet from a side table and filled it with wine from the fountain, washing down a hearty helping of duck's liver pâfe with the bright green liquid and only then stopping to think that crabgrass wine was, perhaps, not what he needed more of. But he was hungry, and the delicious food in his mouth craved company (the responsive thought came to him). He popped several appetizers between his teeth, strawberries stuffed with jalapeño peppers. Who was to know when he might eat like this again?

When he felt full he looked around for Lifesaver, but the light from the tripods now dazzled him. He thought for a moment that it ought not to be so bright. Was it the fact that it was reflected by mirrors?

The incense from the braziers smelled better now that he had eaten. He inhaled deeply, pleased with the way it made him tingle. He got another goblet of crabgrass wine from the fountain and drank deeply.

Yes, he felt much better!

The colors in the room started to shift, so that everything that was red began to turn orange, and everything that was orange began to turn yellow, and everything that was yellow began to turn green; and the greens became blues, and the blues became indigos, and the deep, deep indigos became violet. And then a new color came into existence where the violets had grown.

Piswyck blinked his eyes and found that he was no longer in front of the food table. He was looking up at a woman wrapped in scarlet velvet. She was sitting on a silver throne ornamented with golden cherries. She was the most enormous woman he had ever seen.

It was difficult to tell if she was the oldest, for the fat made the wrinkles irrelevant. Yet there was something very lovely about her, Piswyck thought, a merry twinkle and a wisdom in her eyes that he had never seen in the eyes of any woman before. She smiled at him. He bowed, but found that his flourish was a mite unsteady.

"Madame Roseboom, I presume?" he asked as he came up from the bow.

"And who are you?" the fat lady asked, still smiling.

"A traveler," answered Piswyck. He suddenly had the vague feeling he'd been at the party longer than it seemed.

"Most are," said Madame Roseboom, laughing. "Let's start again! What favor are you here to seek, my pretty young man?"

"I am in need," said Piswyck, trying to stand up straight and be dignified, "of an honest smuggler."

There was a crash of laughter. Piswyck looked around and discovered that he was standing at the center of a circle of people, all gathered before the throne.

"What for?" asked Madame Roseboom.

"To get me to Far Bermuda," answered Piswyck.

"Ah-*ha!*" said Madame Roseboom, leaning forward. "You want to go and visit Smagdarone the Great!"

Piswyck allowed himself the luxury of a sneer. "I had not heard that he was called 'the Great,' Madonna, but it is to his realm I wish to travel. Preferably without his foreknowledge."

Madame Roseboom's eyebrows, which had been plucked into little half moons, rose on her moonlike face to indicate question.

"He is uncle to my betrothed," said Piswyck, "and I am committed to rescue her!"

Madame Roseboom leaned back a little. A small, quixotic smile lit her lips.

"Yet you do not ask for soldiers or magicians," she said, half to him, half to herself. "I suspect this means you are on a pauper's quest." She sighed, then addressed him more pointedly. "So what have you got to offer me, that it may be worth my while to give you my aid?"

The glittering effect of the crabgrass wine slid away like an ebb tide. Piswyck found himself standing alone, as if on the dry and sandy shore; and he didn't know how to call back the sea.

"All that I can hope is that some small talent of mine may amuse you enough that you will grant my boon," he said. "I also have a friend—" He looked quickly around the circle, but Lifesaver was not in sight.

"Never mind the friend for now," said Madame Roseboom, settling back on her throne. "First let us discuss *your*, ah, talents. I am a sporting woman, and it may be that you *can* amuse me. I will make you a wager concerning your talent, and if you win I will grant your wish. Now what can you do?"

"I am a good swimmer and a good gymnast, and an adequate swordsman," said Piswyck. "I can do a bit of hang gliding, though nothing I fear for an air circus. I ride reasonably well—"

"The tumbling," said Madame Roseboom, not letting him continue. "I think that will do nicely! I have here at my court several skilled in that art, but you may be better. The wager shall be this: If you can outshine even one of those I employ I will grant your wish. Is that suitable?"

The sea came rushing back in, with all the attendant colors of its winy spray. Piswyck felt alive and confident again.

"I accept!"

"Good!" said Madame Roseboom. "Now show me your stuff!"

Piswyck looked around to see how much room he had. There was plenty, but even as he looked the audience stepped back to give him more. He pulled off his boots and stripped off his tunic. With only his pants and hose he'd be able to move better; besides which, his instructor had once told him that a bare-chested man had a better chance of making points with the judges. He tried the slipperiness of the floor, found it satisfactory, and started his best routine.

He did cartwheels, somersaults, back flips, all the things he'd been taught for the sake of building his young body into the kind of thing he'd want in maturity. His father had been a gymnast in his youth and a finer looking and healthier man there was not in the world (provided, of course, that the Countess had not yet murdered him). It was an excellent workout, and rather charming to watch, he'd always imagined.

When he finished all the tricks and combinations of tricks that he knew the sweat was pouring down his chest, and there was more than one pair of eyes admiring him. He did a final combination, came up with a flourish of upthrown hands, and waited for the applause.

There was a little.

Then a thin, dark young man in a stretchy suit of motley stepped forward. He was harshly handsome, with a knife-sharp nose and a cruel mouth. He smiled at Piswyck, and something flipped over in Piswyck's stomach. This must be one of Madame Roseboom's hired tumblers, he realized.

With no more ado the young man jumped straight up, twisted about-face in midair, flipped backward at the same time, and came down with his back to Piswyck. He did two handsprings forward and away, then reversed himself with another twisting flip and hurled himself right at Piswyck with a double somersault from a standing start. He landed at attention, toe to toe with Piswyck, and stared into Piswyck's eyes with utter contempt.

"Amateur!" he said, with a little lift of his head. Then he walked away.

Every move the man had made had been perfect and precise. It was a display such as Piswyck had never seen. Around the circle of watching audience there was a chatter of applause and laughter.

Piswyck looked up to Madame Roseboom on her cherry throne. She shook her head, not quite sadly.

"Young men from the provinces frequently lose wagers," she said. "And must pay the price."

This statement brought Piswyck suddenly sober. The effects of the wine had prevented him, he realized, from ascertaining his stakes in the bet.

Madame Roseboom saw the change on his face and laughed heartily.

"Oh, be not afraid," she said. "I am not the Princess Turandot and I am not going to have you beheaded. The price you must pay will be lower than that. Come here!"

She held out her fat, floppy arm to him, motioning with her sausagelike fingers that he was to ascend the steps of the throne. He stooped to retrieve his boots and tunic.

"No, no!" said Madame Roseboom. "Come to me just as you are! Lean and young and glistening with sweat! I do love a man whose muscles are pumped up with blood to full firmness!"

Piswyck froze for a moment, understanding what his stakes had been.

"Yes, yes, my pretty boy," said Madame Roseboom, "that is what you have lost. Now come, sit here beside me. Perhaps you would like to have a few more goblets of crabgrass wine?"

The laughter around the circle this time was an explosion. Piswyck wished desperately for the effects of the wine to return. He felt his face, his neck, his chest, flush with a blush that he was sure went all the way from the roots of his hair to his toes.

"As you wish, Madonna," he said. "But may I at least bring my things *with* me?"

Madame Roseboom nodded her assent. He picked up his clothes, then ascended the throne to sit at her left hand. She put her arm around him and he felt for all the world like a small child being cuddled by a giant, smothering aunt.

She began to fondle him. Then her attention went back to the court she was holding, and Piswyck became no more to her than a tactile toy; something she had won, but which she would play with later.

"Who is next?" Madame Roseboom asked the crowd.

Much to Piswyck's surprise, Lifesaver stepped out of the crowd and trotted forward. Piswyck started to greet him, then thought better of it. He had lost his wager already; perhaps the unicorn could do better with Madame Roseboom.

"Dear Madame," Lifesaver said in his high, strong contralto. "I am newly come to town. My occupation is to sing such songs as keep my always eager belly full. I hope by singing them to entertain. Yet you, I note, have bards aplenty here, and so I feel redundant at your court."

"Surely," said Madame Roseboom, her hand moving idly down Piswyck's rib cage. "*Surely* there are *some* songs I have not heard!"

"It may be as you say. I hope it is," said Lifesaver. "But I observed the game that you just played and thought some relish it might add to song if I might offer wager with my skill. Consider this: if I can sing a lay to which the chorus here is yet unknown, will you grant me a boon that I request, and fill my friend's request at break of day?"

"Your friend?" asked Madame Roseboom.

"Me!" said Piswyck, taking the opportunity to shift the Madame's hand slightly. He was not used to engaging in spectator sports, he realized, and was not quite ready to become used to it.

Madame Roseboom looked from Piswyck to Lifesaver, then back again. Then she laughed.

"I see! So this is the friend whom you mentioned. Dear boy, the unicorn is the wiser of you, for he was careful to ask his boon *after* I have had mine, rather than trying to bet you out of my arms. My congratulations, Bright Beast! It is well done! But if you fail, what am *I* to win?"

"His agile body for another night," said Lifesaver, tossing his rose-pink mane and indicating Piswyck with his spiraled horn.

Madame Roseboom laughed and squeezed Piswyck so hard the breath went out of him.

"Sing on, my friend!" she commanded. "This pretty boy must surely be better in bed than one night will tell! But wait! Where are my bards? Boys, gather 'round! This creature has a song to sing, and you must match him if I'm to win my wager. As the prize is such a pleasant one, I may be wroth with him who fails me. Sing every chorus the creature cants to, or you're out on your ears! Now, Unicorn, sing!"

"But pray a moment more, Madonna mine," said Lifesaver, as if in afterthought. "How many choices shall comprise the bet? Will one song be my chance, or many yet?"

Madame Roseboom looked upward and all eyes followed her. High up in the vault of broken mirrors a tiny window admitted a single bright ray of daylight.

"Here is the way it is," she said, looking down again and fixing Lifesaver with unwavering attention. "At the Mirror Court time runs backward, so day is night and night is day. By the light of that small window we know that it is time for revelry. The outer daylight is our night, and vice versa. Most who serve here would be to bed by noon. Yet I would not constrain an entertainment in the way Prince Paul would do. If you can keep my interest till the sun sets, why let the wager run the whole day through."

"And if before the night the wager's won?"

"I'll honor it and you can sing for fun!"

Lifesaver nodded once, indicating that he understood, then began to sing:

"Goddess, may I sing of wine-dark seas," he began, then stopped. He looked around, then up to Madame Roseboom. "But let these bards play on their harps for me!"

"Done!" said the madame. "Maestri, a little music, please!"

Lifesaver began again, and this time a number of harps of various kinds joined him. By the second verse of the old drinking song about the hero Odysseus, and his amorous adventures with a harpy, the whole room was singing along. It was clearly not a prizewinner, Piswyck lamented as the song came to an end.

"Well done!" Madame Roseboom applauded. "But everybody knows that one! You will have to do better than that, friend. Try again!"

"The Queen of Washington had dark brown hair," Lifesaver began; then, to a melody of undoubted grace and charm, he told more about that esteemed old lady's love life than had most probably ever crossed her mind.

Madame Roseboom smiled. It was a very naughty song and she was clearly pleasured by it; but though it was more obscure than the previous one, there were still lots of singers to join in on the chorus.

Piswyck noticed servants with tall ewers refilling the silver fountains with bright green crabgrass wine. He signaled for some and a boy with orange hair and yellow-painted lips brought him a big goblet. The orgiastic quality of the party seemed to be quieting down as people gravitated to the attentive circle around the particolored unicorn.

"Well sung," said Madame Roseboom appreciatively as Lifesaver finished. "But still no cigar. Another?"

"Her Lips Were Like a Pair of Jellied Eels," Lifesaver sang, and when there were those who knew that one, "She Hid the Major's Cannon 'Twixt Her Legs." This one proved better known than the previous one, but Lifesaver's delivery was so delightful that no one even bothered to ask for the next song, which was "Larry Gathered Cucumbers in May."

Piswyck denied himself the next round of crabgrass wine, considering that his honor as a gentleman might this night be dependent upon his semisobriety. The drugged incense from the lamps had ceased and his head was beginning to clear. There was a dull aching in his hand, where the basilisk's blood had spurted on him, and his shoulder ached. He had almost forgotten the old sword wound there, because of the crabgrass wine, but the fact was that the flight over the mountains had aggravated the wound; his display of *amateur* gymnastics had made it livid.

As his head cleared still more he unwound the dirty and ragged bandage from his hand and looked at the wound. The skin was blistered and it hurt, but the damage was not serious. He remembered what Skylatch had done to treat the wound and poured what wine was left in his goblet over it. That seemed to help.

Lifesaver sang "Webster's Book Is Full of Dirty Words" and "Jeremiah, Susan, Fred, and George," a song with beautifully descriptive language.

Piswyck sobered further and realized, soberly, that when the songs ended he would have to make love to a woman at least four times his age and perhaps six times his size. He began to worry. Could he do it?

He had never before considered such a thing. There were so very many beautiful young women in his native Carsonne that passion had never been a problem. It had occurred to him that perhaps they were as much enamored of his incipient title of marquis as they were by his person, but that had not bothered him. A woman ornamented herself as best she could; what was his title but an ornament? Yet still— In the few years of his young life that lovemaking had held meaning, he had never resorted to an unattractive female.

He wondered if he could do it. After all, it was a matter of honor. He had as much as given his word. But suppose he *couldn't?*

Lifesaver sang "Oh My, Her Feathers Tickled Him So Fine," "Rhinoceros Are Playful in the Dark," and "The Son in the Morning and the Daughter at Night." He was getting into some very, *very* esoteric material now, but still there were straggling voices to join the choruses.

Piswyck raced through his memory, trying to revive every detail of the *Three Hundred Marital Exercises* that his tutor had taught him. It was with some foreboding that he noted Madame Roseboom looking up at the little window in the ceiling, smiling to herself as the last daylight faded from it.

Lifesaver finished "Dim Wang, Your Diddle up the Fragam Wump!" and Madame Roseboom raised her plump hand for silence. She sighed and said: "I have enjoyed your performance much, Sir Beast! But the hour goes on and I fear that you have lost the wager. I will see to clean straw for your bedding, if that is how you would sleep, and whatever victuals you may desire in addition to what is provided upon the tables. But now it is time I took my prize to my chambers and enjoyed the first half of my victory."

"I fear me, Madame, that you may be right," said Lifesaver, his voice a little hoarse from a whole night of singing. "Though yet, there is the slightest spark of day."

Everyone looked up and, sure enough, the setting sun gilded the tiny window with one last glimmer.

"And anyway," continued the unicorn, "I have but one more song. If I may offer it, to gild your sleep?"

Madame Roseboom hesitated, yawned, then smiled.

"One more," she said. "And *only* one. And then to bed!"

"The tale of a magician long deceased," said Lifesaver by way of introduction. "A man who styled himself Listair Mac-Beast."

Madame Roseboom reclined as much as she could on her throne and began to renew her interest in intimacy. Piswyck squirmed. Lifesaver sang.

> *"I've a story to tell of a man born in Hell,*
> *Who proclaimed that he was a Great Beast.*
> *For his place in the sun, sought to shock everyone,*
> *'Swore on little boys' bodies he'd feast.*
> *But it's sad now to tell that his ego did swell,*
> *'Till he puffed himself up most obscene.*
> *He was picked up one day and deported, they say,*
> *For importing a coffee machine."*

Tired as the harpers were, some lifted their instruments preparatory to joining in. It was waltz time, and an ancient Berlinerwaltz at that. How could anyone resist such a lilting air?

Lifesaver opened his mouth to sing the chorus, then stopped. There was a sudden, uncomfortable silence in the room. Piswyck felt Madame Roseboom's arm tighten protectively around him.

After a moment Madame Roseboom cleared her throat and said: "It is late. Everyone is tired. Sing us the second verse and give us a chance to think."

Lifesaver shook out his rose-pink mane and made a formal bow, head down, one hoof forward. Then he straightened up and sang:

> *"How his followers glowed on the dim astral road,*
> *As they blundered about in the dark.*
> *Though their magic was botched, aspirations all*
> *   scotched,*
> *They thought not that to him 'twas a lark.*
> *With no traces of guilt, misdirections he'd built*
> *Into all of the spells he wrote down,*
> *Leaving bodiless seers trapped without their bras-*
> *   sieres,*
> *In the subways of old London Town."*

As if on an upbeat, Lifesaver opened his mouth for the chorus; but again there was only silence, save for a couple of harpers who had picked up the melody of the verse and who each anticipated the direction the chorus would take with a different discordant tone.

The time passed that it would take a musical phrase to play out, then the quiet grew clammy with discomfort. Madame Roseboom shifted on her cherry throne and her smile oozed away. Her eyes slid from one bard to another, barely concealing her writhing concern.

She was about to speak when Lifesaver broke the silence with a third verse:

> *"How he once tried to reign on the gray astral*
> *   plane,*
> *Is not told by his student, a sage.*
> *In his castle, alone, with philosopher's stone,*
> *He invoked Great Ahbramalin Mage.*
> *Standing naked at night by a dragon oil light,*
> *He faced down his own guardian Sidhe.*
> *Left the seals all undone, now the light of the sun*
> *Shines on all of his nightmares set free!"*

At the end of this third verse the silence was absolute. Not even breathing stirred the bards' harpstrings, lest the lightest sound call down the madame's censuring eyes. The light from the tiny window at the top of the chamber was gone and two of the brazen tripods had sputtering bowls as the mirror night took hold. The smell of last night's food and guests seemed suddenly stale.

Madame Roseboom smiled.

"Master Unicorn," she said at length. "It seems that neither I nor my courtiers know the chorus of your song. Yet I still retain a slight hope of winning the bet. Master Unicorn, do *you* know the chorus? For if *you* do not . . ."

Lifesaver tossed his head.

"I think my voice is starting to give out," he said, "But satisfaction now to you I give. The chorus of my song I now shall sing, but first I need your oath on one small thing."

"My oath?" queried Madame Roseboom, obviously displeased at this last-minute requirement.

Lifesaver nodded his head again.

"It is the custom of my place of birth," the unicorn said,

"and never meant as insult or as shame. I only ask you swear to my reward, unaltered as you earlier gave your word."

"I swear it, of course," said Madame Roseboom.

"That you shall bind a smuggler by his life to carry us to sea, and safely so?"

"I swear it," she said, "if you have the chorus you say you have."

"Then swear it as a god would, *by the Styx!*" said Lifesaver coldly.

Piswyck had never heard the unicorn use such a tone of voice before. It was as if his speech came from some dark old cave and brought with it the musty smell of forgotten chaos. There was not a gasp from the courtiers still awake, but there might have been had any dared. The oath of the Styx was the oldest and most powerful of oaths. Not even a god dare break it, for it was an oath upon one's own oblivion.

Madame Roseboom's hand grew cold on Piswyck's bare chest. Her turmoil was like a cloud beside him. She would be discredited as a ruler if she refused the oath, and her future pronouncements would be as empty air.

"I swear it . . . *by the Styx!*" she said, and Piswyck felt the fear in her as the words left her mouth. She was old, after all, and death, he thought, must be familiar in the periphery of her vision.

Lifesaver bowed, then sang the chorus:

> *"He was recently seen with his face turned all green,*
> *And his tongue sticking out, greatly bloated,*
> *Being interviewed by a blue Djinn from Sakai,*
> *As in warm tropic waters he floated!"*

The atmosphere of dread that had come with the oath dissolved. It was as if all the breath in the room had been held in, from the first verse to the last. Sounds which had been missing reappeared: the scrape of a chair, a subtle cough. The Mirror Court came alive.

"Well done!" said Madame Roseboom, rising. The color was coming back into her cheeks, but she was not yet ready to smile. He noted that she was taller than she looked seated. "You have your prize. And for tonight, I have mine!"

Her smile returned and her hand shot out at her side. Piswyck knew that she meant for him to take it. He did, and the musicians started to play again.

* * *

The small leaded windows still showed dark when Piswyck awoke alone in the bed. An oil lamp softened the vision of Madame Roseboom preparing herself to hold court, the business part of which was conducted before sunrise.

He reflected, as he watched her make her toilette, on the wisdom he had got during the "night."

Old women, he observed, had little beauty to offer; but they had great experience if they had not wasted youth. No young woman could have pleasured him the way Madame Roseboom had. In a few brief hours she had demonstrated more technique than he had imagined to exist. There was a thing she did with pearls . . .

But there was also the truth of her affection. A young woman would have been wondering all the time if he were quite the thing she wanted; if she had not better chosen a different swain for this tryst. Madame Roseboom had finished with all that, for she had no swains fighting for her now, and without such luxury she could simply decide what she wanted and, if it were available, have it. He was what she had wanted, and she had devoted her gifts entirely to him, to his exhaustion.

The closeness of death that comes in old age, the young Marquis Piswyck realized, makes every living moment all the more precious. This was why men in danger found themselves aroused; it had not occurred to him before that old age could be an aphrodisiac.

Each time might be the last. Each rising sun, each opening flower, might ring down the curtain. Madame Roseboom had made love to him with just this intensity, and he had learned much of her wisdom, beyond her technique.

Still, the memory of the pearls . . .

"Come," she said gently, drawing aside the sheer pink curtains of the canopied bed where they had slept. "It is time."

Piswyck climbed out of the bed and pulled on his clothes, wishing he had risen earlier and availed himself of a bath in her huge marble tub. When he was dressed he took her hand and followed her, like a small boy with a giant aunt, down the long, ancient corridors to the Mirror Court.

Lifesaver was curled up in the middle of a huge table, surrounded by piles of exotic foods and looking for all the world like an old tapestry. He was munching on a pineapple cut in the shape of a big yellow flower, and only nodded in greeting when Piswyck and Madame Roseboom entered.

Piswyck was directed to sit next to Madame on the Cherry Throne and the petitions began at once. He wondered when she would send for the smuggler, but he supposed that it would be impolite to ask, so he enjoyed her company, this time pleased by her casual fondlings.

He would not like to spend his life as her lap dog, he thought, but for a diversion and an education it was not unpleasant. Watching Madame Roseboom dispense justice and make deals was highly enlightening. She had as sharp a legal mind as he had ever observed in action, and could slice a tort with the best of the barristers before her.

He was amused when a beggar asked her for a new territory because of the sunburn he'd got standing on the corner assigned him; this wish she granted. He was more amused when a noble from Prince Paul's court appeared, unable to get things his way above the law and so forced to crawl beneath it. Piswyck almost expected the madame to grant the noble's petition, in order to mirror Prince Paul's decision, but she didn't. The man went away bemused by her explanation of her decision, as well as frustrated and a good deal poorer than when he'd come in. The cost of law, Piswyck noted, was not precisely mirrored.

Then Skylatch came before the Cherry Throne.

"Madame," he said, his voice grating and ingratiating, "I am a businessman, as you know—"

"I know you, Skylatch," said Madame Roseboom, uncomfortably. "You sell secrets. What is it you offer?"

"The droppings of a little dead bird," said Skylatch.

Madame Roseboom sighed. "I have little time for the dissembling of a businessman," she said. "You will not convince me your product is rare or valuable, Skylatch, so do not try. You can only sell it to me if it is genuinely worth its price. Now proceed, as honestly as a businessman can."

"The little dead bird fell from the grace of the Black Dove Messenger Service," said Skylatch. "It had just flown here from Carsonne."

Piswyck relaxed his muscles even as he felt them tighten, but Madame Roseboom's arm was still around him and she knew men's bodies and why they moved as they did. She glanced at him speculatively.

"Well, my pretty boy, it's from Carsonne you are fleeing, is

it?" she asked. "That does bode most interesting. We have not
heard much word from there since the roads were closed by
the trolls. I wonder what is happening?"

"You may find out, for a small fee," said Skylatch.

"Skylatch," said Piswyck, leaning forward and fixing the
businessman with his best look of intent. "I ask that you remember the small kindness I did you yesterday, and I ask that
you give the message to me."

Skylatch raised his ragged eyebrows in surprise.

"Why, I do indeed remember that you saved my life," he
said. "But I also remember the price you set on it. In exchange
for your service to me I gave you entrance to the Mirror
Court, where it appears to me that you have prospered!"

"But," said Piswyck, "you told me that anyone could have
given me entrance to this court. That it was a paltry item to
trade for your life!"

"Indeed, I did," said Skylatch, ignoring for the moment the
stern look Madame Roseboom lavished upon him for his eval-
uation. "But you must remember that you *paid* the price, my
young Marquis; and a price is a price, a bargain is a bargain. I
am a man of business, you know. If you ate a cabbage that
you found and which was cheap, you would not return to the
grocer the next day and demand another, now would you?"

"He called you *Marquis*," observed Madame Roseboom.

"One of thousands in Serrique, I am sure," said Piswyck,
feeling the tidal sand shaky under him again.

"Give me the message!" Madame Roseboom said to Skylatch, extending her fat hand. "I will pay the price."

"Two hundred gold rodrics?" quoted Skylatch.

Madame's hand dropped.

"Are you mad?" she asked.

"I think it is the value of the message," said Skylatch, a
little too coyly for a man his age.

"What words from Carsonne could be worth two hundred
gold rodrics?" she asked contemptuously.

"A message to you, My Lady," said Skylatch. "A message
that would have fallen with a hawk's dinner, if I had not seen
the kill and rescued the dead bird. A message from a man
called Krakmalnic."

It was difficult for Piswyck to tell whether he or Madame
Roseboom went stiffer at the mention of Krakmalnic. But
what, he wondered, could the Seller of Beasts have to do with

her? Unless she, too, was intrigued by the exotic pets he sold. Or unless, like the Countess . . .

"I will pay the price!" Madame Roseboom said. "Now give me the letter!"

Skylatch stepped forward and handed her the small folded document. She took it gingerly, as if she were afraid it might be contaminated from contact with a businessman; then she gestured to an old steward to pay Skylatch his money. Piswyck felt his blood run cold.

Madame Roseboom opened the little missive and read quickly through it, then she sighed and turned to Piswyck, the light of affection dying in her eyes.

"Why did you mutilate Krakmalnic?" she asked.

Piswyck took a deep breath. "He, and the Countess's men, attacked me, with the intention of killing me. I let loose a baby dragon in order to defend myself. If he was mutilated it was not by my hand."

"Sophistry. It was by your doing?"

"As he intended to kill me, and as he had allied himself with the Countess against my father, my intention was to defend myself. I used what weapon I had. I will not lie to you. I would have been happy enough to see him dead."

Madame Roseboom drew in a huge breath, then let out a great sigh. It was like an ancient mountain sighing, and Piswyck found it difficult to conceive that the great sadness it betrayed could be contained in the same joyful woman with whom he'd just made love.

"He has a call on me," she said at length. "I will not trouble you with knowledge of it, except to say that we were lovers once. Somehow he had news that you were coming here, and more or less what it was that you intended. He demands of me what he has the right to ask: a life; that I surrender you to Lord Death, by as terrible a means as I can devise. This he asks as fair exchange for the mutilation he has suffered."

"My Lady," said Piswyck carefully, "he may have call of demand on you, but he has not the right to ask redress for my action. As I have said, it was he who attacked. I did not plan to mutilate him, but to kill him. And that he has consorted with the Countess against my father makes him my enemy, and therefore subject to the winds of war. You need not involve yourself in a battle between two others."

Piswyck hoped desperately that Madame Roseboom's

sense of legality agreed with his argument. If so, then he and Lifesaver were safe. If not . . .

Madame Roseboom sat silent, looking at nothing. Her eyes were empty for a time as she retreated into the dark chambers of her mind. Piswyck wondered what call the Seller of Beasts might have on her. Considering her profession and the power she had amassed, it might be almost anything. But he, Piswyck, also had some call on her now, for he had been her most recent lover; and surely that must count for something, must it not?

At last the vacancy vaporized from her eyes and Madame Roseboom turned to Piswyck, an incredible exhaustion draining the vitality from her features. "My boy," she said at last, "perhaps the worst of growing old is being in the world with other people. One learns so much, and most of it is softening. I am not so prejudiced as I was when I was young. I can see beauty in more than one kind of face. It has been very long indeed since I disdained a new experience. But the wheels of the gods come around and around, and we are ground up between them, like so much wheat, like so much rice. When two clans war it is sad that all the Romeos and Juliets must die. But it is so much sadder yet for those children who are skewered while standing innocently by, licking their lollipops. Nothing is done anywhere that does not touch us all."

On the table at the center of the room Lifesaver heaved and tossed and brought himself to his feet. He shook out his rose-pink mane and fixed Madame Roseboom with his amber eyes.

"Though oaths conflict, there are still oaths and *oaths,*" Lifesaver said. "The one you swore to me was on the Styx."

Piswyck felt Madame Roseboom shudder next to him. "Why, so it was," she said tiredly. Yet there was something in her tone that disquieted Piswyck. Surely there was nothing Krakmalnic could hold on her so powerful as that oath!

"That you shall bind a smuggler by his life, to carry us to sea, and safely so," the unicorn repeated the oath solemnly.

"Yes, yes!" said Madame Roseboom, waving her hand feebly in assent. "And so I shall. And it had might as well be now, for I can take no more pleasure in either your songs or this pretty man's presence. *Chamberlain!* Go thou and fetch me the Smuggler Spoletta! And a very large flagon of crab-grass wine!"

She dismissed the court immediately, refusing to hear any more petitions and canceling the day's revelry. Some tried to protest, but the anger that flared across her face was sufficient to still them, and soon the Mirror Court was empty save for Madame Roseboom, Piswyck, Lifesaver, and a few servants cleaning up. The old chamberlain brought in a tray with two large goblets and a low golden bowl filled with bright green crabgrass wine. The goblets he gave to Madame Roseboom and Piswyck, and the bowl to Lifesaver; then he withdrew. They all drank, in a silence, slowly.

After a few sips Madame Roseboom said: "I should like it very much if things were other than they are, Marquis Piswyck. But I am bound by so many oaths, tied by so many strings of state. My oath to your unicorn is, for the moment, the most powerful of them. I must see you safely to the sea. But by keeping that oath I am disavowing an older, intimate one I made to Krakmalnic, when he was my young lover. I do not imagine that he is so handsome now, even as he was when I last saw him some years ago, when he was here to buy beasts. You see, he would have married me but for my ambition. He was a fine young wrestler, and I a jolly young whore. We should have made a splendid pair! But I wanted more than to be the mother of an ex-wrestler's brats. I wanted power."

She laughed a dry, distracted laugh.

"It was my aim to marry a nobleman and be the power behind his throne. Or perhaps become an accountant and control the money. Some such. In any case, I could not be much of a mother and devote my attention wholly to my career, and so I cast off the child he got me with."

"The child he got you with, you sent away?" asked Lifesaver, incredulous. Bred beasts had strong feelings about creatures naturally born.

"More," said Madame Roseboom. "I wanted no babe held over me like some hair-hung sword, and so there *was* no child."

Piswyck felt a chill run over him, like wind on the surface of a pond. Lifesaver gasped in horror.

"I know," Madame Roseboom said, observing their expressions. "I had only the right of my own body, not the right of his as well. I could have prevented the pregnancy, I could have fostered the child. But I did what I did, and so I owe Krakmalnic a life, and he has asked for yours. Tell me, Piswyck, were you pleasured by last night?"

For a moment Piswyck was confused. The question came so abruptly at the end of such a revelation.

"I was pleasured greatly," he said after a moment. "And I learned much of wisdom."

"Wisdom?" Madame Roseboom seemed surprised. "Then let me make you an offer. I have no heir. When I die the Mirror Court will fall, and it will be here as it will be with Prince Paul: an empty place for which brigands war. It may not mean much to you, but Serrique is a city filled with people, and they need wisdom to aid them in their daily lives; the robbers and the thieves as much as the princes and queens. When Prince Paul dies they will war for his throne. When I die they will war for mine, unless I can give them an heir in succession."

"You want me to be your son?" asked Piswyck.

Madame Roseboom reared back and laughed a huge hoot that shook her all over.

"They might accept that above ground," she said, "but not here! Here, wisdom must be demonstrated and power secured. No, Piswyck, I would have you as my consort. To assume the rule from me as I live, so that when I die the reins will have passed already. And let me tell you: with the heir Prince Paul has picked, it is likely you will rule Serrique from both thrones before your life is out!"

"Is this a ruse to rob me of your word?" asked Lifesaver coldly.

"No," said Madame Roseboom seriously. "No, indeed, but quite the contrary! If I am married to Piswyck then the law obviates my oath to Krakmalnic! Before owing him a life, I owe the Goddess a life. As I cannot have a child to continue what She began by giving *me* life, I can only fulfill that obligation by giving my worldly accomplishments into the hands of another who will carry them into the future. If Piswyck is my husband, he is safe from my past because he becomes my future."

The words began to look very pretty to Piswyck, rather as if they were gilded all over with cobwebs and the cobwebs were touched with new morning dew, and the dew were conglomerating into little jeweled beads along the strands. He shook his head and knew that the crabgrass wine was getting to him more quickly than he'd anticipated. He put down his goblet.

"My Lady," he said, "I am honored by your offer more greatly than I can express. Indeed, if I were free of mine own oaths I would choose to stay beside you for a season of summers, for your wisdom would enter me as by osmosis, and make me fitter ruler for my land. But time is a harsh taskmaster, and I must be away, and swiftly. My father's life is in danger. My betrothed is in bondage. My heritage and my good name are at stake. One cannot exchange one destiny for another."

She looked at him sadly and laid her hand on his cheek.

"So be it," she said.

The great brazen door of the Mirror Court opened and an errant reflected bolt of sunbeam limned a swarthy man in golden plumes and lime-green satins. His black hair hung in curls to his shoulders and a huge gold ring gleamed in his earlobe. His eyes were black and his smile betrayed a dark heart.

"The Smuggler Spoletta!" he announced, sweeping off his hat and dusting the floor with its plumes in a cavalier bow.

"Ah!" said Madame Roseboom, "so it is! Tell me, my bucko, are you up for a trip to Far Bermuda?"

"Whatsa matter, you crazy?" asked Spoletta, outraged. "That's the other side of the stinking ocean!"

"And suppose I made it worth your while?" she asked.

"What have you got to offer, my weight in emeralds?" Spoletta asked contemptuously.

"I have two passengers who must be taken there with the greatest dispatch," Madame Roseboom said levelly.

Spoletta looked at Piswyck, then at the unicorn.

"At least it's not a gray mare!" he snorted.

"I will offer you the same terms I gave you when you took care of the Conte Palmieri," Madame Roseboom said.

Spoletta's glossy eyebrows shot up.

"And I will give you the orders in writing, sealed with my seal," she continued.

"There was only one of Palmieri," said Spoletta. "There's two of them, and one's a unicorn!"

"Everyone wants double or nothing today!" said Madame Roseboom, exasperated. "Oh, very well! Double the price. But remember, you are bound by your life in this endeavor, and I can make *that* worth half of what it is now, if you fail me!"

Spoletta bowed again.

"When have I ever let you down, My Lady?"

"There was the time with the politician hiding in the well," began Madame Roseboom, but Spoletta interrupted.

"There's no time for telling tales! The sea is moving with

the eternal tides. If I'm to do your bidding we must be off.
Come, the orders, quickly! And the cash!"

"Half now," said Madame Roseboom, "and half when you
return."

"Agreed!"

And so it was that Piswyck and Lifesaver (only slightly af-
fected by the crabgrass wine) found themselves wobbling
down the jasper-paved streets of Serrique behind the Smuggler
Spoletta, their brains occasionally ringing with song, all the
colors around them intensified, the sky starting to become
visible and light once again between the overhanging buildings.

"I like it not. I think there's something wrong," said Lifesaver softly. "Some music hammers just behind my ears."

Piswyck laughed, part laugh, part liquor giggle.

"What I would like to know is how you stumped her whole
court with that last song. I thought for sure you'd lost the bet!
And yet, there you were, with one last song in your repertoire,
and *that* one that no bard in all her menagerie knew!"

Lifesaver snorted.

"The song was but the simplest of the bet," he said. "The
harder part was getting her to think that everything I knew was
what I'd learned. Those hours of singing were to set the trap,
which laid the prize unfairly in my lap."

"I fail to comprehend," said Piswyck, espying the spars of
the ships at the quay ahead.

"I must confess that what I did was wrong," said Lifesaver,
"but Piswyck, it was *I* who wrote that song!"

"And so," concluded Piswyck, "no one at the court *could*
have known it!"

They both began to laugh, and at that moment they
emerged from the shadows of the buildings and the fresh wind
from the sea blew on their faces. It seemed a wonderful day
indeed as they followed the golden-plumed Spoletta innocently toward his ship.

4

With the Black Elves on the High Seas in the Middle Days of Latter Earth

The great green sharks were closing in on Piswyck and Lifesaver, and Spoletta and his men were standing on the deck of their ship laughing and making bets as to which the sharks would eat first, the angry young marquis or the particolored unicorn. Lifesaver had remembered too late the nature of the "Conte Palmieri" dodge, and Piswyck had figured out too late (after the crabgrass wine had cleared from his brain) that when Madame Roseboom had sworn by the Styx she had sworn only to see them safely *to* the sea, not safe *upon* it.

"If we float still as death perhaps they'll pass!" gasped Lifesaver.

"If I ever get my hands on you—" Piswyck shouted at Spoletta, but he couldn't think immediately of any revenge dire enough to balance being fed to great green sharks.

Spoletta grinned down, his black eyes flashing and his golden plumes bouncing jauntily against the backdrop of bright blue sky. For a smuggler he was overdressed.

"Go on, little fishbait!" he said encouragingly. "What will you do, eh?"

Piswyck glanced in the direction of the tall, jade-colored fins that rocketed toward him through the water. There must be *something* to compare with death by maceration, he thought wildly.

Then a peculiar thing happened.

As if out of a deep mist (though there was no mist) a huge gray ship appeared. The prow first, carved like a death's head grinning; sails like gray stone mountains filled with air; long and sleek and tall and close at hand, cutting through the water between the menacing sharks and the desperate Piswyck and Lifesaver. It was headed directly amidships of Spoletta's vessel.

Piswyck stared at the apparition, almost forgetting to tread water.

The high sails were webbing, and over them sea spiders scuttled, dropping freshly spun lines to the decks below. On the decks the Black Elves danced, and the drumming to which they moved swelled out into the sea, blended with the beating of their ship's passage through the brine, made Piswyck's teeth rattle, chilled his bones, inspired terror.

He saw the prow coming on, encrusted far above the waterline with thickly grown fanciful seashells, like a rushing barrier reef. He saw that it was a warship intent on ramming, and turned to look again at golden-plumed Spoletta.

In a terrible moment of sea silence the laughter aboard Spoletta's suddenly small ship died away. A look of puzzlement crossed the smuggler's face, a look that betokened a man looking squarely at his fate but still not comprehending.

Then the gray ship struck and there were screams from men and wood being rent: and after, even more screams as some of Spoletta's men fell into the sea where the sharks were swimming.

A net came down as the ghostly schooner passed, and Piswyck and Lifesaver were scooped up, lifted like a catch of fish, and deposited dripping on the deck. By the time they had disentangled themselves from the net the ocean was silent once again: and the sky had turned a strange silver gray, not unlike the color of the ship on the deck of which they lay.

An Elfwoman came and stood before them. She was clad in a tight-fitting tunic and breeches that stretched to accommodate her movements. Her clothes seemed at first dark gray, but then iridescent. She was classically beautiful, with a high brow, a delicate nose with a little lift at the end, a mouth that was fragile and full at the same time. Her eyes were black as the midnight heavens, and almond-shaped with heavy, curved lashes. Her cheekbones were high and they tilted at the same angle as her fine ears, which were pointed. Her long hair was silvery white, braided up high on her head and wound with fresh brown seaweed. Her skin was black, with the texture of the very finest snakeskin. Her teeth (for now she smiled and they could be seen) were very white and very sharp.

Piswyck remembered how someone had once told him that the Black Elves were cannibals. The snakelike skin brought up the moral point of whether, for Elves, eating human beings (such as himself) could indeed be viewed as cannibalism. Humanity in general took a very liberal view of predation between and among sentient species, he noted.

"We like not to see people walk the plank," she said, and her voice was very high and musical. "A waste of flesh. Not many things that humans do. Why we are here."

Her accent was as strange as her syntax but her statements seemed to have settled the matter for her. She turned and started to walk away, her small hips swaying gracefully with the roll of the ship's deck, somehow in time to the omnipresent music of the drums.

"Wait!" Piswyck called after her.

She turned and raised her eyebrows, displaying plain puzzlement.

"What shall we do now?" he asked, not knowing a thing about the customs of the Black Elves and not wishing to get in any more trouble than he was already in.

"Yes?" she asked.

"Well . . . that is . . . is there some proper thing we should do at this point?"

"You ask me?" she queried. She looked more confused than he felt as she asked it.

"Well, it's *your* ship, and I do not know any of the customs of your people. I would like to thank you for rescuing us, if it is proper to do so. I would also like to know what is going to happen to us."

The Elfwoman's expression changed to one of disgust.

"Ni'Mamba is right!" she said. "All you think of is other times and magics. You expect us to desire everything for you!"

With that she turned and walked away, and this time Piswyck didn't call after her.

"I don't think she was pleasured by your words," said Lifesaver, climbing to his feet and shaking the water out of his many-colored coat. "When only females rule, the logic goes!"

"Are the Black Elves matriarchal?" Piswyck asked, also climbing to his feet.

"But look you at the dance, my soggy friend," Lifesaver said.

Piswyck looked at the mass of Elves dancing in the middle of the broad deck, a dance that included not only pleasurable movements of the body but a number of useful movements as well; the ship's work seemed to be getting done as part of the dance.

"They do seem to be all female," he said. "I wonder if they keep their men locked up, the way the women of Khataris do."

"We can but ask of she who comes here now," said Lifesaver, and with his carnelian horn he gestured toward the afterdeck of the huge ship.

A person of obvious authority was coming toward them. Piswyck could tell she was someone of authority by her clothes, which, in addition to tight-fitting breeches and tunic featured a headdress made from the skull of a shark, encrusted all over with polished sea opals. Back in Carsonne the headdress would be worth a castle's ransom, Piswyck thought, for the sea opals (actually a nacre secreted by a particularly rare abalone and prized for its lustrous blackness shot through with fiery dark blues) were among the rarest gems, a treasure, from beyond the Sundered Seas, that only the Elves could trade. She also wore a cumbersome cloak of dusky green on which hundreds of brightly colored seashells had been sewn, and she carried a staff around which coiled two live, bright red seasnakes.

"I am Ni'Mamba," she said, stopping and making a little bow. Piswyck noted that she stood well above the meter-and-a-half height that was usual for Elves. "I will talk."

She sat down on the deck and indicated that Piswyck should do likewise. Lifesaver continued to stand, not being one of those quadrupeds with a propensity for the sitting position.

"A Mateship has lost its Reckoner," she said without preamble. "One of two. The other fell asleep, so they are lost. We have no Seer here, but a Hearer-Speaker have we, and close we are to them. Swiftly will we fly across the waves, but now they sail upon the Coast of Monsters. If they are saved we will put you on their ship."

She stopped, and once again Piswyck had the feeling that something obvious had been said, and that he didn't understand a word of it.

"Is their ship going somewhere that I am going?" he asked. The Elfwoman smiled.

"Ni'Dbhrda said you were ignorant of things," she said. "How much I did not know!"

Piswyck shook his head. She was making him dizzy with her manner of speech.

"Uh, pardon me if I am forward, My Lady, but there are, indeed, many things I do not understand. If I interpret you aright, you have rescued my unicorn and me while on your way to help another ship. I think that much is clear. But why is it that we will be put aboard the other ship?"

"Ah, that is right," she responded. "You landlubbers are lustlocked all your lives. Your bucks and does cohabit. No wonder you are so confused! And we all women!"

"You mean there are no men upon this ship?" asked Lifesaver.

"No-no!" Ni'Mamba said. "Too many Elves, not enough ships: that is what it would produce!"

"But then, how do you beget your young?" Piswyck asked, for he noted that different levels of age were apparent amid the dancers of the crew.

"By coming together," Ni'Mamba said. "Why . . . have you forsaken *sex* upon the land?"

Piswyck felt himself blushing foolishly. "Well no!" he stammered. "It is just that we do it . . . well . . . whenever an opportunity presents itself."

"On a ship," said Ni'Mamba, "that would be all the time." For once the obviousness of what she said was apparent.

"Is it the Coast of Monsters off Carsonne?" Lifesaver asked, and Piswyck was grateful to him.

"If that is what you call the land by the Waters of Hercule, then yes," said Ni'Mamba. "Long ago, before we sundered the seas, it was a place where people played."

Piswyck sat bolt upright and felt a shaft of ice run down his spine. "Before *you* sundered the seas?" he asked, not quite believing what he had heard.

"Oh, yes," said Ni'Mamba. "Didn't you know that? We

thought you would have figured it out, after so long. But short
lives do not make for long minds, as the saying goes."

Piswyck felt his emotions whirling like a hurricane inside
him and he fought to control them. There was not a human
alive in Latter Earth who did not chafe at the loss of the stars.

"But *why?*" he asked.

Ni'Mamba cocked her head to one side and looked at him
quizzically, the way a spaniel looks at its master when the
master is making a game of holding back a bone. Then she
sighed, a sigh that clearly expressed her reaction to the stupid-
ity of short-lived human beings.

"Before I was born," she said, "in the Old Era, at the close
of what some call the Fourth Age, you humans ruined life for
us on the land. You raged your silly wars and cut down the
forests. For a thousand revolutions of the sun we felt ourselves
persecuted by your kind. We moved away from you, farther
and farther west, until there was no room left on our home
continent. You built hideous weapons of cold steel that poisoned us if we were cut with them. You made *guns!*"

She said this last word as if it were the most obscene in any
tongue, and Piswyck, who had read about guns, thought she
might be right in such a judgment.

"Then you built machines that puked out smoke and bile,
and you poisoned *everything!* The land, the rivers, the sea, the
sacred sky . . . Even those of our ancestors who had moved to
the far coast of the other big continent could not keep ahead of
your ravages. You made the world a cesspool! When at last
you built an airship, a balloon, and sent up a cock, a rabbit,
and a dog, we knew that we could no longer live upon the
land. We set to sea, and shrouded our great ships with spells
of invisibility that were woven into the dances of our daily
lives. For a time we were safe.

"But on the land your iniquities continued. With ships of
your own, fast ships before the wind, you plied a trade between the continents. The princes of Old Afrique sold their
poorer relations not only among themselves but to the even
more cruel traders who had gone to steal the Westron continent from the humans who lived there. Then those cruel black
kings were themselves taken slave, and their ancient empires
toppled. All this in but a short season of our Elvish lives!

"Some of your people thought slavery wrong, but instead
of striking down those who perpetrated this thing, they set
about to make rules against it.

"Ha! You humans! *How* you make rules!"

She reared back and her laughter was like glass shattering, and just as painful. When she continued, her contempt was like poison from the mouth of a serpent.

"Some of your sailors did not choose to abide by these *rules!* Some of them kept taking slaves and transporting them across the seas. Your rule-makers didn't like that, so they built great ruleships and sought to hunt them down. But *that* made things all the worse, for then if the slavers spied a ruleship they would throw their hapless victims into the sea to drown. Just as that feathered man did with you!

"Oh, how we grew angry! We would not see those poor chained beings taken by the eatingfish, so we pulled them from the water. Then would we strike the slaveships, breaking them in half, dancing with joy as the slavers and murderers drowned! The anger of Elves is mighty when it is aroused, however long it may take to kindle!

"But what could we do with the slaves we had rescued? Some we took home. Some grew sick from eating our foods. But some were initiates of the African magicks, and those stayed aboard. Their lives were short, but we bred with them, and from them we got this fine new color to our skins. It is most useful in the full blaze of the sea sun. They also gave us the secrets of their lore!"

Ni'Mamba paused for a moment, looking directly at Piswyck. Dark lightnings seemed to flash behind her eyes. One of the red seasnakes had coiled over her shoulder, a ruby necklace promising death.

"While we studied the secrets the slaves brought us, the landpeople studied secrets also. They pried open atoms and released the fire of heaven upon the world. When one of *our* ships was lost to one of their *tests,* we began to act.

"All our ships upon the seas in one great dance! All our minds and bodies in one great spell! And not only the Elves, but other species as well. All the other people who share this planet, and to whose worth the human race is blind!

"Had you kept to knowledge—had you kept to exploring the stars—

"But you retreated from the stars and set to making bigger bombs, and so the die was cast.

"With all the magick of the Eldar Worlds, of Elves of Old Afrique, we wove a spell that sundered all the seas, and made mankind's technology a shade. And useless that technology shall remain, until . . ."

Ni'Mamba smiled and the passion of her narrative ebbed away. It was now just a story, a history, an exciting thing to be told around a campfire.

"Until?" Lifesaver queried.

Ni'Mamba looked at Lifesaver and said: "The humans have not done badly with what was left them, to make such a creature as you."

"Until the alphabet runs out!" said Piswyck, and his voice was harsh, betraying more emotion than he wanted to show.

Lifesaver and Ni'Mamba looked at him in question, but the moment had passed. Piswyck regained his self-control.

"It is an old prediction," he said simply. "One of those family stories that heap importance upon every genealogy. The first of my line was Astwyck the Great, whose son was Boswyck. They fought the Battle of Baldebourg together. Boswyck named his son Chaswyck, and so on down the line. My father's name is Oswyck and mine is Piswyck. My son shall be named Queswyck and it will continue until Zedwyck, who will be the last of our family. But with *him,* the prediction goes, the seas shall right themselves and the world return to the innocent state it was in before."

The second of the red seasnakes slid up over Ni'Mamba's shoulder and ran its tongue along her cheek.

"Perhaps I shall meet this Zedwyck some day," Ni'Mamba said after a moment. It was not lost on Piswyck that she would live a great deal longer than he. "If I do, I will tell him of Piswyck, his ancestor, and of the particolored unicorn who kept him company."

"For now," said Piswyck, taking a deep breath and hoping to bring the conversation back to his personal welfare, "I am in a rather delicate situation. My heir is yet to be conceived. His future mother is held captive by her uncle in Far Bermuda, and I was on my way there when this untoward incident befell me."

"Far Bermuda?" Ni'Mamba asked. "Yes, indeed I know that isle. It is full now of powerful magicks, wreathed in spells such as we have not seen from humans in many years. Did you know that the magician who rules there recently transported a whole *castle* thence from the Old Continent?"

Piswyck felt a wave of despair flow over him.

"Perhaps they are right then, to call him Smagdarone the *Great*. If his magic impresses even you—"

She laughed.

"I am impressed by the power of a hurricane, but that doesn't mean I can't control one! I am impressed by the poison in the teeth of these little snakes, but that doesn't mean I am afraid of them! You must know that magic is a question of living *with*, not ruling *over*. You must let the wonder of everything flow through you. There are many rivers, and you must but choose which one is best to carry your boat."

Piswyck nodded.

"That sounds like what my father has tried to teach me," he said.

"Is your father then a magician?" Ni'Mamba asked.

"Yes," Piswyck answered. "But he is now held captive by the Countess in Carsonne, so there is nothing more that he can teach me. That's another reason I must acquire powers: to rescue my father. Ever since the Countess discovered that she knew the whereabouts of the Appearing Egg . . ."

"The *Egg?*" cried Ni'Mamba, leaping to her feet. "This Countess has the Appearing Egg?"

"Well," said Piswyck, now even more confused than before, "whether she actually *has* it or not is a moot point. The Egg appears where it will. But she can use its power because she knows where it will appear. She can be present and—"

"Yes, *yes!*" snapped Ni'Mamba. "I know all about the Egg. Certainly much more than you do, probably more than this Countess does. It is important that you have told me this! Indeed, very important!"

"But why?"

"Because it means that I am free to give you some of the instruction you will need to combat the sorceror of Far Bermuda, that is why! Provided we live through the monsters of the coast!"

She whirled and was gone so swiftly that Piswyck could not even gain his feet. He looked astern after her, then turned to Lifesaver to comment on the way Elves rushed in and out of conversations.

But beyond the prow of the Elfship was a sight such as Piswyck had never hoped to behold, and all his conversation deserted him.

It was said that the coast of Carsonne had been a place of dark workings in the Great Days of Science, before the Sundering. Strange experiments had taken place there, and some said the means of making genomythological creatures had been developed in the laboratories deep under its ocean. Whatever might be the truth, there was no doubt that the results of the final experiments had been disastrous. The waters now boiled with the thrashings of gigantic beasts perpetually at war with one another, things so hideous they *could not* have evolved through a sane and gracious Nature.

In some parts of Carsonne, near the coast, there had developed a problem with the locals deifying one or another of the monsters, which occasionally rampaged near the shore, and making sacrifices. It had been the policy of the Marquis Oswyck to apprehend such people as planned to offer up their cattle, their daughters, or their sons, and send them off to the mountains for a holiday in the hope of renewed sanity. But with the rule of the Countess now consolidated, and the Countess herself turning loose trolls upon the land, there was no telling what might transpire.

In no case would any inhabitant of Carsonne have considered putting to sea along the infamous coast; yet Piswyck now found himself aboard a vessel not only headed for that coast, but sailing immediately in amongst the monsters.

Ahead, and to the port of side of the ship, two things fought amid the waves, two things too huge to imagine. One was like a lobster as much as it was like anything else, but built awry of its proper symmetry. The other was like a great crocodile with flashing scales of brazen plate, a gorgeous creature with far too many teeth.

Farther away and to starboard there was a boiling dome of water from which a sickly green mist arose. Whatever lay at its center was doing battle with an enormous serpent whose skin was mottled white, as if it were infected with leprosy. There was a huge whirlpool near this battle and Piswyck shuddered to think of how quickly even the great gray Elfship could be sucked into such a maelstrom and broken up.

The Elfwoman Ni'Dbhrda appeared next to Piswyck and Lifesaver.

"If these scaresights, below you may go," she said kindly, her feet still moving in the ship's great dance.

"If one of those things attacks us," Piswyck said, a little offended that she should think him a coward, "you may have need of my sword arm."

"Also with swords," Ni'Dbhrda snorted in contempt, "you

fight hurricanes?" She spun around and danced back to the center of the ship, vanishing into the mass of Elves who moved there.

"I do not think she likes you much, my friend," said Lifesaver.

"You're very good at understatement, do you know that?" Piswyck responded crossly. "I'd say she viewed me as somewhere down the evolutionary scale from a sea urchin!"

The unicorn sighed.

"Sea urchins, friend, alas, are good to eat," he said, and lowered himself to the deck.

Piswyck leaned on the gunwale and watched the fantastic display of fauna as the Elfship sailed on. The dancers on the deck wove in and out of patterns, sometimes grabbing lines that fell from above, product of the spiders' industry; sometimes tugging, hauling. Some Elves danced upon their knees as they scrubbed the deck. The music of the drums beat on, their sound a pulse for the ship, the drums the very heart.

When they sailed close to a huge dark shape that seemed to rest *above* the water, unmoving, the drums grew soft. The songs that sometimes emerged from the dance grew soft as well, their patter a susurrus of syllables in tongues too ancient to fathom. Piswyck gazed up at the monster in wonder, for it looked like nothing so much as a giant flea.

As it was the only thing in sight that was not engaged in battle, Piswyck fell to wondering if it, like its minute paradigm, was a creature with no place in the food chain. That led him to consider its source of nourishment, and that in turn led his imagination to begin constructing an enormous seadog, a creature immense beyond imagining. (This was a very tricky exercise, belonging to the *"Can God make a rock so big that God can't lift it?"* category.) This musing upon paradox might have led him to an elightenment of some kind if an Elfwoman had not danced up and put down a tray of food before him, then danced way. The sense of hunger quickly replaced the sense of wonder at that point, and enlightenment was postponed by the arrival of what, to Piswyck and Lifesaver, was breakfast.

It was tasty enough fare (if one liked a mildly fishy taste to everything) but some of the crunchy, saladlike dishes were a little too rubbery of texture. There was also something gelatinous with no flavor at all, which sucked all the other flavors out of the mouth; and the longer one chewed it, the tougher it got.

The meal provided the first occasion on which Piswyck had seen Lifesaver wear an expression of utter distaste. But the unicorn, being aware of their delicate position as guests and having escaped being eaten too many times of late, cleaned his wooden plate in silence.

There was a certain charm, Piswyck thought as he ate, to having breakfast with a dance show to one side and a horror show to the other.

Dusk was settling in, dusk beyond the grayness that prevailed beneath the invisibility spell, when they at last spied the distressed Elfship. It was closer to the land than it should have been, a circumstance that puzzled Piswyck, for reckoning should not have been necessary to steer clear of the shallows.

He felt a pang as he realized how close he was to home. *His* Carsonne, land of the dark blue wine, of new bamboo and leatherleaves . . .

They drew closer and he could make out the Elfmen dancing on the deck. The light of stars now pierced the grayness of the sky through the invisibility spell, and soon it would be night. It was not a good time to sail among monsters, he thought, noting that a number of the Elfmen were armed and that others stood in the prow watching the waters.

Then the surf began to boil and bubble and a huge chartreuse tentacle rose up out of the depths. It was followed by another, and then another, and then the first tentacle grappled onto the prow of the Elfmen's ship.

"Look!" Piswyck cried, to nobody in particular. "One of the monsters has got the ship!"

The creature was not as big as some of the denizens they had passed, but it was big enough; and as its body surfaced it proved to be ugly enough as well.

"A giant chartreuse octopus, Great Gods!" gasped Lifesaver.

"Wrong!" said Ni'Mamba, appearing at the rail. "That is not a giant chartreuse octopus, that is *the* giant chartreuse *heptopus,* the only one. He is well known throughout the world, for he is the only monster of this coast who travels. His name is Ralph."

She appeared to be serious.

"Can't we *do* something?" Piswyck asked as the Elfmen started to hack at the tentacle with their bronze swords.

"Oh yes," said Ni'Mamba calmly. "And we will, as soon as we reach them. For now must we keep the spells full. Even so, some of the monsters are so stupid that they see us anyway."

Not understanding her at all, Piswyck was forced to take what she said on faith. The gap between the two ships grew slimmer and the drumbeats grew faster. As the Mateship (and Ralph) loomed very close indeed, Ni'Mamba raised her staff in some kind of signal.

An instrument that sounded like a clamshell being struck against a lead pipe was added to the music. Voices lifted in song, then were joined by the eerie skirling of the Elvish bagpipes. Piswyck felt the hair on the back of his neck rise up. An Elfwoman appeared from the hold, balancing a flat-bottomed amphora on her head. Another Elfwoman followed her, then another, all balancing the big jugs.

"If there is something we can do to help..." said Lifesaver, letting the sentence trail off as Ralph and the Mateship loomed near.

"Oh yes," said Ni'Mamba, "you can. You can sing, and you can dance."

"Uh, I'm not very good at dancing," said Piswyck. "I know the court dances, and I can shuffle dance, but something as elaborate as—"

"What kind of magician do you think you can be without dancing?" demanded Ni'Mamba, outraged. "Do you think the mind alone can channel the forces of Mother Nature? Do you think you can sit still and spin spells? You must master your body before you can master your spirit, foolish boy! Great gods do not ride little horses! Now get out there and *dance!*"

"But suppose I ruin the pattern?" he asked.

"Do you think you are strong enough for that?"

She put her hand to his chest and pushed him, and he found himself hurled across the deck, barely keeping his feet under him. She was so small, and yet she was stronger than any man he'd ever fought!

"With four legs I can't dance, but I can sing!" said Lifesaver, and before Ni'Mamba could challenge the information he started, perhaps not with perfect accent, but great accuracy of pitch.

"Now we are ready!" Ni'Mamba cried, and it was a good

thing, too, for that was the precise moment when the ship slid alongside its mate, its prow punching right into old Ralph.

Piswyck looked around, dazed, and saw what looked like a simple circle dance. He slid in, they made room for him, and he concentrated on imitating the step.

But the step wasn't as easy as it looked, and the battle that ensued *was* distracting.

Ralph threw a tentacle over their ship as well. He glowed slightly, giving the whole scene a dim and bilious yellow-green ambience that was nauseating, and he didn't smell good, either.

The music rose to fever pitch, which was somewhere above high B-flat, and the cross-rhythms went crazy. The Elf-women with amphoras on their heads headed for the prow, toward where the tentacles were waving and seeking prey.

Piswyck forced his mind away from the mayhem, forced his thoughts into his feet. His father had taught him to make a little fire, a precious small piece of magic indeed, but it was nothing like learning to dance. Left, forward, back, move the hip . . .

Something touched his mind, something strong, then it grabbed hold.

Come in! it beckoned, *Come into the dance! This is how it is, how it goes!*

He was afraid for a moment; then he let go, realizing intu-itively that whatever was calling to him, touching him, was one with what was happening on the ship.

That is right, do it slow, you must learn, you must know, let your spirit stretch and grow . . .

He danced.

And as he danced he felt himself fall down the well inside himself, saw a colored vision of the Greater Magic, the stuff his father always mentioned. First a stillness, then a beat, then a haze of light that resolved itself into the pattern of him*self*.

A pattern, a series of patterns, of complex patterns one within another, all related.

When he perceived the pattern, it *changed*.

When he *thought* about the pattern, it changed.

For *Thought* itself was a part of the patterns, as was *Feeling, Knowing, Being*. These things, these active parts, were like hands and feet and stomach and spleen. They danced with one another; there was no other way to see it.

And as the sacred spiral dance (which everybody knew)

was a paradigm for the molecule of DNA (ancient words, words of power, letters in an almost forgotten alphabet), so might the dance of his Being's body be a paradigm for other things, things too small, too great, to see with only the eye of the mind. *Thought* moving in an orderly relationship with *Feeling,* partnering with *Being;* change partners and come to *Knowing.* It was as simple and as straightforward as knowing (without being conscious of it) that your liver and your pancreas are working together!

That's it, you've got it! Now turn, now whirl!

And once you were good at that dance, you could dance with other people, other things! You could move outward, perceive and alter other patterns of atoms, hazes and screens of electrons and . . .

Slowly now! Don't go too fast. Those things are for Mages, ideas too vast!

He swelled, he spread, he touched beyond the ship.

There! That lump of psychic mucus, *that* was Ralph!

Here! Flickering lights, the souls of a school of tuna!

And . . .

What was out there? What was it out there that was so great and strong?

He felt his heart beating, heavy, felt it slow as he touched a great spirit, a mind, a being who sang with the tidal rhythms of eternity.

Have I touched the soul of the Earth? Do I hear the music of the spheres?

He felt the sweat run down his sides, felt his feet ache as they pounded against the bare boards of the deck. He saw Ni'Mamba on the foredeck, her arms waving. The Elfwomen took down their amphoras, unstoppered them, climbed up to points where they could look down on Ralph. Ni'Mamba cried out with the piercing voice of an osprey. The women poured out the contents of their jugs, and from where he danced Piswyck *knew* what they were pouring, *knew* that it was the Elfire they poured down on Ralph's head, into his huge shining eyes.

All Hell broke loose.

No, all Heaven!

The sea errupted in a billion hues, glowing, flashing, sputtering, and spewing up in fountains like fireworks against the night sky. Myriad rainbows bent backwards through their own light, prismed off themselves, shot in all directions. It was beautiful. It was blinding.

Ralph couldn't take it.

Anointed with the very glory of celestial triumph, merely garish Ralph slid off the bows of both ships and with a great gout of noxious black ink shot into the nether depths.

The dance and the song swept to frenzy.

Piswyck began to whirl, to spin, to shout and sing words he did not know. He felt as if his body would fly apart, his spirit explode. He knew that what he was feeling was the joy of the ships, of all the Elves combined, flowing through him like currents of lightning, and he wondered if he could take it.

As it happened, he couldn't.

So he passed out.

He was deep in the waters of the ocean, or so it seemed. A tidal presence moved through him, calming him, letting him know that he was not dead.

—You must not judge all the soft and leggy ones by Ralph . . .

It was not a speaking in his mind, nor yet was it words, but the thoughts, akin to concepts but more amorphous, emerged, like bubbles from the bottom of a warm pool.

—Ralph is not so much of our world as of yours. It was because of beings like Ralph, your human inventions, inadvertent, that we chose to sing with the Elves . . .

"But who are you?" Piswyck questioned. *He sensed it was the same presence that he had felt during the battle, the slow calm great calm.*

—We are the Big People, the Deep Singers, the Travelers of Dark Ways, the Poets of the Eternal Shade. We are philosophers. We contemplate Life. For that thing only did our bodies and brains evolve, and we do it well. But your kind required more of us. You feared us. Foolishly! That you ate our flesh we allowed, but that you made us into soap and bound your weapons with our skin we found unfitting. We chose to sing with the Elves . . .

"But why am I here?" Piswyck asked.

Everything had the reality of a dream, clear and sharp and bright with unrememberable colors, objects just beyond a veil, ready to take back to the land of wakefulness.

—You must learn not to judge classes by single examples. Ralph is not like the others of his kind. Neither are any other

special cases, nor even single instances. Your doubts are a part of your nature, as are ours. We are not long-lived like the Elves, but our songs are long, both yours and ours. Our songs support the Sundering, so be careful not to break them. Consider well what songs you will sing, for a wasted song is a terrible thing . . .

The presence withdrew from him, as if it were backing away. And yet it was not wholly gone. It was as if it stood just outside the chamber, behind an arras. He could feel it breathe.

He rose with it, holding an enormous breath, upward toward the light. Upward, where the sun was playing on the ripples of white-capped waves.

When Piswyck awoke he was lying on the deck of the Elfship, curled up against Lifesaver. The unicorn's body felt warm and comfortable, like a many-colored blanket that had been with one through storms. He yawned and sat up, stretching his arms out, then extending his legs. It had been a good sleep. He stood and scratched a little more than usual upon awakening as the salt water had dried on his skin and in his clothes.

"What's wrong?" he asked casually as he noticed the expression of dissatisfaction on the unicorn's face.

"Breakfast!" snorted Lifesaver.

Piswyck looked around and saw an elaborate feast set out on wooden plates nearby. He walked over and squatted down, picking up something unidentifiable between his fingers and tasting it. It was delicious!

"This is good!" he exclaimed.

"They do not cook with fire upon this ship," Lifesaver expounded. "Their meals are eaten raw, or at most dried. Raw squid is more than I can eat today!"

Indeed, the central plate was piled high with an artistically arranged mass of sliced flesh and tentacles, but there were other things as well.

"It serves but to remind me of old Ralph," Lifesaver continued. "And worse than that, I'm seasick to my ears!"

With this statement the unicorn hurled himself to his feet and trotted to the rail, there to purge himself most ungraciously of whatever he had last eaten. It served to dampen Piswyck's appetite for squid, but not for most of the other delicacies; for he found that he was famished.

When Piswyck finished eating (and Lifesaver finished puking) he looked around and noted that the deck of the ship was

all but deserted. Four Elfwomen danced a round dance near
the tiller, but aside from that the ship seemed to be in the
charge of the sea spiders high in the rigging.

"Where is everyone?" Piswyck asked as Lifesaver slumped
to the deck.

"The males and females all are now below, indulging in an
orgy if I'm right," the unicorn replied mournfully.

"An *orgy?*"

Suddenly Ni'Dbhrda was there.

"Ni'Mamba told you a Mateship it was to rescue," she
said. "When we cross, we partymate. Soon little Elves again.
Come, I want you!"

Though her syntax wasn't clear, her intentions were. As
she was the third woman since he'd left home to settle on
Piswyck as the object of a freely expressed desire, he wondered if he would ever again have the privilege of making the
first move.

"So long as it is customary and proper..." he began,
climbing to his feet. But Ni'Dbhrda grabbed his hand and
pulled him toward the hold.

"Customary and *very* proper!" she laughed.

She led him down into the cool darkness of the hold and he
was at once enveloped in the scent of spices and the sound of
soft singing. There was another sound, like the brushing of a
bow over strings, or perhaps papers blowing in the wind, but
he could not identify it. A small laugh, muffled, now and then
punctuated the music.

They moved in darkness amid moving bodies and then she
stopped, turning, pressing her small form against him. Her
hands flew over him, stripping him with a heady abandon, as
if she were shucking an ear of corn. He tried to perform the
same service for her, but she was too swift. With a move she
was naked against him and he felt terribly tall and awkward,
like a dinosaur trying to make love to a butterfly.

Her lips fastened on his and the hunger of her lonely life at
sea was unleashed. One of her small legs fastened around him
and she climbed him like a mast. Then his mouth began to
tingle, to vibrate, and he realized that she was singing as she
kissed him, a buzzing delight that almost made him laugh with
pleasure.

They sank to the deck and he felt soft warmth under him,
not boards. Her breath carried little whispered and sung words
into his mouth; then her lips left his and slid down his body.

He realized that the sound he had not identified was that of dry, snakelike skins moving against one another.

Her mouth was like a swallow flying over him. He felt her youth in her passion, her age in her experience. His blood pounded and his mind retreated, his desire growing greater than sunrise, greater than dawn. They were tumbling (like gymnastics underwater) and then they were colliding with other bodies, and up and down lost its meaning.

Brushing, touching, pounding, sweating, singing. Somewhere along the way he realized that it was not only Ni'Dbhrda he was making love to but the whole company in darkness. The sweet spicy smell was intoxicating, the touches on his flesh like golden fire.

The explosion racked through him but it did not bring surcease. He was not in a wave that fell upon the shore but one that built and rode across the endless sea. The crest grew higher and higher, dizzying.

When he first recognized an Elfman instead of an Elfwoman he thought to withdraw, to grab hold of his mind and sense, but. . . . All Elves were black in the dark and the dark was not merely the hold of a ship but the great dark cave of the Eternal Mother. Soon he was not shouting with release but singing wildly, at the top of his lungs, his breath as much of sex as was his body.

Fragments of songs, words he did not know, ages of ecstasy boiled down on him, out of him. How wonderful! To have so many years in which to develop one's amorous abilities. What privilege! To share these deep and heady poetries.

He knew that when the wave finally broke he would *die*. Nothing of satisfaction could exist beyond these moments.

But, to his surprise, it was not that way at all. The wave never did break. Instead, he drifted into dreams; dreams of many-colored landscapes, of shifting abstract patterns, of flying over valleys and plains and seas. If there was anything more wonderful than making love with the Elves, it was the sojourn in the Land Beyond, to which the wild Elvish passion was the gate.

He slept.

When he awoke he was alone and his groin was aching. His head was pillowed softly on a pile of sponges. Indeed, the whole of the hold was padded with sponges, floor, ceiling, and walls. He rolled over and groaned, and thought that it had been a *lovely* night.

That very morning the Elves transferred Piswyck and Life-saver to the Mateship, providing them with a small area curtained off from the rest of the sleeping quarters by a thin wall of spidersilk. Piswyck was provided with new clothes as well, a tight, stretchy outfit of the same iridescent gray stuff the Elves wore. It felt good against his skin, but it was so thin and fit so tightly that any time he thought about the night before, it would show.

When he was dressed they were taken back up on deck to be introduced to Bahamfalme, an Elfman who occupied the same position aboard the Male ship that Ni'Mamba held on the Female. He, like she, was taller than average. His shark-skull headdress was encrusted with baroque pearls of many tints and his dark green cloak was sewn with white scallop shells. His staff looked for all the world like a real dogfish, its scales glittering in the sun, save that it did not move.

Bahamfalme bowed a little, then settled to the deck. Piswyck followed suit.

"This is how it is," Bahamfalme said, and his voice was remarkably deep for such a small person. "Our ships will sail side by side to the West. I will teach you men's magic. Ni'Mamba will come to the ship from time to time and she will teach you women's magic. It is wrong that she should do it, but sometimes you have to do what is wrong to do what is right. That is how it is. The only harm it will do, we hope, is to you. When we are within reach of Far Bermuda we will put you both in a little boat and you can sail ashore. We will hold you invisible until you land, then you will be on your own against the wizard. Now let us eat!"

Despite the indication that what he would learn might do him harm, Piswyck felt his spirits lift. At last somebody was going to help him in his fight against Smagdarone and the Countess!

A number of (young?) Elfmen came up from below bearing wooden bowls of food and set them on the deck. It was the usual uncooked seafood, but Piswyck's exertions of the night before had given him an incredible appetite and he set to with gusto. Lifesaver was more selective about what he ate, Piswyck noted, but the unicorn ate nonetheless, and a goodly amount.

When all the dishes had been delivered, the servers sat down on the deck to join the meal. They sat in a circle and

Piswyck felt himself pressed by Elves from both sides. The one to his left smiled at him and introduced himself:

"I am Londea. I am to help you and be with you while you are aboard our ship, as I speak with you better than most. I will help you stay out of the way, keep you from being dangerous in the dances. Also will I share your bed, if that is your desire."

Piswyck nearly dropped the chunk of raw tuna he was about to pop into his mouth.

"From how you were last night, I think you might enjoy me," the Elf said nonchalantly, reaching for a chunk of the same food.

Piswyck felt himself go red to the very core of his being. It had never occurred to him, in the heat of passion, that anyone would remember . . .

"Of course you do not have to decide right now. It may be that some other will be your choice. It is the usual way that two or three will serve each other's needs in the long times between Partymate, but there are those who cannot settle down. So take your time. We have a long voyage."

Piswyck caught Lifesaver's eye. Was the unicorn raising an eyebrow at him? And if so, was it speculation or amusement?

"Uh . . ." Piswyck said. Then he thought better of continuing the sentence and shoved the tuna into his mouth.

"I must go and join the dance now," said Londea after a moment, and Piswyck felt relieved. "I will speak with you later. There are many things for you to learn."

Londea was up and away as swiftly as Ni'Dbhrda had been, or Ni'Mamba. For a long-lived people, Piswyck thought, the Elves did things with remarkable speed.

He kept on eating, now less from hunger than to occupy his confused mind. He let his eyes follow Londea, but soon could not make him out among the dancers. He stared for a few moments, then turned away, afraid that everyone in the circle would take his interest as . . . well . . . *interest!*

But looking around the circle, he decided *everybody* seemed to be eyeing him casually; and rather than meet other eyes he reverted his gaze to the dance.

The Elfmen's dances, he noted fiercely, were more springing and bouncing than those of the Elfwomen. Both sexes used their feet to keep the rhythm, but the steps of the Elfmen were more often in triple time counting than in double. Whereas the Elfwomen moved sinuously, the Elfmen leaped,

kicked, made gestures straight of arm in reaching for a rope or
scrubbing the deck. He could see that their dances were those
of warriors; athletic dances, taking no more energy perhaps
but exercising different muscles.

The supper over, the Elves drifted away and Bahamfalme
told Piswyck and Lifesaver that he would begin their instruction on the morrow. Piswyck was relieved again, and hurried
down into the hold, followed by Lifesaver, who was still
somewhat seasick.

During the night Piswyck discovered, as he lay on a bed of
sponges, that Krackmalnic the Seller had not lied about Lifesaver, at least in one important point. Given the proper diet,
the unicorn suffered mightily from gas. And worse: when seasick, Lifesaver snored in iambic pentameter.

The great gray ships sailed west and Ni'Mamba and Bahamfalme taught Piswyck and Lifesaver magic: the magic of the
Elves and the magic of Old Afrique, which were not like the
magic of the humans that he had learned. These magics were
filled with songs and dances, the drawing of pictures that the
wind took away, and the memorization of many poems. There
were no books of spells nor any charmed objects to be
charged, for the Elves had no room aboard their ships for the
detritus of sorcery, and they held in contempt what could not
be held in the mind.

"Writing," said Bahamfalme, "has robbed you of much of
your brain!"

It was not that the Elves had no writing. Indeed, Bahamfalme wrote in water on the deck to show them what a beautiful script the Elves possessed. But there were parts of the
brain that were like empty treasure houses, waiting to be filled
up. The commission of knowledge to paper often lost that
knowledge, and the unused chambers filled up with dust.
They were both set to memorizing long epics, sometimes in
languages they did not know, just for the practice.

"It is like praying," Bahamfalme said wisely, if a little
obscurely.

Both the marquis and the unicorn had limitations.

—Piswyck found that he could memorize dances more easily than poems, a fact that surprised him greatly. Lifesaver
could memorize the poems just fine, but though he could
memorize the steps of dances the fact that he had four feet
instead of two made the learning all but useless.

"In this I am as clumsy as a book," he told Bahamfalme, and the old Elf laughed (as he often did) and said that even useless knowledge was pleasurable.

The days stretched and Piswyck's mind and body stretched in new directions. He thought back to the time he'd spent learning to hang glide, and wished that now he had Bethzda's sure hands to massage away the pain in his aching muscles. He also wished that she were there to repeat their long nights of making love, for the Elfwomen's ship was now strictly taboo, despite the fact that it sailed only a hundred meters away.

He spent much free time leaning on the gunwale, watching the Elfwomen dance their sensual dances, longing for just a glance from Ni'Dbhrda, or any of them. When Ni'Mamba came over to teach him forbidden things from the repertoire of the women's magic, the Elfmen all retreated to the far end of the ship and he felt as if he were not only a person of another race, but almost a being of another species. He grew increasingly lonely, with a loneliness that Lifesaver could not assuage.

Sometimes as he leaned on the rail he would catch sight of Londea watching him. Then Londea would grin, his white teeth flashing, and Piswyck would blush all over again, knowing just what was on Londea's mind. But Londea never made any overt move toward him, never advanced his cause, and that, perhaps, made Piswyck all the more uncomfortable.

He couldn't simply come out and tell the Elf that he was not interested. It might be an insult to an Elf. And Londea was so friendly, so helpful in explaining anything he asked! He felt like a fool, and simply because he felt no desire.

One day Bahamfalme taught him a dance he was sure would kill him. He was amazed that the serene old Elf could do it, that anybody could do it, and he tried to persuade his teacher that it was beyond his ability. But Bahamfalme was patient, and by sunset Piswyck felt as if he had been stretched on the rack and whipped with morningstars at the same time. He hobbled down to his bed and collapsed, moaning softly, and was glad that Lifesaver was still above, learning one more song.

He lay there for a long time hurting; then he felt a hand upon his shoulder. He started, and Londea laughed.

"Will now you let my hands pound out the pain?" the Elf asked.

Piswyck felt he would have offered a gallon of his blood to ravenous vampires if they could have done it, so he assented, and soon Londea's hands were, indeed, pounding out the pain. It was a massage such as he had never known, one so rough and thorough that he cried out several times; but the pain did go away, and more, a tension that was not of the learning ebbed with it. When at last he lay upon his back, looking up at Londea in the dusky light, he was able to smile.

"Now there is a little more," Londea said, laughing gently, "and then you will feel fine. Will you allow it?"

Piswyck still felt no desire for the Elf, but he did feel a certain gratitude, and a growing friendship. Shyly, with the hope that Londea would understand if he didn't respond, he nodded.

For a week Piswyck sat in the prow of the ship and dissolved clouds. Then he spent another week condensing them. He learned how to take a wooden staff and make so much energy flow through it that he could bring down lightning to strike where it touched the ground, and survive. These were very showy techniques, he commented, but were they of any use?

Bahamfalme showed him how to move the clouds in circles, how to hurl the lightnings, how to build a storm front. Then he learned how useful it could be to control the winds when a ship was becalmed.

Ni'Mamba tried to teach him how to talk to her seasnakes, but he never got the hang of it. They sensed his distrust, and though they would not harm him, they would not be his friend, either. Lifesaver they loved, and would wind around his carnelian horn by the hour, enjoying the sunlight.

Bahamfalme showed him the little spell that turned an ordinary dogfish into a rigid staff. Piswyck considered this feat more an act of prestidigitation than magic, and wondered of what use it could be; but he didn't comment on it, he *learned* it.

Piswyck learned about the properties of various natural substances, and how they related to the world magically. He had known that silver was ground for all things magical, for his father had taught him about entropy, the Great Evil, the Heat Death that the universe thrust perversely upon itself; but now he learned about the insulating properties of spidersilk, and how different kinds of woods resonated with different kinds of psychic forces. He learned to scry without the necessity of a cumbersome crystal ball, and he quickly learned to tell whether someone was actually doing it or not.

"Vanity, thy name is *Unicorn!*" he proclaimed one day when he found Lifesaver looking at his reflection in a bowl of water, rather than concentrating on the depths beyond.

As the weeks grew long, his mind grew sore. He had not been aware that such was possible, but it was. There were whole parts of his brain that he had never used, and now he used them repeatedly, finding that the power of the mind was much greater than he had expected.

"There is a danger to it," Bahamfalme told him one day, "and it is this: you will come to enjoy the power, to take pleasure in it. You will want to devote yourself completely to the practice of magic, and that you must avoid."

"But why?" Piswyck asked.

"Because to do anything to the exclusion of everything else is a perversion, a corruption of what Holy Life is about! You are here to *live*, Piswyck, to exercise *all* of your talents, not just one. There are those of your people who lock themselves in towers and give up all other aspects of existence, just so they may accrue power. But what have they got when they finish with their lives? Jewels to lock with them in the tomb, but no taste for beauty. A banquet with an untrained palate! They are fools, who learn to rule a world they cannot enjoy."

There was a day when Piswyck and Lifesaver were shown the chamber below decks where the Lifeworking was done. To enter it they had to sing their minds into an appropriate state for nearly an hour, and once in, their minds slid sideways, adrift in mystical clouds of dim light. It was in this chamber that the best magicians on the ship worked, doing things too subtle for beginning magisters to comprehend.

They saw the Elfire grow, a microscopic sea creature mutated under patient Elvish wills; and someone, who seemed invisible at the time, hung a small vial of it around Piswyck's neck, suspended by a silk cord, wrapped securely in a silk bag. It was a tiny amount, only a seed culture, but it was a great gift. With it came the songs to make it grow, so that in the future Piswyck would be able to make his own. It took a very long time to grow, he noted, but he vowed that when he got the chance he would attempt it; and until that time he would keep his gift always with him, a living gemstone at his breast.

"You must sing a part of the song to it each day,"

Ni'Mamba later told him. "It is very unstable stuff, and unless you sing the song it will revert to its origins. You would have nothing but a plankton which has been in the sea for millennia. Then would it not give off light unless it died. Have you not seen glowing footsteps behind you upon the beach? That is what it is!"

Another day Londea introduced him to the Reckoners, the two Elves who held in their minds the ship's position by dead reckoning. It was the death of a previous one that had led the Maleship to the Coast of Monsters, and Piswyck was glad to have the mystery of their nature cleared up for him. They simply sat awake, one at a time, and *knew* the ship's position. He had heard of fishermen who dead-reckoned their boats for a day of work, but he had always assumed that dead reckoning on the high seas was a fable. He found himself amused to see another cherished scientific myth crumble, and amazed that anyone could sit awake for a week, then sleep when his partner took the shift.

"It is a hard work," Londea told him. "They of course maeterlincks are, so they can only play one day at a time, and then must even so watch the sea."

Piswyck smiled at Londea, and was very glad that he was not a Reckoner.

The gray ships went west before the breeze and Piswyck felt his mind and spirit stretch, embracing the open-skied spirit of the seas and the wild-hearted ways of the Elves, at least so far as the journey was concerned. He was aware that the subjective quality of his short life must be very different from theirs, but for the moment it mattered not. The food seemed more palatable the more he ate it (although Lifesaver still farted and snored at night) and, although the practice of magic was draining, it was also a kind of revivifier.

At the end of the day he would be exhausted and hungry but he would also be refreshed and energetic. He thought back to that part of his youth when he'd studied gymnastics and remembered how he had continued the practice into his dreams, running, tumbling, continuing the excitement of the day. The juices that poured through his spirit felt much the same as those that had pumped through his muscles then, and he liked it.

Londea's company at night, although still not what he would have chosen under most circumstances, was not unwanted. The young Elf never mentioned the disparity in their ages, but it was clear to Piswyck that Londea had considerably more experience than he—perhaps more even than the redoubtable Madame Roseboom, he thought one night when Londea arrived with a long string of bright baroque pearls.

And then, almost too soon—but perhaps not, as the magic was beginning to draw him—they were near to Far Bermuda. At first it was a misty dot upon the horizon; then a heat-shifting shape that seemed no more than a mirage. But it was there, at last unwavering ahead: the place where Smagdarone the Great held Miranda a virtual prisoner.

A small boat was prepared and lightly provisioned. The trip would be short once they left the ship.

Ni'Mamba hugged Piswyck, then hugged Lifesaver, and Bahamfalme followed suit. Piswyck was a little disconcerted when Ni'Mamba's snakes licked his cheek, but it made him happy.

He was happier still that Ni'Dbhrda was allowed to come to the Maleship and bid him good-bye, and his emotions overflowed completely when Londea presented him with a small bronze dagger as a present.

There was another round of hugging, and Lifesaver got a wreath of seaweed draped around his neck; then everybody kissed everybody. Piswyck and Lifesaver got into the little boat, and it was lowered over the side, between the two great gray Elfships.

And that was when Ralph decided to strike.

Now to understand what transpired next one must seek to understand something of Ralph's position.

The octopus is well known to be the most intelligent of the mollusks and there are, indeed, many naturalists who sincerely feel the eye of the octopus to be the most amazing product of the whole course of evolution. That the octopus evolved so much, with so little to begin with, has astonished humanity ever since the native savvy of the beast was discovered; not enough to stop humankind from eating its fellow sentient being, but certainly a level of astonishment adequate to indicate that humanity, also, might have something to offer.

Ralph, due to his peculiar genetic background, had been born one leg short (making him the world's only giant heptopus) and therefore an outcast from the octopus race. An intensive study of octopus culture would be necessary to give one even an inkling of what a dreadful fate this was, but, suffice to say, it gave him a *very* bad attitude.

The Elfire had given Ralph a headache, which, in a creature consisting mainly of head, was quite a pain. It had taken him a long time to recover but, once recovered, he knew exactly what he wanted to do.

He wanted to get his seven tentacles on the two Elfships and destroy them as thoroughly as he had destroyed the ancient city of San Francisco!

He had trailed the ships across the broad ocean at a leisurely pace, giving them plenty of time to think themselves safe. He could have caught them almost immediately, but that was not Ralph's way. He liked to savor his revenge. He liked to watch (and later remember) the expressions on the faces of his individual victims as he dismembered them one by one.

The contemplation of this prospect had put him in an excellent mood as he rose above the waves on that fateful day, and it was with great relish that he reached out a long tentacle to each of the ships, grasped the prows, and turned the two ships toward one another. It was a little disappointing to him that they had come to a stop, apparently to put down the little boat that floated between them, but it didn't really matter. This time he had his eyes almost closed, barriered against the Elfire.

He was prepared!

Piswyck and Lifesaver were not prepared, nor, Piswyck thought in sudden panic, were the Elves. The Elfire took a long time to grow in quantity and there was certainly not enough of it ready to defend the ships. Ralph, in all his chartreuse glory, looked about ten times as big from the perspective of the little boat as he had from the deck of the Elfship, and as they were sailing straight toward him he kept looking bigger by the second.

"Sashimi looks its best when it's on ice," said Lifesaver, with only the faintest tremor in his voice.

"Turn your boat around!" cried Londea from the deck above.

That sounded like a good idea on the surface, but there was no hope that Ralph would let the little boat escape so easily, and he was between them and the island. Besides, Piswyck had no desire to desert his friends. There had to be something he could do!

Two more tentacles came up out of the water and seized the ships; then one of Ralph's heavily lidded eyes swiveled around and caught sight of the little boat. It opened just a

small amount and they were treated to a stunning display of
heptopoidal emotion. Lightning-blue veins shot through the
chartreuse of Ralph's mantle and a tentacle was lifted to deal
with *them*.

"I think we'd better take battle stations," Piswyck said,
drawing the little bronze dagger that Londea had given him
and realizing what a silly weapon it was under the circumstances. Lifesaver lowered his horn and braced his feet.

The huge tentacle hovered over them, curling and uncurl-
ing, poised like a fork over a plate of hors d'oeuvres. Then,
with speed stunning in a thing so large, it whipped down and
wrapped around Lifesaver, lifting him neatly out of the boat
and holding him up twenty meters above the water.

The unicorn neighed, for the first time sounding something
like a horse; then he twisted in Ralph's grasp and jabbed his
horn into the tentacle.

Aboard the ships the Elves were pouring forward, male and
female alike armed with brazen swords and axes. They hacked
and hewed at the tentacles looped over their vessels, and
Ralph felt it. With a churning of the waters he began to draw
himself up, out of the ocean, using his weight to pull the
prows of the ships downward. It would be only minutes before
his sheer bulk would scuttle them!

The little boat in which Piswyck stood had not stopped
moving. Even as Ralph started to rise out of the brine it slid
close to him, bumping against him far too near his mouth.

High in the air Lifesaver's screams grew faint. The tentacle
was tightening slowly, crushing the life out of him.

There was nothing for Piswyck to do but attack.

With his best battle cry (and how he wished it were still old
Alberta, his nurse, on the receiving end of his training) he
leaped from the little boat onto the body of the heptopus,
plunging his dagger in not so much for the damage it could do
as for something to help him hold on.

For the first time in an eternity the sound of the Elfdrums
faltered. There was a sound of breaking wood, then screams
from the ships. Piswyck held on to his knife and glanced toward the decks, terrified lest the screams be coming from
Ni'Dbhrda or Londea.

From the rigging high above the water the sea spiders were
descending, and Ni'Mamba and Bahamfalme were crying out
orders that clearly told the Elves to move back. The huge
spiders reached Ralph's tentacles and began to sting, injecting

him with their deadly venom. It might not be enough to kill him, Piswyck thought, but it would certainly hurt!

Some of the sea spiders started throwing webs toward Ralph's eyes, but the heptopus had learned his lesson in the previous battle. He kept his tentacles at fullest possible extension and the webs fell short.

Piswyck looked up and saw that Lifesaver was hanging limp where Ralph squeezed him. Balancing carefully, he pulled his dagger out of Ralph's hide; then, stretching himself as far as he could, he plunged it in again, farther up. Like a mountain climber in a rainstorm, Piswyck began climbing the heptopus, moving toward the nearest eye.

The sea spider venom took effect, and Ralph, in self-defense, made his skin go tight and nubbly all over. He turned crimson with anger, and with a yank pulled the prow of the Elfwomen's ship slightly under. Water started pouring in.

The nubbly texture that Ralph had assumed suited Piswyck just fine. He was able to move faster, almost running up the monster's skin. When he slipped he used the dagger to catch himself, but it was a quick journey now to where he wanted to be.

Panting, and holding on to the dagger with one hand, Piswyck used his other hand to open the silk pouch that hung around his neck. He pulled out the little vial and uncorked it with his teeth. There was only a tiny bit of Elfire in the container, but it was the only hope he had. Properly applied, it might be enough.

He yanked his dagger free, reached around the rim of the huge eye, and plunged the blade into Ralph's eyelid.

The sudden opening of Ralph's eye was nearly enough to pull Piswyck's arm from its socket, but he held on, jerked upward, perilously hanging directly before the amazing orb.

Ralph didn't like things that attacked his eyes. He tore them apart very slowly.

The heptopus tossed the unicorn aside and brought the great tentacle toward Piswyck, mayhem roiling up in his slimy soul. But that was the exact moment when Piswyck poured the little vial of Elfire onto the surface of the big eye, planted his feet against the eyeball, pulled his dagger free and dove out and away.

It was a reasonably good dive under the circumstances, but it was from a rather great height for his ability and it plunged him to a greater depth than was reasonable or safe. His old diving instructor would have cautioned him against attempting it.

Down he went into the water, and down, so *fast!* He held his breath against both the need for air and the sudden pressure. He let his body go loose, letting go of form, concentrating on the simple business of keeping air in his lungs, of being buoyant enough to return to the surface.

The water around him churned, a mass of turbulence. He opened his eyes and caught flashes of chartreuse, of scarlet, of thrashing; and then he was enveloped by a black and oily cloud. He lost all sense of direction, and fear gripped him as he realized that he might be caught in the undertow if one of the ships went down, or even of Ralph's sudden exit if his maneuver had worked.

His lungs ached and he had to let some of the stale air out. He couldn't swim toward the surface because he didn't know where it was. His head began to ring and then to buzz. He had to let more air out, and then more, and then the darkness started to crawl inward, pushing back the barriers of his mind, encircling him like the flashing teeth of sharks. A ringing of stars overtook him.

Thus it was that Piswyck, unquestionably the hero of the day, missed one of the most visually impressive battle finales in maritime history.

Ralph blinked.

This served to spread the small amount of Elfire smoothly over his eye.

The Elfire exploded into light and color, sending painful rainbows deep into Ralph's neural cortex.

Ralph let go both ships in a paroxysm of agony, then discharged all the water from his sack at just the wrong moment. He floundered around in the water, his tentacles clutching at his blinded eye and his mantle shifting rapidly from chartreuse to scarlet to blue and several other colors less distinct.

The Elfwomen's ship rocked backward as it was released and the water it had taken aboard fore sloshed toward the stern in a huge wave, sweeping almost everyone overboard and nearly taking on water aft before it righted.

Ralph managed to refill his water sack, then shot off toward the safe, deep waters of midocean, not only hurt but humiliated.

The drums and bagpipes of the Elfmen's ship sounded and

nets and lines began flying from the deck. Spiders shot webs
to floundering Elfwomen and a big fishing net dipped down to
scoop up the unconscious Lifesaver. Londea and Ni'Dbhrda
both dove into the water where Piswyck had dissappeared, but
were too late to rescue him from his dive; the porpoises had
already got him and were bringing him to the surface.

There were no Elves lost overboard. A little thing like
being swept into the sea was not worth considering dangerous
to a race that lived amid the waves and storms. More difficult
was getting the water out of Piswyck's lungs and restoring his
breathing.

More difficult than that was administering artificial respira-
tion to Lifesaver. The Elves were too small for mouth to muz-
zle, so they had to lift and squeeze, and that was a lot of work.

It was several days before both Piswyck and Lifesaver
were up and about, and ready once more to head for Far Bermuda. It might have been less if both Ni'Dbhrda and Londea
had not been allowed to nurse Piswyck.

"Young Piswyck," Ni'Mamba said as she embraced him in
farewell again, "you will do well in the great wars that must
ensue. Brave enough you are to jump a heptopus, and that is
brave enough. And you, Lifesaver, you too are brave, and you
sing with a good measure and a strong heart!"

"Yes," said Bahamfalme, "that is right. What she says is
how it is. But always remember that the world is full of illu-
sions, and that bravery alone cannot prevail against them all.
You must discriminate between what is true and just, and what
is only fashionable."

Londea and Ni'Dbhrda kissed Piswyck again, everybody
hugged Lifesaver, and Bahamfalme presented Piswyck with
another vial of Elfire; then, once again they were lowered in a
small, well-provisioned boat. This time the Elves had talked
with the dolphins and determined that the waters for a long
way around were safe.

The little boat moved out, sailed toward Far Bermuda, and
Piswyck and Lifesaver bade the Elves farewell.

Slowly (but much too quickly for the space it made in
Piswyck's heart) the great gray ships seemed to thin, to become transparent, then to vanish as if in a mist; but there was
no mist. After a while there was only the bright blue sky and

the horizon, and a hot yellow sun. There was not a cloud to be seen.

"I wonder if we're out of hearing range," Lifesaver asked quietly.

Piswyck turned to look at the unicorn and detected a certain mischief in his friend's amber eyes.

"I think we are," he said. "But why do you ask that?"

"I have a song that I have just composed," said the particolored unicorn.

"And it would not be appropriate for our friends to hear it?"

"I do not know if they would understand."

"Let's hear it!" Piswyck said, leaning back and munching on a piece of dried sea vegetable.

Lifesaver cleared his throat, then began to sing:

> *"When Humankind decreases,*
> *The Otherkind comes out.*
> *My wonder never ceases*
> *At what this world's about.*
> *The Elves show up on steamships,*
> *The Gnomes show up on trains.*
> *It seems to me that time slips,*
> *And scrambles up my brains."*

Piswyck, puzzled, tried to interrupt at this point and point out that the Elves had *not* shown up on steamships, that in fact steamships had not been a functional means of transport since those very Elves had sundered the seas so many generations ago. But Lifesaver ignored him and launched into the chorus of the song, which was:

> *"This water's not for drinking,*
> *This sand will not lie still.*
> *My ship I think is sinking,*
> *Yet utter this I will:*
> *I do not like the ocean,*
> *I do not love the sea.*
> *Such maritime devotion,*
> *Is not the thing for me!"*

Piswyck interrupted again, making the point that it might very well be bad luck to sing about one's ship sinking while one was aboard one's ship; but Lifesaver plowed on with the next verse.

> *"The dogfish howls at sirens,*
> *The catfish claws the rug.*
> *The starfish's environs*
> *Are deeper than a jug.*
> *The blowfish gets too stuffy,*
> *The oyster spits a pearl.*
> *The lionfish gets rough, he*
> *Wants to impress his girl."*

And Piswyck said: "I don't know what kind of a song this is, Lifesaver, but it seems like a lot of nonsense to me!"

Lifesaver fixed him with a cold stare.

"It is an antichantey, Piswyck mine," the unicorn said. "About the sea, and what I've come to feel. I've rendered it directly from my gut!"

He then launched into the chorus again, as if to make his point completely clear.

> *"This water's not for drinking,*
> *This sand will not lie still . . ."*

"Well, really," said Piswyck, "it hasn't been so bad. I mean, not in the long run . . ."

> *"My ship I think is sinking,*
> *Yet utter this I will . . ."*

"While it's true that we got a little wet along the way, think how much we've learned . . ."

> *"I do not like the ocean,*
> *I do not love the sea . . ."*

"And besides, it was a kind of rite of passage, for me at least. You do get the joke, don't you? The pun on passage? I thought that was pretty good!"

*"Such maritime devotion,
   Is not the thing for me!"*

They kept on that way, Lifesaver adding more verses and repeating the chorus, and Piswyck talking to him; well, really trying to get his bearings again in a non-Elvish world, right up to the point at which their boat slid up onto Far Bermuda's soft pink sands, and they espied a mango tree just jeweled with fresh ripe fruit.

5

The Wizard of Shinbone Alley

The flavor of ripe mango was almost delightful enough to prevent Piswyck and Lifesaver from noticing the approaching monster. For humans, mangos are messy things to eat. For unicorns they are tricky, because the skin is poisonous and it is by no means easy for a unicorn to skin a piece of fruit. Still, Lifesaver was doing a valiant job, holding the mango down with one carnelian hoof and pulling the skin delicately off with his teeth. Piswyck was grateful for the clothes the Black Elves had given him, for aside from the way they stretched to outline, with embarrassing clarity, the contours of his body, the soft iridescence of their grayness seemed impervious to mango juice. It would be a dreadful thing, Piswyck thought idly as he picked at the stringy pulp caught between his teeth, to present himself in Bermuda looking like the remains of a fruit cocktail. He glanced down the beach (which was actually sparkling *pink,* and not white as he had first presumed it) and noticed a shadow drifting toward them, not unlike the shadow of a cloud; save that there were no clouds in the sky. He looked up and saw that which cast the shadow.

If it had been floating in the water he would have called it a jellyfish, or perhaps more formally a Portuguese man-of-war. It was, however, floating in the air and much larger than either of those simple sea creatures. Its canopy was perhaps three meters across and suffused with the loveliest pastels one could imagine: pink, lavender, soft orange, mauve. Its mass of long tendrils were of darker hue, but of the same general colors, tending toward smokey purples and brick reds, but still not vibrant.

Lifesaver noticed the creature at about the same time Piswyck did, and abandoning his mango he said: "I think we'd better leave the fruit and run." And he pranced backward across the pink sand.

"Seems right," said Piswyck, and he dropped his fruit and scrambled up onto the unicorn's back. They headed off at a gallop away from the creature, but a quick glance over his shoulder showed Piswyck that the thing was gaining on them.

"Up from the beach," he said at Lifesaver's ear. "Perhaps we can escape it in the trees!"

Lifesaver did as he was bid, charging under the cover of subtropical foliage, but this proved a mistake. Most of the trees were mangroves and their dense and wandering roots and branches stopped progress almost instantly. Worse, another look back showed the flying jellyfish to be unhampered by the growth; its long (and probably deadly) tendrils slid through the forest like well-conditioned hair through a comb.

"It can't get both of us. Get off and run!" cried the unicorn, finally able to go no farther forward.

Piswyck slid from Lifesaver's back, but he was not about to abandon his friend and steed. He drew the small bronze dagger Londea had given him and charged right at the jellyfish, thinking grimly that he might be able to inflict enough pain to scare it away, even if it killed him in the process. This, he realized, was on the assumption that a jellyfish could feel pain.

But just before he reached the mass of tendrils sliding through the foliage toward him, somebody leaped out of the undergrowth, nocked an arrow to the string of a very long bow, and let fly directly into the canopy of the hovering horror. There was a loud *plunk* as the arrow pierced its mark, then a shrill whistle as the monster shot off across the sky, bobbing and jerking and staggering like a child's balloon with the knot released.

The young man who had rescued Piswyck turned and smiled. "It was a special arrow," he said. "Hollow. Lets the gas out of them quick, and away they go!"

"Uh, thank you!" said Piswyck, suddenly a little out of breath. He hadn't noticed how fast his heart was beating.

"It would have been tragic to see that thing get you, but then, I wouldn't have known much about the tragedy because

I don't know you. So I thought I would prevent it. I'm Frog-stool."

Piswyck guessed that Frogstool might be an underdevel-oped twenty-five years in age. His hair was tight and curly, blond but with paler, almost white patches in it. His skin was dark brown, and he was thin, almost bony, both of face and physique. It appeared that he was trying to grow a beard, valiantly in the face of incapability, but the effort only served to give him a scruffy look. His clothes were cut in the dagged-tunic fashion of mythic Sherwood Forest but patterned with the mottled greens, browns, and olives of traditional camouflage; this caused Piswyck to take him for some kind of forester.

"I'm Piswyck, and that is Lifesaver. We are both most grateful to you for saving us. What *was* that thing?"

"A floater," said Frogstool, his voice a little reedy for a baritone. "Smagdarone has set them to patrolling the shores. It has ruined the fishing, and you can imagine what it has done to the sport of suntanning. One hopes that Smagdarone comes to a bad end, and soon. If he does, I'll be able to write a play about it."

"Oh, are you a writer?" Piswyck asked.

"No," said Frogstool, "but as soon as I have time to do some writing I will be. I have lots of stories in my head. I collect them. Tragedies in particular are my favorite, and my very favoritest of those are the ones that I have personally witnessed. That is why I felt the most delicious inclination to let the floater get you. But, as I said before, I wouldn't have known much about the tragedy because I don't know much about you. That would make it a rather weak tragedy, don't you think?"

"A death is not a tragedy unless the audience can know what might have been," said Lifesaver, trotting up to them.

"How true!" exclaimed Frogstool. "At last, someone who understands. You must both tell me all about yourselves at once, just in case something dreadful should happen to you!"

Piswyck was now inclined to think that he and Lifesaver had just been rescued by a lunatic, or at least someone with highly questionable ethics, but Lifesaver continued the con-versation: "Those tragedies are best that speak of love. The unexpected twist of fate that robs the lovers of their long-expected goal. Yet tragedy, to rend its poignant tear, must be exception to the happy rule. Most lovers *do* unite and come to good. What *should not* happen predicates what *should*."

"How profound!" said Frogstool, obviously impressed. "May I take it then that you two are embarked upon some quest of love?"

"You may," said Piswyck. "But before you learn more of us, I must, and rather rudely I fear, inquire more about you. Matters are delicate for us just now. We would not wish to involve you in a way detrimental to either you or us. Tell me, if the floater was something of Smagdarone's, was it wise for you to kill it?"

Frogstool shrugged. "Wise or not, he has made such a mess of our little country that I think almost any of us would be happy to see him eaten by his own creations. Why . . . well, come, it is easier to show you than to tell you!"

Frogstool led them through the woods for a few minutes; then the ground rose slightly and they came out in a clearing.

"There now, across the trees, in the distance. Can you see it?"

"The castle?" asked Piswyck. "One would be hard put *not* to see it!"

The castle in question was a glimmering confection, a fairy-tale castle with a peaked roof, a very tall tower, some shorter spires, a kind of fore-tower, and an autumnal-red gate-house that seemed to belong to another building entirely; and which yet was not architecturally offensive.

"Neuschwanstein!" said Frogstool.

"Bless you!" responded Piswyck politely.

"No, no! That is the name of the castle! The New Swan Castle, built centuries ago by Mad King Ludwig of Bavaria and quite a tasty ornament when set amidst the crags and peaks of its native land. But Smagdarone has had the effrontery to move it here to Bermuda, where it is quite the most un-Bermudan piece of architecture one can imagine! It simply *dominates* the landscape! Which I suppose is what a castle is supposed to do; but we have simpler tastes here, and a tradition of architecture quite our own of which we are rather proud, and we can do nicely, thank you, without either Mad King Ludwig *or* Smagdarone the Great!"

"But what is that which glistens 'round its base?" asked Lifesaver, calling attention to a shining wall of something fluorescent orange-pink which ran around the whole base of the castle, giving the impression that the whole affair was no more than a saltity of marchpane in the middle of a jelly mold.

"That is Smagdarone's strongest line of defense," said Frogstool. "It is a five-meter-high wall of modified tissue, essentially similar to the jellyfish but much more deadly. If anything approaches it shoots out a pseudopod and drags it inside, to its death. If we were closer you could see within the clear gel the remains of various foolish animals, and occasional unlucky humans, being slowly digested."

Piswyck shuddered. "How then does one get into the castle?" he asked.

"Only at Smagdarone's bidding," said Frogstool. "He has some kind of control over his creations and when he wants to ride out to the hunt the wall of jelly opens for him."

"And what of flying over to get in?" queried Lifesaver.

"If you look closely you may be able to see the floaters that patrol the sky around the castle. They are rather charming to view, like delicately colored balloons adrift above the keep, but you have seen how they attack at the first opportunity. And anyway, how would you *fly* over the walls?"

"Perhaps in a hang glider?" suggested Piswyck.

"There are two flaws in that plan," said Frogstool. "The first of course is the floaters. The second is that there is nothing in the islands from which to build a glider. Spidersilk is, in this part of the world, prohibitively expensive, and rare. New bamboo is not grown here. And even if you built the contraption, I doubt there is any place from which you might launch it adequately. In ancient times people used to fly them by being towed from speed boats, but of course the motors have not functioned since the Sundering. I trust it is Smagdarone's niece, the Lady Miranda, who is the object of your love?"

"Well, yes," said Piswyck.

"Then I should take you immediately to Kimowatt," said Frogstool. "You will be safe with him until you can devise your means of getting into the castle. I should warn you that although most people who live here oppose Smagdarone, he *has* offered a very large reward for you and your unicorn, and there are many who would be happy to collect it."

"*What?*" cried Piswyck and Lifesaver, almost in unison.

"Oh yes," said Frogstool. "For several months now there have been posters, and in addition to the reward he has promised a terrible punishment to anyone caught harboring you.

That is why Kimowatt has had me keeping an eye out for you."

"But how did he know that we would be coming? How——"

"I know none of that," said Frogstool, "but I do know the danger you are in. We'll hide here among the mangroves until after dark, then make our way into the Town of St. George. Things close down early in Bermuda, so if we bind some leaves around Lifesaver's hooves we should be able to get to Kimowatt with no difficulty."

"Who is this Kimowatt?" Piswyck asked, feeling that things were decidedly slipping beyond his control and not liking it.

"Kimowatt, Grower of Bones, he is called," said Frogstool. "That is all that I will tell you for now because I will want to see the expressions on your faces when he tells you the whole story, and why he is so implacable in his opposition to Smagdarone. It will be wonderfully dramatic, don't you think?"

By moonlight the Town of St. George was even more like a saltity than was Neuschwanstein. The houses were neat and square, with a restrained elegance, but the rooftops were marvels unto themselves: glistening white miniature steppyramids.

"There's no water in the islands," Frogstool explained quietly as they moved through the very narrow streets. "The roofs are cut from the limestone of which most of Bermuda is made, and kept very clean. Rainwater pours down them into channels that lead to a big tank in the basement, and that is how we get our water. When you dig the limestone for the roof you are also digging the basement tank. We've only had to import water twice since the year sixteen oh-nine of the Christian Era."

"Are Christian teachings then abandoned here?" asked Lifesaver, gesturing with his horn to a huge ruined church building as they passed it.

"Oh no!" said Frogstool. "Most of the people here are Anglican. That is our *unfinished* cathedral. The project was begun in eighteen seventy-four, but there was a schism in the church and work halted. The cathedral we use was eventually built in the City of Hamilton, but we liked the look of this unfinished one so much that we have kept it around for decoration. Don't the cacti and palm trees have a charm to them, growing there in the nave?"

There was a certain musical quality to Frogstool's narrative, a lilt to his reedy baritone that made Piswyck wonder whether what he was saying was the truth or merely a charming folk tale; or perhaps outright dissimulation.

"Here now, down Duke of Kent Street," said Frogstool as an intersection jogged and they crossed it. "If it were daylight we could stop at the museum. We are very proud of our past and we like to preserve as much of it as possible."

Piswyck could well believe that, for the citizens of Bermuda seemed to have done a very good job and there was virtually nothing in evidence that appeared to have been built since the Sundering.

"And now into Blockade Alley," said Frogstool as they turned again, and then: "Shinbone Alley! Named because there was once a barracks at the top and the soldiers used to drink here to immoderation and get into many fights. Over there is Somers Gardens. Maybe tomorrow you can go to see Sir George."

"Sir George?" queried Piswyck, not at all happy with the idea of encountering local officials if there was a price on his head.

"Not all of him, of course," said Frogstool. "He died in sixteen ten and his nephew buried his heart over there in the gardens. They sent the rest of his body back to England. I think it was the fashion in those times."

Piswyck was now convinced that Frogstool's veracity was in serious doubt. Quaint and curious traditions are everywhere the stock and trade of the tourist industry, whether one travels to a great metropolis or a country inn. But if Frogstool were to be believed, Bermuda was catalogued entirely of such impedimenta!

They stopped at a heavy wooden door and Frogstool knocked; a curious pattern of knocks.

"The wizard keeps such hours as other people shun," said Frogstool by way of explanation. "It makes his experiments easier."

"The wizard?" asked Piswyck.

"Kimowatt," elaborated Frogstool. Then he pointed upward to the plaster of the wall above the door. It was still dark, but there was enough moonlight for Piswyck to discern, embedded in the plaster, the complete skeleton of a rather large pteranodon.

"Grew it himself!" said Frogstool with a certain smugness.

The door was thrown open, a blaze of yellow light poured through it, and within the doorway, holding a many-branched candelabra, stood a very tall man, stark naked and dripping wet. He had dark blond hair, cut flat across his forehead in bangs, and longer at the sides in the manner of a page or herald. His eyes were wide-set and gray, his nose straight, his mouth broad and thin-lipped. His body was lean and corded with the kind of muscle displayed in the paintings of El Greco. Piswyck was reminded at once of the description of the hero of *Davy*, one of the literary classics his father had pushed upon him: *well-hung, with a natural-born goofy look*. The thin lips broadened in an enormous smile as his eyes focused on them.

"So you've found Piswyck and his particolored unicorn," the naked man said, his voice a brightly inflected tenor.

"Rescued them from a floater," said Frogstool proudly.

The naked man looked to Piswyck for confirmation, raising his eyebrows. Piswyck nodded assent, thinking to himself that the man must have the most mobile features he had ever seen; certainly the most instantly expressive face.

"All come in!" the man said, and he stepped back from the door so that they could enter. "I am Kimowatt, Smagdarone's most ardent enemy!" He shut the door behind them. "And his brother."

With that, Kimowatt held the candelabra high and headed off down the hall, apparently expecting them to follow, which they all did.

The hallway was decorated in the manner of the eighteenth century, with fine wood floors and portraits on the walls. At its far end Kimowatt opened another door and they followed him down a circular stairway cut out of the living limestone. The stair had certainly been cut a long time before, as there were minute stalactites already growing from the ceiling. How far they decended Piswyck could not guess, but when they reached the bottom he gasped in astonishment.

There was an enormous cave and in it a laboratory such as might have existed in the ancient Modern World. Huge glass tanks, globes, retorts, and other apparatus were everywhere, and in them moved liquids of divers viscosities and tinctures. The whole was lit with rich candlelight so that it shimmered and glowed, a veritable ballroom of arcane science. Bubbling sounds issued from unseen sources to make the music, and the smell of the sea was thick in the warm air.

"As close to the bottom of Lake Geneva as I can make it," said Kimowatt, and he sat down on one of several hassocks tufted with thick white lamb's wool.

"The bright ensorcelled caverns of the mage," quoted Lifesaver, and Piswyck saw a look of awe in the unicorn's amber eyes. There was no doubt that it was in just such a cavern that he had been conceived, bred, and born.

But Kimowatt's face fell at the sound of the quote. "No, not a mage, only a wizard," he said sadly. "That is the very heart of the matter. Both Smagdarone and I aspired to be mages, but the enmity between us, the intense competition, flawed us for the profession. Neither of us was able to pass the tests, and so here we are. He is competent at tissue growth while I excel with bones, but neither of us is capable of building life complete and whole."

"You truly then have been beneath the Lake?" asked Lifesaver in awe.

"Oh yes," said Kimowatt. "Smaggy and I were sent there when we were very young, by our mother, the Lady Nea. But high moral character is the first requirement and I am afraid neither of us had it high enough. It was a lack of that in the scientists of old that caused the Sundering in the first place, did you know?"

"The Black Elves," said Piswyck, "told us that it was the way humankind spread poisons all over the land."

"Ah, so it was the Elves who got you here, was it?" said Kimowatt. "Everybody wondered about that, just how you would get here after Madame Roseboom's stratagem failed. The Countess was pretty sure it had failed when Spoletta did not return to Serrique."

Piswyck felt the hair on the back of his neck rise.

"Just how much does *everybody* know?" he asked.

Kimowatt grinned, displaying his delight in the prospect of revelation.

"The Countess and Smagdarone are very close in some ways," he said. "And of course I have my spies in the castle. It would seem that the Countess has great confidence in your ability to survive, young Marquis. For some dark reason of her own, she fears you greatly."

"As well she might!" said Piswyck. "She has imprisoned

my father, taken our lands, sealed the borders of Carsonne with trolls—"

"You started in to speak of *Sundering, sir?" Lifesaver interrupted.

"Yes," said Kimowatt. "The Sundering. It was indeed pollution that put the Elves at odds with us, but not only the chemical kind. When they finally took action it was the damage to the bioelectrosphere of the planet that was their chief concern."

"The *what?*" asked Piswyck.

"It has to do with the way life is organized," said Kimowatt, and in his eyes there kindled the same kind of scientific passion that Piswyck had seen in his father's eyes whenever the senior marquis had spoken of the lost Ancient Science. "Everything that lives is organized under the influence of the Earth's magnetic field. That field is so delicate that only the flux of electrons in a superconducting substance can be used to detect its finer tunings. Of course there are many organic superconductors, like the little *E. coli* in your intestines, but science did not know about that when the irresponsibility began. The big things came easy, like the industrialization of knowledge; it was not until long after the first atomic fission that they were able to make a superconductor in the laboratory by bathing semiconductors in liquid helium and thus discover that, indeed, the human brain and all other living things produce magnetic fields, albeit only about a billionth as strong as that of the Earth. But, under the influence—"

"Wait a moment, you've lost me!" cried Piswyck, almost breathless from racing after Kimowatt's words.

Kimowatt grinned more delightedly. "It's *magic!*" he said. "You don't really have to understand it to use it, not at the simplest levels. What you might *wish* to understand is that humankind had increased electromagnetic radiation around this old planet over a hundred million times in a little over fifty years. The little compasses in our heads went all askew; the little clocks in our cells got mistimed. The very clocks that governed our biocycles. In general, all life was endangered and the people doing it were not even willing to think about the problem. They were having too much fun inventing new things and making money from their inventions. But the Black Elves, out there on the seas in their invisible ships, they knew all this stuff because their magic was just another technique for using the same knowledge. Biological perception rather than mechanical perception, a thing which the Ancient Science had invested much energy and emotion in denying. That denial didn't do much good when the Elves sundered the seas and made all our machines stop! But the Ancient Science, and thus humankind, had *learned,* and though our machines stopped, our knowledge didn't go away. There *were* humans who had been working on the biological methods, magicians, and the Ancient Science had finally given them appropriate models to manipulate. They were able to continue with the biological sciences in places like the labs under Lake Geneva; and though we can no longer build a spaceship, we *can* now build a unicorn, if the operator has a concentration pure enough. That is why our particolored friend here exists. But the requirement for high moral standard is also now a part and parcel of the study, for the mages simply will not train anyone who treats knowledge irresponsibly. That is why Smaggy and I sit around experimenting with things neither of us can ever hope to master. The accumulated knowledge of how it's done is closed to us."

"You speak, sir, much as my father does," said Piswyck.

Kimowatt seemed pleased.

"That is to say," Piswyck continued, "in phrases that I do not have the background to understand. May I assume that all this talk of biology is somehow allied to the little things I do inside my mind when I make fire or summon clouds?"

"Precisely!" said Kimowatt. "But that little bit of energy you are organizing in your brain and using to influence other energy fields is not the sum total of the energy involved when you cast a spell; and that is where moral integrity enters. The synergy of electromagnetic forces which you muster is still part of the greater, overall system. The most important rule of magic is that there is no such thing as a free lunch. The laws of thermodynamics are always operative in our universe, and when you use energy, of whatever kind or degree, it has to come from somewhere."

"The heat that is drawn from my body when I make fire," Piswyck suggested.

"Exactly. But note this: in manipulating the tiny electrical currents that stimulate DNA replication and the like I am using very small amounts of one kind of energy, but possibly setting in motion others. The mages of Geneva take into consideration the results not only of that primary energy use when they work, but the synergistic effects of the creatures they create. What will be the *effect* of growing a particolored unicorn?"

He paused a moment to let that sink in; then, sighing, he said: "Personally, I think the Priest-Kings of Geneva are a little stuffy, and that some good original research could do the world a lot of good. Are you hungry?"

"So long as supper isn't seafood, yes!" responded Lifesaver heartily.

"Good!" said the wizard. "So am I! Frogstool, go up to the kitchen and bring us a couple of those cassava pies I baked on Monday."

Frogstool went up to get the food and Kimowatt stood and stretched. "Most people here take cassava pies only at Christmas, but I like them year 'round," he said. "But then, I am a little odd by island standards. They get upset if I answer the door naked; but frankly, it is such a bother to get dressed, and so uncomfortable when one has been lying in a sensory deprivation tank in order to focus concentration. I hope my nudity does not offend you?"

"Uh, no," said Piswyck, still trying to follow the scientific narrative.

"I may not address myself to the local customs as well as I should," Kimowatt laughed, "but at least I have had the good taste not to litter the landscape with Bavarian castles!"

Frogstool brought the pies, a large basket of fruit, a jug of wine, and a tablecloth, which he spread over a table stained with unappetizing substances of unknown origin. They ate, Piswyck and Lifesaver voraciously, particularly appreciating the meat in the pie. Then Kimowatt showed them around the laboratory while Frogstool sat on one of the white hassocks, bored with the details, which he knew already.

"You must understand how a thing *grows* to understand what it is that I do here," Kimowatt said, pointing to a glass vat where something small and indistinct was suspended in liquid. "I assume that you understand elementary embryology... No? Well, in the earliest stages of growth every gene on every chromosome is active and available to every cell. As the critter develops some genes are turned off, so to speak, differentiating, and the cells form three tissue layers. The mesoderm (which is the one I can *almost* handle) turns into the muscles, the bones, and the circulatory system. Smaggy is stuck with the ectoderm, which turns into the skin, sense organs, and the nervous system. Neither of us is any good with the endoderm, which becomes the glands and the guts. I almost got veins and muscles once, but in the long run there wasn't much point in it; you can't run a critter on muscle and bone alone. I suppose I am a fool for continuing my experiments in the face of my own colossal ignorance, but I do enjoy trying. Can you understand that? And if I ever get control of it *all*, why, then, my pterodactyls will live and fly the Earth again. That is my pet project, if you will pardon the pun. Dinosaurs have fascinated me since boyhood and I would really like to grow a few. But, as you can see, I get nothing much but well-developed bones and some scummy protomuscular tissue, sometimes rudimentary veining, and it dies. Which does leave me with the bones, a nice skeleton it is true, but somehow not quite the same as a live pteranodon. Here, take a look in this tank! Another flyer, and if it were to succeed... But even so, the biggest thing that I have yet grown!"

The exhibit in question was a huge aquarium in which a sluggish soup moved and in which soup definite outlines could be seen of a flying reptile much larger than the one skeletally displayed over the front door of the house. A pinkish goo enclosed the bones and something that might have been about to be blood was in evidence, but nothing more.

"How long will it take before it is finished?" Piswyck asked.

"Well, it never *will* be finished, as I just explained. But what growth there will be is almost done. As I have no chance of bringing it to life I've just bypassed the normal development cycle and taken it to full adulthood. By tomorrow the tissue will start to atrophy I'm sure. Frankly, the thing is done. Nothing to do now but dry it off and mount it somewhere."

"Could you grow another one like it?" Piswyck asked.

"Oh, I think so," said Kimowatt. "I have this part of the technique pretty well in hand now. But it *so* infuriates me to think that they could be growing full-sized tyrannosaurs under Lake Geneva *now* if they weren't such fuddy-duddies!"

"If you can grow another one," said Piswyck, "how would you feel about giving this one to me?"

Kimowatt looked at him and blinked.

"Well, it would certainly be ornamental, no matter where you put it, but... Are you thinking of seizing Neuschwanstein from Smaggy? There *are* some places in the castle that could use a dinosaur, now that I think of it!"

"I am thinking of using it, if it would not offend you too much, in a project I have in mind. Frogstool says there is nothing in Bermuda from which to build a hang glider, yet I observe that you are making very good replicas of the stiff parts of one of nature's best."

Kimowatt blinked again, and the light came on in his eyes and in his smile.

"Why, so I am! Tell me, what will you use to cover the wings? And what about stress? This creature is designed to fly with its body at center, while a hang glider has its center of gravity much lower. You have to remember that these bones have never been stressed, although they will react as any other piezoelectric substance. I suppose if you need vertical strength I could grow you a femur from an allosaurus or something, then saw it in half—"

"No need to worry about that," Piswyck interrupted. "I'll only need the glider once, and I don't think I'm in much danger of flipping upside down; so we won't need a kingpin on top. We can make it a rigid-wing flyer, which will eliminate a lot of other parts. The main thing will be to find something to cover the wing."

"*And,*" added Frogstool, "getting past the floaters. Not to mention the question of getting you up in the air!"

"I think that I can help to get you up," said Lifesaver. "I took advantage of our time at sea to brush up on the speech the dolphins use. They travel fast enough that, in a pod, they'd surely have the strength to tow you up."

"That leaves only a covering for the wings," said Piswyck.

"And getting past the floaters," Frogstool added insistently.

Kimowatt tilted his head slightly, the way a puppy will when pondering some great and momentous decision. He turned and walked slowly across the laboratory, letting his muscles sink cat-graceful with each move, then sat on one of the hassocks. Piswyck wondered what it was the wizard did to keep in such remarkably good shape. He didn't seem the type inclined to sports, yet there was no fat on him. It was not a swimmer's build, certainly, nor a gymnast's; those were the types that Piswyck had always believed to produce the most universally developed physiques, and he knew them.

"The fact is," said Kimowatt, "that Smaggy is just a little bit more advanced in technique than I am. He was offered a chance to train as a healer—a chance that I'd have taken—but turned it down. He can't grow anything from scratch, but he *can* manipulate living things pretty well and make changes in them; then reproduce them. The floaters, so far as I know, are his masterpiece, even more so than the jelly wall."

He paused a moment, whether to marshal his argument or provide a dramatic respite Piswyck could not tell.

"Unless I am mistaken, the outer membrane of the floaters' canopy must be fairly tough, or rather tight of texture. Otherwise they could not effectively keep in the hydrogen they produce to keep themselves aloft. Am I right, Frogstool?"

"Indeed you are," said Frogstool, his interest now clearly kindled.

"Further," said Kimowatt, "we know that they don't attack one another. Suppose we were to cover the wing of the hang glider with the membrane of a floater's canopy? What might be the odds that the floaters around the castle would think the glider one of themselves?"

"It would depend," said Frogstool, "on whether they recognize one another by shape or smell or some other sense; perhaps even electromagnetic field. Whatever the case, I think it worth the risk, for it's the only suggestion I've heard that might work."

"If we could find the one that Frogstool shot—" Piswyck began, but Kimowatt shook his head negatively.

"He only let the air out of it. They heal very fast. That thing is probably back on patrol by now . . . unless Smaggy has them report back to him somehow, in which case we are in trouble! But I don't think they're intelligent enough for that, so we probably aren't."

"Then we'll have to hunt one down," said Piswyck.

"Yes," said Kimowatt. "Hunt it down, kill it, then see whether our plan will work. If they are like most of the jelly-fish family their skins will dry quickly to a very thin substance. That means we'll have to stretch it on the glider quickly, else it will be subject to tearing."

"And," added Frogstool, "we will have to hunt it in the dark. Otherwise somebody will notice and try for the reward."

"So tomorrow we will begin to construct the frame," said Kimowatt.

"With that in mind," Lifesaver declared with a yawn, "I think we ought to sleep."

"Agreed," said Kimowatt. "Frogstool, take them up to Captain Avery's room and draw the shutters tight, so that they can sleep by day."

"Who is Captain Avery?" Piswyck asked.

"The gentleman who committed suicide in that room in twenty thirty-eight of the Christian Era," replied Frogstool, and as he took them up the stairs he told them the story.

A gibbous moon glistened on the warm waters of Tobacco Bay, and a gentle breeze rustled the leaves of the forest up from the water. The air was sweet with night-scented blossoms, and, had Miranda (or any other pretty girl) been beside him, Piswyck would have considered it a perfect night for melancholy romance, his very favorite pastime since early adolescence.

However, the matter at hand was a jellyfish hunt, and a skyborne jellyfish at that. Frogstool had outlined the strategy and armed them with crossbows, each bolt of which was drilled and threaded near the base with a long length of spider-silk; a costly commodity, but the only thing strong enough to hold the game and light enough to travel with the bolt.

"There's bound to be one along soon," said Kimowatt, who had dressed for the occasion of leaving his house in formal starched white shirt, white tie, and tails; and whose patent leather shoes were now full of pink sand. "They circle about the islands widdershins until they catch something. Then they stop and sting it to death—not a pretty sight, I can assure you, especially if it's someone you know."

"Then," said Frogstool, "the floater lowers itself down to ingest the kill. When Smagdarone first loosed them we tried to kill them off by hobbling a sheep on the beach, waiting until a floater was down and feasting, then throwing a net over the damned thing, staking the net down, and burning it. But Smagdarone can breed floaters faster than we can breed sheep. After a while we gave up the fight, realizing that the only way we were going to rid ourselves of floaters was to rid ourselves of Smagdarone."

The moon got higher, crossed the sky, and was lowering again before their intended victim finally appeared, coming at them gracefully around the little headland to the north. For all its deadliness it was quite beautiful, Piswyck thought. Lavenders and pinks and soft corals glowed faintly in its canopy, while the hellish tendrils luminesced with mauves, aquas, and a soft, smoky ruby color that was particularly attractive. It was a splendid specimen, with a canopy over three meters across and tendrils that dangled more than eight meters down from it, not touching the ground but near enough for a quick and terrible descent.

"Wait until it gets fairly close," cautioned Frogstool. "Make sure that the ends of your cords are fastened securely to their pegs. The barbs on the ends of the bolts should keep them from pulling loose once they're in, but you will have to drive the anchoring peg into the sand, and quickly as well as securely. The hard part will be getting away fast, before the floater can run down the line. I think of it as being like marlin fishing, or maybe hunting the great white shark, though that is perhaps not the best description possible. Come on, let's scatter, so that we have three good positions."

At that moment Kimowatt fired, so it was a good thing that they were already moving. The bolt plunked into the floater, and Kimowatt knelt to hammer his stake into the ground; there was a hissing noise, indicating that the floater was releasing gas to propel itself.

Piswyck looked up and saw the floater move in the direction opposite that from which the bolt had entered. It reached the end of its new tether, jerked, then reversed direction and with remarkable speed shot straight toward the place where they had all stood not a moment before.

Piswyck and Lifesaver came to a halt and Piswyck aimed his crossbow. He fired, but his bolt missed. He cursed quietly and began to turn the rachet of his crossbow, cranking the string back for a second shot. While he was thus engaged another plunk in the darkness told him of Frogstool's hit.

Now the floater was as mad as a jellyfish could get. It hissed and shot at the source of its second wound, faster than before, and Frogstool got clear just in time. Piswyck finished cranking his bow, nocked his bolt, checked its tether string, and took aim. The floater still had the option of moving back and forth between its two tethers; Piswyck's bolt would provide a third point of anchor and make it possible to reel the thing in. He fired.

His bolt hit.

As he bent to hammer in his peg he wondered just how the floater propelled itself. Did it use the hydrogen it generated for staying aloft, or did it take in air and squeeze it out somehow, so as not to lose its buoyancy? He got up and ran, making a mental note to ask Kimowatt about the floater's propulsion; then he tripped over a mangrove root and fell flat on his face.

"Piswyck!" Lifesaver cried, ahead of him. There was just the trace of a whinny in the unicorn's voice.

Piswyck looked up and saw the floater coming at him, almost over him, the deadly tendrils about to brush across his prostrate body.

Then the tethers grabbed and the floater was jerked back and upward, just enough (and just long enough) for Piswyck to scramble backward before the tendrils lowered once again to the place where he had lain. He fell at Lifesaver's hooves and let the air out of his lungs with a rush that might have propelled him had he been airborne.

Now the floater throbbed with pastel biofluorescence as it struggled with its three-point anchorage. It hissed and jerked like a kite caught in crosswinds, but the bolts were secure and it could not escape. Kimowatt and Frogstool began reeling in their ends and as soon as the creature was clear of his end, Piswyck also reeled in. Soon the floater was down on the ground, a flattened globe of soft yet angry colors atop a mass of darkly pulsing tendrils.

"How do we kill it?" Piswyck asked when Kimowatt came up to him.

"Slowly, I'm afraid," the wizard answered. "We cut off the part we want and let the rest dry to death. It may die somewhere along the way, but I don't know for certain. Death is such a thorny philosophical problem."

Piswyck remembered the slow death of the water troll and asked if there were any quick way to dispatch the thing; he had no taste for slow murder, even of this low a life form.

"A bit late in the proceedings for scruples," Kimowatt responded. "Haven't you ever eaten oysters on the half shell?"

"Well, yes," said Piswyck. "But what has that got to do with it?"

"Well, think how *they* must feel, lying there with half their protective shell ripped off, partially maimed; and then you swallow them alive, perhaps chewing their little bodies in the process, and digest them to death. You are aware that they are still alive when you eat them, aren't you?"

"No," said Piswyck, and he felt a little queasy.

"Well, never mind. Just remember that the floater would have no qualms about killing you with pure pain, or just paralyzing you enough to eat you alive, if it had the chance. Life is not always pretty, young Marquis. Now come, we have to get the skin back to the lab and stretch it over the bones before it dries, and also before everybody in town is awake to see us. I've brought some knives attached to very long handles, so we should be able to skin the thing without getting too close to the tendrils."

Piswyck considered that being cut apart alive was probably no worse than being burned alive during dinner, and that both were probably preferable to being digested to death. He took one of the long knives and joined in the butchery.

Piswyck had never built a hang glider, and neither had Kimowatt or Frogstool. But Piswyck *had* watched old Amerdeen build the big one for Lifesaver, and there were picture books from ancient times in Kimowatt's extensive library depicting both rogollos and rigid-wing gliders. They had chosen a likely picture for their model in assembling the bones of the unliving pteranodon into a frame, and now they used the same picture for guidance in stretching the rapidly dehydrating floater skin over that frame.

Frogstool, like most hunters, was adept with a needle, and soon they had something that resembled a flying contraption. It didn't give Piswyck a lot of confidence, but if it could get him over the wall of man-eating jelly and into the castle it would serve its purpose.

"Now comes the question of getting you up!" said Frogstool as he put the finishing touches on the wing. It was clear that he still entertained a certain amount of cynicism regarding the whole project.

"Tonight I'll go and sing beside the sea," said Lifesaver confidently, and as that was the only solution to the problem that presented itself they spent the rest of the day eating and sleeping; except for Frogstool, who was assigned the job of keeping watch against Smagdarone's agents. Time, after all, was likely to betray them.

Yet when night came the sweetness of Lifesaver's songs did not attract the dolphins. Nor the next night, nor the next. Either there were no dolphins close enough to the shore to hear him or those who heard the songs were unresponsive. By the fourth night Piswyck was questioning Kimowatt and Frogstool in the hope of finding other alternatives.

"Even a moderate hill in the vicinity would give me a chance to run down and launch," he said. "If there is a bit of wind in the right direction I'll have no trouble getting up. And so long as there is land between me and the castle there is likely to be lift.''

"Oh," said Kimowatt, troubled, "but there is *not*. Perhaps it is not so obvious from this far away, but the castle is on an altogether different island from this one."

"A different island?" queried Piswyck, startled.

"Why yes," said Kimowatt. "Bermuda is not just one island, it is almost a hundred and fifty little ones. We are on St. George's, but Smagdarone has put his castle up on Coney Island, across from Ferry Point. It's not a great distance, but it is across the water. Smaggy said he wanted the castle there because Castle Harbour has so long needed a really good castle, and this way he can guard the entrance, though precisely from what he wasn't clear; and besides, there's more entry to the harbor from the other side than between Ferry Point and Coney Island. But that is the sort of conceit in which Smaggy likes to indulge!"

"Just *how far* is it across the water?" Piswyck asked.

"Well, I've never had reason to measure it, but I'd guess about two hundred and fifty meters, more or less."

Piswyck was relieved. "If I can get up high enough to fly over the castle walls in the first place," he said, "that should be no problem. But we still have to find a way to get me that kind of lift! Is there any place where we can test the glider? Any way to determine a good place to spiral up?"

"I'm afraid Bermuda is a little small for keeping anything so public as hang gliding a secret," Kimowatt smiled.

"Then it will be one try, win or lose," sighed Piswyck. "Tell me, is there anything between here and there in the way of farming? A plowed field would give me the lift I need."

"Nothing," said Kimowatt. Then his brows knit just slightly. "Some sheep graze down by Love Lake, and just before that there is a little rise, maybe twelve meters' rise at the most. Would that be enough to get you up?"

"I could certainly use it to get off the ground," said Piswyck. "But I would still need a source of lift."

"There is nothing under cultivation in that area," said Frogstool, who was now sitting with a spoon, scooping out the soft flesh of a large papaya (he called it a paw-paw) and devouring it. "But that does not mean that it could not be plowed preparatory to planting something where nothing has grown before."

"Well, splendid!" said Piswyck. "What crops grow here?"

"Easter lilies and onions," said Frogstool. "There used to be quite a trade with the United States and Canada for the lily bulbs, but of course, after the Sundering . . . I wonder how things are going in the States after all this time?"

"Onions, I think," said Kimowatt. "I'll tell Quincy Tucker that I need a lot of onion juice for one of my experiments and ask him to go down there and plow."

"He'll only get around to it when he's ready," cautioned Frogstool. "You know that onions don't like being pushed."

"I don't think we have to worry about the crop, Frogstool," said Piswyck irritably.

"That's not what he meant," said Kimowatt. "He meant that native Bermudans, who sometimes call themselves 'onions,' don't like to be rushed. But don't worry about it, I'm sure I can find some discreet way to get Quincy plowing in a hurry."

Kimowatt didn't tell Piswyck just what way he had of persuading Quincy Tucker to plow the land with all speed, but persuade he did, and none too soon. Three days after the plowing, early in the morning when Lifesaver had just returned listlessly from further serenading the uncompliant dolphins, Frogstool rushed in with the news that Smagdarone had ridden out to the hunt, headed south.

"I would not think there'd be much *room* to hunt," said Lifesaver.

"Wild boar," said Frogstool. "In the forest that grew up where the Old Port Royal Golf Course used to be. But never mind that! This is the chance we've been waiting for. If we hurry, we can get Piswyck up in the air and into the castle while Smagdarone is away!"

There were many reasons not to attempt the assault so soon, but none so pressing as the need to get it over with; so they threw such cautions to the winds and moved the hang glider out into Shinbone Alley. It was light enough that Lifesaver could carry it easily on his back for the whole distance, and though he complained, he agreed that it was the best way of doing it. And a pretty procession they made in the cheerful light of dawn: Kimowatt, dressed in black tie and tails; Frogstool in his Robin Hood camouflage; Piswyck in Elfin iridescent; and Lifesaver, a particolored unicorn bearing a bone-white hang glider covered with a fading pastel jellyfish skin.

Down Shinbone Alley, past Somers Garden, past the oldest building in Bermuda ("That's the State House," quoth Frogstool, the irrepressible tour guide, "built in sixteen twenty and still rented to the Masons for the sum of one peppercorn a year. The price of peppercorns has fluctuated greatly over the centuries, and right now that is a pretty good bargain for the government!"). Across King's Square, from which they could see Ordnance Island with its stocks, ducking stool, and replica of the *Deliverance*. ("Of course it was built only as a tourist attraction in the old days, but keeping a ship like that in repair is always a good idea. You can never tell when you may need to sail away!") Down Water Street, past the Tucker House. ("There are still a lot of Tuckers in Bermuda, but *that* was the home of *Henry* Tucker. Sometime I must tell you the story of Henry Tucker and George Washington and the gunpowder plot.")

Piswyck found the Town of St. George particularly charming by daylight, with its pink- and green- and blue- and coral-colored buildings and its view of St. George's Harbour. He also enjoyed hearing the bits of history that Frogstool offered, though just how much of what the forester said was true seemed doubtful. He found it odd that the townspeople did not come out of their houses to see the little procession, but Kimowatt explained that this was due to Piswyck's manner of dress.

"I'm afraid your clothing reveals more than is considered decent," Kimowatt said. "Knees are acceptable here in the proper season, but outlines definitely are *not*."

They took Mullet Bay Road, with the Atlantic waters of Nearon's Cut on one side and the enclosed waters of Mullet Bay on the other. Lifesaver, never gracious about bearing burdens like a common animal, let Frogstool know that he was *not nearly* so amused by local color as was Piswyck. After that they traveled in silence for a while, until the road turned to Ferry Road and they were moving along above Ferry Reach.

They came to the hillock Kimowatt had described, and to the plowed field. They ascended and took the glider off Lifesaver's back, and Piswyck ascertained that what was best in the way of wind (there wasn't any, not really) was coming from the ocean, from the northeast.

"I'm afraid those cattle are going to be in your way," said

Frogstool, pointing downhill toward the ocean, where a half dozen milk cows were chewing their morning cud.

"I'll run down and tell them all to move," said Lifesaver, shaking his rose-pink mane, and away he trotted.

"I've made you a special bow," said Frogstool, unwrapping a length of cloth he had been carrying. "A crossbow takes too long to fire and a longbow would be awkward, so this one is shorter. It will fasten to one of the down bones of your glider, and on the other bone we can tie this quiver of hollow arrows. This is just in case the floaters don't mistake you for one of their own!"

There continued to be an edge of cynicism in his reedy baritone, but Piswyck detected also a note of genuine concern.

"Oh, by the by," said Kimowatt casually. "There's one thing I would like to ask you before you take off: Just what are you going to do once you get into the castle?"

"Why, rescue Miranda, of course!" said Piswyck.

"Oh," said Kimowatt. "And beyond that you have no further plan?"

"Why, no," said Piswyck.

"Ah, youth!" exclaimed Kimowatt softly.

"My father," said Piswyck, a little offended by what seemed to be patronization, "advised me never to make too many plans in detail. The philosopher Heisenberg determined long ago that you cannot pin down Reality."

"Be that as it may," said Kimowatt, showing a small amusement with his lips, "if you should find a way to take out that jelly mold around the castle there are a number of us who might be available as a sort of 'army of liberation,' if you understand. If you can get a message out, I can get the army ready to come in."

"Ah!" said Piswyck, pleased to know that he was not fighting the war alone. "I see. I'll try!"

He fastened his harness hook and lay down on the ground for a preflight check. The harness was made of leather, an old-fashioned straightforward material that would never go out of fashion so long as the whole of humankind did not adopt ethical vegetarianism. The hook was wrought bronze, a product of Frogstool's skill at following Piswyck's design.

"I'm ready!" said Piswyck when he was finally satisfied.

"That's fortunate," said Frogstool. "Look back along the road, toward the town!"

Up the distance of Ferry Road they looked. A small crowd of men and women were coming toward them.

"What now?" asked Piswyck.

"If I mistake me not," said Kimowatt, "that is Norbert Lightborn, Smagdarone's resident toady and spy, leading something in the way of a posse. Notice the pitchforks and scythes?"

"Wonderful!" said Piswyck. "A mob out to kill us!"

"Perhaps," said Kimowatt. "But perhaps only to cut up your glider and capture the three of us; or rather the four, if they can catch Lifesaver. Remember, they are following the carrot of a reward, like good asses."

"I think I'd better start my run," said Piswyck, wondering if he should perhaps stay and help his friends, but quickly dismissing the possibility as a stupid one.

"Go quickly," said Kimowatt. "We can take care of ourselves, and once you're gone they have nothing to gain."

Piswyck bent, checked the little trailing thread in front of him to see if there was *any* breeze, and headed the glider into what small movement of air there was. He fixed the waves just beyond the shore as his goal and started to run. Slowly, three, four, five steps to get him and the glider moving; then he increased his pace.

One nice thing about a hang glider, he thought as he picked up speed: if he stumbled he wouldn't fall. The glider would keep him at the same height until it eventually glided down.

The harness caught at his thighs, tightened, gripped his chest. His heart was pounding, his legs were pounding; he felt the lift. His feet were barely touching the ground, then they were off. He kept running, felt the slight breeze against his face, felt the glider lift him. The ground receded slowly; he was up. He stretched his legs backward, pulled in on the control bar to pick up speed, and the lift died.

Just why he never knew. At that moment he didn't care. The ground came up; he tried pushing out to flare, but it was too late and he was too low. With agonizing comedy he settled down, moving horizontal and fast; and with no effective way to stop he found himself being dragged along the ground like an anchor, facedown, through ten meters of fresh morning cow flops and dewy grass.

"Misbegotten issue of a turkey fart!" he swore out loud as the glider came to a stop. He raised himself up on his elbows,

then climbed slowly to his knees. He hated it when he had to carry the glider back up the hill.

The glider was nose down so he ran his eyes quickly over the bones to be sure none of them were damaged. Then he looked morosely back to the top of the rise.

Frogstool was standing there, but Kimowatt was running down the hill, probably wondering if he was hurt. He waved to indicate that he was all right but Kimowatt kept running, right up to him, and unwinding a heavy length of spidersilk as he came.

"I'm glad that Lifesaver insisted on this," the wizard said, reaching down and starting to tie the cord to the nose of the glider.

"On what?" Piswyck asked, not knowing what was going on and still a little dazed from his ignominious landing. He started to unfasten his leathern helmet.

"Leave that on!" commanded Kimowatt. "The posse is too close for another try from the hill; besides which, Lifesaver has some help."

Kimowatt lifted the nose of the glider and, ahead of him, Piswyck saw the particolored unicorn dancing back and forth in the surf, emitting high-pitched whistlings that had escaped his notice amid the birdsongs of the morning air.

In the water, near the shore, a pod of dolphins danced upon their tails.

Kimowatt ran down the beach, and as he ran he untangled the other end of the very expensive spidersilk cord. It divided into many smaller strands at that end, and these Kimowatt gave to Lifesaver, one at a time; and Lifesaver gave them individually to the dolphins.

Piswyck, sensibly unquestioning of such good fortune and timing, hefted the glider upon his shoulders and prepared to run. It crossed his mind briefly that he would have to get off the ground before he reached the water unless he wanted to revive for himself the ancient art of water skiing without water skis; but then, by this time he had faced many challenges with equally unlikely odds. And there was, in the long run, nowhere to go but forward. He said a quick prayer to Hermes, who was oft considered a god of the air, and the towrope tightened.

He started to run toward the water but the glider was suddenly faster than he was. He pumped his legs harder and caught up. He felt lift. Still no wind, but rapid movement through the air was doing the job. Across the beach—still running—then he was literally running across the tops of waves (soaking his shoes)—he was up—he stretched out; and *still* the dolphins pulled, a wide line of splashing bright bodies with a fan of spidersilk lines converging upward to the nose of his glider.

He rose. He flew higher. Then the line was at its length. The dolphins let go and the fan of spidersilk fell aft of him. He pulled the slip knot Kimowatt had made and the tow line fell away, expensively, into the ocean. He shifted his weight and the glider banked, turned; he straightened it out and headed back for the land.

On top of the hillock he could see that the posse had arrived. There would *have* to be lift over the plowed field! Kimowatt and Frogstool were arguing mightily with an unpleasant fellow who looked as if he should be named Norbert Lightborn, whether he was or not. Piswyck pulled in on the bar, got speed; but still it was a downward slant!

He headed for the hillock. The plowed field was on the far side, beyond the posse. He came in low, lower . . . He glanced up the shoreline and was glad to see Lifesaver galloping away from the altercation toward which he was flying.

Now he could hear the voices that were raised in argument. He saw Norbert swing on Kimowatt. He saw Kimowatt move with lightning speed, deflecting the blow. With candid grace Kimowatt decked Norbert with his left foot. That told Piswyck what exercise it was that kept Kimowatt in such good shape. It also gave him confidence that the mob would not be able to prevail against Kimowatt's martial arts.

Then he was upon them, perhaps four meters up, and the wind of his wings whooshed over them. In fear, the mob fell flat on its collective face, while Kimowatt and Frogstool looked up and laughed.

Piswyck passed on toward the plowed field and suddenly there was warm air on his face. The glider jerked as he came into the thermal current that rose from the freshly turned soil. He banked; there was lift; he moved into a spiral, cored upward. He was suddenly elated, suddenly excited to be up in the air again, suddenly hoping it would not get foggy all of a sudden.

Up and up.

He saw Lifesaver gallop farther and farther, saw the unicorn disappear into the woods before a floater noticed him. He saw the argument below die as it became obvious the posse had lost its prey. He saw Smagdarone's castle glittering in the sunlight, its deadly ring of jelly even less appetizing than it had looked at a distance.

And when he judged that he had enough altitude, he headed for it.

As Piswyck approached Neuschwanstein he noticed at once that the floaters would not be the major problem.

There was only one place suitable for landing his hang glider and that was the courtyard of the castle. It was painfully small, not a target he would have chosen, but it *was* possible if his landing were near perfect. He would have to flare just right or he would run into a stone wall. This was complicated by the presence, in said courtyard, of a tree and a semi-inflated circus balloon.

The balloon was painted in gay colors, and near it was a winch with an enormous length of rope. Piswyck remembered having ridden in such a balloon when he was a boy. One paid a pittance and got into the basket and the rope was let out, giving one the thrill of aerial ascent while still fastened securely to the ground. From such a balloon, Piswyck thought, Smagdarone could view virtually all of the Country of Bermuda.

He sighed, half for the memory, and half because the balloon was in the way. He would not only have to make a perfect landing, he would have to negotiate the space between the walls and the balloon and the tree. The air currents around the stone castle would be tricky enough. If the balloon was a hot-air type . . . But then, he didn't know a thing about balloons, except that they could be monitored in the air because there were so few of them.

He wished that he were safe at home, reading all about an adventure such as the one he was having rather than actually having it, curled up in a big chair in front of the enormous fireplace in his father's library. Why was it, he wondered, that he had never been trained to be an adventurer? His father had taught him a great deal over the years—but not nearly *enough!*

He caught himself thinking this and wondered whether his blood sugar was low.

Music drifted on the air. At first just a tinkle, then many notes. He listened intently and fixed its direction and nature.

Someone in the topmost tower of the castle was playing a very
loud music box. The tune was the ancient "Carousel Waltz."
Remembering how much Miranda loved that antique dance,
Piswyck was suddenly confident that his true love must be just
ahead, in the tower, playing the music.

He noticed something else.

The floaters, like pretty pastel balloons (somehow pastels
had always seemed to Piswyck less honest than primary circus
colors) were moving widdershins around the castle in slow,
stately time to the music. His first response to this fact was to
wonder if Tchaikowsky had ever written a "Waltz of the Jellyfish," but he immediately dismissed this thought from his
mind as being too silly for consideration under the circumstances. His second response was to note that the floaters obviously responded to sound, a fact that might or might not be
relevant.

He gauged his timing, hoping to come in between two of
the floaters *en progress*, then pulled in just a tiny bit on the
control bone, starting his descent. The tree in the courtyard
was to the left, the balloon to the right; but if he could fly in to
the right of the gatehouse, then bear a little left, he could land
between them; or, barring that, land farther into the courtyard.

Closer, then the tinkling music dimmed as the air currents
shifted subtly. Abruptly one of the floaters changed course,
heading toward him.

Piswyck was completely in control of his feelings, so he
calmly took the bow from its place, pulled a hollow arrow
from the quiver, nocked it; and waited patiently, letting the
creature continue as it would. The glider would stay on course
without his help unless there was turbulence, so he was not in
the least upset. He waited for the opportune moment, then let
the arrow fly.

As expected, the arrow pierced the floater's pastel canopy
with a plunk and the creature shot off, bobbing across the sky
erratically until it finally crashed into the castle wall and fell,
insensate.

It fell, unfortunately for the floater, directly on top of the
jelly ring. Piswyck shuddered as the orange-pink horror
slurped up around the fallen floater and soundlessly drew it,
now struggling slightly, into the clear and highly enzymatic
substance of its body to be digested like any other protein,
related by family or not.

Now Piswyck's hope of being able to go placidly back to

the business of piloting his glider was shattered. At the plunk
of his arrow the other floaters had stopped their dance. With
the crash of their sibling to its doom, they abandoned their
procession and moved swiftly toward the airborne invader,
picking up speed as they came.

Piswyck nocked another arrow, waited as long as he dared,
and let fly. Then another. There were at least ten floaters coming; he didn't have time to count. The first arrow struck but
the second missed. The closest floater loomed huge as it came
at him, and he barely got his fourth arrow off in time to stop
it. That was when he noticed another problem, namely that he
needed to do some course adjustment or he would smash into
the same wall that had flattened his first victim.

He drew his arrow, let it fly; then, steadying himself with
his right hand, he threw his rear end to the right, changing his
center of gravity so that the glider moved toward a theoretical
target to the right of the castle. His turn started, he nocked
another arrow and shot another floater.

The trouble was that he was now losing altitude. He had to
stay high enough that he could get over the walls, but he also
had to maneuver. He pulled in on the control bone, gained
speed, and hoped that he would find some lift. He shot another arrow, missed, adjusted course a little, then shot again.

The next floater sailed in at him, its deadly tendrils dangling, and he thought that he was dead. But as the floater
passed over him he realized that he had forgotten one small
thing. The glider itself formed a canopy over him. The tendrils struck the leading edge and the glider bucked slightly;
then they slid across and beyond, their suppleness defeating
their purpose for once.

It might not work a second time, he thought, but it had
worked once, and that was enough to have kept him alive. He
drew his bow for the next encounter, then checked his course.

He was missing his landing window completely!

He came in too close to the castle wall, but by throwing his
weight full right he missed it. Now there was nothing to do
but proceed widdershins, as the floaters were doing, around
the castle. Or else make a complete turn and go back.

He decided to go back. There would be less loss of altitude
and he would be facing the floaters head on rather than having
them come at him from the rear. He let the glider continue its
turn, then flew straight across the front of the gatehouse.

He shot the air out of two more floaters as he flew, but then he had gone past the entrance he had planned on, too close for a turn and too fast.

Heat rising from the road that led up to the gatehouse caught him and he gained a little altitude. Abruptly, roughly, but he gained it. He glanced to his right and noted that a low wall bordered the courtyard briefly to the left of the tree. If he could go around the guard tower and approach from that direction . . .

Around the guard tower, directly ahead, came several more floaters, bunched roughly together but at different altitudes. They were making a wall of themselves! He couldn't brush under their tendrils and he couldn't shoot them all down quickly enough. He threw his weight left, headed away from the castle, and let fly three arrows in rapid succession, hoping to do as much damage as possible.

He'd lost track of how many floaters he had wounded. He didn't know how long it took one to recover, or how many more there might be in reserve. But he did know now that they could organize themselves into different defensive patterns, that they were doing so even now. He would have to get past them fast if he was going to do it.

He glanced down and saw the glistening ring of orange-pink jelly and his heart skipped a beat. Even as the air battle proceeded it had shot out a pseudopod and seized a goat, which cried and struggled as it was drawn back toward horrid death. And there were pseudopods reaching *upwards*, long thin tendrils of death from below, toward *him!*

How high could it reach? The canopy of the glider would offer no protection from that direction!

He had only one chance now. He knew he couldn't make it all the way around the castle and still have enough altitude to get in. He shifted right and brought the glider around, flattening his flight, then nudging it farther into a rightward curve. He shot more arrows, took out more floaters, saw more of them coming from behind the castle.

He headed straight for the low wall with the tree just beyond it. He was too high, but he could get lower. He said another quick prayer to Hermes, pushed out on the bar, and stalled; just slightly.

The glider went up, almost stopped, then dove again. The floaters from the front of the castle moved toward him. The floaters from the back speeded up. He pushed out again, mushing his airspeed again. Again an almost-stall, then the fast dive.

It was going to be close!

His stop-start was confusing the floaters nearest him as they tried to adjust their courses. He was heading right for the stone wall, and if he miscalculated even a little he would crash into it, and he and his glider would fall straight down into the man-eating jelly.

He let fly one final arrow. The stone wall was right in front of him, coming up fast, and he pushed.

A moment of giddiness, a feeling of falling as gravity ceased to be, as forces equalized. The glider moved up, up, over the stone wall, the wall not a meter below his belly—then it was over.

He brought his feet down under him and there was a tree right before him. His feet touched the stone pavement; the glider stopped, settled, and he was down. Inside Neuschwanstein's walls!

And there, running across the courtyard toward him, past the half-inflated circus balloon, was Miranda!

"The *floaters!*" he cried, suddenly terrified for her safety and unable to look up past the glider's wing to see what the creatures were doing.

"*Piswyck!*" Miranda gasped, and her big dark eyes went wide. "You look a perfect *mess!*"

Piswyck wondered what peculiar weight of karma always brought him to important interviews covered in manure.

6

The Mystery of Miranda's Missing Missive

"Miranda, the floaters!" Piswyck repeated, pointing upward and not wishing to have traveled half the world only to watch his lady love eaten by a giant airborne jellyfish.

"Oh, *Piswyck!*" Miranda said, and she stamped her dainty foot on the pavement in exasperation. "They can't harm us here! What use would they be as guards if they attacked people within the castle walls? And what on earth *happened* to you? You're all covered in—"

Her pert nose wrinkled in distaste and Piswyck felt his heart melt all over again, just the way it had the first time he had seen her.

She was a little less in height than he was, and her chestnut hair fell down over her shoulders to her waist in glistening silky waves. Her eyes were brown, with flecks of golden light in them, and her brows arched over her eyes with a wonderful delicacy. Her nose, Piswyck felt, was perfect, even when wrinkled. Her lips were full and pink and sensual, with just a tart twist perpetually upon them to keep them from being too sweet. Her complexion was golden from the sun, as if she drank goblets of summer sunlight to make it warm and dark. Her breasts (revealed somewhat by a daffodil-colored blouse, which had slipped down off her shoulders alluringly) were luscious. Her waist was tiny, a fact about which she was vain and which led her to wearing tightly cinched skirts. The skirt she wore now was a cerise-colored crinoline cut tight at the top to show off not only her tiny waist but her gracefully swelling hips. It stopped its downward cascade just below her knees to reveal the strong, graceful legs of a woman who did not dally with languidity. Her small feet were encased in black patent leather slippers, slashed and purfled to show the yellow velvet lining that matched her blouse.

Piswyck wanted to rush her, to take her in his arms and smother her with kisses. But it would not be advisable, he admonished himself, considering her reaction to the cow manure with which he was covered.

"I had a little trouble with my takeoff," he said lightly, and let the fear of the floaters drain away out of him with a single great exhalation. "In fact, I had a lot of trouble getting here." He tried to brush away some of the manure, but not even Elfcloth was impervious to mashed solids dried in the wind. He gave up and unfastened his harness hook, then stepped forward, out of the shelter of his hang glider.

"I should think you *did* have some trouble getting here!" Miranda said, as if something unpleasant had just occurred to her; and with that she turned rapidly and walked away from him, headed quickly toward the stone stairway that went up from the back of the courtyard.

"Miranda!" Piswyck cried, stunned to confusion by her behavior. "Miranda, wait! What's the matter?"

His relief at having landed safely had put him off guard and slowed his reactions. She was halfway up the stairway by the time he almost caught up with her, at which point she whirled, and looking down at him with the greatest possible scorn said: "What's the matter? What's the *matter?* Piswyck, do you know how long it took me to do the embroidery on that Montana Bib? Do you know how hard it was to save up the money for those pearl buttons without Uncle finding out? It's not as if he gives me a very large allowance! And it's not as if I were particularly adept at stitchery." She began to cry, even as she ranted at him. "The fact is, I am *terrible* at stitchery, and that salamander took me *months* to embroider! I only did it because I thought you cared for me, but to find out that you merely tossed it away, leaving it to be grimed and defecated upon . . ."

"Miranda," Piswyck cried, finding himself a little more than upset, "I didn't *toss* the bib away. It was already covered in shit when I ripped it off and threw it very hard into the face of a man who was trying to *kill* me! And the reason it was all covered in shit was ... Wait a minute! What are you talking about? How do you know what happened to that bib?"

Miranda had reacted badly to his little show of temper, and instead of displaying contrition she rose to his supposed challenge. "I'll show you how I know!" she snapped, and quicker than his mind could change tracks she turned and ran up the stairs.

Piswyck was a little tired after a busy morning of escaping a posse, hang gliding, and battling monsters in the sky. He was not so quick as he might have been in chasing after her, and he was barely able to keep her in sight as she led him through a maze of incredibly decorated rooms, corridors, and up a stairway that he *ached* to stop and appreciate (there was a huge central column carved in the shape of a white palm tree, its capital colored with green, red, and yellow where the fronds were furled, and its outstretched fronds lush green against a vaulted ceiling of sky blue spangled with five-pointed golden stars in different sizes). She finally led him into a small but ornately decorated room where he found her unlocking a carven wood desk. She pulled out a bundle of white linen, unwrapped it, and held out at arm's length the moldering remains of his long-lost Montana Bib, the embroidered salamander barely distinguishable amid the stains.

"There!" she said in triumph and with scorn. "Look at it! Just look at it! Just *look* at what all my work has gone for!"

The fact that she had it was more important, for the moment, than her feelings about it, so Piswyck was a little rough of tone as he spoke to her: "Miranda, how did you get that?" There was a puzzle emerging as a picture in his mind, had been since his arrival in Bermuda.

"The Countess sent it to Uncle Smaggy in the hope that it would dissuade me from my hopeless passion for you," Miranda said bitterly.

"The *Countess!*" snarled Piswyck, the very mention of his arch-enemy firing a rage in him. "That wanton bitch! She has imprisoned my father, stolen my lands, and now she wants to come between me and my lady!"

"Your lady?" inquired Miranda haughtily. "I was not so sure you considered me worthy of that title! I was not even aware that I had granted you the privilege of serving me thus!"

"You sent me that bib as a pledge!" he cried, outraged.

"And you threw it way!" she charged.

"I told you, the man was trying to kill me! I had to do something, and quick. He had a sword, while I had only a dagger in my boot."

"You might have found something to throw at him other than my pledge of love!"

"There was no time to pull off my pants!" he stormed, and his voice dripped sarcasm as well as anger.

"It was bad enough that you should dispose of my gift that way," she shouted, "but my letter—" And abruptly she fell into a chair, buried her face in her hands, and wept.

Piswyck's father had warned him that women were capable of the most amazing transitions from one emotion to another, but the warning never prevented Piswyck from being astonished when he encountered one of those transitions. He was angry now; and a moment before Miranda had been angry, too. But suddenly she was sitting there sobbing uncontrollably. What had happened? And what was she saying about a letter? The only letter he'd had from her in ages had been the one old Alberta had given him, and that had been lost even before he'd had a chance to read it. The loss had seemed unimportant at the time, for he was going to see Miranda in any case.

"Miranda?" he ventured, damping his temper. "What do you mean about a letter?"

"Couldn't you just have *burned* it, as I wrote that you should? It was so foolish of you to let it fall into Uncle's hands. You cannot imagine what it has been like." And she wept some more.

Now, men whose fathers had not given them instruction in the ways of women might have taken Miranda's wild vacillations of mood to be a sign of fickleness or unreason. Not so Piswyck, for his father had adhorted him that the understanding of women was important; nay, was one of the great philosophical unattainables toward which a man must always strive. In Miranda's passionate (if seemingly unreasonable, given the circumstances) anger, followed immediately by equally passionate despair, Piswyck easily discerned a person whose every resource had been drained to empty. He had not expected that Miranda should have endured any hardship at her uncle's hands, and that she *had* troubled him.

He thought back to what old Alberta had said about the contents of the letter and realized that he had underestimated its importance. He felt a touch of guilt about losing it, but not much; he had been preoccupied with escaping first the Countess's men, then the burning stockyards. He was not even sure *when* he had lost the letter. Perhaps now the mystery of its loss and content would be cleared up.

"Miranda," he said patiently, "if you mean the letter that summoned me here, I never even read it. I got it from Alberta, who told me that things were worse with you and advised me to come rescue you; and then, sometime during my escape from Carsonne, I lost it still unread."

Miranda looked up at him and emotions moved across her pretty face the way the shadows of clouds move across a pasture in summer, only much faster. She took out a little handkerchief embroidered with strawberries and dabbed at her eyes, then blew her nose into it unceremoniously.

"That letter," she said, "revealed more than my heart. It told of all of Uncle's plans."

"And what might those plans be?" he asked.

"Uncle Smagdarone," Miranda said, carefully so as not to start sobbing again, "plans to conquer the world. He is breeding floaters by the thousands—no, by the *millions*—in what amounts to a seed form. When he is ready, when he feels he has enough of them, he will send them against all the capitals of the world and . . . simply take over!"

For a moment, time and space seemed to stop for Piswyck. There was a kind of eternal and spiritual silence around him. No emotion showed itself within him. He was like an emptied cup waiting on a shelf for the dust of the Ages to fill it. Finally he said: "Miranda, that's the silliest thing I ever heard!"

"It's *not* silly!" Miranda cried, and she burst into tears again. "It's true, and he's going to do it!"

"Miranda," said Piswyck, "you can't take over the world with a bunch of flying jellyfish! If people are indoors they'll be safe from the floaters."

She turned her face up to him and it was flushed, but she sniffed and addressed him as if she were a school teacher lecturing a small and ignorant boy (and how he hated it when she did that).

"There is more than one way to rule the world, Piswyck. You can rule it with brute force, the way the military leaders did of old, or you can rule it economically, the way the great corporations did at the end of the Age of Science. You can also rule the way the Countess does, pitting people's pride against their own foolishness; cultural rule that makes everyone a slave of almighty fashion. Uncle Smagdarone plans to rule the world through sheer nuisance. He can produce the floaters faster than you can imagine, and I do *not* underestimate your imagination. They are not only deadly, they are voracious carnivores. They will eat anything that doesn't eat them first, and I don't know of anything that will eat a floater. Now, people may be safe in their persons when they are indoors, Piswyck, but they cannot stay indoors all the time. They must go out into the fields to raise crops and harvest them. Otherwise everybody will starve to death. *That* is the menace Uncle Smagdarone represents. Total world famine as the floaters gobble up every farmer and every animal in sight. It will take the fall of only one country to bring the others to their knees. No ruler can withstand the mobs of the hungry at his castle doors."

What she said made Piswyck a little uneasy, but the plan looked too simple to be effective.

"You don't seriously think that the rulers of the world will give over their power that readily, do you?" he asked.

She continued to lecture: "Piswyck, there *are* no rulers of the world. This planet is covered with tiny warring states run by ambitious cockroaches too greedy to make meaningful alliances. The people Uncle will deal with are *incapable* of acting in concert."

"Even so," said Piswyck, "an army for destroying the floaters—"

"Would be worn out the first day. Uncle can make floaters tremendously fast. More than that, he can move his troops about at will. They are all linked to him telepathically. It's made him a little odd of late."

"Wait!" said Piswyck. "He is in rapport with the floaters?"

She nodded.

"Then he knows I am here! Has known since the very day I arrived in Bermuda! He knows I'm in the castle!"

"Oh," cried Miranda, "if *only* you had read my letter!"

Piswyck felt despair sweep over him like a riptide. Not so much because of the sudden realization that he was now trapped inside his enemy's castle, and that his enemy knew him to be trapped. Nor yet because he still had no genuine plan as to how he should rescue Miranda or get hold of her uncle's secrets in order to rescue his father and save his homeland from the ravages of the Countess.

No, it was because he suddenly realized how *little* he knew his beloved.

He had never before seen her wavering between anger and tears. She had always been bright and cheerful, positive and charming. One of the things he liked best about her was that she was not the kind of woman who would leap up on a chair at the sight of a mouse. They had gone hawking together and she had handled her merlin with the surety of a full-time professional. They had gone hunting and she had brought down a stag bigger than the one he took that day. She rode steeplechase with the best, and she fenced fiercely.

He had never seen her cry before, except that night when they had plighted their troth by the Fontaine de Barenton, by moonlight amid the hazels and willows, beneath the ancient oak. There was a nightingale in the oak that night, and they had sat silent, their fingers entwined, her head on his shoulder, and listened to its song.

"Miranda," he said, putting his hand on her bare shoulder and manfully ignoring the electric current he felt from the contact, "what has gotten into you? This is no time for us to argue, or for you to sit around weeping. We have to get out of here!"

It was the wrong thing to say.

"No time for me to sit around weeping?" she flared. "Well, just what do you have in mind? Can you take the two of us out on your hang glider? Did you build it big enough? Do you think we would get far if you did? Just what weapons did you bring for fighting Smagdarone the Great, Piswyck? I wrote all this to you in my letter, and you didn't even read it! I expected you to arrive with an army at your back!"

Piswyck was stung to the core. Even though it wasn't his fault, she had a point.

"I asked you to come here so that we could stop my uncle from taking over the world," she continued, "but you come fluttering in over the walls more like a spy than a conquerer. A spy on bat's wings! If you want me to stop weeping, Piswyck, for the gods' sakes, think of something that I have *not* thought of!"

And she fell to weeping again, not without good reason, Piswyck now understood.

That, of course, put the ball squarely in his court; but at least he was now empowered to play, and knew a little about

the rules. He pretended confidence, and threw in just a little
arrogance in order to be convincing.

"All right," he said. "What are your uncle's strengths and
weaknesses? What are his weapons, beyond the floaters and
that wall of digestive-enzyme aspic he's thrown up around the
castle?"

Miranda once again got control of herself. What he had
pretended seemed to be what was needed. His father had often
told him that it was frequently not so important that one have
the *right* solution as that one have *some* solution. Inactivity
was often deadlier than merely being wrong.

"The servants in the castle are loyal to him," she said,
"mainly out of fear. More than one of them has become a
subject for his hideous experiments as a result of minor in-
fringements. He has a huge library of magical lore from which
to draw spells, so you will see that his power is not limited to
his manipulation of biology. If you should meet him in battle,
beware the little swagger stick he carries: it is really his hunting quetzal, a small flying dragon with poisonous fangs. ·He
keeps it inert because it is hard to control, but he can loose it
at a word. It is deadly, and it can find you almost anywhere."

"Could you get me into his library?" Piswyck asked. "If I
could find the spells he used to move this castle I'm sure I
could get us out of here, at the very least. My father has
taught me a little about magic, and—"

"Oh, but *he* didn't move the castle, Piswyck. The Countess
moved it for him," Miranda said.

Now Piswyck was really dumbfounded.

"Why on Earth would she do that for him?" he asked, half
rhetorically. "And how? She has the Appearing Egg, but the
Egg could never move something as massive as this castle.
And she has never been known as a magician. She must have
acquired great powers since I left Carsonne . . ." His voice
trailed off as a terrible thought stole over him like a shroud.

"My *father* . . ." he whispered. "My father would never do
a thing like this, a thing to unbalance the forces of nature so
thoroughly. But he has a great store of knowledge. What
might she have done to him to gain his aid in an enterprise
such as this?"

"Oh, Piswyck," said Miranda, and every trace of her dis-
traught condition vanished as she sought to meet his need. She
reached out her hand and put it on his arm, ignoring the dried
cow manure.

After a moment he snapped out of the numb terror he felt at the thought of the Countess doing nameless things to his father and asked: "Again, *why*, though, should she have done something this large for Smagdarone?"

"I'm afraid I know the answer to that," Miranda said, and she took her hand back and cast her eyes downward. "Uncle boasted of it to me, the way he boasts about everything. It seems the Countess had a vision from the Egg, and in that vision you were bound helplessly in his laboratory. Uncle Smaggy and I were still living in that chilly old Fort St. Catherine at that point, and he asked her to describe the laboratory in the vision, more for his amusement than anything else. She did, and he told her he had no such grandiose equipage as she had seen. Well, the Countess became quite serious and offered to have built for him just the laboratory she had seen, and set atop it any fortress he might choose for its defense. Uncle Smaggy laughed and named Neuschwanstein, and asked her the price."

She paused and shuddered a little.

"The price, Piswyck, was that he should accomplish the vision as she had seen it. You are to be bound in his laboratory as you were in the vision, and he may do with you as he pleases, so long as you do not escape and you do not die."

It did not make sense.

The Countess had reason to fear him, yes, for he was the son of her enemy and would no doubt be a great deal of trouble in the future. But, Piswyck was forced to admit, she did not have to be *that much* afraid of him. He was no more important than many of her other enemies. Why was she willing to expend so much energy to secure his defeat?

He wished that he knew more about the Egg.

It was a talked-about bauble, but the talk was shadowy and veined with speculation. It was known that it appeared in the world where it would, then disappeared. That if one were present, physically, when it appeared, it had the power to grant wishes within certain limits; it certainly did *not* have enough power to relocate Neuschwanstein. It was also known that the Countess somehow knew the whereabouts of the Egg's next appearance, and had harnessed that knowledge.

He had not known that the Egg could give visions; but if it could, a possibility suggested itself that might explain the Countess's concern. Suppose that the vision of him bound in the laboratory was but one of two, or perhaps more? Suppose this bondage was the alternative to some future terribly inimical to the Countess?

But what could he possibly do that would make her move a castle as big as a mountain to stop him?

"Miranda," he said, returning to the present problem, "Can you get me into your uncle's library?"

She shook her head in the negative.

"It's guarded with locks and spells," she said. "He's taken me into the laboratory to show me his work, but I've never been into the library. I've never even seen him entering it."

"Very well then, the laboratory?" Piswyck asked.

"More locks and spells, but I *have* seen him loose the spells that close it, and, if the locks are no more difficult to pick than the others around the castle, I will be able to help you with that."

Piswyck refrained from asking why his lady love advertised herself thus as an accomplished picklock because he was afraid that she would tell him, and that it would take too much time to tell.

"To the lab then," he said. "If nothing else, we may be able to slow down his plan for world conquest before he gets to take me prisoner. I do hope that he is an honorable man, or at least that he fears the Countess's wrath."

"Why is that, love?" Miranda asked, leading him off down the hall.

"Because of the clause in the contract requiring him to keep me alive."

They went down more hallways, and Piswyck had to admit that Neuschwanstein was certainly the most . . . well, the most whatever-it-was that he had ever seen.

They passed across the end of a throne room that was gorgeous almost beyond comprehension, certainly at a glance. It had a vaulted ceiling of blue (more gold stars); an enormous gilt chandelier; a mosaic floor with a design of fanciful animals and trees; a colonnade of red marble pillars surmounted by Roman arches inlaid with arabesque mosaics surmounted by another colonnade of what appeared to be lapis lazuli pillars (both sets of pillars were topped with gold chapitles) surmounted by more Roman arches with more mosaic arabesques surmounted by richly colored Biblical paintings on a field of gold leaf. It wasn't a very big throne room to contain so much, Piswyck thought as they hurried past, but perhaps there hadn't been a lot to do but look at the walls.

"What about the ring of jelly around the castle?" he asked as they hurried down a stairway leading to the cellars. "How does he control that? Is he also in rapport with that thing?"

"I don't think so," said Miranda. "When he rides out he uses some spells and the jelly divides for him. I'm always a little frightened for him when he rides between those high quivering walls of jelly."

"Frightened for *him?*" Piswyck asked.

"Well, he *is* my uncle, and my guardian. When my parents died it was Uncle Smagdarone who took me in. Grandmother Nea was still alive then, and she kept him and Uncle Kimowatt pretty well under control. Since her death, of course . . . Well, they never got along very well, and now Uncle Smagdarone has this foolish passion for ruling the world. He thinks things will be ever so much better if he can just get them organized and operating under a single code of ethics. He really has a noble heart, and the best of intentions. He just happens to be stark raving mad."

They reached the bottom and the stairwell opened into a tunnel that was quite new and faced with brick. It had a quaint Industrial Revolution look about it and it occurred to Piswyck that if Smagdarone ever gave up raising jellyfish and trying to conquer the world he could always install some orphan girls and open a shirt factory. They followed the tunnel a way, past several side doors, then came to the end and what was obviously the door to the laboratory. There were locks on both sides and arcane symbols chalked all over it.

"Let me see," said Miranda, and she stepped forward, raised her hands in an attitude of ritual address, and closed her eyes.

This part would take a subjective eternity, Piswyck realized, for she would have to use her mind to examine the spells as best she could and see if there was anything she could do, then do whatever she had seen her uncle do as well. It would be difficult for her and boring for him. He accepted that.

But by the time he was entertaining himself by making up folk tales about the mortar between the bricks he was also fidgeting like a eunuch at a beauty contest. Smagdarone knew he was in the castle, of that much he was certain. He must surely return, and soon!

Miranda spoke several words of power; but nothing happened. Perhaps she had not got the intonation right, he thought. Intonation was very important in the use of magic words. If the sound waves did not vibrate as an analog to the brain waves that would perform the substratum work of the spell, then nothing would happen. He continued to stand quietly, hoping she could find the keys to the spells. She continued to stand in her ritual stance, and as the minutes slid by she tried several more words of power.

In the end she gave up.

"I'm sorry, Piswyck," she said. "I thought perhaps I knew what he was doing when he opened this, but there must be something more to it."

"Let me try," he said, and he stepped forward, raised his hands, closed his eyes, and opened his mind to the traces of force that crisscrossed the doorway.

It took him only a minute to discover that part of the spells were encoded in Algol, a defunct language he did not speak.

"There's one more chance," he said, rubbing his eyes with his thumbs and forefingers. He walked up to the door and seized the handle. And found himself hurled backward against the brick wall opposite.

"What on earth did you do *that* for?" Miranda asked in astonishment as she helped him up.

"Because I was stupid," he replied. "Every once in a while a magician will just chalk the marks up and set the spells without activating them. It saves time and it usually works, unless someone comes along and tries to break in who doesn't know what all those marks are for."

"I don't think you'll catch Uncle Smaggy in that kind of slovenly habit," she said.

"Tell me," he asked, rubbing his hand where the bolt of energy had shot through it, "are there any air shafts?"

"Air shafts?" she asked.

"Ventilation shafts," he elaborated. "I've never heard of anybody building a burglar-proof enclosure that wasn't conveniently equipped with ventilation shafts big enough for a whole tactical squad to crawl through."

"Now that you mention it," she mused, "the air in the laboratory isn't nearly as stuffy as you'd think it would be. I suppose there must be some way for fresh air to get in, but as I've never thought about it I have no idea where the shafts would emerge."

"It would take too much time to look for them," Piswyck said. "Tell me about the balloon instead. Is it a hot-air balloon?"

"No," she said, "it's filled with hydrogen, which Uncle gets from the floaters. He hasn't been up for a while, which is why it's only partially inflated."

"Can you inflate it?" he asked.

"Heavens no! One of those floaters would eat me up like an hors d'oeuvre. Uncle says it's difficult even for him to get one to come down and let him drain the gas out of it. They don't recover their full buoyancy for a couple of days, but they do recover. He says it makes him feel like a vampire; even worse, that it's like sucking his own kin, because they do have some of his genetic material in them. That's how he established the rapport. In a way the floaters are just extensions of his own person."

"Not to mention his ego," Piswyck added wryly.

"Well, what *now?*" asked Miranda in exasperation.

"Let's try the library. You do know where it is, don't you?"

"Come on," Miranda said, and once again they were racing through the tunnel, up the stairs (her legs were not only beautiful, he noted from behind her, they were in *very* good shape, probably from running around in the castle) and then through the corridors of King Ludwig's toy palace. Dark and beautifully carved woods were everywhere, as were rich and gorgeous paintings, mostly depicting Germanic legends of old; though some of the legends seemed more pan-cultural than Germanic.

"That fellow in blue, with the body a bit too broad for his handsome face, is Tannhäuser," said Miranda, pausing briefly before a mural. "The naked queen is the goddess Venus, and those other naked ladies are her court. In this story she has been exiled to a lovely grotto because she refused to convert to Christianity, and she is now doomed to an eternity of absolute pleasure."

"He seems to be having trouble concentrating," said Piswyck, noting that the troubador's eyes were focused far away, and not on the voluptuous body of the goddess.

"One certainly wonders about his sexual orientation," said Miranda. "The ladies in the picture are all much better proportioned than he is, and clearly ready for action, but he just kneels there holding on to his silly little harp."

They hurried onward.

"I suppose the painter may have been conscious of King Ludwig's tastes. The poor king was very lonely, and perhaps the painter wanted to give him a companion, if only in a painting. They say Ludwig had very little idea of his own drives."

"Oh?" queried Piswyck. "Was Ludwig enamored of his own sex exclusively?"

"As far as anyone can tell, yes," said Miranda, heading down yet another corridor. "That's what all these paintings, this very castle, are about. Ludwig was deeply in love with the composer Richard Wagner, and built this place while inspired by one of his operas, *Lohengrin*. He had a fiancée named Sophie, whom he insisted on calling Elsa, after the heroine of the opera. It's a shame he was not able to marry her because he loved heroism and she was surely more of a hero than anyone else who ever entered his life. She died in a fire at a charity bazaar, steadfastly refusing to leave the burning building until all the girls in her booth had been rescued. Her body was so badly burned that only her dentist could identify her."

"Lifesaver doesn't like Wagner," said Piswyck. "He says the music is too thick, like beef stew. He prefers music like pastries. Cream puffs, or that dish where they roll up filet mignon in puff pastry. He says that's why he likes Mozart."

"Who's Lifesaver?" Miranda asked.

It came as a shock to Piswyck that Miranda didn't know about Lifesaver. Everybody else in Bermuda seemed to take it for granted that they were companions.

"Lifesaver is my particolored unicorn," he said, realizing that the beast should now be classed as his best friend.

"A *particolored* unicorn?" Miranda queried. "Isn't that a little gauche? Or garish? I would think that if you had decided to keep a unicorn you would have got a white one, with a golden horn and hooves. Or at the very oddest a black one, with perhaps a horn of ivory."

Her words cut Piswyck to the quick.

"He is neither garish *nor* gauche," he said hotly. "He is the most beautiful creature in the world! And you should hear him sing!"

"Well, there's no accounting for tastes," Miranda shrugged, and stopped. "Here's the library."

There were more locks and spells on the door of the library than there had been on the laboratory, but that was not surprising, considering Smagdarone's reputation as a magician.

Piswyck stepped forward gingerly, closed his eyes, and held up his hands in the same ritual gesture as before the laboratory. He put aside the veritable itching he felt to get within and calmed his mind so that he could examine the force patterns that underlay the elaborate designs sketched in blue chalk.

He recognized immediately the sigil for binding the demon Aznoterus, and another for invoking the protection of the god Anubis, Egyptian Guardian of the Way. Across the right of the doorway there was an eagle with lightning bolts for summoning the terrible damned spirits of the Joint Chiefs of Staff; but he was doubtful whether that one would work since the seas had been Sundered. Still, Bermuda was, in theory at least, less than a thousand kilometers from the States. On the other hand, what did *that* mean? No one had been able to sail across that short distance in centuries. If one tried, if one sailed west, one ended up sailing back east, and the journey could take varying amounts of time—some of them fatal.

From what he had learned from the Black Elves he made out two *vevers,* one for the Baron of Saturday and the other for—*Marinette!* That one sent shivers up his spine. Smagdarone was invoking some powerful stuff to keep his library locked!

He calmed his mind and reached out delicately, feeling the pattern of each set of symbols. There were a number he did not recognize, but, he knew, sometimes a magician would weave a program so complex that it would be far too much trouble to keep it in mind. In that event the magician would likely as not impress some kind of mnemonic amidst the desiderata of the actual evoking emblazonments. If there should be such a token here, and he could find it, and if it should be in a language he could decipher...

His mind touched something that might be what he wanted. He began to examine it.

"Oh!" came Miranda's cry, and Piswyck's eyes popped open, first with annoyance, then in alarm as he saw her pointing mutely down the length of the corridor. He looked to where she pointed, saw: then he looked quickly in the other direction to see if there was still a chance of escape.

There was not.

Across the lower end of the hall a line of guards with beautiful black skin and ruby-red livery stood, crossbows cocked and aimed directly at Piswyck. At the upper end was a similar

line with like weapons at ready, but in the center of that line
stood Smagdarone the Great.

Of course Piswyck remembered him. They had met but
once, at the very festival at which Piswyck had met and fallen
in love with Miranda. But the memory of his features was
vague in Piswyck's mind, and now Piswyck realized why.

Smagdarone was physically rather unprepossessing. He
was about Piswyck's height, much shorter than his brother
Kimowatt. His sandy-blond hair was cut cherubically in curly
locks that covered his ears. His eyebrows and mustache were
also sandy colored; his eyes blue, his nose unremarkable in a
round, mildly pleasant face. He was totally undistinguished.
He could have been mistaken for a grocer or a hostler or any
of a thousand other people in a crowd. His medium-sized
mouth had medium-sized lips, which curled sightly in a smile
he no doubt hoped would look cruel, or perhaps triumphant,
but which only looked like a smile.

His clothing set him apart.

Had Louis the Sun King gone bad he might have designed
such clothes. History could be grateful that he had not. To say
that they were ostentatious would have been a faux pas on the
side of understatement.

Smagdarone's feet were encased in shoes of black patent
leather, formed to imitate the claws of a griffin. Three gilded
toes clawed forward and one back. His calves were decently
displayed in black silk hose. His breeches were of red corded
silk appliquéd with a design of dragons' legs, with each foot
clutching a copper orb, which covered his knee caps. He wore
a long black vest (or perhaps it was more properly a waistcoat,
as it fell to mid-thigh) which was worked to resemble a
dragon's belly, the raised work in dark burgundy and the rib-
bing in metallic gold. Over this was a splendid long-skirted
coat of red corded silk, the skirting cut in bat's-wing scallops.
Embroidered on either front panel of the coat was half of a
winged black dragon edged entirely in gold bullion. It was
obvious that when the coat was fastened the design became a
two-headed dragon. The dragon's tail curved down and
around the skirting of the coat to double back on itself in an
intricate interlace. The cuffs of the coat were long and black
and cut like dragons' wings, and at the sleeve and throat there
were falls of black chiffon embroidered with gold so that they
almost looked like lace. On his head Smagdarone wore a tri-

corn hat of red corded silk, the edges of which were cut like
bat wings and edged in black ostrich plume.

Under his arm he carried a swagger stick in the form of a
small dragon with wings oddly placed just behind the head. It
looked like dark wood worked with gold, but Piswyck remembered Miranda's warning and carefully noted the quies-
cent hunting quetzal.

"Welcome to my house," Smagdarone said in a medium-
strength tenor voice that had no real distinguishing character-
istics. That he quoted *Dracula* did not escape Piswyck's
notice.

"Good morning!" Piswyck said brightly. "Or is it already
afternoon?"

"I see that you have made my brother's acquaintance,"
Smagdarone continued. "I am pleased to see that someone has
at last found a use for those infernal skeletons he grows."

"Oh, my glider! Well, yes sir, it did seem foolish to mount
yet another one of them on his wall."

"I approve!" said Smagdarone. "If my brother had half that
much imagination and daring we might be better friends. It is
also nice to know that my niece seeks more in a man than a
pretty face."

"Uncle Smaggy!" Miranda exclaimed.

"I have asked you *not* to use that diminutive." The great
man winced.

"Oh, I *am* sorry, Uncle," Miranda said contritely. "I was
just so surprised by what you said! Does that mean that you
now approve of Piswyck?"

"It means," said Smagdarone, "that I approve of your
choice of him. He seems a fine young man, well set up,
good-looking, and clearly clever to have braved so many
dangers and have solved so many problems in order to be
united with you. I only regret that you will not be able to take
advantage of my approval, as he will be otherwise occupied.
Guards, if you would please be so good as to bring him
along?"

Smagdarone turned to his left and vanished at the corner of
the hall. The four guards at the opposite end of the hall
marched to form a square around Piswyck, carefully aiming
their crossbows at delicate but nonvital parts of his anatomy.

"Oh, *Uncle!*" Miranda cried, and ran to chase after Smagdarone.

Once again they threaded the maze of halls and descended to the catacombs under the castle, this time by a different flight of stairs. Their destination, to Piswyck's surprise, was not the laboratory but a spacious chamber with high walls, filled almost entirely by a swimming pool of Olympic length. There was no doubt that it was an Olympic pool because high up in the left and right walls, which rose up smoothly from the bottom of the pool with no intervening deck, there were niches with white marble statues of the Twelve of Olympus.

To the left of the entrance to the chamber was an elaborate sculpture in the shape of a white marble swan from whose beak spurted a needle spray. The spray ended in a large white marble scallop shell, so Piswyck assumed this to be the shower. At the far end of the pool the cavern was carved out like a nave, with a little white marble dais on which rested an assortment of white-painted rattan lawn furniture with cloth pillows in green-and-white stripes. There was a silver dinner service set out on the small round table, complete with silver warmer dome and coffeepot.

Piswyck had no doubt that the orange globe floating in the air over the dais provided tanning rays as well as artificial sunlight, and wondered just what kind of thing it was. Certainly magical, for no piece of technology that elegant would function.

There were no doors in the nave, so clearly the only way to reach the other end of the pool was to swim. Not a comfortable prospect, considering that the lane dividers in the pool were six giant red seasnakes, lying rigidly in the water from end to end.

"Strip!" said Smagdarone, politely but firmly.

"Oh, *Uncle!*" said Miranda, and she stamped her pretty little foot again and turned her back modestly while Piswyck pulled off the stained Elfsuit.

"Now if you would be so good as to use the shower? We can't have the pool water polluted," Smagdarone said reasonably.

Piswyck stepped under the shower and was pleased to find it of tepid temperature. There was a gilded soap dish with lavender-scented soap and he set about washing himself, happy that whatever was to come, he would not have to endure it covered with cow manure.

"Uncle, I *love* him," Miranda said persuasively. "Doesn't that count for anything?"

"Well, of course it does, my dear," said Smagdarone. "It just doesn't count for enough. I have made my arrangement with the Countess, and I am a man of honor. One can always find someone else to love, Miranda, but one cannot always erase the stain of a welshed deal. Would you hurry with that shower, young Marquis? I've had a very trying day."

"Sorry," said Piswyck, rinsing the soap off quickly and stepping out of the shell onto the marble floor. "I've had a pretty difficult day myself."

"I understand your discomfort," said Smagdarone. "Let me assure you that you won't have to endure it for much longer. Now please get into the water and swim to the other end of the pool."

Piswyck glanced at the seasnakes, then at the guards with their crossbows. Smagdarone might be planning to have him die in the water and use some sophistry to get out of his contract, but Piswyck doubted it. If the Countess was able to move a castle, she was a formidable enemy, even for Smagdarone the Great. He stepped off the edge of the pool and plunged in, feeling the cool water close over his head, opening his eyes in the wonderful semigreen aquatic light; then stretching out and starting his stroke. Even if Smagdarone unbound the spell that held the seasnakes, venom in such quantities must surely be a quick, if painful, death.

Piswyck had always liked swimming even more than tumbling. He thought, as he moved his arms and legs in an easy rhythm, that if one could combine the freedom from gravity, the gentle support of the water, that one got from swimming with the sense of boundless space and freedom that one got from hang gliding, one would have achieved an ideal sport to pleasure the human spirit. Swimming was soft, primally sensual as the water enwrapped the body intimately, caressing it; but it forced the mind in on itself. There was not much of a horizon, so the mind made its own horizons. That made swimming an ideal meditative sport. It required the body and mind to act in perfect coordination, and, once the form was achieved, it induced in one that restful alpha state so conducive to centering.

Hang gliding, on the other hand, offered *all* horizons, and in three dimensions. One could almost see forever. But the mind had to be focused on the environment lest a mistake prove fatal. The bonds of the harness helped to keep one aware and provided sensory stimulation at positive odds with the sensuality of the wind pouring past and the glory of the view. If swimming was nearly totally interior, then hang gliding was nearly totally exterior; yet curiously, it too led (because of the intensity of focus that was required) to that alpha state and to centering.

There must be some magical and philosophical significance to that, Piswyck thought as he reached the far end of the pool, grabbed the marble lip, and hoisted himself up out of the water.

"You will find towels on the back of the chaise longue," Smagdarone called to him.

Piswyck got the towels and began drying himself off, turning as he did to face his captor. At that moment Smagdarone made a gesture, clapped his hands together, and the six giant seasnakes softened and started to swim. Piswyck backed away from the water's edge.

"You needn't be afraid of my little pets," Smagdarone said cheerfully. "So long as you stay out of the water they will leave you alone. There is a pleasant little supper prepared for you under that silver dome, and you will find blankets there in case you feel chilly; though I doubt that you will, it's quite warm in here. You will spend a pleasant enough night, and tomorrow I will have things prepared to receive you in the laboratory."

"Uncle!" Miranda nearly screamed. "You *cannot* use Piswyck for your experiments!"

"My dear child," said the wizard, not displaying the least offense at her manner, "of course I can. And I shall. The Countess has seen it in a vision. Now, I know that you will be angry with me, and that you will probably stalk around the castle for weeks, sulking and not talking to me. But in the end you will get over it. Hearts mend much more quickly than you think. Remember Wolff's Law? Remember how I cut open that salamander and sliced his little heart in half, then sewed him up again? Healed in only four hours! Yours will not heal so quickly: Wolff's Law, you know; but it *will* heal. Even if you never forgive me, in the end you will treat me with respect, and eventually affection, and that lack of forgiveness in this one small matter will be overshadowed by the love you will feel. Now run along, my dear, up to the dining room. We shall dine on exactly the same delicious meal that Piswyck is having, and everything will be fine. Run along now!"

Miranda stood for a moment in fury, then deliberately

turned and threw Piswyck a kiss, perhaps as much in defiance
of her uncle as out of love for him. Then she stormed out.
Smagdarone listened for a few minutes, until her footsteps
died away, then signaled to one of the guards. The guard left
the room to return a moment later with an ornately carved
rosewood chair, which he set down, facing the pool. Smagdarone sat in the chair and crossed his legs.

"Piswyck," the wizard said, "when you sent word that you
wanted Miranda's hand in marriage I turned you down. I had
in mind for her something a little better than a minor marquis
in Carsonne. You would have been wise to take my refusal
and seek another, but you did not. As it has turned out, your
constancy has been good for me, although bad for you. I am
sure Miranda has told you the whole of my bargain with the
Countess; she seemed at great pains to communicate that information to you in this letter. . ." He reached into a pocket in
his waistcoat and pulled out the sweat-stained, long-missing
missive. "And whether or not you have read it, I am sure you
arc all fillcd in on thc facts. Do I assume correctly?"

"I believe so," said Piswyck. "Although I hope that Miranda has not been wrong about your having to keep me alive."

Smagdarone gave an effusive little chuckle.

"No, my boy, she was quite correct about that. I may not
kill a single cell of your body. The Countess was quite explicit
about that. She does not want any taint of your blood upon her
dainty hands, heavens no! But neither may I allow you to
escape! Now doesn't that put me in a pretty predicament? Do
you have any idea how hard it is to guarantee that a prisoner
will *never* escape? Why, Fate herself sits up nights trying to
devise new means to escape from perfect prisons! Yet I *have*
devised a means to meet all of the criteria of the contract."

Piswyck wasn't exactly dying to hear what awaited him,
yet his curiosity was piqued.

"The Countess saw you bound in my laboratory. And why
should you be there? Why, as a subject for my experiments, of
course. And what experiments might I perform upon you?
What experiments that would not kill a single cell of your
body? Why, experiments in tissue culture, of course! I will not
have to kill any of your cells to separate them, now will I
Piswyck? In fact, I can make you relatively immortal, albeit in
pieces. Although you will not be aware of the fact, you will be
a part of my grand conquest of the world, perhaps a stone in
the very foundation of the new world culture. I don't know

yet, because I haven't examined your germ plasm, but you seem to me to be in good condition, and I don't really foresee having to reject any of you for genetic reasons, do you?"

Piswyck sought desperately in his memory for any story or tradition that would link him with congenital family madness. If only his mother had been a nymphomaniac! (As she'd died at his birth, she very well might have been for all he knew.)

"I promise that I will do well by you, Piswyck," Smagdarone continued. "I've already worked miracles. The floaters were just various species of jellyfish when I began. Some had rudimentary eyes, rudimentary sensory cilia; but now they can almost hear, and *see* fairly well, although I expect in the near future to get a sharper picture through finer tuning of the process. Oh, Piswyck, I have just begun, and you shall be a part, or rather *parts,* of it all! Doesn't it make you feel proud?"

Piswyck refrained from answering this last rhetorical question by main force.

"I have even considered that when my technique becomes flawless I might clone you, and give Miranda at least the simulacrum of the young man she desires. But I fear that by the time I can do that she will probably have forgotten all about you, and be madly in love with someone else. Don't let that discourage you, my boy, for I fear they are all, all like that eventually. *Così fan tutte,* as Mozart would have said."

Piswyck was glad to hear, at least, that Smagdarone was not a *total* degenerate.

"Pardon me, sir," Piswyck said when Smagdarone paused, "but what will the Priest-Kings of Geneva do when they find that you are performing these highly forbidden experiments? They have many years of experience in these matters, after all, while you are having to work out the whole history and practice on your own."

The joviality left Smagdarone's eyes and he stood slowly. His head tilted to one side, a gesture that was oddly familiar and yet chillingly alien the way he did it.

"The Priest-Kings of Geneva will give me anything I ask," Smagdarone said quietly, "when my armada of floaters descends from the sky and eats every man, woman, and child in the areas that grow their food."

The wizard said no more but left quietly. The servant took the chair after him and all the guards filed out behind the two of them, leaving Piswyck alone at the other end of a pool full of giant red seasnakes.

He sighed and sat down on one of the white wicker chairs. For a few moments he contemplated death by slow and tedious dismemberment. Then he corrected himself: not death, but piecemeal immortality. Should there be any slimmer comfort he could not imagine it!

He stared into space for a while, then tried to turn off his mind so that his body would stop producing the kind of hormones that were upsetting his stomach. Eventually he realized that his eyes were following the graceful movements of the seasnakes as they swam back and forth in the pool.

He could always go for a swim, he thought. Would that invalidate the bargain between Smagdarone and the Countess? Could he, by aquatic suicide, turn the Countess against the wizard and perhaps avert airborne disaster of an invertebrate kind? He doubted it. The Countess was only concerned with keeping his blood off *her* hands. If he killed himself, however heroically, she was still in the clear. He could not imagine her carrying ethics to an inconvenient extreme. No, diving and dying would not stop Smagdarone's heinous hijinks.

He pulled his eyes away from the seasnakes and surveyed the table. He wasn't really hungry, considering what Smagdarone had just told him. But . . .

He lifted the silver dome that kept the meal warm.

Broccoli with white sauce, onions with cream sauce, and little triangles of white bread, toasted and covered with something unidentifiable. He poked a fork at the toast and tasted. *Welsh rabbit.* He thought back to the tale of the English king hunting in Wales who had been served cheese melted on bread and told it was Welsh rabbit because the king had forbidden the Welsh to hunt rabbits in his forest. He poured some wine into a silver goblet and tasted it. *Pink Chablis!*

This—*this*—was the meal that Smagdarone was even now sharing with Miranda in the dining room?

Now Piswyck *knew* that he was up against a villain!

He replaced the silver dome and stood, stretching his muscles for the pleasure of it. They might not be connected to one another for long, so he had *better* enjoy them while he had the chance. At the other end of the pool, lying on the white marble where Smagdarone had dropped it, was Miranda's letter.

He raised his eyes in frustration to the ceiling, ready to cry out in rage. Then he noted more consciously what he had only noted peripherally before.

Along the upper portions of the walls of the chamber were

niches containing white marble statues of the Twelve of Olympus. That they were not painted in a semblance of life told Piswyck that Smagdarone had not placed them there as objects of worship but as mere classical decorations.

That did not make any difference. *Wherever* an image of any deity was raised, *there* was its temple; and there were some gods who didn't even require that much. Piswyck ran his eyes along the figures rapidly, wondering to which one he should pray, since praying seemed the most likely way to get out of his current predicament.

And besides, it would take his mind off the dreadful supper that waited.

He looked first to Zeus. Zeus was the archetype one invoked for power: the power of government, of law, and ideas, structures, and energies. He was the progenitor of abstract power, but he did not rule the physical world per se. That was the business of Hera, his wife. She had got a bad reputation during the dark ages of monotheism, but actually she was a good goddess to worship, for she ruled the material aspects of those things that Zeus ruled in the abstract. That was why their eternal yin-yang argument raged. One could institutionalize lust in marriage, but one could not bridle it and make it stay there.

Then there was Athena, the sympathetic daughter who sprang full blown from Zeus' mind; no doubt in answer to his desire for a woman who could *understand* as well as rule. She served, in a way, as a more temperate version of Ares, that most misunderstood of deities. He was either the most beautiful or the most terrible of the Twelve, and his mystery was that of the pure male energy that could build cities or tear them down. (If only, Piswyck thought, he could know the *Serenity Prayer!*) And Aphrodite, the pure female energy. She, too, could be destructive or creative. She was so much more than sex and beauty; and yet, she usually caused her worshippers to forget that she was.

Hephaestus was there, poor god deformed in body and spirit, the divine cuckold who yet gave birth to all the comforts of civilization and the Age of Science, and whose inability to love more his loves than his machines might be a paradigm for humankind before the Sundering; and Demeter, the mother of Persephone, who brought springtime and rebirth. Demeter could be a fearful goddess, for in her resided the rage of the mother protecting her child, the madness of the mother who loses her child. Opposite her was Poseidon, over whose realm Piswyck and Lifesaver had just sailed; but Poseidon was also called Earthshaker, master of earthquakes, god of horses. He was like unto Zeus in power, but like Hera his kingdom was physical manifestation.

Dionysos was there, but Piswyck shied away from calling upon him. Passion, ecstasy, death, and rebirth were Dionysos' realm, and all those seemed already much too present in his life, at least for the moment.

The figure of Artemis was made so that she was facing him directly, and in her proud face he found a bit of courage. It was to Artemis that young girls prayed, as young boys prayed to her brother Apollo. It was with Apollo that boys learned sports and poetry and music and dancing. With Artemis the girls learned sports and poetry and music and hunting. Both were archers, both shot straight to the heart of any matter. They helped to clarify goals. And Apollo it was who knew the mind of Zeus. He was the god of prophecy. Perhaps, Piswyck thought, a prayer to Apollo would bring a dream with an answer to his current dilemma.

But then his eyes fell upon Hermes, to whom he had prayed that very morning for success in the air. God of magicians, actors, and thieves. Dream walker, messenger of the gods, the psychopomp who conducted one beyond the grave. Hermes was a god of wisdom. He had been called thrice-great since ancient (really ancient!) times. He was a trickster, guardian of the crossroads; but he was the helper, the stranger who saved you along the way.

Piswyck took a deep breath and held his hands out before him, palms up, in the ancient (really ancient!) gesture of prayer.

"Hermes, and all you Great Gods," he prayed. "Hear me! I am in an *awful* lot of trouble!"

7

Some Aspics of Magic

The prayer did not protect Piswyck from broccoli with white sauce (it was boiled!) but it did calm his mind enough to let him get some sleep. Whether it was an answer to his prayer that awoke him or merely the clearing of his thoughts, he did not know; but he made a quick prayer of thanksgiving to Apollo, to Hermes, and to the rest, then drank the still-warm coffee from the silver pot and began to put things together in his mind.

Smagdarone might be meticulous in his magical workings, as Miranda said, but he was sloppy in some other things. He had left Miranda's letter lying on the floor where he had dropped it. He had also left Piswyck's Elfsuit lying where Piswyck had discarded it before his shower. Presumably a servant was delegated to clean up such things, but for the moment Piswyck was glad the servant had not. The Elfsuit, caked with cow manure, contained two things that it was important Smagdarone should not confiscate: the bronze dagger Londea had given to him, and the little silk purse, worn as a scapular and thus caked to the front of the suit, containing the vial of Elfire.

Now that the fog of exhaustion had dissipated from his mind Piswyck could think about the knowledge he had acquired in his travels, and he knew what he must do next. Bahamfalme had taught him a spell for turning a dogfish into what appeared to be a wooden staff. At the time he had considered the spell mere prestidigitation, but now it might be a

matter of life or death. If it would stiffen a dogfish into the
semblance of wood, he reasoned, there was a good chance
that it could stiffen giant seasnakes back into lane dividers.

He moved to a position in the middle of the dais and lowered his left hand, opening his fingers toward the floor and
sensing through them whether or not the energy of the Earth
was available. If Smagdarone had warded beneath the castle . . .

The familiar tingle came to his fingertips. The wizard had
not warded; he probably made use of that energy himself,
Piswyck thought.

He raised his right hand in the ritual gesture Bahamfalme
had taught him. He summoned energy up from the Earth,
modulated it through his own consciousness, changed it, and
let the resultant force flow down his arm. He visualized it as a
tight bolt of clear purple light. He aimed two fingers at one of
the seasnakes and spoke the ancient African words that he had
learned, letting the invisible purple light shoot straight from
his fingers to the serpent.

When he had done this with Bahamfalme's dogfish the
sensation had been like getting a bite on the end of his fishing
line. A little pull as the dogfish resisted; a little tug as he
brought the creature under control; and then it had been as
wood.

With the giant seasnake it was different. It was as if he had
hooked a great green shark. His whole body was jerked forward by the force of resistance. He had to plant his feet wide
to keep from being yanked into the deadly swimming pool.
The snake cast back and forth, writhing against the force that
sought to bind it, darting its eyes to see what so disturbed it,
hoping for a glimpse of something at which to strike.

Piswyck leaned back, spread the fingers of his left hand
wide, holding them just below crotch level. He drew hard on
the Earth, sucked energy up and channeled it. He pictured the
words of the spell written on the air in the Elvish script, letters
of purple fire a meter high.

Slowly the snake came under his control. Fighting every
centimeter, it moved to its place in the pool, end to end, facing away from Piswyck, still bewildered by what was happening to it but finally stilled. Piswyck moved his right hand in
the gesture he thought of as "tying the knot" and broke the
contact. He flexed the fingers of his left hand, cutting the flow
of energy from the Earth. The snake still struggled, still

wiggled back and forth a minute amount, but it was under control.

He sagged.

This was exhausting, and he still had five snakes to go!

He sorted through his memories to find the technique for increasing his personal strength, as opposed to drawing energy in for use. There was a little dance . . . Oh yes. He hummed a couple of bars to get the tune right, then began the step, turning, shifting side to side, singing the words quietly as he danced. After a moment he felt the strength come, like sunlight soaking into his skin; but it came from inside, not outside. He remembered Bahamfalme's deep, rich voice saying: "You call upon the soul of the sun, not upon his body. That is how it is!"

When he felt warm enough he addressed the stiffening of the second snake, and after that the third. It was a debilitating process, and each time he had to do the little dance for a longer while in order to get strong again. But eventually it was done and the swimming pool looked much like any other save that its lane dividers were red, and that they quivered slightly with malice.

He knew that the spells, as he had done them, were far from perfect; so he made a practical test of his work. The snakes had their heads all toward the far end of the pool, so the first experiment seemed safe enough. He knelt and put his hand in the water, then stirred it gently. The snakes continued to strain, but that was all. Piswyck stirred the water a little more violently. Still they did not break ranks.

He got one of the chairs and put its legs in the water and sloshed it back and forth. This disturbed the snakes a bit more and they twisted, but still the force held them. Finally he got the last piece of boiled broccoli with white sauce from his plate, drew his arm back, and hurled it the length of the pool. It hit the water with a splash and in an instant was in the fanged mouth of a seasnake, who promptly spat it out.

But the snake only moved quickly to bite and was back in line almost as quickly. The spell was holding, even though there were limitations. This caused Piswyck to formulate a theorem, which he fervently hoped to be correct. He took the chair and sloshed it very hard and very suddenly and two of the snakes jerked against their bonds. When the sloshing stopped, they calmed.

Well, then. It seemed that the snakes were prompted to

strike by sudden movements, not merely by the presence of something in the water. All he would have to do was swim the length of the pool with utmost slowness, disturbing the water not at all, and the snakes would be able to avoid striking him.

It was a slim hope, but it was a better one than being sliced up and distributed as sweetmeats in man-eating aspics.

He ate what was left of the previous night's meal (creamed onions and limp, cheese-soaked toast), then danced some more to get his strength up. He knew it was a bad idea to eat before swimming, but he thought cramps would be easier to take than amputations, and he didn't know when he might get to eat again. He did a couple of minutes of slow, deep breathing; then he lowered himself slowly, in very tiny increments, into the cool water of the center lane.

He focused his thoughts on Hermes and Apollo: Hermes to protect him as he made his journey across the pool, Apollo to give him the perfection of form it would take to swim slowly and silently. He stretched out carefully in the water and arched his back so that his buttocks and legs rose to the surface; then he lifted his left arm carefully up and out of the water, bending his elbow, letting the water drain off it quietly, and stretched his right arm out before him. He flattened his right hand into a paddle, bent his right elbow, and began to pull backward on the water as his left arm stretched up and forward.

He remembered thinking many times, how foolish it was that his swimming coach placed such emphasis on training for form. It had always seemed to him that one's main goal was moving through water fast. Now he was grateful for all the slow—infinitely slow—work he'd been forced to put in. Water ballet had seemed silly to him in those days of youth; now he blessed the memory of the little shrine to Saint Esther Williams that stood before the entrance of his coach's house.

To either side of him he felt the presence of the seasnakes, testing, struggling, dimly aware of his presence but not impelled to action by it. He felt himself sweat, felt the sweat washed away by his passage through the water. His forward hand dipped, slowly knifed into the water, pulled backward. His legs moved up and down, not really kicking, not aiding in his progress, but helping to eliminate drag on his body by their movement. When his face came up out of the water he breathed lightly, not gulping the air in. When it submerged he did not blow out his breath but let tiny bubbles trickle from the corners of his lips. He was not getting adequate oxygen, but that could be remedied if he made it out of the pool alive.

His lungs were aching to dispel *more* carbon dioxide when his hand finally touched the marble lip of the pool, and he stopped. Now was the most dangerous moment, the moment when he was closest to their mouths. Deadly, those mouths curved with the cold smile of the serpent, only awaiting the stimulus of a little splash, a sudden gasp. Piswyck let all the air out of his lungs very slowly, then took in a fresh breath with equally painful slowness.

Now he must get *out* of the pool.

He remembered the great care with which he had come up out of the water to battle the troll when they'd rescued Bethzda. He hoped that he could repeat his performance now. But this was not a matter of walking up a sandy silted bank. He had to rise vertically out of the water, and do it without sloshing. He slid his hands forward, spread his fingers to see if there was any roughness to the marble that would give him friction. There was a little, but he feared not enough. It would have to be his muscles that raised him.

He put his weight on his elbows and began to lift with his shoulders, the muscles at the sides of his chest. His pectorals helped a little, but he had no purchase for using the muscles that one normally used to lift. He felt the sword wound in his shoulder strain. He got his chest above the level of the water, but now what? He shifted his weight slowly to his left elbow, felt the sword wound like a knife, then put his right palm flat on the marble. His biceps were useless (he'd always been proud of them) and his triceps and the muscles behind his shoulders were not developed for this exercise; still, he made them work, strained them, and lifted himself carefully, slowly up in the unnatural posture. When he could lock his elbow to hold himself he moved the other arm up, equalized the strain by putting that hand flat, then repositioned the right arm. Now to get his lower half out of the water!

With slowness as great as what he'd used before, he brought his right knee up, over the lip, then his left. This stretched his groin and he hoped fervently that he didn't get a hernia out of the effort. When he finally had nothing but his feet in the water, he bent forward, touched his head to the ground, and with his best style at tumbling did a forward somersault that yanked his feet up and away and threw him flat on his back. He heard the water splash where the snakes snapped, and lay perfectly still until it calmed. Then he climbed wearily to his feet, feeling his body strained as it had not been since he'd learned to do Elvish dances. He wished that Londea were here to pound him!

But, for the moment, he was on his own.

His next move was rude, but he had no desire to travel either naked or covered in manure. He washed his Elfsuit in the swan fountain, squeezed it out, and put it on wet. He also washed the dagger and the silk pouch with the Elfire and trucked them both inside his tunic. The manure began to clog the drain and he considered cleaning it out; but if Smagdarone had to worry about the plumbing maybe he wouldn't be quite so efficient in his hunt.

Piswyck took the Elfire out for a moment, sang the requisite bit of song to it, stuffed it back in, next to his heart, then addressed the seasnakes again. It would be better if Smagdarone wondered just how he got out rather than knowing that he had the ability to stiffen serpents. Piswyck uttered the counterspell and released them; then, as the dirty water from the fountain overflowed and began to trickle across the floor, he hurried out of the pool hall.

He had no idea how long he'd slept so he had no idea what time it was. Yet even if it were late at night, or the early hours of the morning, it did seem odd to him that there were no guards posted. Was Smagdarone so confident as all that? Where were the servants? In his own castle his father had ordered the servants so that they did all the cleaning and polishing during the hours of sleep. It cost him a little more in candles and lamp oil, but it was a great convenience to both the residents and the staff never to have to come into conflict over the use or occupation of a room.

He heard music. It was distant, but it was clearly music and not an illusion. There was a string orchestra, albeit small, and a tenor voice. He followed the sound, ever cautious, until he found himself peering in from the passage past small white pillars topped with gold.

There was a concert in progress.

The glass windows across the hall showed it to be dark outside. Within, all was opulence and warm light. Gilded chandeliers with many candles hung from the ceiling, massive torchiers blazed with many more candles. The room was elaborately paneled and painted, its parqueted floors laid with purple carpets. Chairs had been set up in neat rows with a center aisle, and what must surely be the whole staff of Neuschwanstein sat in rapt attention, the Black people on one side of the aisle, the White people on the other; a most curious arrangement, Piswyck thought, in a castle devoted to genetic admixture.

At the front of the audience, in the middle and slightly ahead of the first full row, Miranda sat looking uncomfortable in an electric-blue gown of cut velvet.

At the head of the hall, up four steps; at the center of a line of four darkly polished marble pillars; before a cheerful mural of green woods and large rocks; Smagdarone stood, dressed in the gear of an old Germanic knight. His surcoat was electric blue (no doubt to match Miranda's dress; or probably the other way around); he wore some pieces of silver plate-armor; and he carried a helm of silver under his arm, crested with swans' wings. Though Piswyck was not an admirer of Wagner (one did not get to see those huge and costly operas in a little country like Carsonne) he was not so illiterate as to avoid recognizing Lohengrin.

The tenor voice was Smagdarone's, a voice not well suited to Wagner. Weak in the upper range, edgy in the lower, but who was going to criticize him? Certainly not *this* audience!

The piece came to an end and everyone applauded enthusiastically. Piswyck flattened himself against the wall.

"Thank you, thank you," Smagdarone said as the applause died down. "And now, also from Act One, *Zum Kamps für eine Magd zu stehn.*"

Some instinct deep inside told Piswyck that Smagdarone was planning to sing the whole opera, or at least all the major parts assigned to the lead tenor. If that should be the case, he would have plenty of time to explore the castle and accomplish various deeds.

He left the concert and made his way through the halls back toward the library. The encoding of the spells on the door of the laboratory had been in Algol, but in the brief look he'd got at the library door, just before Smagdarone and his troops had captured him, he had seen a mnemonic in Latin, a language with which he had a nodding acquaintance. Though most contemporary magicians chose to work in defunct computer languages (they were good for nothing else since the Sundering, but ideally suited to that) the Marquis Oswyck had been at great pains to give his son a grounding in the sweep and grandeur of human history, and to give him as well a sense of the history of science (as it had risen and as it had fallen) and of magic.

Piswyck arrived at the library door with no difficulty. Neuschwanstein was not so large or complex a place as it had seemed at first, and he was beginning to find his way about in it. He stood facing the door, calmed his body, slowed his breathing, closed his eyes; and with his mind's eye looked over the glittering traces of force that crisscrossed the portal.

He found the mnemonic readily, which did not surprise him, but he *was* surprised at how easily he was able to decipher it. His Latin had not been that good in school. Was it possible that something had happened to his consciousness because of his study of the Elvish magic? It was well known that patterning governed one's ability to process data; perhaps he had been somewhat repatterned.

He manipulated the symbols just the way the token indicated that he should, and the spells fell away. Now to the locks. Just in case, he reached out and tried the handle of the door, and . . . it opened.

Miranda did not know her uncle as well as she thought she did!

Piswyck thanked Hermes in his aspect as patron of pickpockets and thieves, then went into the library and closed the door behind him.

Orange light spilled from another of the sun globes that Smagdarone seemed to favor. In contrast to the rest of the castle, the library was a mess, with books piled everywhere. Shelves of books reached from floor to ceiling, tables were stacked with them, pedestals held single volumes open to specific pages; there were boxes full of books and even piles of them on the floor. The smell of old books was thicker than the smell of old dust and the air was heavy with both. The room was a warren of psychic cobwebs. How was Smagdarone able to concentrate in such a place?

Directly under the orange globe was a library table with the traditional human skull and such devices as one might use for calculating horoscopes and tides. The table had legs carved like gargoyles and it made Piswyck feel a little homesick. He went to it to see what Smagdarone had most recently been perusing.

There was a large volume on Atlantic weather patterns. He glanced quickly through it to see what kind of things he might encounter on his way home. It didn't look promising because the hurricane season was approaching. Just what he needed! But at least they blew in the right direction. There was also a picture book called *Jazz Greats of the 1950s,* a lavishly illustrated Japanese cookbook (wasted on Smaggy if last night's supper was any indication of the man's tastes), and a tourist guide to Paris. What use *that* might be, Piswyck could not imagine, considering that Paris had sunk beneath the waves so long ago. Under a thick volume criticizing the writings of Henry James he found something he considered of value: a slim book of spells for controlling the weather. Although he knew a certain amount about that subject he could always learn more; and it were better to abduct such knowledge from Smagdarone's ken, given the chance, and thereby perhaps balance forces in the one area where he had some expertise, than to leave the volume where the wizard could use it against him. He put it inside his tunic.

He went to the shelves next, hoping to find a selection of easy-to-memorize spells to be used in magical battles. There were several, but most of them he'd seen in his father's library, and none of them were encoded in systems with which he'd had experience. He felt much like a lute player confronted with keyboard tablature. It could be transcribed, but not without much more time than was at his disposal.

Farther along the shelves he found a treatise on the significance of color in psychological attitude by the long-discredited Professor Pinsley, a handwritten monograph on the sex life of a common parasite in the intestines of the Antarctic flea, and an ancient telephone directory (in English and Arabic) for the city of Mecca. Smagdarone was nothing if not eclectic!

He moved to one of the pedestals and looked at the tome displayed there. It was a grimoire dealing with shape-changing, and Piswyck could not resist the urge to page through it, though why it should be thus set out he could not fathom; was Neuschwanstein beset by werewolves? He quickly found the answer, on a page marked by a stem of dried and pressed nightshade: a spell for causing transmogrified beings to return to their original forms, and in the margin a series of copious notations, including spells that formed a palindrome when paired with the one printed. He quickly memorized the central incantation, noting the mudhral positionings and trying them with his hand above the page, though not actually speaking the words.

It was while thus engaged that he noted a buzzing in the air, a sound like that of a hummingbird hovering. He froze, then slowly raised his eyes, moving no other muscle.

Across the room was the hunting quetzal, its ruby eyes fixed on him, its serpent tail hanging down and thrashing at the tip, not unlike the way a housecat would thrash its tail. Its gold wings were a blur just behind its head, and as he watched it opened its mouth to reveal tiny fangs like those of a cobra.

It moved, arrowing across the room toward him.

But Piswyck's hand was in position. He moved two fingers, uttered the Elfspell he had already used five times that day, and an invisible purple ray hit the quetzal between the eyes. It stiffened into a rod even as it flew, and as its wings were not meant for gliding its angle of descent was extreme. Its body struck the edge of the pedestal in front of Piswyck and it broke in half, clattering to the floor.

Piswyck licked his lips with the tip of his tongue and exhaled. Just *why* did it have to be snakes? Couldn't Smagdarone have chosen cats or birds or something else for his familiars?

The door of the library was still closed. It was possible that the quetzal had tracked him and entered through ventilation ducts, but the air in the library was so stale that he doubted that. It was far more likely that Smagdarone had left the hunting quetzal to guard the library. And against whom? Why, a possibly escaping Piswyck, that was whom! A Piswyck who could get through the spells on the door, but who would have had a difficult time getting in if the locks had not been left open.

It would certainly be a neat trap, he thought. The Countess would be absolved of any guilt; she had written into the bargain that he was not to be killed. Smagdarone would be absolved; he had left his prisoner secure and his library guarded, two totally unrelated circumstances. Piswyck shook his head at the depths of intellectual dishonesty to which people were willing to descend; then he continued to search the library.

Though it was filled with lore, there was not much that he could use. He was not able to resist a green leather-bound compendium of the complete works of William Shakespeare, hand-tooled with elaborate gold interlace (he added it to the book of weather spells inside his tunic) because it had been left negligently on the floor. It was only when he found a

cabinet containing book-binding materials that he got an idea
of what to do next.

In with the binding press, the long needles, the flats of
leather, and the waxed linen thread there was a big pot of
glue. He fetched the two halves of the broken hunting quetzal
and used the glue to put it back together, then set it carefully
on the library table. Smagdarone would certainly wonder why
his quetzal had gone stiff on him; let him be more upset that
the quetzal was dead when he next set it to hunt.

He looked around one final time, decided that there was
nothing more he could immediately use, and left the library.
He reset the spells, then hurried down the corridor.

In the concert hall Smagdarone's voice was rapidly wearing down, and there was enough fidgeting from the audience
that not even an egomaniac such as *he* could ignore it for
much longer. Miranda was slouched in her chair, fanning herself with a small blue ostrich-plume fan and looking openly
bored. How could Smagdarone stand it?

Piswyck hurried past, found a room with pen, ink, and
paper, then headed in the direction of the castle's highest
tower, taking the writing implements with him..

By the time he had climbed the unfinished brick stairs to the
top he was wondering if perhaps he had not done better to
work from the courtyard walls, or at least a shorter tower. But
by then it was too late, and besides, he was charmed to discover the top room of the tower filled with a collection of
music boxes, most of them the very large kind that worked
from metal discs. The music box, with its spring-wound
mechanism, was one of the few items of technology that the
Sundering had not rendered impotent. The discs manufactured
in Latter Earth did have to be hand made, rather than stamped
out by machine, but they worked and made music.

He resisted his urge to put on a melody and set to work at
once writing his messages, all of which were the same. On
each piece of paper he printed the words: *Defend yourselves
with Fire and the Umbrella.* That seemed clear enough. He
then folded the hundred or so messages into paper gliders,
took them out onto the balcony that ran around the tower, and
began sailing them off in the one direction that would get
them over the jelly wall and farthest from the castle. It was a
clear night with blazing stars, and well past midnight, so the
air was still. With luck Kimowatt had someone watching the

castle 'round the clock. Without luck there were still enough copies of the letter that at least one should get through.

That chore done, Piswyck went back inside.

Smagdarone had boasted that the floaters could almost hear. That explained their quaint dance in the sky to the tune of the "Carousel Waltz." Piswyck now wondered what effect other kinds of music might have on them. He searched through the wooden cabinets of metal discs but was deeply disappointed. There was nothing agitating or even confusing. Songs, dances, even a few renditions of choruses from Wagner, but nowhere any evidence of the virtuostic stuff for which music boxes, unlimited to a mere ten digits, were ideally suited.

In the center of the room was a spectacular specimen inlaid with exotic woods in floral patterns. Piswyck lifted the cover carefully, stooping to see where the activating pin was, then covering it with his thumb as he raised the lid all the way. The interior paneling was as exquisite as the exterior, being done mainly in cocobolo and chestnut on a field of white oak, the whole varnished with clear red to make it glow like the inside of a furnace. The disc mounted on the mechanism was something called "Lara's Theme," which Piswyck vaguely remembered to be another waltz.

Being surrounded by so much music made Piswyck acutely aware of Lifesaver's absence. He had been away from the unicorn for less than a day and yet it seemed an eternity. Smagdarone's faulty tenor was no substitute for Lifesaver's clear and flawless contralto, and whatever their relative merits, it was clear that Wagner was no Mozart.

Piswyck closed the music box carefully, walked across the little room, and stared out the window into the darkness. Far below and to the north Bermuda's forests spread a dark blanket of mangrove, palm trees, and cedar. He tried to imagine Lifesaver out there in the redolent cedar smell of the woods, cedar mixed with salt air. Or perhaps Lifesaver was safe inside Kimowatt's laboratory, eating cassava pie by candlelight amid the retorts and alembics. Thinking that a line or two of iambics might ease the emptiness, he pulled out the Shakespeare, but at that moment a bell began ringing madly in one of the other towers: the alarm!

He looked around the room quickly. There was no place for him to hide, only a couple of cane-backed chairs and many music boxes. He made a quick examination of the music boxes, found one with a little more dust on the cover than the others (he couldn't blame the maid for not climbing the stairs every day) and opened it carefully, holding down the pin. Into it he put the Shakespeare, the book of weather spells, the dagger, and the vial of Elfire. Having nearly lost them once he wanted to make sure they were secreted safely in the event he was captured again. He closed the box, then headed down the circular stairs toward the castle proper. In so large a place there must surely be rooms that were used for storage and in which he could hide.

He left the tower and hurried through what seemed to be an abandoned corridor, right up until he heard the commotion of armed guards coming rapidly down the hallway ahead. As there was nothing else to do, he opened the first door he came to and ducked in.

Two women, one white and one black, were undressing for bed. Whether or not they agreed with Smagdarone's policies on vivisection, they had good reason to be startled by a young man bursting in on them, one dressed (by Bermudan standards) quite indecently. They began to scream.

The small one, Piswyck thought, had the better and the stronger voice, but this was not the time to compliment her. He murmured a quick apology and opened the door to leave, just in time to meet the squad of scarlet-liveried guards.

This time Smagdarone didn't bother with the swimming pool. He had Piswyck taken directly to the laboratory and held under guard while the requisite bondage equipment was prepared. Miranda had heard the bell and come along against her uncle's direct orders, so the wizard was more than a little perturbed as he oversaw the construction.

"The *whole thing* will have to be drained!" he muttered in Piswyck's general direction as he directed the servants to set up a big wooden X frame and had them drill small holes all over it. "The poor snakes are sick and vomiting! Don't you have any compassion at all? You might have killed them, polluting the water that way!"

"They might have killed *me*," Piswyck said, attempting to cast a reasonable light on his activities and maintain some semblance of decorum in the midst of adversity.

"Well," said Smagdarone, "but that's what they're *for*, don't you see? In case you should try to escape. It's not their fault they failed, and that you did escape. Did you have to penalize them further by giving them upset stomachs?"

"At least it isn't diarrhoea," Piswyck suggested helpfully.

"It may be by morning," Smagdarone said morosely. He helped adjust the upright beam behind the X frame, making sure it was firmly affixed.

Piswyck glanced at Miranda. To his surprise her eyes were smiling at him, even though her mouth was set in a frown.

"There now!" Smagdarone pronounced, stepping back from the contraption. "That ought to hold you. Gentlemen?"

The guards nudged Piswyck, and, as there were no less than twelve crossbow bolts aimed at various delicate parts of him, he thought it best to cooperate. He stepped up to the rack, spread his arms and legs obligingly, and held still while Smagdarone personally secured metal bands around his wrists, his biceps, his ankles, his calves, his thighs, his waist, his chest, and finally, around his neck. He was, however, still at liberty to turn his head left and right.

Smagdarone cranked a handle at the side of the device and it rotated, moving Piswyck so that he hung from his bonds facing the floor. From this uncomfortable position he watched the wizard leave the room and return a moment later with a small glowing crucible, presumably quite hot from the way he handled it with heavily padded gloves.

"Uncle, *no!*" cried Miranda.

"Hush, child!" said Smagdarone. "I'm not going to pour the molten metal on him, I'm going to pour it on the nuts and bolts that hold him, so that they cannot be unscrewed."

He did just that, and Piswyck felt the heat transferred through his bonds as each seal was accomplished. Then Smagdarone cranked him back up to vertical.

"But uncle," Miranda said, looking on, puzzled. "How is he supposed to . . . Well, there are some things even prisoners have to move about to do!"

"My dear," Smagdarone answered dryly, "techniques not awfully pleasant, but efficient nonetheless, were developed centuries ago for use in hospitals. He will be able to, at least for as long as he has to."

He picked up what appeared to be a surgical knife from a table. "Now, I believe we are ready to bring about the final fulfillment of the Countess's vision."

"Uncle, would you really slice my one true love into pieces

right before my eyes?" Miranda asked with shocked horror, and not a little bit of morbid fascination.

"Not unless I have to," chuckled Smagdarone. "But rest easy for the moment, my dear. In order to fulfill the Countess's vision I have only to put him in the exact situation in which she saw him, which was naked."

He took the knife and began to cut Piswyck's Elfsuit off his body. When he was finished, Piswyck hung stripped in his bonds, a singularly embarrassing spectacle, he felt, for the eyes of his intended; and she *did* look at him.

"Now," said Smagdarone with satisfaction, "we can all get some sleep!"

With that he gestured and the guards filed out; he gestured again and Miranda left; and finally he stood in the doorway alone, the light of the sun globe that illuminated his workplace giving him a cheerful look. He coughed, the result, no doubt, of singing most of *Lohengrin,* and gestured grandly to indicate the whole of his (truly magnificent) assemblage.

"Piswyck," he said, and his blue eyes sparkled, "when I have learned enough—and that will not be long now—in this laboratory I can create life!"

Neither was this quote lost on Piswyck; but at the moment literary allusion was not his prime concern. He watched as Smagdarone pulled the door shut and enchanted it once again. Then his heart sank. He had really loved the feel of his exquisite Elfsuit, now that he had gotten used to it, and it was *ruined!*

He tried to force himself to relax in his bonds. But if he sagged the metal bands cut into him. It would have been more polite of Smagdarone to leave the rack at a slightly backward angle, he thought. But then, it would have been more polite of *him* to have cleaned the drain. He shuddered to think how Smagdarone would react when he found his hunting quetzal dead. Hunting quetzals were not only expensive but on the list of restricted species, and therefore hard to obtain. If the Priest-Kings of Geneva had got word of Smagdarone's illicit activities he would *never* be able to obtain another, not at any price.

For lack of anything more stimulating to do, and because he was too uncomfortable to sleep, Piswyck began to examine the laboratory. It was much larger than Kimowatt's, and it was built in the fashion called Art Deco, which gave it a wonderfully smooth and scientific look. There were great glass tanks, the contents of which seethed, no doubt filled with the seed culture of floaters which Miranda had described. There were smaller tanks under bell jars in which pink amoebalike things writhed, no doubt progenitors of the jelly ring around the castle. There were tables covered in knives and other such implements whose names he did not know.

The floor was milky marble of a green hue, inlaid with numerous intaglio, not least conspicuous of which were the great pentagrams encompassing each of the giant tanks of floater seed culture. Piswyck had wondered what procedure Smagdarone used to suspend the creatures' growth until they were needed, and now he knew: a straightforward stasis spell. Around some of the smaller tanks were areas of plain white marble upon which changeable blazonings could be chalked, and these Piswyck assumed to be the experimental sections.

The pale green walls were punctuated by frescos, but it took Piswyck several minutes, because of the elongated and stylized manner of Deco painting, to realize that all of them depicted Smagdarone in the guise of one heroic figure or another. One showed Smagdarone as Christopher Columbus discovering the (long-lost) New World; another showed him as Jesus healing the sick. Here was Smagdarone as Lenin leading the Russian Revolution, and there he was as John Glenn entering his spaceship. A particularly unlikely depiction was Smagdarone as the Prince Regent Awakening the Spirit of Brighton.

But there, between Smagdarone as Henry V at Agincourt and Smagdarone as Pancho Villa dying in a bin of artichokes, was a cabinet with a glass door such as one might use for the storage of pool cues. And in the cabinet, neatly displayed, were five (count them, *five*) wizard's staves.

Two of them were carven like serpents out of wood; but Piswyck was willing to bet they were not wood at all. One was wrapped in brightly colored ribbons (Smagdarone a devotee of Apollo?) and one was carved like a dragon with many eyes along its body; it had the face of a moonstruck cow. The last was made of gold and silver and there was a great jagged crystal affixed at the top.

Out of curiosity he let his left hand go limp, spread the fingers downward, and tried to draw energy up from the Earth. It seemed unlikely, but . . .

There was the slight tingling. It could be done. That his arm was bound upward and that he had to twist his wrist unnaturally made it difficult and slow, but he could pull the energy up. For a while he did just that, holding it inside himself. It did not occur to him to wonder why Smagdarone had not warded against this, once the fact was established. The energy of the Earth was like any other magical energy, neither good nor bad, only available. Gods answered those who prayed to them in response to their own whims. All swords had two edges.

He bent two right fingers in the closest approximation he could manage to the proper mudhra, then spoke the words. The two serpent staves in the cabinet loosened and fell into coiling cobras.

Well, at least the case was closed.

This little exercise over, Piswyck was quickly bored again. It wasn't that he was in a hurry to get on with his next appointment (being cut up in little pieces by the sorcerer), but rather that most of the stuff in the laboratory was unintelligible to him without an explanation. How he longed now for one of Kimowatt's extended lectures!

A pair of eternities passed and he was wandering down the pleasant (and sometimes not so pleasant) lanes of his memories when the door opened and Miranda stepped in. She shut the door behind her and smiled.

"Uncle was terribly upset about what you did to the swimming pool," she said. "So upset that he paid not the least attention to my watching him as he opened the door to bring you in. I find it very handy to have people think I'm shallow. I get to see lots of things that would be carefully concealed from sharper wits."

"Miranda, darling, you are marvelous!" Piswyck said, and he felt a positive gush of love for her. "Got any idea how to get me off this rack?"

"Not yet," she said. "He didn't bother fastening you up with anything magical and I can't think of anything physical that I could use. If only he had made some small provision to get you down in one piece . . . Oh, I don't know! Even if we could get you free, we'd still have no plan of escape! The best we can hope for is to keep you intact a little longer."

"Miranda," said Piswyck, "I *do* have a plan. I did not waste my little taste of freedom. I've sent messages to your Uncle Kimowatt and he is preparing an army to attack the castle. I told him to use umbrellas to keep the floaters off and fire arrows to explode them. I don't know why fire arrows haven't been used before!"

"I can tell you that," said Miranda. "It's because of the forests. Bermuda Cedar was almost extinct before the Sundering, but now we have our trees back. If you shoot a floater with a fire arrow it explodes, scattering burning debris all through the woods. This is too small a country to handle much in the way of forest fire. Still, they might be willing to risk it to get rid of Uncle and this castle. They do so hate it."

"Can you think of any way to inflate that balloon? Not with hydrogen but with plain old hot air?"

"I'd have to squeeze out the hydrogen that's in it," she said.

"Never mind that," Piswyck said. "We can make do with half hydrogen and half hot air, if you can avoid using flames or sparks. Is there any way?"

That little wrinkle appeared between Miranda's brows as she thought intensely. Time got longer. Then: "Why yes, I believe I do have a way to do it. Back when we were living in that drafty old Fort St. Catherine Uncle liked to give barbecues for the local nobility. He built me a little solar barbecue cooker. Unfortunately, when we moved in here everyone was so offended by the architecture that they stopped coming to the barbecues. But I think I can find it. I could use it to heat air as readily as spareribs, perhaps in one of his old alembics, perhaps with a one-way valve that would suck in cold air as the hot was expelled into the balloon. I'm not entirely ignorant of the Ancient Science—"

"Good!" Piswyck interrupted. "Then be ready to do it at a moment's notice. I will also need you to go up into the topmost tower, the music box room, and retrieve some things I left there in one of the music boxes. There are two books, a bronze dagger, and a little silk purse on a silk cord. They are very important. Don't open the pouch or you'll damage the spell. You will also need to provision the basket under the balloon for a very long journey. Enough food for three."

"Three?"

"Yes, and one of them is a unicorn."

"Piswyck, I don't think that basket will hold much hay. Couldn't we send for your unicorn later?"

"Miranda, he is a unicorn, not a horse. He eats the same things we do, although his tastes are a little more refined. We are certainly not leaving Bermuda without him, either. He is my very best friend in the world."

"Oh, very well," she said. "But it will be crowded. Have you any other little tasks for me to do? Assuming we can get you down from there."

"We'll need warm clothing for the journey. It gets cold in the upper air."

"Blankets for the unicorn?"

"Yes."

"All right," she said. "Now let's get back to the problem at hand. Have you any ideas for getting you off of that rack?"

He had not exactly forgotten his immediate dilemma, but he had felt better for a few minutes. Planning for the future was an appealing way to escape the present, though not always effective in the long run.

"The staves in that cabinet," Piswyck said, not really gesturing with his head because he couldn't. "Do you know what they are for?"

Miranda turned and stepped toward the cabinet, then jumped back with a shriek.

"*Snakes!*" she cried. "Oh, Piswyck, I don't mind most of the impedimenta of magic, but I *don't like snakes!*"

Piswyck knew exactly how she felt.

"Sorry," he said. "Just a minute."

He took a deep breath, drew up some energy, and reversed the spell, returning the two cobras to their rigid state. "*Now* can you tell me what he uses them for?"

Miranda looked up at Piswyck with unabashed surprise, and a definite measure more of respect. Then she looked back at the cabinet and took two steps closer to it.

"The two cobras," she said, "are the ones he carries on festival days in the grand parade. I'm sure he uses them to intimidate people, but he also uses them for things he does down here. The one with the ribbons is a Wand of Apollo and he also uses that in his experiments. It's some kind of healing device. The wooden dragon he uses to summon clouds on hot days, and to make it rain when the cisterns get low. As for the gold-and-silver one, that's for mechanical operations like wardings, drawing walls of power, channeling energy and the like. He mentioned to me once that the crystal vibrated at the same rate as something or other, but I don't remember what. Can you use any of them?"

She was quick to realize that he could do things now that she didn't know about.

"Bring me the one made of gold and silver," he said.

She opened the case and lifted out the staff, giving a little shudder when her hand brushed one of the rigid cobras. She closed the case carefully, then brought the staff across the room and held it before him.

"Put the butt on the floor," he directed, "then hold it firmly, but as far away from your body as you can. I'm going to try and scry the crystal."

"Be careful, Piswyck," she said, holding the staff as he directed. "Uncle has a lot of power and you may be letting yourself in for something you can't control."

He thought she might be right. He was filled with horror and disgust that Smagdarone should have bent the healing Wand of Apollo to the use of his perverse experiments, but that (as Bahamfalme would have said) was how it was, and his horror would not alter the fact. Nor would his retreat from the task at hand serve to improve the situation.

"My dear," he said quite soberly, "if I don't get control of *something*, and quick, I won't have options like fear and caution. I'll simply be dismembered. So hold the staff well and don't drop it unless things get dangerous."

Miranda nodded, then did as she was bidden. Piswyck closed his thoughts off from everything but the clear crystal mounted atop the gold-and-silver staff; then he looked deep into it and let his eyes unfocus partially. He tried to see not what light would reveal but what was laid down amidst the matrices of the quartz, encoded along the lines of its molecules.

It was like looking into water once you let go of the rest of your environment. It was with water that the Elves had taught him to scry, and it was natural that the simile should occur to him. Clear, pure water.

But the crystal was not water, however clear it might be. There were straight lines within it, lines that only became visible when you thought yourself down and down to a level where blocks of atoms lined up with the neatness of stones in a cathedral wall. Order was the nature of the crystal, order born of its nature and given character by its imperfections.

Those imperfections were important.

Why was this crystal different from every other crystal?

It was the imperfections. They made it not merely a place to store words, not merely a place for clarifying the mind, not merely a means of transmitting thoughts. They gave it the power to shadow energies, form analogs to forces both larger and smaller, made it a closet in which to keep the blueprints of the world. Locked inside, Piswyck knew, were the patterns of all the spells Smagdarone had cast with it.

He moved from vista to vista, looking out on what seemed infinite corridors of linear growth. It was frozen but it was not cold. Changes ran along the lines like pigeons made of light, holding ideas by their movement, holding information. It was incredibly beautiful and he felt the temptation he had expected to feel, to lie down in one spot and become a part of the perfected beauty of the crystal world. He was not weak enough to give in, not at this moment or in this crystal, but he felt it. He had other business in these glittering gardens, in this palace of light. If only he could remember . . .

Oh yes.

He formed the idea of a pattern for channeling physical energy, raw force, the kind one used to seal a door, the kind one used to enclose a demon. He moved to the place where those patterns dwelt, but upon seeing them he startled, for they were such pitifully small things; he needed much more, much greater strength.

Obligingly his need attracted him across the charges and he was where he wanted to be, before a vision so beautiful, so terrible, that he hurt with it, loved it, wanted it, feared it.

Dazzling!

With such he could . . .

What?

Rule the world?

He laughed and took only what he needed, left the rest beckoning and glittering at him, crying to him: Why Not? Why Not? Why Not?

He shook his head and blinked his eyes.

"Can't do it?" Miranda asked. "Maybe if you try again . . ."

"It's done," Piswyck said. "Find a chair or something, so that you can prop up the staff and get away from it."

"What? But you just blinked your eyes!"

"It doesn't take long, once you get into it. Now quickly, we haven't got much time."

She hurried around the laboratory until she found a chair, then brought it to him; she propped the staff up as he instructed, with the top of the crystal pointing roughly toward him.

"Now go out in the hall and wait," he said. "Just in case I blow myself to Hell."

"What?"

"Just do what I say, and hurry! I don't know when your uncle is going to pop in on us again."

"Oh, he's sleeping soundly," said Miranda, but she hurried across the room, opened the door, and was stepping out into the corridor when he called to her again.

"Miranda? I've changed my mind. Don't wait in the hall. Go and start doing the things that I told you to do. If this gets out of hand the hall won't be safe."

She looked at him fearfully.

"And I love you," he said.

It seemed to startle her. She stood for a moment as if indecisive, then she said: "I love you, too!" and left.

Now there was nothing for it but to act.

He would find out just how much alteration in his consciousness the Elfmagic had made. If he could control the energies the crystal had shown him, he could cut through the metal bands that held him; but he would be drawing those energies from other sources, among them the spells that held the various containers in the laboratory in stasis. If he made a mistake it could get messy. There were many things going on around him that he did not understand.

He thought for a moment about hydrogen. How much of it was generated by seed floaters? Was each tank a bomb waiting to go off? He thought about how Smagdarone had brought the molten metal in from outside rather than heating it nearer to its use. He might just blow the whole castle off the face of the planet.

But if he didn't try, Smagdarone would slice him like a tomato and grow his parts in test tubes.

No contest.

He reached for the crystal with his mind and began to whisper the words he had seen written in the matrices. The crystal began to vibrate, first to his subtler senses, then on the etheric level, and finally on the physical plane as the monody of the long and oft-repeated text resonated in it. He visualized a line of force reaching from the end of the crystal to the metal band around his right wrist, a force that would reach just *through* the metal and not a millimeter farther. He licked his lips, then spoke the words that would release the charge.

From the tip of the crystal a beam of light shot; not spiritual light, not etheric light, not even symbolic light; but real, *physical* light that his eyes could see, blinding terrible light that came not from the proper realms where light dwelt but from the twisting of the universe to abnormal purpose. And it seared, it sliced, it burned.

Piswyck screamed as molten drops of metal fell upon his wrist, as the band melted and peeled back like the petals of an orange orchid opening. The moment it was possible he jerked his hand free, gasping with pain as the light died.

The door flew open.

"Piswyck!" Miranda cried, and she stared at him, her eyes wide and frightened.

"Go!" Piswyck commanded, and his voice was the voice of power that his father had tried to teach him, that he had tried to use fully that day in the burning stockyards, that finally welled up out of him as from the depths of some bottomless cavern.

Miranda stared at him for but a second more. Then she whirled and shut the door, and he knew that this time she obeyed. A corner of him was astonished. A larger part of him ached and made tears flow down his cheeks. A third part of him knew that he disturbed great tides, and that Smagdarone would know. He must make an end of it, and quickly.

He visualized the beam again, this time directed at the band around his right bicep. He steeled himself to the pain he knew would come and began the incantation. He pronounced the words of release and again the searing light cut through metal to free him. He got his arm clear quickly, but there was a burning seared mark in the flesh that was like a slave bracelet, and his instincts told him that the dire magic was putting its brand upon him.

In agony he cut his left wrist free, then his left bicep. He held off shock by main force as he seared through the bands on his ankles, his calves, his thighs. He was trembling all over when he cut the band in two places to free his waist, and in two more to free his chest. Those bands fell, clanking to the ground, inflicting additional burns as they touched him in their fall. Holding himself on the wooden rack with his burned arms and legs so that he would not choke, he at last aimed the force of the crystal at the collar around his neck; and as it peeled back, burning, he lurched forward and fell from the rack, knocking over the chair, sending the staff clattering, his whole body a single scream.

"*Gods!*" he sobbed, lying on the floor, his limbs segmented by fire. His breath came in gasps, his mind reeled with pain.

But it was not yet ended.

He heard an ominous sound, a bubbling, a gurgling, and he looked up through his tears at the tanks in which the seed floaters grew; and indeed now they *grew!*

What had looked like translucent broth was now as thick as oatmeal as the power of the stasis fields failed. He could see tiny floater bodies resolving, and near the surface some were already lifting up, becoming airborne.

He glanced at the experimental areas and the sights under the bell jars sickened him. No longer free-floating amoeba shapes but thick, darkening jellies that had consumed their medium, that were climbing free, straining at the glass containing them.

Piswyck dragged himself to his knees, grasped the gold-and-silver staff, and used it to pull himself to his feet. He hobbled across the room to the cabinet where the other staves were kept and opened it. He must do all he could, and quickly, to stop the sorcerer's further depredations. He took the two cobra staves and lifted them in turn, throwing them like javelins up and over and into two of the floater incubators. Then he pronounced the spell that loosed them and shuddered as the baby floaters attacked the snakes. He didn't like to do that, but it was the quickest way he could think of to dispose of two of Smagdarone's tools and at the same time distract the inhabitants of the floater tanks. With luck, Smagdarone would have some rapport with the cobras as well as the floaters and find himself mentally devouring his own parts.

The Wand of Apollo he could not bear to have used so ill. He carried it to one of the tanks with an aspic, set it up, then backed off to aim the crystal-topped staff. He asked Apollo for forgiveness, then directed a bolt of energy directly at its center. The Wand shattered, hurling splinters and colored threads in all directions.

Piswyck took the wooden dragon and the gold-and-silver staff and headed for the door. He pulled it open and looked out into the hall but nobody was yet in evidence. He moved through it and turned to face the laboratory.

Abruptly the bell jars full of creeping slime began to shatter one after another. Now he realized what the Wand of Apollo had, in part, been used for. He watched in horror as the different cultures, so irrationally fixed in his mind as enzyme aspics, began to throb and expand and take on the fluorescent orange-pink color of the one around the castle, and move toward him hungrily.

Unthinking, he aimed the metal wand and fired a bolt of destructive energy at the closest of the crawling nightmares. But by now the baby floaters had grown, had lifted, had generated enough hydrogen to be dangerous. The jelly was blasted, but there was a spark, and suddenly Piswyck felt himself lifted by an explosion and hurled back against the brick wall, the staff wrenched from his hand even as consciousness was wrenched from his mind.

He awoke a moment later and stared straight into Hell. The explosion had shattered the glass tanks and the laboratory was filled, floor to ceiling, with rapidly growing floaters. The floor itself was quickly being covered with the nightmares in aspic, which reached upward with new and untried pseudopods to try to capture the floaters.

They were doing a good job, except for the part of the jelly that was moving through the door, toward him, creeping across the fallen crystal-topped staff, getting ready for a really *big* meal. Piswyck scrambled up, grabbed the dragon-wood staff, which was as yet untouched, and ran, still dazed, up the passage.

In the castle above, the shouting had begun. As he reached the top of the stairs, he encountered two of the scarlet-liveried guards, their faces a mixture of anger and fear. He didn't give them time to draw their swords but swung the staff in a great arc, feeling the shock as the butt end hit one man's head and shattered it like a watermelon. He pulled back and rammed the other end up into the second guard's throat, and was spattered with blood as the bones broke. He was past them and running again even before their bodies had given up life.

By now he was confident of the castle's layout, even if he didn't know where to look for anything, and he knew in which direction he had to go. He found the door by which he had entered and rushed out, down the stairs, into a rapidly lightening morning. The balloon was just as he had first seen it, a fat mushroom, as it was not yet day enough for Miranda to inflate it. His hang glider was gone.

He ran past the balloon, found the stairs that led down to the gatehouse. Behind him he heard shouting; he glanced over his shoulder and saw guards coming after him, and then Smagdarone coming out of the door, robed now as the sorceror he was, all in black embroidered with golden sigils.

He looked up and saw that the sky was full of floaters, hovering and massing beyond the gatehouse. He looked ahead as he reached the bottom of the stairs and saw two gate guards drawing their swords. He ran toward them, not letting himself think about the odds on a single man with a quarterstaff against two men with steel. And they had clothes to protect them while he was still naked.

He looked desperately for the mechanism that would open the gates, then approached the swordsmen. He gave them no time to gauge him. He planted the butt of the dragon staff on the ground, grabbed the top of it, and pole-vaulted upward. Whatever his opponents were expecting, it was not that. His bare foot kicked sideways and the force of his leg at extension caved in the bridge of one man's nose, crushing his face and hurling him backward.

Then Piswyck fell, rolled, and was up again, facing the remaining guard with a little better odds. He crouched, holding the staff crossways, panting, fighting the pain of all his burns, not thinking about death.

"Stop!" came Smagdarone's voice from the edge of the courtyard above, and in that one word Piswyck heard all about Smagdarone that he had not known before. The voice was the same tenor, but all the charming eccentricity had fallen away, leaving only the sharp edge of the man who planned the conquest of the world, who experimented on living men and women, who was willing to unbalance the forces of nature for his private gain.

Smagdarone the Great.

"As he wants to go out so badly," the sorcerer said, *"open the gates!"*

The guard opposite Piswyck backed off, glanced up fearfully at his master, then ran to do as he was told. Piswyck stood breathing hard; then he heard the ancient mechanism creak as the castle gates opened.

"Go!" Smagdarone commanded, and there was bitter cruelty in the command. "Go!"

Piswyck looked out the gate and there it was, but worse. Within the high wall of orange-pink fluorescent jelly he saw the figure of a man, the skin flayed off him so that his veins and muscles were exposed; and he was still alive. He twitched and writhed and his white eyeballs stared, unseeing, and he was somehow still *alive*.

The wall of jelly bulged, then extended a long, thin pseudopod toward Piswyck.

Piswyck glanced up at Smagdarone and saw that his hand was extended in a gesture of control.

"The Countess has had her vision fulfilled," the sorceror said as the pseudopod lengthened, and anger tinged his voice. "You have been bound in my laboratory even as she saw you. And I will not kill a single cell of you, so she *must* be satisfied. But now, I am *tired* of you, Piswyck!"

Piswyck looked back at the approaching pseudopod, and at the horror of the flayed man; and *he* was a little tired of Smagdarone.

He raised one hand, made the gesture described in the book, and spoke the words of the spell against werewolves, the spell that returned transmogrified creatures to their original form.

The air seemed to shiver, as if mighty waves of heat rose all around. There was a moan, a palpable deep sound that could be heard. Outside the gate the monster aspic quivered, shuddered, then quickly began to melt.

Above and behind him Piswyck heard Smagdarone gasp. Then the wizard recovered from his surprise and began to chant the spells that Piswyck had seen scrawled in the margin of the ancient book, the spells to return the jelly to its neatly molded shape.

Piswyck turned and faced him and held up the dragon-wood staff. He spoke now in the Elvish tongue, and as he spoke he used the power he could feel in the wood to summon the air. Not a great deal, but enough to form a tiny, intense whirlwind. He forced the whirlwind at Smagdarone's face, twisted it into the sorceror's mouth, and in so doing, crammed the words of the counterspell back where they came from.

Smagdarone looked down at him, and if he had been a really good Lohengrin the lightning from his eyes would have struck Piswyck dead. As it was he shut his mouth and turned and fled, no doubt to prepare his attack from safer quarters.

But that was enough.

Behind him Piswyck heard a commotion. He whirled, and there, running across the still wet ground where the monster had melted, was Kimowatt, followed by Frogstool and an army of irate citizens. Kimowatt was in tweeds with a pith helmet, and Frogstool carried a banner bearing the ancient motto of the nation: *Quo Fata Ferunt*.

And as they came, their voices rang out in their battle cry: *"For Bermuda's architecture and St. George!"*

And they all carried umbrellas.

8

Escape From Coney Island

The initial assault on the castle cost the citizens of Bermuda heavily. Whether Mad Ludwig had meant Neuschwanstein to be defensible was no longer a moot point; the stones of the courtyard around the semi-inflated circus balloon were slick with blood. Still, Smagdarone had put too much faith in his omnivorous aspic and his flying jellyfish, and as Piswyck had taken out the aspic and the citizens were carrying umbrellas, the sorcerer's first two lines of defense were thoroughly breached. By mid-morning what history would alternately describe as "The Bumbershoot War" and "The Battle of Coney Island" was in full sway within the walls. There were skirmishes in painted corridors, ambushes from gilded chambers, and a general bloodthirsty search for the wicked wizard who had sought to conquer the world, a social impropriety almost as great as the despoiling of Bermuda's architectural heritage.

There was also Smagdarone's heavy dependence on the crossbow. While it was much easier to train a soldier to shoot a crossbow than a longbow, the crossbow had to be cranked back, so it reloaded more slowly. The longbow was ready to fire again with just the nocking of an arrow and a draw. This fact had allowed Frogstool's squad of archers to strike down the defense of the courtyard above them and get up the stairs, and was now allowing them to inflict heavy losses.

But the tide of success on which the citizens' militia rode was slowing. Smagdarone's troops were generally better trained with the sword, which meant that close-fought battles with even numbers tended to go to the enemy. Piswyck realized immediately that success would depend on finding the sorcerer and somehow disabling him; by killing him, for instance.

Nor had Piswyck yet found Miranda, either alive or dead amidst the carnage. Surely she must be somewhere in the castle! And where was Lifesaver? He had not come in with the assault, a very sensible thing as a particolored unicorn must rank high among the world's best targets. But where was he?

If Miranda got the balloon inflated, and if the tide of battle turned irrevocably against them, and if they had to escape (really *had* to!) there would be no time to search.

Another thing that bothered Piswyck was his clothing. Fighting in the nude was not only dangerous but indecent. He had stripped a corpse for the basics, and he was glad that a loin cloth was infinitely adjustable; but the padded tunic he wore now was a size too large and the arms dragged at him, impeding his skill with a sword. The cannons were even worse, and as he ran down yet another hallway he wondered if it would not be better to fight bare legged than to risk tangling his knees in the baggy cloth. He would almost have rather taken one of the tweed jacket and knicker suits favored by most of the citizens, but he could not imagine fighting with a sword while wearing a tweed sport coat.

A door opened ahead and he snapped his sword up into position, crouching, bunching his legs in case he had to make a leap. Why must life be just one damned sword fight after another? he wondered. But the face that peered around the doorjamb was not the threat he expected. It was Miranda, wearing the silliest hat that he had ever seen.

"Piswyck!" she cried, coming out and running down the hall toward him, her arms full of bundles.

The hat was crushed yellow velvet with black trim and a black veil of net. It sat on her head at an angle and bore a slight resemblance to an antique sailing ship, save that it was ornamented all over with little stuffed blackbirds, creatures whose dull jet eyes and lackluster plumage were no tribute to the art of the taxidermist. Her gown matched the hat, an affair of crushed yellow velvet, black-and-yellow brocade, a little coat with padded shoulders that fastened with French corded frogs, a long gathered skirt with a slight bustle; but no birds. She had done her hair up on the top of her head in tubular

curls in a fashion proper to the outfit and looked every centimeter the proper Victorian lady set to go riding in the park.

"Thank heavens I've found you!" she gasped. "Here, put
on these clothes. That thing you're wearing is entirely the
wrong size, and somebody might mistake you for one of
Uncle's troops."

She was right, of course, but as she opened the bundle and
handed him things Piswyck was not sure whether bright yellow wool would be an improvement. There was also some of
the black-and-yellow brocade that ornamented her dress.

"I'm not sure this is the right time to change . . ." he began,
but she wouldn't hear him out.

"Don't be foolish! You can't fight in something that binds
your arms and legs. Now give me your sword; I can use it
well enough, even in this skirt, if we're caught with your
pants down."

There wasn't time to argue, and Miranda *was* good with a
sword. He quickly stripped and put on the outfit she had provided, pleased that she had picked one to match hers even if
he did look like a fool in the bright yellow wool trousers with
silk stripes up the sides, black-and-yellow brocade vest,
skirted yellow wool frock coat with black piped lapels, and
(underneath) rainbow braces.

"Have you got the stuff from the tower?" he asked as she
handed the sword back to him and tied a casual but elegant
bow in his black crepe cravat.

"Not yet," she said. "I went to the kitchens first and got
food. Abelia, our cook, was quite nice about it. Helped me
pack everything in hampers and dishcloths, just as we would
for a picnic. She's so good; she never asks questions. Then I
took the food out and loaded it in the basket under the balloon.
After that I went for clothing, and, well, here we are. Oh yes,
I started filling the balloon with hot air. My little solar barbecue works just fine!"

"Have you seen Lifesaver?" he asked.

"The unicorn?" She looked Piswyck over to make sure he
met with her approval.

"Yes."

"No. But I'll tell him the plan if I see him. You did say that
he could speak with humans, didn't you?"

"Of course he can speak with humans!" said Piswyck, a
little irritated. "In iambic pentameter, as a matter of fact."

'Oh, *Lord!*' exclaimed Miranda, rolling her eyes. "Now

that's going to be hard to take!" She straightened his cravat just slightly. "Now do be good and see if you can pick up another sword for me, will you? I'm off to the tower."

She reached up and kissed Piswyck on the cheek.

It was the first intimacy they'd shared since his arrival, despite all the time he'd spent naked in her presence.

"I had hoped we would not have to rush off so suddenly," he began, taking her by the shoulders and looking into her beautiful eyes.

"I never had any doubt but that we would," Miranda said sadly. "I know my uncle. I only hope that we *can* leave!"

"If we could just *find* him!" said Piswyck in frustration, and he released her, fearing he might get carried away.

"Oh, that's easy," Miranda said. "He'll be in his laboratory, preparing a counterattack."

"But he can't go there," said Piswyck. "It's full of rapidly growing floaters and even faster growing aspics."

"You seem to be forgetting some aspics of his research," Miranda said, but he ignored the pun. "Those things are cooked up with his very own genetic material. They'd eat you or me for an appetizer, but they're *part of him*. I've seen him *play* with those blobs of pink slime, just the way one would play with a pet octopus."

She shuddered, but in Piswyck's mind there appeared the vision of Ralph the heptopus as a playmate.

"One more thing," he said as she turned again to go. "Is the wooden dragon staff I hid in the balloon basket still there?"

"Oh yes," she said. "I wouldn't want us to leave that behind after what you did to Uncle down by the gate. I watched it all from above!"

Then she was hurrying down the hall, her little bustle bouncing behind her.

Piswyck watched until she turned the corner, then headed back the way he had come, with the intention of finding either Kimowatt or Frogstool and appraising his comrades of Smagdarone's whereabouts. They couldn't go down there to attack him, but perhaps they could force his own troops back upon him. He would then either have to expend energy controlling the ravenous aspics or let his own vassals be eaten.

He didn't have to go far to find Kimowatt. The wizard of Shinbone Alley came rocketing down the hall toward him followed by four fellow Onions, three men and a woman. The men all wore standard tweed shooting suits, but the woman wore jodhpurs with her tweed jacket, and there was a longbow slung across her back next to an empty quiver. Her hair was starting to gray, was cut short, and there was a fierce determination in the set of her wide mouth. Kimowatt waved at Piswyck, motioning him to go back, but before Piswyck could follow this semaphoric advice the reason for it came tramping around a corner: a squad of Smagdarone's swordsmen.

"Smaggy's come out!" Kimowatt gasped as he came abreast of Piswyck and the two of them began to run together. "He's in the throne room, all covered with that horrible pink slime, standing under a cloud of immature floaters. He looks like a statue of Saint Gregory being regal beneath the papal canopy! And he got five of my best as the stuff boiled up out of the basement!"

The six of them made it through a door at the end of the hall and slammed it shut. There was no key in the lock, so two of the men grabbed an ornately carved piece of furniture (Piswyck couldn't remember what it was called) and heaved it against the door. Piswyck and Kimowatt lifted a couch and added it to the barricade; then they looked around for another exit.

"If he has floaters with him he's doomed!" said Piswyck, panting. "Have you got any fire arrows left?"

"Good heavens, man!" said Kimowatt, registering shock. "We couldn't use those things. Do you know what it would do to our cedars?"

Looking back on the assault, Piswyck realized that he hadn't noticed any of the expected aerial explosions. He also remembered the old adage about people who would not save the forest for the trees.

"If we don't stop Smagdarone, and do it now," he said, holding down the passion in his voice, "there won't *be* any cedars. Neither will there be any citizens to enjoy them. Besides, he's indoors now!"

"Quite right!" said the woman. "Lemuel, give me some of your arrows!"

One of the three men (apparently Lemuel) gave her some arrows and she looked around. She grabbed hold of a blue velvet drape and unceremoniously tore it down.

"Baroque trash!" she muttered as she began to rip it up and wrap the strands around the tip of an arrow.

There was a crash against the door and it buckled. It

seemed the enemy wanted in. Kimowatt opened a door at the opposite side of the room and they all dashed through, Lemuel and the lady working on the arrows as they ran.

"There's one flaw in your plan, Piswyck," Kimowatt said as they passed through a paneled room decorated with marble busts. "Somebody will have to go to the throne room and shoot the arrows in. That's going to be quite dangerous. That slime moves fast and there are a great lot of floaters. Even if you blow Smaggy to Kingdom Come, you may get eaten for your efforts."

Piswyck was charmed by the way Kimowatt had moved the pronoun from "someone" to "you," thereby delegating *him* to what was clearly held to be a suicide mission. Yet there were some things that Kimowatt didn't know, and at that precise moment Piswyck was beginning to feel rather as if he *wanted* to be a hero. He said nothing and let Kimowatt wonder whether he had got the point.

They closed more doors behind them, moved more furniture, and got the fire arrows made. Two guards in scarlet livery appeared ahead of them, but Kimowatt ran at them, leaped into the air, and with an amazing twist of his body killed them both; one with a snap of his hand, the other with a kick.

"Just what martial art *is* that?" Piswyck asked as they sped past the corpses.

"Pinoi Tekabo," said Kimowatt, "and down that corridor is an entrance to the balcony of the throne room."

"Just the place I want to be," said Piswyck. "Are the arrows ready, ma'am?"

"They are!" the woman said. "There are four of them, and take a few more with points, just in case you need them."

"Wish me luck!"

"All the luck in the world!" the woman said, and with a warm but restrained smile she thrust out her hand and shook his with a firm grasp. It was such a quaint and antique gesture that Piswyck was deeply touched.

"Try to keep the war indoors!" he called as he headed down the corridor. "Miranda is working in the courtyard."

He approached the entry to the balcony warily, not sure how much surveillance Smagdarone could manage while controlling his creatures. The lapis blue pillars came into view, and, at the far end of the throne room, the gorgeous paintings of angelic splendor that ornamented the dome of the nave above the dais. He held his bow at ready, one of the fire arrows loosely nocked. He moved in and the floor of the throne room became visible to him.

Smagdarone was standing on the white marble dais, just at the top of the white marble stairs. Above his head was indeed a thick canopy of floaters of various sizes, the largest being only about a meter across. Far from looking like Saint Gregory, however, the wizard, clothed in transparent orange-pink jelly that came up over his head in a hood, reminded Piswyck most of Rodin's statue of Balzac. He could picture that monumental bronze, somehow abandoned for an eon, left where the mangroves could dangle their roots around it (the tendrils of the floaters reminded him of mangrove roots). On the other hand, the way that Smagdarone leaned on the gold-and-silver staff with the crystal on top reminded Piswyck of Eisenstein's vision of Ivan the Terrible waiting for the people of Moscow to come to him through the snows on their knees. Smagdarone would surely enjoy that kind of gesture on a national scale.

The jelly that formed his imperial mantle flowed down the steps, licked at the gold ballisters to either side, and thickened at the base of the stairs. In the main mass of the stuff Piswyck could see the slowly digesting remains of some people who had got caught, plus such other organic dainties as had come under its fancy.

The metaphors, alas, did not hold up. Smagdarone's hair was too short for Balzac and he was a little too pudgy for Ivan. The look in his eyes, however, was that of one who looked on other realms than the one before him, and by that token Piswyck knew his mind was within the crystal, working some magic.

Piswyck hated the idea of killing a man in other than a fair fight, but it didn't look as if he was going to have a chance to take on the sorcerer hand to hand. He set the fire arrow slowly on the floor, then took one of the pointed shafts and set it to the bow string. He drew the bow and took careful aim at Smagdarone's heart.

For a moment he thought about how Smagdarone had taken Miranda in and cared for her when her parents died. The man had his good side, surely, and his death would cause Miranda pain. He hesitated. Then he remembered that Adolf Hitler was said to have been very charming, and he let the arrow fly.

It struck precisely where he had aimed it.

But it did not pierce.

It stuck in the jelly as if it had hit wood, going in no more than the breadth of three fingers.

Smagdarone noticed.

His eyes focused, lowered to the arrow sticking in right above his heart, then raised to the balcony where Piswyck stood.

Piswyck was remembering the many mistakes he'd made in trying to kill a water troll.

"Too late, *amateur!*" the sorcerer laughed, and the cloud of floaters took flight in a gush of expelled gas straight for Piswyck.

It occurred to Piswyck that he might have done better in this instance to have tried the spell that had dissolved the jelly mold around the castle; that, at least, would have taken out one aspic of Smagdarone's defense systems, leaving only the floaters to contend with. But now there were only seconds, no time for casting a spell against that which was now on the attack.

Piswyck grabbed the fire arrow, nocked it, and fired it into the heart of the cloud of floaters coming toward him. There was no time to light it. He danced backward through the door into the corridor, stepped sideways so that he was clear of the entrance. Then he threw his mind back into the room, using the only piece of magic his father had ever really taught him.

Inside the room the arrow struck a floater; the creature started to flap and wobble in the confines of its cloud; then the heat that Piswyck was moving from his body into the blue velvet shreds on the arrow made a spark. It was only a little spell, to make a *very* little fire, but in the cloud of floaters full of hydrogen it was enough.

It was the same size explosion as the one he'd set off in the laboratory, but this time he was sheltered by the wall. It shook him, but he stayed conscious to watch the gout of fire erupt through the doorway, replete with bits and chunks of dismembered jellyfish, which splatted twitching against the wall opposite.

From the throne room came a howl like that of a werewolf in Hell, and by this sound Piswyck knew that Smagdarone was not utterly destroyed. He risked ripping down a tapestry, which he threw on the partially living mess on the floor. He stepped out on it and looked into the blasted throne room.

The jelly cloak had protected Smagdarone from the explosion, but he was *not* happy. Piswyck could imagine him figuring the repair bill for the throne room. The jelly mass was leaving his body quickly and slithering toward the balcony, part of it already flowing up the walls, and fast.

Now Piswyck uttered the spell that had so thoroughly destroyed the jelly mold, hurling its force toward the attacking aspic.

Nothing happened! The slime kept flowing toward him. Obviously Smagdarone had made some quick changes in the rules governing his creation; a very sensible precaution, all things considered.

Piswyck turned and ran.

He pounded down the corridor, turned a corner, and suddenly there was the unit of Smagdarone's troops that had earlier been pursuing him. They were sweating, no doubt from breaking down doors and moving furniture, and seeing him seemed to make their day. They smiled.

He stopped, panting.

They looked at him with the communal leer of a wolf pack arriving for dinner. Piswyck raised his sword, a little bit foolishly, considering the odds.

Their faces changed.

Piswyck glanced back over his shoulder.

The pink slime was coming!

The guards turned and ran, en masse.

Piswyck ran after them.

How silly could things get? he wondered. *A lone warrior chasing fifteen men down a corridor, all of them pursued by ravenous pink jelly!*

They emerged into a large chamber painted with large murals. Kimowatt, the lady in jodhpurs, Lemuel, and the other two men were there. Their swords were drawn. Smagdarone's fifteen ran right past them and out the other door.

"What in Latter Earth . . ." Kimowatt began, his eyebrows raising and a smile of bewilderment spreading on his wide mouth.

"Run!" Piswyck cried. "It's after me!"

Both Kimowatt and his followers displayed a commendable lack of curiosity about what *it* might be, and soon the sorcerer's guards were being followed by Piswyck, followed by Kimowatt and friends, followed by the pink slime; which delayed its chase just slightly to gobble up a bowl of petunias that rested on a credenza in the large chamber, an even worse way for petunias to die than being hurled into the void of space; but then, the pink slime had only the most rudimentary awareness of literary allusion.

The liveried guards ahead dashed through a door and slammed it behind them. Piswyck crashed into it, tried the knob, found it locked, hammered on it.

"You bastards!" he snarled, and looked around for another exit.

There was the sound of laughter from the other side of the door, then the laughter died and there was the sound of clashing swords.

"You bastards!" Piswyck heard Frogstool cry beyond the door; then he was running to the small door to his left: it might be a while before Frogstool could give him entrance. He pulled the small door open just as Kimowatt and party arrived, the slime visible down the hall in hot pursuit. A long descending stairway met his gaze.

"Down here!" he said. "And last one through close the door!"

"That stuff can get through the crack around the door!" Lemuel said.

"But not as fast as it can get through an *open* door," said the woman in jodhpurs.

If there had been a railing they might have taken the steps two or three at a time, but there was no railing and the stairs were small and of an odd size. If they did not intend to end in a pile at the bottom, like steak tartare waiting for the sauce, they had to run it a step at a time in little quicksteps. Piswyck rapidly discovered that this was another of those activities requiring a human to use odd and unfamiliar combinations of muscles, and that it was *exhausting*.

He reached the bottom.

To his left was the brick-lined tunnel leading to the laboratory and the swimming pool (maybe). To the right was a wall with a large oil portrait of Smagdarone as John Kennedy placing a wreath on the Berlin Wall. There was a curious sofa straight ahead, upholstered in dark mauve tufted cotton worked with white needlepoint pictures of Victorian acts of pornography. Beyond that was another stairway, leading up. He ran around the sofa and headed up the stairs. The slime would gain speed sliding down the stairs, but it might be slowed crawling up.

"Not another stairway!" cried Lemuel, reaching bottom.

Piswyck got to the top panting. He seized the doorknob and prayed that it was unlocked. He turned it and the door opened inward. He stumbled through, his legs rubbery from the climb, and found himself confronted by a large black woman in a white starched uniform wearing the funny hat of a master chef. She was slicing eggplant on a hardwood counter as he staggered in, and she turned to face him, her round face registering first surprise, then upset.

"And what do *you* want?" she demanded, brandishing her long, sharp knife right in front of his face.

"What's for supper?" Piswyck asked lamely as the rest of his party piled into him from the rear.

The very *first* things that Piswyck's father had told him, when he was a very, very young marquis indeed, were the two rules governing the life of any noble: (a) One never annoys the cook. (b) One lives in terror of the gardener.

"What's for supper?" the woman repeated, and her eyes grew wide with outrage. *"What's for supper? I'll tell you what's for supper! Last night that miserable man wanted boiled broccoli! Tonight he wants steamed eggplant! Can you imagine that? Me, Abelia Cambridge, trained at the Cordon Blanc, having to steam eggplant! If it weren't for all those monsters in his foolish Hall of Science, I'd—"*

Piswyck comprehended the situation instantly and decided it was well within the bounds of propriety to interrupt the lady.

"The monsters are loose and following us up the stairs," he said. "Throw the eggplant on the floor to slow down the slime and get everybody out of here fast."

Cooking being the most complex and subtle of all human art forms, and its superior achievement requiring a mind able to adjust quickly to infinitesimal variations in a multiplicity of media, Abelia Cambridge apprehended the circumstances faster than white sauce could scorch.

"That's the first sensible thing anybody's said since I came to work here!" she said, and with a sweep of her knife she sent the whole pile of vegetables scattering toward Piswyck's feet.

"Everybody out!" she yelled, in a voice that even Wagner would have admired. *"The monsters are loose!"*

Piswyck and company slipped and stumbled over the eggplant, and Lemuel closed the door behind them. The kitchen help scurried toward the exit with as much speed as if they'd been serving dinner to a restaurant critic.

"Is there a meat locker in this place?" Piswyck asked as Abelia shooed her charges out.

"Right there, Honey!" she said, pointing. "There's even something in it. It used to be a freezer before the Sundering. Can you imagine that? Being able to freeze things in Bermuda?"

Piswyck hauled open the huge steel door. He was always awestruck by such artifacts of the Ancient Technology, but there was no time now to admire. He looked inside and saw half a side of beef, some venison, part of a wild boar, and rack after rack of sausages. He grabbed some of the sausages and began laying them out on the floor in a line toward the door.

"Lemuel!" he said. "Open the door and kick some of the eggplant down the stairs. And tell me how far the slime has gotten!"

"It's stopped to eat the settee," Lemuel said, and Piswyck presumed he meant the curious sofa.

"All right, shut the door again; then all of you get out of here!"

The door was shut, most left, and then Abelia and Kimowatt were standing at the exit, making a final survey of the battleground.

"Good luck, Honey!" Abelia said.

"Don't do anything foolish," Kimowatt added; then they left also.

Piswyck pulled the huge steel door open to its fullest, then climbed up as high as he could on the cupboards behind it. He hoped desperately that the sensory apparatus of the creeping glop was still at the primitive food-search level. If so, then it ought to follow its instincts right into the freezer, where the most meat was available. Of course, it didn't have a nose or a head or anything, and it might just delegate a pseudopod to gobble him as well; but what he was doing seemed the best chance. He waited.

It was not until the stuff had seethed in around the door, eaten its way along the line of sausages, and was starting to flow into the freezer that he thought of the hundred and thirty-six things that could go wrong with his plan. The seals on the ancient food locker might have decayed beyond containment. The glop might be too voluminous to fit entirely inside. It might not *need* to go all the way inside to make its meal. It might even be suspicious.

He watched as more and more of it flowed into the room,

burbled across, flowed into the locker. From where he was hiding he could not see how much had built up within, nor could he see how much remained to enter around the door. He wished he had told Lemuel to leave the door open; then at least he would know part of the equation.

It flowed, and it occurred to him that it would have been rather pretty if he'd been watching it through a microscope. As a tiny little thing it would have been attractive. As a macroscopic organism, however, it was just plain unpleasant. An affront to Blessed Nature, and far, far too pink.

The last of it came in. It left behind a clean floor (it had one virtue), with not a trace of either sausage or eggplant, as it flowed forward, forward, and then out of sight.

Piswyck braced his feet and pushed at the huge steel door. It stuck!

Why was it, he wondered, that nobody ever got around to oiling hinges?

He jumped down on the floor, his feet tingling with the same kind of feeling one had when one's parents discussed snakes, and put his shoulder to the door. He pushed. He heaved. It began to move. The hinges let out a horrible shriek as they scrunched their rust. They hadn't seemed that rusty when he had opened the door. Perhaps with all the kitchen help talking excitedly he hadn't noticed. He hoped the jelly couldn't hear. He planted his feet, grateful for the patent leather shoes Miranda had got him, and threw all his weight against the door.

It swung, and with a mighty clunking sound it slammed shut. He shivered and sighed. The stuff was not pouring out around the edges. But then it occurred to him that no matter how tight the seal on a room might be, some idiot architect was likely to have built in ventilation shafts. He turned and ran out the door, just in case.

He glanced into rooms as he ran and before long he came upon a small but luxurious study in which Abelia Cambridge sat at an ornate writing desk scribbling furiously on cream-colored vellum paper. She looked up at him and, without his asking, she answered his question: "My resignation. I don't share *any* kitchen with *monsters!* Kimowatt went *that* way." She pointed with her goose quill, then went back to writing.

"Thanks!" Piswyck said, and headed the way she'd pointed. Once more he heard the sounds of battle, sword on sword, the clash of steel. He drew his weapon and advanced.

Kimowatt, Lemuel, the lady in jodhpurs, and about a dozen more, were being driven down the grand staircase of the castle by a force of more than twenty of Smagdarone's scarlet-clad swordsmen. A number of dead and wounded lay upon the white marble in pools of blood, and blood also spattered the dark green and dark red walls, staining the interlace and stylized swans of gold. The gold stars still shone down from the azure dome, but the marble palm tree was now awash with drops of blood.

Piswyck leaped to the fore, his legs tired but his sword arm comparatively fresh. He parried a cut, slashed, killed, killed again. He was only one man, but his appearance was opportune and gave the impression that fresh troops had arrivied. His fellows rallied. Kimowatt, at the other end of the line of skirmish, gave a grisly yell and kicked at the same time he cut, and two more men fell, one clutching a slashed artery in his arm, the other rolling with arms crossed at his groin. Kimowatt's art was nasty.

The odds evened, then reversed. The battle began to move *up* the stairway. Then Lemuel yelled and spun backwards, falling against the wall. There was an arrow sticking out of his shoulder.

Piswyck looked up higher and there, at the top of the stairs, stood Frogstool, drawing his bow again.

"You *fool!*" Kimowatt yelled, seeing the forester at the same moment. "You got one of *us!*"

"I know," Frogstool called down, and his eyes burned and his voice was choked with a fathomless sadness. "I meant to."

"What?" Piswyck cried.

"If you were to win it would be a triumph," Frogstool said, "and all I would have would be the Tragedy of Smagdarone the Great. Frankly, he lacks heroic proportions. But *you*, Piswyck, you are the very stuff of which art is made! I will be able to render you magnificent! More, I will be able to write with a deep and tragic affection, for I have come to love and admire you greatly, tragic flaw and all."

Piswyck had no time to wonder what his tragic flaw might be; he had to defend a cut, parry, and strike again.

"Frogstool, this isn't art, it's *life!*" he yelled.

"Art imitates life," Frogstool called down, and he drew his bow and shot again, wounding another of his countrymen. Now Smagdarone's troops were rallying, perceiving an ally behind them.

"You're wrong!" Piswyck shouted. "It's the other way around! Life imitates art, and slavishly. Look at what you are doing, and all for the sake of a play! Must people always do things just the way they see them on the stage or read them in books?" He thrust to the left, missed, defended, slashed to the right. *What was that sound?*

"Piswyck, art and life are ultimately the same thing," said Frogstool. "The trick is to make one's life a work of art, don't you see? And don't you see that this is my one chance to be in on something great and beautiful? If I let you live, it will only be one more chapter in one more dreary serial!" He drew his bow and took aim at Piswyck.

The sound, somehow familiar, was getting louder, closer.

"Do you think Smagdarone will let you live to write your play?" Piswyck demanded, still fighting, both with sword and tongue.

"He'll have to," said Frogstool with grim satisfaction. "Who else would there be to sing his praises, to put him in the history books?"

"He can do his own singing!" Piswyck cried—and then he recognized the sound that had crept into his awareness, could tell that it came from above, was coming down the corridor behind Frogstool.

"I'm sorry, friend," said the forester, and he gave his bow just that little extra tug preparatory to releasing the arrow. If it struck true Piswyck knew he would be at the mercy of his opponents' swords. "I can't let you talk me out of my one chance at greatness!"

Then the clatter of hooves sounded clear.

At the top of the stairs Lifesaver appeared, his carnelian horn catching the light, his amber eyes glowing, his rose-pink mane streaming, his black-and-green tail twitching, as he thundered down the marble stairs.

Frogstool heard even as he released the arrow, and the distraction was enough to send the arrow scattering against a wall. But Frogstool turned as he heard. Thus it was that he presented himself full to the spiral horn on the lowered head of the unicorn, and received the thrust straight into his chest.

It must have been the expressions of shock, the awe that Smagdarone's men saw on the faces of their opponents, that brought about the stop, the terrible pause and silence that sometimes comes in the middle of battle. Into that brief si-

lence Frogstool's last words fell, with the clarity of a single
drop of water breaking the surface in a deep old well.

"How profound," he said, his voice not even harsh. "I am
my own best subject after all!"

His hands moved toward his chest, as if he would clutch
the spiraled horn, but they never reached it. His life left him,
he slumped, and Lifesaver dipped his head to let the ruined
man slip off and to the ground.

The unicorn's head came up. He shook his rose-pink mane
and ruby drops scattered from his horn out into the air, fell
below the artificial heaven like terrible rain. He lashed his
black-and-grass-green tail and somehow his bright colors, his
oranges and olives and mauves, were not festive at all; they
were the colors of banners carried to war, the colors of flowers
on graves, the colors of death in the jungle. He spoke, and his
contralto had an edge of steel and contempt.

"The comedy is over now, my friend, as one more wasted
human life does end!" And then, harshly, and *not* in iambic
pentameter: *"La Commedia e finita!"*

Steel struck; the battle was engaged again. But now there
was a formidable foe behind Smagdarone's troops, a foe who
could rise up and come down with sharp hard hooves to cut
and break and smash in skulls. Those who survived the first
few moments surrendered and were locked in a nearby room;
and those of the victors who were in condition to do it began
to treat the wounded.

Piswyck walked wearily up the stairs to where Lifesaver
stood over Frogstool's body. He was joyous at seeing his
friend, and yet he approached slowly, not throwing his arms
around Lifesaver's neck the way he wanted to, not crying out.
There was at this moment something about the unicorn that
clutched at his heart. It was as if Lifesaver's innocence had
been killed. It was as if a part of his own life had been cut
away.

Piswyck did not want to face his own feelings just yet.
They were too mixed.

Finally he reached out and patted the place on the unicorn's
neck where deep garnet verged on dark rich blue.

"There is more bloody handiwork ahead," Lifesaver said.

"I know," said Piswyck. "Do you have any ideas about
how we can win this war?"

"We'll cripple him if we can burn his books," the unicorn
said.

"Oh, no you don't!" said the woman in jodhpurs, coming up to them quickly. "His books must be seized and put in trust for the future, whatever harm he may have done with them!"

Piswyck still had no idea who she was.

"I'm always reluctant to damage books, ma'am," he said. "But we're dealing here with human lives, and I'm not sure we can get the books out of Smagdarone's reach in any other way. And by the by, I'm Piswyck and this is Lifesaver."

"How do you do?" the woman said, changing tone for the introduction. "I'm Madeleine Forsythe, the librarian for the Town of St. George." She turned her consternation back on. "As for human lives, you must always remember the words of Heinrich Heine, who said: *'Wherever they burn books, they will also, in the end, burn human beings.'* Books, Piswyck and Lifesaver, are the essences of human beings, those human beings who wrote them. Their bodies are dust but their books live on!"

Piswyck never ceased to be amazed at the varieties of human passions, and their depth.

"Very well," he sighed. "Your point is well taken. We shall *not* burn the library if there is any other way. And I'm very pleased, at last, to *meet* you."

"Kimowatt!" Madeleine Forsythe called down the stairs. "Come along now! This nice young man and his unicorn are going to help us liberate the library!"

Piswyck hadn't been aware of this fact, but it seemed a logical next stratagem so, as the able troops gathered, he prepared to do as Madeleine desired. Swords in hand, they headed down the hall, Kimowatt leading, Madeleine next to him, and Piswyck and Lifesaver forming a rear guard. The people in between included the remaining two furniture movers from the original party and a few stalwart survivors of the battle of the stairs.

But halfway to the library they encountered Abelia Cambridge with a suitcase in her hand and a traveling hat on her head that matched her fresh, voluminous dress, a dress covered with a colorful array of printed tropical flowers that made Lifesaver look subtle.

"Hear that thumping?" she asked in alarm. "That's the jelly monster hurling himself against the freezer door. It can't be long till he breaks out. You folks had better *all* get out of this castle as fast as I'm getting. Another thing, there's more floaters in the basement! I tell you, Smagdarone is the wickedest wizard in the west! Nobody in her right mind should work for him! *Steamed eggplant!*"

Piswyck had never heard foodstuffs used as cursewords before, but he liked the idea: especially after the broccoli. He decided that he admired Abelia a lot, as she passed by him and headed for the front of the castle, cursing a whole stew of ill-prepared vegetables.

"Take an umbrella!" he called after her. "It'll keep the floaters off!"

She turned and smiled at him, a smile as sunny and bright as her outfit.

"You know, boy, you have some *good* ideas!" she said, and, giving him a little salute, she changed direction, presumably going to get an umbrella.

"The others are now halfway down the hall," said Lifesaver, fidgeting beside him, and Piswyck observed that this was true; the rest of the party had continued on while he spoke with Abelia.

He turned and walked beside the unicorn, hurrying a little to keep up, and thought that it would take only a moment to catch them. After all, it was no more than twenty meters.

But ten meters ahead there was a cross corridor, and out of it erupted yet another squad of Smagdarone's scarlet-liveried regulars. Piswyck shouted a warning to the party ahead; then the battle was on.

But this time the split attack didn't work so well. Lifesaver was a given, not a surprise appearance, and they were fighting on the flat. The enemy concentrated on Piswyck and Lifesaver, whom they outnumbered, and steadily pushed them backward, toward the front of the castle, ignoring the assault from the rear. It was only a matter of moments until Piswyck and Lifesaver were shoved out the front door of the castle, onto the steps that came up from the courtyard, and the door slammed and bolted in their face.

Piswyck turned and realized why.

In the courtyard the huge balloon was now fully inflated, held down by a tether rope attached to a winch, a plump and bulbous puff of beauty. He recognized its colorful design and had to admire (just briefly) Smagdarone's sense of *quod libet*. It was a copy of the famous balloon in the ancient motion picture of *The Wizard of Oz*, a work of art that many scholars argued to be the single greatest cultural loss of the Sundering.

Of course there were faded still photographs on display in
museums and virtually every hand-printed picture book on the
history of art recalled its glory, but . . .

Next to the balloon's wicker basket stood Miranda in her
yellow-and-black traveling outfit, and next to her, in black
velvet with gold sigils, stood Smagdarone, bereft of his jelly
coating but still holding on to the silver-and-gold staff with the
crystal on top. They were arguing mightily, but in low voices,
the way well-brought-up people always argued about family
matters in public; so Piswyck couldn't hear what they were
saying.

"I have a very bad feeling about this," he said to Lifesaver
quietly, realizing that the guards had driven the two of them
like cattle to the abattoir.

"I wonder what great Mozart would have done?" the unicorn queried.

That gave Piswyck an idea.

"Sing the hymn to Isis and Osiris," he said, running
through his mental catalogue of the spells the Elves had taught
him.

"That hymn is most profound, but for a bass!" Lifesaver
objected, scandalized.

"We all have to make sacrifices for our art," Piswyck replied. "Now sing it!"

Lifesaver opened his mouth and began (in the original German, which seemed right in Neuschwanstein) the mighty paen
asking the protection of the powerful Egyptian deities of
Death and Rebirth, perhaps the only time in history there was
any genuine justification for its transposition; and Piswyck
began to reach across the symbolic gulfs to tap the forces
those deities personified. It might be a little strange to use
German music to call Egyptian deities from Bermuda, but
then Mozart had specified that the hero of his opera was Kor-
ean. As most of Piswyck's training was in a symbolic logic
based on Elvish linguistics (which drew from Celtic and African roots) and as Ancient Egypt had been in Ancient Africa, it
was not really so strange after all.

So long as it worked.

Piswyck sought the pathways through the ether that the
languages made, let the music carry him, looked into the
realms where mind held sway, and . . .

Smagdarone noticed them. He turned from his argument
with his niece, stepped forward, and held up his staff.

Piswyck had second thoughts about the wicked wizard's ability to play Lohengrin. Certainly his eyes *now* held enough anger to bring forth lightning.

Miranda clutched the edge of the wicker basket and threw Piswyck a look of fear.

Piswyck reached across the gray ether of magic.

The crystal on Smagdarone's staff began to sparkle in response to words the wizard muttered, words in a language Piswyck did not know.

Piswyck visualized the winged disc of the sun, Horus, son of Isis and Osiris and avatar of Hermes (who had already done so well by him). He pictured the disc flying down, interposing itself between him and Smagdarone. He made the disc a mirror.

The lightning flashed, not from Smagdarone's eyes but from the crystal atop the staff. And it was *real lightning*, the kind that struck things with the forked tongues of electric snakes.

But Piswyck's shield (almost to his surprise) was good, was just as real as the lightning, albeit invisible. The bolts struck the Horus mirror and rebounded at an angle, ravaging the tree that stood at the far edge of the courtyard.

"Uncle!" Miranda screamed. *"Do you want to kill us all? There's still hydrogen in this balloon!"*

Smagdarone glanced at his niece and for a moment Piswyck was afraid she was the next target. Even sorcerers were subject to family problems, he reflected. Then the wizard walked with calm dignity a good ten meters more from the balloon. He bowed with some restraint, then faced the tree he had inadvertently destroyed. Its leaves and branches were now in flame.

He aimed his staff, chanted loudly, and a great globe of fire erupted from the tree and sailed across the air toward Piswyck and Lifesaver.

Lifesaver's voice quavered slightly but he kept up the hymn.

Piswyck raised both hands in gestures of power and moved the great mirror toward the fireball. At the last moment he gave it a little extra push, throwing all his strength behind it. The fireball hit the mirror, and like any other ball it bounced. Back, up, and arcing high, it went over the castle walls, sailing out over Bermuda's precious cedar forests.

The citizens are not going to be happy about that, Piswyck thought. *On the other hand, it was kind of fun!*

Smagdarone lifted his staff, raised the free hand in a gesture, and spoke a word. The air thickened and changed, became a wave. Piswyck recognized the word, a Word of Power to invoke thunder. He could almost see the densifying air become a wall of noise.

He raised both his hands and spoke the Words the Elves had taught him for throwing back the thunder during gales at sea. His own thunder spoke, louder yet than the wizard's and crashed against it. Smagdarone's thunder was hurled back upon him.

Smagdarone was knocked to the ground and the burning tree behind him crashed backward.

"Come on!" Piswyck said to Lifesaver, and the two of them galloped down the stairs, running toward Miranda.

"Piswyck, no!" Miranda cried, pointing, but it was too late. They were already at the bottom of the stairs, already moving across the pavement when Piswyck spied the hastily sketched blue chalk pentagram and felt the tingling of the stasis spell that rose from it. It was the very same spell that Smagdarone had used to hold the floaters and aspics in stasis outside of Time, and almost before Piswyck could become aware of what was happening it had happened. He and Lifesaver were suspended midstride, hovering in the air a few centimeters above the pavement, caught neatly in a trap.

They could not move, they could not speak. But they could see the sorcerer climb slowly to his feet, taking his time for their benefit. He adjusted his robes and walked toward them, smiling.

"As I said before," the wizard said contemptuously. "*Amateur!* You were taken by the oldest trick in the book! So now, Piswyck, I'll *destroy* you; and your unicorn, too!"

He reached inside his robe and drew out his swagger stick, which was actually his hunting quetzal. Piswyck thought with some distress that they were *really* in for it now. Smagdarone was going to be madder than a caged cat at a cock fight when he found out the quetzal was dead..

The wizard held the stiffened serpent to his breast and ran his finger over its head, with just the affection one always saw in people stroking their pets. Then he spoke the familiar words that loosed the spell; and a curious thing happened.

Had Piswyck thought about it at the time, he might have

assumed that the glue in a sorceror's book bindery would have
special properties; properties intended to restore old bindings,
properties that might (just *might*) effect a rejoining better than
that of ordinary glue. If he had considered such an effect, and
if he had been feeling compassionate toward the hunting quetzal (which he had not) he might have been more careful about
gluing the two halves of it back together. As things stood, he
had not considered the matter at all, and he had glued the
halves askew. The nerve and muscle fibers were therefore
misaligned when the quetzal was restored to motion, and it
went into convulsions.

It started fanging Smagdarone.

"Aaarrrgghhh!" the wizard screamed, throwing his pet
from him, and he fell upon the ground writhing in pain.

The stasis spell dissolved. Piswyck and Lifesaver staggered, their forward momentum regained, and then they were
once more running toward the balloon and Miranda.

"Well, I guess that takes care of him!" Piswyck panted as
they arrived.

"Oh, no it doesn't!" Miranda snapped. "Get into the basket, both of you! Uncle couldn't have survived working with
so many blasted serpents so long if he couldn't handle a little
snake bite. It'll take him a few minutes, but he'll just absorb
the poison, transmute it, and then the old bastard will be as
good as new and twice as mean!"

Piswyck was a little startled by Miranda's vehemence.
After all, her uncle wasn't *that* old. He clambered into the
basket.

Then he clambered out again. Getting a unicorn into a basket was not as easy as getting a man or a woman into one.
Lifesaver had managed his front half all right, but his efforts
to bring his back half over were fair to shred the wicker.

"Wait!" Piswyck told him. "We'll help!"

Piswyck pushed on the olive-green left hindquarter and
Miranda struggled with the scarlet right hindquarter. They had
to be wary of his carnelian hooves, but they got him up and
in, if uncomfortably. Then they followed him.

"Give me the staff!" Piswyck said; and, reaching with the
butt end of the wooden dragon, he struck the lock of the
winch, loosing its control.

The balloon lifted, its tether rope unreeling with alarming
speed. They grew giddy as the world fell away below.

They reached the end of the rope and their innards continued to climb, even though the balloon stopped and jerked downward slightly. They held on tight against the unfamiliar sensation and Lifesaver mumbled: "My stomach will not take too much of this!"

The balloon sank with a sickening sensation like falling; then it was going up again, this time not so fast.

"I *knew* that unicorns weren't meant to fly," Lifesaver moaned.

"Quick, Miranda," Piswyck said. "Give me the book of spells from the tower!"

"*Oh!*" said Miranda. "I don't have it!"

"*What?* You don't *have* it?" cried Piswyck.

"Well, I went up to the tower to get it, and I found the things you said would be there. But then Uncle Smaggy came up the stairs. I stuffed them into another music box, all except this one."

She rummaged through the stores she had loaded and drew out the green-and-gold bound copy of the complete works of William Shakespeare.

Piswyck sighed.

"Well, I don't like having to lose the Elfire—"

"*Elfire?*" Miranda asked.

"—but I think I can get us out of here with this almost as well."

He paged furiously through the volume.

"That is," he said, finding what he was looking for, "provided you brought a knife!"

He was so busy reading the text he had found that it took him a moment to register the silence that answered him. He looked up. Miranda was blushing.

"I'm afraid I forgot *all* the tableware," she said.

By now the balloon was not bouncing up and down. In fact it was hanging perfectly still at the top of the rope. Piswyck looked around. They were above the courtyard, halfway across the castle from the tower where Londea's dagger rested in a music box. Almost level with the lightning rod on top of the tower.

"Give me the staff again," Piswyck commanded, and Miranda handed it to him. It was crowded in the basket, so it took him a moment to face south, across the larger island, but that was all right; he didn't want to think about what he had to do next.

Piswyck could summon clouds well enough with Elvish

techniques, but that took time. Smagdarone had only to crank
them down again unless they could cut the rope that kept them
earthbound. What was needed now was not a graceful joining
with the forces of nature but a good old-fashioned spell. And
spells were only complexes of emotional patterns, programs
of responses set in order for swift accomplishment. With a
little tinkering the text he now had before him would work
admirably; if he had become a good enough magician.

He raised the dragon-wood staff in his right hand, and
holding the book in his left he lifted his voice and began to
paraphrase the Bard:

> *"Ye Masters of the Wind and Sea, Do Thou bedimn*
> *This Noontide Sun! Come forth thou mutinous*
> *   winds*
> *And 'twixt the green sea and the azur'd vault*
> *Set roaring war! Oh Ye dread rattling thunders*
> *Hurl forth your fire, and rift now Jove's stout oak*
> *With his own bolt! The strong-bas'd promontory*
> *Will I make shake, and by their spurs pluck up*
> *The palm and cedar! Waves at my command.*
> *Rear up your breakers! Clouds, let rain pour forth*
> *By my so potent art! By this rough magic*
> *I here adjure, and when I have requir'd*
> *Some heavenly movement, which even now I do,*
> *To work my charm upon those forces that*
> *This airy charm is for, I'll bring a wind,*
> *Circle it many fathoms o'er the Sea,*
> *And wider than did ever shimmer sound*
> *I'll draw my storm!"*

The people of Bermuda weren't going to like that bit about
uprooting palms and cedars, Piswyck realized, but maybe the
storm would douse the forest fire he saw burgeoning where
the fireball had fallen. Already a cool wind was blowing from
the south.

"Piswyck, he's getting up!" Miranda cried, looking over
the side of the basket.

Now the wind was up, Piswyck knew how to direct it. He
closed his eyes and used the force of the staff to adjust the
wind direction, just slightly, causing the balloon to move toward the tower.

"If we don't get away we're going to crash!" said Lifesaver, noticing their movement.

The real question was going to be just how far the balloon would go before the preliminary wind died. There was always a lull before the next breeze. If the balloon swung too far it might be pierced by the protuberances of the tower. If it did not go far enough . . .

"I need more wind!" Piswyck decided.

"Piswyck, what in Latter Earth are you doing?" Miranda asked, but he didn't have time to answer. He aimed the staff southeast.

"Blow winds, crack your cheeks!" he cried, and the breeze stiffened from just where he wanted it.

Now the balloon swung like a great upside-down pendulum, higher at the center of its swing, lower at each end, and Piswyck handed Miranda the staff.

He climbed up on the rim of the basket, facing the tower.

"Piswyck, you *can't!*" she cried, but Piswyck knew he could.

The balloon moved closer, moved downward; the balcony of the tower was ahead and below and—

He leaped.

Across a dizzying distance, then his hands grappled stone. He slipped, clawed, caught; then he was through the crenellation, on the balcony. He shuddered. He didn't look back or down.

He ran into the little room, went directly to the music box where he'd stowed the stuff, flipped it open. It began to play "The Man on the Flying Trapeze." There was nothing inside but the music-making mechanism.

Of course! Miranda had been forced to move his things. He looked around and realized it would take him a half hour just to *open* all the music boxes in the room. He ran back to the balcony.

The balloon was now approaching its farthest point from the tower. He would have to shout against the wind, but he hoped he could be heard.

"Miranda, which one did you put the dagger in?"

She couldn't hear him!

Then she pointed downward and Piswyck followed her direction.

Out of the door of the castle the pink slime was flowing into the courtyard.

Well, that took care of any notion Piswyck might have of running down the stairs and re-entering the balloon from below!

"Miranda, *which music box has the dagger?*" he yelled.

For answer this time she pointed toward the back of the castle. He hurried around the balcony to see what she was pointing at, then wished he hadn't. An armada (yes, really an *armada)* of young floaters was rising into the sky behind Neuschwanstein.

He rushed back to the balloon side of the tower and now the balloon was moving back toward him. But what he hadn't noticed before was that the balloon was not moving so fast. As it came toward him he made a quick calculation and realized that its arc would not be sufficient to let him leap back aboard.

But of course! His own weight had been subtracted, thus changing the balloon's mass.

"Piswyck, what are you asking me?" Miranda called across the shortening distance.

"Which music box has the dagger?" he yelled again.

"The one right in the middle, of course!" Miranda answered.

He turned and ran in, flipped up the lid of the very largest music box of all, and it began to play "Lara's Theme." He took out the dagger, the book, and the vial of Elfire, and slammed the lid down. He put the Elfire around his neck, inside his shirt under the cravat, and the book and dagger into inside pockets. The wool frock coat was not an ideal garment for gymnastics, but it *did* have pockets!

He ran back out on the balcony. The balloon was moving away again. Even were it not, it was not coming close enough to the tower for him to make the leap. Then Miranda started jumping up and down in the basket and pointing down. Piswyck looked, then let out a sigh of relief. The pink slime was starting to slither up the rope toward the balloon.

Smagdarone had slipped!

The slime was a threat, but it was also added weight. It would pull the basket down to where he could leap across.

Miranda pointed again, this time above Piswyck's head. He looked up and dodged back into the tower room just in time to avoid the lowering tendrils of a huge floater. As he looked out the open doorway more of them arrived, and yet more of them invaded the air around the balloon.

Piswyck was a good gymnast, but not good enough to leap through the air from Neuschwanstein's tower to a moving balloon while carrying an umbrella. Besides, he didn't have an umbrella. He didn't even have a supply of arrows!

He did, however, have music boxes.

He flipped up the lid of the big one and let "Lara's Theme" waltz out.

La, La, la-La . . .

Primitive as they were, the floaters responded to music. They began to move in a way that could only be described as a dance. Widdershins, slowly, an aerial ballet that would have been beautiful from a distance.

The balloon moved back toward him. The slime crept up the rope. He only hoped that its weight did not drag the balloon down *too far*. He only hoped he didn't fall several hundred meters to the ground!

Closer the balloon came, like clockwork the floaters danced, closer, tick tock . . .

He looked. He gauged. He waited.

La la la la, la laaa.

He took a breath that might be his last, thanked Hermes for all his help, made a token prayer to Saint Genesius, then ran like Hell across the room, out onto the balcony, leaped through space—

—and grabbed the edge of the wicker basket!

"Help!" he yelled, and at once Miranda was hauling on him, pulling him in over the edge, her hands seizing him in some very embarrassing places as he tumbled headfirst in amidst the supplies.

The balloon moved back on its swing and Piswyck scrambled to get upright.

"I think this ride is going to make me sick," said Lifesaver, and he abruptly threw up over the side.

Piswyck pulled the dagger from his pocket, then leaned out over the edge. He made the mistake of looking down, got dizzy, and was glad he hadn't done it before his leap. He began sawing at the tether rope.

"Oh dear," said Miranda. "Your unicorn just threw up all over Uncle Smaggy!"

There was a flash in the sky, then thunder too close. Piswyck noticed the coolness of the air and how strong the wind had become. He looked south and there were great dark clouds boiling up. The light was acquiring a faintly green tint.

In Hertford, Hereford, and Hampshire, Piswyck thought inanely, *Hurricanes Hardly Happen. But in Bermuda they can come up damned quick!*

The pink slime was less than a meter away when Piswyck cut through the last strands of the rope and the balloon shot up, now much more buoyant in the suddenly cooler air. He had to hold on tight, thus he couldn't see whether or not the enormous weight of the rope, covered in ravenous aspic, fell upon the sorceror.

He only saw that it fell.

Lightning flashed again, and this time it struck one of the floaters. The hydrogen within ignited and the sky was lit with a bursting bubble of flame The shock wave from the explosion buffeted the balloon slightly, but they were already much higher than the jellyfish armada, and still rising. The wind from the south had caught them now, and they were rapidly being blown away from Bermuda.

Piswyck felt as if he'd cut his own natal cord and was now being born into the real world. Neuschwanstein was receding rapidly, the mists of the rising storm obscuring it, its outlines lit clearly only when another, and then another, of the floaters exploded.

"Oh look, Piswyck!" Miranda said, pointing east. "You can see the Town of St. George, still clear of the storm! And there's Fort St. Catherine, where I used to live with Uncle! Maybe if we look southwest we'll be able to see the City of Hamilton."

Piswyck shuddered, looking down upon the great expanse of the ocean, looking south toward the oncoming hurricane whose energies he hoped would carry him home. The battle that still raged in the castle was now invisible, too small to be seen. The bursts of light from exploding floaters were not even as spectacular as the lightnings that ignited them. Bermuda was a green and lovely jewel bordered with pink sands, and not even Neuschwanstein could despoil its beauty.

Is it over? Piswyck asked himself. *Is it truly over?*

The answer came back.

No. He had the particolored unicorn. He had rescued Miranda. But his home was not his own. His father was still a prisoner.

The Countess still ruled Carsonne.

And what of Smagdarone?

If the falling rope and slime had not killed him, and if he survived the war, he still had failed in his promise regarding Piswyck. The power of the Egg, augmented enough to move Mad Ludwig's castle, was as formidable an enemy for him as it was for Piswyck.

And what of Kimowatt?

Had he reached the sorcerer's library, seized the precious books, made himself his brother's equal in magic as well as science? If so, then Smagdarone was surely out of the action. If not . . .

And what of Madeleine Forsythe, the librarian? Would she let Kimowatt keep the books even if he got them? She seemed a very responsible lady, and tough. Surely her ethics were high enough to raise up those of the wizard of Shinbone Alley.

And what of Abelia Cambridge? Had she got her umbrella in time? Had she escaped the monsters that roamed the castle halls? Would she find a suitable position in the employ of someone who wouldn't want steamed eggplant?

All this, and more, flowed through Piswyck's slowly numbing mind. He kept his feelings about Frogstool still at bay. There was time enough for that later, as they rode the hurricane.

"Piswyck," Miranda said quietly, and he came out of his reverie to note that she was looking back at Bermuda, her fingers white as she clenched the rim of the basket. "I think I'm going to cry."

"With relief?" he asked.

"Oh *no!*" she sniffed, and she stamped her dainty foot; but it didn't work well on wicker. "Because I'm leaving *home!*"

And cry she did.

Piswyck was too tired to understand. He looked to Lifesaver, but the unicorn, still a little queasy, only muttered, *"Così fan tutte!"* under his breath.

"Well!" said Piswyck, and he turned away from Bermuda to face the direction in which they were traveling. "You may be leaving home, but I am *going* home. And the Countess had best beware!"

The hurricane blew swift and they were off.

Fantasy from Ace
fanciful and fantastic!

☐ 53721-9	**MOONHEART** Charles de Lint	$3.95
☐ 51662-9	**A MALADY OF MAGICKS** Craig Shaw Gardner	$2.95
☐ 67919-6	**THE PRINCESS OF FLAMES** Ru Emerson	$2.95
☐ 76674-9	**SILVERLOCK** John Myers Myers	$4.95
☐ 10264-6	**CHANGELING** Roger Zelazny	$2.95
☐ 89467-4	**WIZARD OF THE PIGEONS** Megan Lindholm	$2.95
☐ 51944-X	**MARIANNE, THE MAGUS AND** **THE MANTICORE** Sheri S. Tepper	$2.95
☐ 77523-3	**THE SONG OF MAVIN** **MANYSHAPED** Sheri S. Tepper	$2.75
☐ 52552-0	**MERLIN'S BOOKE** Jane Yolen	$2.95
☐ 31759-6	**THE HARP OF IMACH THYSSEL** Patricia C. Wrede	$2.95

Available at your local bookstore or return this form to:

ACE
THE BERKLEY PUBLISHING GROUP, Dept. B
390 Murray Hill Parkway, East Rutherford, NJ 07073

Please send me the titles checked above. I enclose _____ Include $1.00 for postage
and handling if one book is ordered; add 25¢ per book for two or more not to exceed
$1.75. CA, NJ, NY and PA residents please add sales tax. Prices subject to change
without notice and may be higher in Canada. Do not send cash.

NAME_____

ADDRESS_____

CITY_____STATE/ZIP_____

(Allow six weeks for delivery.)

COLLECTIONS OF SCIENCE FICTION AND FANTASY

☐ 52567-9	**MERMAIDS!** Jack Dann & Gardner Dozois, eds.	$2.95
☐ 05508-7	**BESTIARY!** Jack Dann & Gardner Dozois, eds.	$2.95
☐ 85444-3	**UNICORNS!** Jack Dann & Gardner Dozois, eds.	$2.95
☐ 20405-8	**ELSEWHERE** Volume III Terri Windling & Mark A. Arnold, eds.	$3.95
☐ 51532-0	**MAGICATS!** Jack Dann and Gardner Dozois, eds.	$2.95
☐ 48184-1	**LIAVEK: THE PLAYERS OF LUCK** Will Shetterly and Emma Bull, eds.	$2.95
☐ 16622-9	**DRAGONFIELD AND OTHER STORIES** Jane Yolen	$2.75
☐ 06977-0	**BODY ARMOR: 2000** Joe Haldeman, Charles G. Waugh, Martin Harry Greenberg, eds.	$3.50
☐ 22564-0	**FAERY!** Terri Windling, ed.	$2.95

Available at your local bookstore or return this form to:

ACE
THE BERKLEY PUBLISHING GROUP, Dept. B
390 Murray Hill Parkway, East Rutherford, NJ 07073

Please send me the titles checked above. I enclose _____ Include $1.00 for postage and handling if one book is ordered; add 25¢ per book for two or more not to exceed $1.75. CA, NJ, NY and PA residents please add sales tax. Prices subject to change without notice and may be higher in Canada. Do not send cash.

NAME_____

ADDRESS_____

CITY_____ STATE/ZIP_____

(Allow six weeks for delivery.)